HALF MOON BAY

Books by Meryl Sawyer

UNFORGETTABLE

THE HIDEAWAY

TEMPTING FATE

HALF MOON BAY

THUNDER ISLAND

TRUST NO ONE

CLOSER THAN SHE THINKS

EVERY WAKING MOMENT

Published by Zebra Books

HALF MOON BAY

Meryl Sawyer

KENSINGTON BOOKS
http://www.kensingtonbooks.com

KENSINGTON BOOKS are published by

Kensington Publishing Corp.
850 Third Avenue
New York, NY 10022

All Kensington Titles, Imprints, and Distributed Lines are available at special quantity discounts for bulk purchases for sales promotions, premiums, fund-raising, and educational or institutional use. Special book excerpts or customized printings can also be created to fit specific needs. For details, write or phone the office of the Kensington special sales manager: Kensington Publishing Corp., 850 Third Avenue, New York, NY 10022, attn: Special Sales Department, Phone: 1-800-221-2647.

Kensington and the K logo Reg. U.S. Pat & TM Off.

ISBN: 0-7582-0476-0

First Zebra Mass-market Printing: March, 1999
First Kensington Hardcover Printing: November 2002
10 9 8 7 6 5 4 3 2 1

Printed in the United States of America

The best way to love anything is as if it might be lost.
—G. K. Chesterton

*This book is dedicated to my Key West friends who know
that Margaritaville is a state of mind, not a place. A sunset
at Cherry Cove is just as spectacular as the sun setting on
Key West.*

*Kathy and Phil
Gina and Paul
Sally and Jerry*

*And, of course, Jeff. Thanks everyone for all your help—
especially with the love scenes.*

KEY WEST

Bel Aire Clinic

ATLANTIC OCEAN

cemetery

Paws 'N' Claws

Louie's Backyard

Mallory Dock
Sunset Pier

Truman Annex
Bahama Village

SUNSET KEY

HALF MOON BAY

southernmost point in
continental United States

PROLOGUE

Character determines fate. Amy Conroy crouched in the dark shadows behind the Stop 'N Go gas station, silently repeating her mother's favorite saying. Once, the words had meant little to her, but now she was convinced the motto had given her courage. And the will to survive.

Beside her a rat scuttled out from under the trash bin. He sniffed her toes, then slithered across Amy's sandals, his long tail brushing her bare leg. She remained rigid, holding the little dog to her chest. It was almost midnight; if the right car didn't come along soon, they would be forced to hide until tomorrow evening.

She had exactly twenty-three cents left in the small tote she had slung over her shoulder. It wasn't enough to buy a bag of popcorn to share with Jiggs. In their cross-country trek to Florida, she'd scavenged in trash bins more than once. She could do it again.

"All right, Jiggs! Check that car. The perfect trunk—and Dade County license plates," she whispered to the dog. "It's going our way."

An older-model sedan drove into the gas station and parked at the side of the building near the rest rooms. Amy had observed this countless times during the three weeks it had taken her to make her way to the opposite side of the country, where Dexxter Foxx could never find her.

An attractive blonde got out of the car and hurried into the jiffy mart. A few agonizingly long minutes later, the blonde sauntered out, the paddle with the key to the ladies' room in her hand. As she struggled with the lock, Amy got a good look at her. The woman was

Amy's size, but a little taller, and her blond hair was slightly longer than Amy's.

She guessed the blonde was a bit older than she was. Thirty or perhaps thirty-one. There was a hardness about her, a brittle edge evident in the grim set of her mouth and the angry way she shouldered open the door.

Amy quickly looked around—the coast was clear—then dashed up to the car. The pit of her belly clenched, the way it always did when she was hitching a ride.

"Get a grip," she muttered to herself. Glancing over her shoulder one final time, she popped the lid of the trunk, praying it was empty. It was.

"No barking," she cautioned the little dog, who rarely barked.

Nothing more than a small notebook was in the large trunk. She put Jiggs down beside it, and he scuttled to the corner, while she looped fifty-pound-test fishing line around the latch. A second later she was inside and had the lid closed. "Whew!"

Amy had traveled across the country in the trunks of unsuspecting motorists. She knew her cars, knew which ones had big enough trunks, knew which ones could be opened from inside, knew exactly how to keep air circulating.

"The tricky part is getting out without being caught."

Amy stretched out as much as she could, then took the penlight and the small screwdriver from her tote. She was in shorts and a T-shirt, but it was beastly hot inside the trunk.

"Jiggs, with luck, this is our last ride inside a trunk."

The dog licked her leg, and she stroked his bad ear. Jiggs was no prize, but neither was Amy. She had experienced a small twinge of envy when she'd looked at the woman driving this car. She was very attractive, the type who turned men's heads. Amy turned heads too.

Turned them away.

A birthmark like a splash of port wine covered the right side of her face. Once, it had bothered her, but years of torment taught her to control her emotions. And ignore men.

Until Dexxter Foxx.

"Dexxter is capable of anything," she whispered to Jiggs. A federal marshal ruthlessly murdered proved how cunning and dangerous an enemy she had made.

Footsteps interrupted Amy's thoughts. "Here we go."

Amy waited until the car was zipping toward Miami before she turned on the penlight and used the small screwdriver to undo the tail light near her face. Hot, but fresh air streamed into the trunk. She moved Jiggs up so that both their noses were near the air vent.

She flicked off the penlight, concerned that other motorists or— God forbid—the Highway Patrol would notice. Outside Phoenix, the car she'd been traveling in had been pulled over. She had been ready to yank on the fishing line to release the trunk latch, but luck—*character determines fate*—had been with her. The officer had cited the driver for a faulty tail light, yet neither of them had bothered to open the trunk.

"Less than two hours to Miami," she whispered to Jiggs.

Smiling to herself, she began to nod off. Amy didn't dare fall asleep now. She needed to select just the right opportunity to release the latch and jump out of the trunk. Getting in without being seen was difficult; getting out was a work of art. She'd had several close calls, but so far she hadn't been caught.

To keep herself awake, she located the small notebook that had been in the trunk. Taking care not to let light shine through the gap from the tail light, she switched on the penlight to see if anything interesting was in the spiral notebook. A business card was paper-clipped to the first page.

"Matthew Jensen. *Exposé* magazine." She read the card to Jiggs, who responded with his usual affectionate lick. "Interesting."

She stared at the card for a moment, an idea crystallizing in her mind. She took the card and reached for her tote, but it was at her feet. She couldn't get it without disturbing Jiggs, so she tucked the card into her bra.

Using the penlight, she scanned the contents of the notebook. It detailed the blonde's long—X-rated—affair with Matthew Jensen. He was crazy about this woman, giving her expensive gifts and taking her to romantic places like Bermuda, where they made love in the surf.

Amy closed her eyes, allowing herself to imagine life without the ugly birthmark. Maybe one day, some man would . . .

The car swerved, jolting Amy, and she realized she must have drifted off. A quick check of her watch told her hours had passed. They had driven through Miami some time ago. They must be south in the Keys somewhere.

"Jiggs, we're going to have to backtrack—again."

A surge of something too intense to be mere disappointment filled her as she remembered the other time she'd miscalculated. She'd thought the car was heading west across Texas, but when it stopped she found herself in a garage in a tiny town in Oklahoma. It had taken her days to get on track again.

"Surely, it won't be that long. We're out of money," she said just as the driver threw on the brakes.

Amy bounced into the tail light, then slammed against the roof of the trunk with a bone-jarring whack. The car fishtailed and she rolled over Jiggs. Terrified of crushing the little dog, she scrambled backward and accidentally yanked on the line. The trunk's lid flew open. A split second later she was airborne.

CHAPTER
ONE

"We need you to identify the victim."

Victim? Even now, hours later, standing in the Key West airport, Matthew Jensen could still feel the sudden weakness in his limbs at the policeman's words. Oh, Christ, no—not Trevor.

Before he had managed a response, the disembodied voice on the phone had answered his silent prayer. Trevor Adams had not been in a near-fatal automobile crash. His best friend was safe.

It was a woman who was critically injured.

Matt had hung up, then he'd tried to reach Trevor. He'd left a message on his friend's machine before flying to Key West. Matt had told the police he was coming, but he hadn't expected the officer in charge of the case to meet him so late at night.

He slung his carry-on bag over his shoulder and followed the man to his squad car. Outside the deserted terminal, the balmy air brought with it the loamy scent of the tropics, night-blooming jasmine and fragrant magnolias. This was the Key West he always enjoyed, the land of endless summer.

Now that he had quit his job at *Exposé* magazine, he wanted to spend time with his buddy from college, Trevor. Matt hadn't planned to come to Key West so soon, but he felt responsible for the comatose woman. The only identification she had was his business card. Undoubtedly, he knew her.

Matt studied the young officer leading him into the parking lot. During his years as an investigative reporter, Matt had encountered dozens of cops. This kid was green, hardly out of the police academy. He supposed it didn't matter. Not much went on in Key West. The main problem was tourists who'd guzzled too much tequila at Jimmy Buffett's Margaritaville.

"The wreck was a real mess," the officer told Matt as he drove the squad car out of the airport. "Two people were killed. Your friend is the only one who survived—if she lives."

"I'm not sure who this woman is. None of my friends told me they were coming down here."

"She was driving an older-model blue Buick. Does that help?"

"No. Most people I know fly to Key West."

"A truck carrying diesel fuel plowed into her car just as she drove off the Oversea Highway. For once, not wearing a seat belt paid off. Everyone was thrown clear. The gas truck exploded. The other two people aren't much more than charcoal chips."

Matt pictured the Oversea Highway. The long, narrow road was flanked by the ocean as it passed through a seemingly endless chain of the tiny islands known as keys. Most were uninhabited, while the others were havens for sport fishermen.

"The trucker wasn't supposed to have a passenger. He'd been cited twice for picking up women. Near as we can figure, he'd given a hitchhiker a ride."

Matt stared out the window, the disturbed feeling he'd had since receiving the call intensifying. He didn't want this injured woman to be someone he knew, a person he cared about. Every fiber of his body warned him that he couldn't take on anyone else's problems right now.

He had more problems of his own than he could handle.

They drove down Flagler Avenue and turned onto Kennedy Drive. Matt had visited Trevor many times, but he'd never been in this part of town. Lying low, surrounded by a shimmering Caribbean-blue sea, Key West was warm sunshine, the smell of frangipani, and the sound of rustling palms swaying in the gentle breeze.

But paradise always had its dark side, the ugly underbelly tourists rarely saw. This wasn't the Key West he knew where the quaint, narrow roads were lined with charming Victorian homes originally built by ship's carpenters trying to outdo one another. Along these streets, shanties splintered to their bones, paint a long-gone memory, crouched beside boxy structures dating back to the sixties.

The hospital was a concrete bunker with weeds sprouting through cracks in the asphalt. The officer led Matt inside and took him down a long corridor to the ICU. A sleepy-eyed nurse glanced at them, but didn't bother to get up.

"She's in here."

Matt followed the officer into the small, dimly lit room, where one other patient was also being treated. The antiseptic smell and the low drone of the machines that clicked and sputtered and gurgled reminded Matt of the hours he'd spent at his mother's side. The memory triggered a raw ache, a profoundly depressing sensation that knocked him backward in time, to when he was a young kid and vulnerable to the point of being helpless.

For an instant he imagined himself in a hospital bed. No friggin' way! Just the thought made him hesitate, breaking his stride.

Get the hell out of here.

The officer shot him a questioning glance. He strode forward, tamping down the uncharacteristic surge of anxiety. The woman needed him, Matt reminded himself.

They stopped beside a bed, and Matt gazed down at the lifeless form. Except for the swell of her breasts, it was impossible to tell if it was a man or a woman. Her face and head were wrapped in gauze, with nothing more than slits at the eyes and an opening at the nose for oxygen prongs. One leg was in a cast from the knee down. Her right hand and arm up to her shoulder were in a contraption hitched to the ceiling by a pulley.

A suffocating sensation made it difficult to breathe. "How am I supposed to identify her?"

"Uh . . . well, we . . . ah, thought . . ."

The officer pulled a card from the small notebook he was carrying and handed it to Matt. He instantly recognized his business card. And the telltale lipstick print across his name.

Rochelle Ralston. A wild flash of anger ripped through him. Son of a bitch! He'd come all this way, worrying that a friend was near death, only to find it was Shelly.

Aw, hell. The business card should have tipped him. Shelly had stolen a stack of his cards. She'd left him dozens of them—complete with her hot-pink lip print. She'd written personal messages on each one.

At first he'd laughed at the notes. Then the messages became menacing. *Why are you ignoring me? Why don't you return my calls? Why won't you admit you love me?*

He realized how warped Shelly's mind was. She was totally obsessed with him and convinced he loved her as much as she *thought* she loved him. They'd had one lousy date and a few kisses. That's all. She didn't know him well enough to love him.

"Your card was inside her bra." The cop turned the color of an eggplant. "We thought . . ."

Damn it all the way to hell. This was vintage Shelly, all right. A wacko who refused to take no for an answer. "I'll love you until you die," she had told him over and over and over.

Matt had been forced to get a restraining order against her when she'd threatened his sister, mistaking Emily for one of his girlfriends. If Shelly had actually carried out those threats—she was dangerous.

The young officer studied the toes of his shoes. "We thought there might be some identifying mark on her body you would recognize."

A pristine white sheet covered the woman, molding her full breasts and outlining her slender hips and legs. The cop expected him to lift the sheet and check for some damn mole or scar. There wouldn't be any point, because he'd *never* seen Shelly without clothes.

"Can't help you there. I had only one date with her." He didn't mention how crazily she'd behaved afterward.

The young officer read from his notebook. "The med sheet says blond hair, blue eyes, five feet three inches, one hundred and twelve pounds. Approximate age, thirty. Does that describe her?"

"Yeah, I guess. Shelly was taller though." He thought a moment, recalling numerous times when she would appear out of nowhere, chasing after him. "She always wore high heels. I guess that made her look taller."

"Oh, I almost forgot. She has a dog. It was thrown clear. There wasn't a mark on it. Two people dead, one critically injured, and a dog survives. Go figure."

"She never mentioned a dog."

He gazed down at the inanimate shape that had once been the vivacious yet deeply disturbed Rochelle Ralston. Shelly was so helpless now. Myriad tubes and wires attached to every part of her body confirmed how close to death she was.

All alone.

He didn't give a rat's ass, he told himself, but it was impossible to see anyone like this and not feel . . . something. The unwelcome tightening of his throat reminded him that this was another human being—struggling to hold on to life.

"It's Rochelle Ralston," he heard himself say. "Who else could it be?"

"Both vehicles rolled. No one was wearing a seat belt, so it was hard to tell who had been in which vehicle. Like I told you, the others were fried. We'll use dental records to ID them. The trucker shouldn't be much of a problem, but the John Doe may take time. We're still waiting for forensics in Miami to let us know if it's a man or a woman."

Matt couldn't keep his eyes off Shelly's body. It didn't seem possible that anyone so critically injured could survive. She hadn't regained consciousness and might never come out of the coma. Hard to believe. The woman he knew had been animated, full of life and energy.

A pang of something he didn't want to label sympathy pierced his emotional shield for a second. Get out of here this minute. Don't get involved.

He turned his back and walked out of the room.

The officer dropped Matt off at Sunset Pier near Mallory Dock. The dock was empty now, but at sunset tomorrow the place would be jammed with tourists as eager to see the fire-eaters and acrobats and jugglers as they would be to watch the sun slide into the ocean in a radiant blaze of color. It was well after midnight, and Duval Street was booming with the dawn-to-dusk revelry that made Key West famous.

There seemed to be more than the usual commotion coming from the Hog's Breath Saloon. Like the Hard Rock Café up the street, this open-air bar offered T-shirts whose sales rivaled its drinks. Above the din filling the sultry air, he heard the muted wail of a saxophone playing the blues.

A trio of guys stumbled down the street toward Margaritaville, singing an off-key rendition of "Margaritaville" that would have made Jimmy Buffett cringe.

" 'Wastin' away in Margaritaville' does not cover it," Matt mumbled under his breath. "Were you ever that young?"

"No." He answered his own question. When he'd been their age, he'd worked two jobs just to stay in Yale. He'd never had the time or the money to indulge himself by vacationing in Key West. By the time he did have the money, his career had consumed all his time.

It had been his life.

Had been. Past tense. His whole life had taken a drastic turn. His career was a thing of the past.

He walked down the ramp to the dock where the Sunset Key launches were moored, hoping Trevor had received his message and had left a boat for him. The way his luck was going, Trevor hadn't checked his answering machine.

He smiled to himself when he spotted Trevor's launch with its distinctive navy and white striped bimini to protect riders from the sun. Matt knew where Trevor kept the key hidden and found it. He was ready to cast off the mooring line, when the last note from the soulful saxophone drifted over the water.

The blues always affected him in a melancholy way, arousing strong sensations of loneliness and depression. Tonight even more so. Man, oh, man. Seeing Shelly had disturbed him more than he'd first realized.

He started the engine and motored away from the dock. Sunset Key was due west of Mallory Dock, about a five-minute ride by boat. The exclusive island didn't allow cars, but it had brick paths for bicycles and golf carts. Accustomed to the go-go pace of Manhattan, Matt had always found Sunset Key a little too secluded.

Now his mind-set had changed. He was ready to kick back and take it easy for a while. Trevor's home on Sunset Key was the perfect place to do it. Trevor had purchased three lots at the southern tip of the key and had built a magnificent conch-style mansion with several guest suites.

A trust from a wealthy aunt and insightful investments in the stock market had made Trevor Adams a very wealthy and somewhat eccentric man. He loved an entourage. At any given moment, he had three or four people temporarily living with him.

The visitors were usually a bit "challenged." Key West attracted artists and musicians as well as misfits. Trevor must have felt like a misfit for most of his life, and he identified with them.

"This is it," Matt muttered to himself as he pulled up to Trevor's dock. "Half Moon Bay."

A new sign had been hung since his last visit. The locals called this end of the key Half Moon Bay because of the crescent of white sand shaded by towering palms that was now Trevor's private beach.

Trevor never locked his home, and Matt was sure his friend had left him a note on the entry table, the message center of the house. The note would tell him which suite to use, but something drew him toward the water.

He dropped his bag on the grass and pulled off his loafers. Barefoot, wearing shorts and a polo shirt, he headed across the sand to the sea. Like a never-ending phalanx of soldiers, the waves marched up to the shore, one after another.

Matt stood in the warm, ankle-deep water and gazed out at the indigo sea. Ribbons of moonlight glistened on the water. Half Moon Bay, with its flowering trees and stately palms and nesting ospreys, usually gave him a lift. Not tonight.

"Forget Shelly," he told himself. Yet in his mind's eye he kept seeing her helplessly trapped in a hospital bed, unable to move or speak.

"Don't be such a bastard," he cursed himself out loud. "No human being deserves to be in a coma—near death. All alone."

CHAPTER
TWO

"Unfuckingbelievable! What a view."

Dexxter Foxx stood at the plate glass window of his Seattle office and looked out at the city's lights. The neon sign just visible from where he stood blared: FOXX ENTERPRISES. His company, symbolized by the awesome view and the sign, filled him with a sense of accomplishment and pride.

The view from the top.

Dexxter was only too well aware that he had not started at the apex of the financial food chain. He had been born Dexter Foxe in a backwater burg in eastern Washington. By the time he'd entered community college, he was sick of saying, "Dexter Foxe. That's fox with an E."

He'd been doodling in the math class he was flunking when he'd added a second x to Fox. Right then and there he'd decided to become a double X. Dexter with two Xs and Fox with two Xs.

"Distinctive," he'd said to himself. "Classy."

About that time he also realized he was never going to make money honestly. He was destined to earn his money the old-fashioned way. Crime paid.

Welcome to the real world, he'd decided, the world of Dexxter Foxx.

So far it had worked. With the technology explosion, there were too many computer-related companies around to be sure just what everyone was doing. People believed he was a successful software manufacturer.

Everyone except Amy Conroy.

Amy had discovered his scam and knew Foxx Enterprises was nothing more than a front. She'd idolized Dexxter. He'd been convinced she loved him and would do anything for him. But the second Amy's mother had died, the snitch had stunned him by squealing to the Feds.

"Ungrateful bitch," Dexxter muttered to his reflection in the dark glass. "She did it because she was crazy about me, but I never paid any attention to her. Did she seriously expect me to take her out? Who would want to be seen with someone around who looked like her?"

Amy was attractive—pretty, actually—if you saw her in profile from the left side. But the gross birthmark on the right side of her face gave him the willies. It didn't detract from Amy's brains though. She had a mind like a microchip.

Too damn smart for her own good.

Behind him, the door to his office opened, and he saw Irene's reflection in the glass. She had finally decided to answer her pager in person. "Where have you been?"

"Around."

He turned toward her. Irene's flushed face and her tousled jet-black hair told him where "around" was. The dilated pupils that made her dark eyes appear ebony confirmed his suspicions. She'd been in the sack with one of her young, buff studs.

"You left without giving me today's report on Amy."

Irene sidled up to him and stood a little too close. He eased back, knowing one encouraging move or word, and they would be more than business associates. He had known Irene since third grade. Though liposuction and diet pills had improved her figure a little, to Dexxter she was still the fat little girl who tagged along wherever he went.

He'd needed Irene's money to start Foxx Enterprises, but he had no intention of becoming involved with her. Business was business. Let Irene screw all the studmuffins she wanted.

"Amy vanished into thin air," Irene informed him. "Zane's the best in the business, but since he blew up that crappy little house where witness protection had Amy hidden, she hasn't been seen."

"With a face like hers, Amy can't hide. Zane just isn't looking in the right places."

Leaning close, Irene brandished the gunboat boobs she had, compliments of silicone implants. "Where would you suggest Zane look?"

He walked over to his desk to put some distance between them. At times Irene irritated him so much that he wanted to throw her across his huge mahogany desk, rip her clothes off, and blister her ass.

Or something.

"Check all the plastic surgeons in the Sacramento area, where she disappeared. I'll bet you money, the FBI arranged to have that miserable birthmark removed. After we had the federal marshal killed, Amy went ahead with the surgery. That's why we can't find her."

Irene sauntered up to him. She was nothing but a whore, he assured himself. Still, he was bound to her like a Siamese twin. If she went to jail, he went to jail.

"Zane's sources say the FBI doesn't know where Amy is. They're looking for her too." Again she stood too close, giving him more than a glimpse of her tits.

"Somehow she had the scar removed. That's the only reason we can't locate her."

"Dexx, did it ever occur to you that if you'd volunteered to give Amy the money to have laser surgery to remove that hideous birthmark, we wouldn't be in this mess?"

He ignored the shadowy hollow between her breasts and met her gaze with a shrug, unwilling to concede he had deliberately not offered to help Amy even though she adored him. He liked controlling her, enjoying it more than he ever admitted to anyone.

Amy had needed money desperately. Her mother had suffered with Parkinson's and Amy had to have a job. Everything she'd earned went to helping her mother. Without the livid birthmark, Amy would have been as beautiful as she was brilliant.

Only someone with shit for brains would have risked losing her.

Life had dealt Amy a crappy hand. No family except for a sick mother, and a birthmark that revolted people. Still, she possessed a streak of pride and a will too tough to admit defeat. And the guts to cross him.

"There is one thing," Irene said as she ran the tip of her finger up his jacket from the cuff to the collar.

He moved away. "What?"

"When Zane rigged the explosion that killed the federal marshal, he assumed Amy would be inside the house, but she wasn't."

"That's old news."

"So where was Miss Big Mouth when Zane detonated the bomb?"

Irene didn't wait for him to guess. "She was stealing her neighbor's dog."

"What are you talking about?"

"According to the drunk who lives next door, Amy was nuts. Several times she'd accused him of abusing his dog. He heard the explosion and came to the window. He saw Amy taking off with his dog."

"That's crazy. I don't remember her even mentioning she liked dogs."

Irene cocked one ebony brow in the same infuriating way she always did, saying, "Did you ever discuss pets?"

"Never." He silently admitted that he hadn't known Amy nearly as well as he'd thought. She idolized him, hanging on every word, but he'd been careful not to encourage her.

He never dated business associates. Like the sword of Damocles, the threat of sexual harassment hung over every executive's head. He had the smarts to use professionals. Pros gave you what you wanted—without question. Without the threat of lawsuits.

"So Amy snatched a dog. Big fucking deal," he said rather than admit he should have paid more attention to Amy. If he'd strung her along, Amy wouldn't have gone to the FBI.

Irene clicked her long maroon nails on his desk. "Plain and simple, Amy Conroy deserves to die."

Amy floated, suspended in no-man's-land between heaven and hell. Everything around her was devoid of light, of sound, so unbelievably bleak. And cold.

She tried to concentrate, but her mind was almost blank, unable to hold a thought for more than a second. She was vaguely aware of . . . something. But what was it? For a second, she struggled with it, then gave up.

Character determines fate.

A thin, reedlike voice whispered those words. She tried to focus on what it might mean, but it was too dark and she was so chilled her teeth would chatter. If she could move her jaw.

"You might not make it," an inner voice warned. Her hold on life kept slipping, moving beyond her grasp with each breath. It wouldn't take much to slip over the edge into total nothingness.

And leave this world forever.

Again something caught her attention. What was it? Sound. No sounds. A glimmer of hope warmed her frigid body. She wasn't alone in this black void. Thank God, someone was with her

"How seriously is she injured?" Matt asked the doctor as they stood beside Shelly's bed.

"She has a broken leg and arm. Her shoulder was badly dislocated." The chubby doctor with a stethoscope slung around his neck spoke in the detached tone Matt recalled from his youth when his mother had been terminally ill.

"Evidently, she put out her hand to break her fall. Big mistake. It was crushed. I doubt she'll ever write with that hand."

"What about head injuries?"

"All the tests show normal brain activity even though she's still unconscious. Her jaw was broken in two places, so we wired it shut. The right side of her face was sheared off. She will need reconstructive surgery. Luckily, her right eye wasn't damaged."

Matt ventured a glance at Shelly's lifeless form. He'd been at her bedside for hours, but she hadn't once moved. Finally, the doctor made his morning rounds, and Matt was able to inquire about her condition.

"Shelly's going to make it, isn't she?" he wanted to know.

The doctor shrugged. "She's been unconscious almost thirty-six hours. The mind is a strange thing. Sometimes it just gives up. Have you tried talking to her, encouraging her?"

The man had no idea what he was asking. Shelly had made his life hell, then threatened to kill his sister. He was here only because he knew Shelly had no one else.

"That often works. You're her . . . ?"

"Just an acquaintance," he snapped, then tempered his voice as he noticed the doctor's shocked expression. "Shelly's family was killed in the ValuJet crash. I'm the only one around here who knows her, and I don't know her very well."

"Try encouraging her. You're all she has right now," the doctor said as he walked away.

Matt watched the man examine the other ICU patient, another unconscious woman. Whatever was wrong with her didn't require the massive array of bandages cocooning Shelly.

Matt stretched, attempting to work out a kink in his neck. He was so damn tired that the ICU kept blurring, his eyes closing, begging for sleep. He should go back to Trevor's, get out of his raunchy clothes, and take a shower. Then he could hit the fancy sheets Trevor used on his beds and get some rest.

He glanced at Shelly, telling himself he would come back later. She looked so forlorn. Totally alone.

"Aw, hell, why me?" He dropped into the chair beside her bed. "Why me?"

He forced himself to take her hand, carefully avoiding the IV inserted into a vein. Her fingers were icy against his palm. He stared at her small hand, noticing Shelly had given up the shocking pink nail polish she usually wore.

Her fingers were slender and delicate. Everything about her was dainty, he thought as he glanced at her body. It was covered only by a crisp white sheet. When they'd been in Manhattan, he hadn't realized how petite she was, almost fragile.

He warmed her hand with his, closing his fingers over hers until all he saw was the IV shunt. "Shelly, it's Matthew Jensen. Can you hear me?"

Her chest rose and fell, indicating she was breathing, but she gave no sign she recognized his name. Through the slits in the gauze he could see her long lashes. They never moved. "Come on, Shelly. You have to wake up."

Still holding her hand, he moved closer to her bandaged head. He began talking about life in New York, about the business. Shelly had worked on the fringe of journalism. Her last job had been with a tabloid that specialized in alien abductions and Elvis sightings.

"Shelly, I know you're not going to believe this. I can hardly believe it myself. I quit *Exposé*."

Matt had left two weeks ago, but saying the words made it seem depressingly final. He'd battled his way to the top of the heap, making a rag sheet called *Exposé* into the country's leading newsmagazine.

He couldn't believe he'd walked away.

Why did you do it? This isn't like you. He thought Shelly was silently questioning him, which was impossible, of course. She was still deep in a coma, but he lied to her anyway. He didn't want to verbalize his problems even to a woman who couldn't hear him.

"Life's too short. I want to kick back for a while. I'm here to visit my roommate from college. You remember me mentioning Trevor Adams. I'm going to spend some time with him."

★   ★   ★

The sounds morphed together. Amy had no idea what was being said. Then a deep, steady voice registered in her confused brain. A man's voice. It seemed close, near enough to reach out and touch, yet it was coming to her from another world.

She didn't understand anything he was saying.

Still, the low, crooning sound comforted her. She liked the voice with its measured cadence and masculine undertone. She needed to know someone was with her. Wherever she was. She wasn't trapped in this black abyss by herself.

She dimly realized she wasn't as cold as she had been. Her body seemed to be warmer now. Surely that was a good sign, an indication the darkness would soon lift.

The sound abruptly stopped, and a deep chill invaded her bones again. She tried to call out, to summon the voice back. But her brain refused to function. She was floating in darkness once more. Abandoned.

Matt stood above Shelly's inanimate form. For a second he thought her eyelashes had fluttered. Leaning down, he looked closely, almost expecting to hear her say "I'll love you until you die."

That's what she'd said the last time he'd seen her. It had sounded like a veiled threat, but he had ignored it. Now she was the one near death.

He must have been mistaken. Her pale lashes were still closed. She couldn't speak even if she wanted to; her jaw was wired shut.

He'd been encouraging her for over two hours. Nothing. Not one sign she knew he was there. He was beat, too exhausted to go on.

"Give it a break, Jensen," he muttered to himself as he left the ICU.

CHAPTER
THREE

Weightless, Amy floated, drifting along in cryptlike darkness. She didn't seem to be as cold as she'd been earlier. When was that? Minutes, hours, days? She didn't have a clue, not much registering in her confused brain except that the world around her seemed unusually quiet.

Something vital was missing. She wasn't sure how long she remained suspended in a vast wasteland of nothingness before it dawned on her what was wrong. Where was the rich masculine voice that had soothed her earlier?

Had she just imagined it, or had the voice really existed? Her brain was barely functioning, but she knew who she was, knew she was alone in the world. Who had been talking to her?

"Come on. Open your eyes. You can do it."

The words sifted through her brain, mingling, jumbling, then finally forming one coherent thought. Him. The caring voice had returned and a warm glow flared inside her.

Her fog-shrouded brain tried to calculate how much time had lapsed since he last had tried to entice her to rejoin the world of the living. Her attempt to judge time failed, but the mesmerizing voice continued to coax her out of the darkness.

"Come on, babe. You can do it. Try."

Amy cracked one eye. The light blinded her, and she snapped her lid shut, waited a few seconds, then allowed her eyes to slowly drift open. Something was covering her eyes, making it difficult to see where she was. She seemed to be peeking through a cloud.

No, not a cloud. Gauze. Her eyes were bandaged, she realized through a hazy watercolor wash of drugs and pain. All she could see was a sliver of light seeping through the gauze.

A man was beside her bed. Silhouetted in the diffuse light of the gauze, the man's eyes were moody brown, unreadable. He embodied the frightening but irresistible combination of sensuality and danger.

Tension was evident in the rigid set of his broad shoulders and in his square, tight jaw. Yet he was holding her hand in both of his with such tenderness that her pain seemed a small price to pay.

No man had held her hand. Ever.

Why now? And why did this man seem familiar?

Her baffled mind attempted to decipher the facts, but the ruggedly masculine man distracted her. He wasn't looking at her face. He was staring into the distance, something unsettling in his gaze. Suddenly, her brain began to function.

"Oh, my God. What is *he* doing here?" she silently asked herself.

She closed her eyes, raw emotion filling her soul with a hot rush of humiliation too intense to ever be forgotten. She must be imagining this. It couldn't be Trent Hastings, could it?

There had to be a logical answer, but her groggy mind refused to sort out the facts. She drifted along for a moment, drawn back in time remembering Trent Hastings's melt-your-heart grin.

In a dreamlike trance, she tumbled backward in time—lost in the dark void of unconsciousness once more. Suddenly she was sixteen again, walking down the high school corridor.

Alone.

By then Amy's birthmark had forced her to develop protective emotional armor. Polite people looked away, pretending not to notice her, but an amazing number of others did not. She was accustomed to stares and giggles and pointing fingers. She kept quiet, not wanting to draw attention to herself.

"Why can't you make friends?" her mother had asked, genuinely puzzled.

For many years, she'd been alone, never wanting or needing companionship. Then puberty struck—although she hadn't known what to call it back then—and she became aware of boys in an entirely different way.

Despite her better judgment, she found herself watching Trent Hastings, the school's star quarterback. And pretending he would invite her to the prom. Night after night she dreamed about dancing with him. She'd even dared to imagine he kissed her.

By the light of day, stark reality wrenched her back to earth. Trent was handsome and had his pick of girls. He'd never even noticed her, not once looking her way.

Then one day Trent glanced in her direction as she walked up to her locker. Seen in profile, Amy knew her nose was a touch too long, but she had inherited her mother's natural blond hair and full breasts. She kept her good side to him, hoping he'd go by with his friends without getting a close look at her.

"Hi, there," Trent said as he passed.

Amy kept her head down, not wanting him to make fun of her the way so many boys did. Please, God, let him keep walking. Out of the corner of her eye she saw him stop and leave his friends. Her heart plummeted to the pit of her belly, triggering a sickening lurch. She managed to get her locker open and stuck her head inside, pretending to be searching for something.

"You must be new," he said as he came up to her. "I haven't seen you around. I'm Trent Hastings."

Amy had wished herself invisible dozens of times, but never—ever—had she wanted to disappear more than she did right now. Her good side toward him, she managed to say, "I'm Amy Conroy."

With an adorable smile, he leaned one shoulder against the bank of lockers. "So, Amy, do you like football?"

For a moment she pretended she was an ordinary girl flirting with the school hero. It felt . . . right. Just once in her life she would like to be normal and have some boy smile at her and ask her out.

It wasn't too much to want, was it? She didn't yearn to be special. Average-looking without the hideous birthmark would be pure heaven. Imagine walking with her head high, not driven by sheer pride, but because it was the natural thing to do. Then talking to boys would be easy too.

But in the back of her head, she heard her mother whispering: *Character determines fate.*

She wasn't an ordinary girl; she was extraordinarily repulsive. That was her fate, and there was no sense pretending otherwise. Or feeling sorry for herself. She mustered the courage to face him.

"I've never been to a football game."

Trent's cocky smile vanished in a heartbeat. He looked as if he'd just been clobbered by a three-hundred-pound tackle. He stepped back, muttering, "It's a great game."

Amy's cheeks were flaming hot as she turned toward her locker again. Behind her, she heard Trent talking to his friends.

"Jee—sus! I thought beauty and the beast were two people, not one."

Pain arced through Amy's body in a searing explosion that singed every nerve ending and left her sweating beneath the sheet. She tried to shriek for help, to cry out against the blinding agony. But her mouth wouldn't open. The scream stalled in her throat and she gagged.

Oh, my God! She couldn't move her lips. She couldn't say one word.

What was wrong?

Her mind scrambled to interpret the messages it could barely understand through the miasma of pain. She had been dreaming about Trent Hastings and something silly that had happened long, long ago.

Before Dexxter Foxx.

She forced her eyes open as all-encompassing terror hit her, making it nearly impossible to breathe. Her former employer wouldn't stop until he killed her. Like a puzzle with just one piece missing, the past fell into place. The piercing screech of brakes and the explosion of glass reverberated in her ears, an echo of the crash.

The dead federal marshal. The trunk with the notebook in it. Flying through the air. Screaming for God to save Jiggs.

On the verge of sheer panic, she stared through something cloud-like, obscuring her gaze. She blinked hard, but her lashes were restricted by something that was not a cloud.

Through slitted lids she noted the banks of machines, wires, tubes. A stringent smell assailed her nostrils, a too-clean scent. Then she noticed a woman in a nearby bed.

A patient, obviously. She must be in a hospital.

"Thank God," she said to herself. "I'm alive. Maybe Jiggs made it too."

For a moment she marveled at having survived the crash and thought about the little dog she'd rescued. Her initial elation vanished, wiped away first by another wave of pain, then by the realization she was trapped in a bed. Something was clamping her jaw shut, and the right side of her body was hooked up to a pulley attached to the ceiling.

She could move her left arm and leg—if she ignored the harrowing pain—but it would be impossible to get out of the bed. Fear coursed through her almost as powerful as the pain. Nowhere to run, nowhere to hide. Dexxter would find her now.

"You're as good as dead," she silently told herself.

Voices coming closer interrupted her thoughts. Through the narrow slit in the gauze she saw a man in a white coat with a stethoscope draped over his shoulders. She assumed he was the doctor, but who was the man with him?

He was taller than the doctor and had rugged, squared-off shoulders and a powerful chest that tapered to a trim waist. He was the man she'd seen by her bed earlier. Her dazed mind had confused him with Trent Hastings, a boy she'd known in high school.

Through the screen of gauze and lowered lashes she studied him and discovered this man bore only a passing resemblance to Trent. Thick, dark, tousled hair. An angular jaw bristling with several days' stubble. Long legs in khaki shorts and strong arms hanging down beside them.

He wasn't handsome, but he was attractive in a masculine way she found slightly threatening. Other than Dexxter and the priest who had given her mother last rites, she had zero experience with men. This man was more than she could handle—if she'd been in any shape to do it.

"You've been talking to her and she's not responding," the doctor said.

"I was here all morning, then I took a quick break for coffee," answered the stranger. "I came back and spent the last three hours trying to persuade her to wake up."

Who was this dangerous-looking man? Why was he here? The scowl that grooved his brow and the grim set of his mouth were chilling. He had to be one of Dexxter's men.

She shut her eyes, aware of how close they were to her bed and not wanting them to know she was conscious. An alarm bell sounded inside her brain. The stranger was waiting for her to die. If she didn't, he would kill her, just the way Dexxter's man had murdered the federal marshal.

"Look at the monitor," said the man.

She realized pulse-pounding fear had accelerated her heart rate. One of the machines off to the side was furiously bleeping. She held her breath, hoping to slow the frantic beating of her heart.

Her eyes were shut, but she could sense them hovering over her, watching, ready to detect any movement. Like a kettledrum's tat-tat-

tat, her heart beat against her temples. She struggled to steady her breathing, to appear comatose again.

"A fluctuation," she heard the doctor say. "It happens."

If she could have smiled, she would have, but she was a prisoner bound by gauze and chained to the bed by myriad tubes and wires. Still, she'd managed to fool them.

A deeper voice with a husky catch dashed her hopes. "Look at her hand."

With a start, she realized her left hand was balled into a fist. Soothing fingers brushed her knuckles, then carefully traced around the IV shunt. She held her breath again, uncertain what the stranger wanted. He seemed too gentle to be one of Dexxter's hired guns, but she couldn't let down her guard.

Slowly, with unimaginable tenderness, her hand was cradled by two warm, masculine hands. "I think she's regaining consciousness."

His words almost made her open her eyes to look more closely at him, but she didn't dare. It could be a trick. Pretending to be unconscious was her only hope.

The next few minutes stretched into two lifetimes as she battled to control her breathing to keep her heartbeat normal. All the while, strong, warm fingers stroked her hand.

"Shelly, come on. Wake up."

Who was Shelly? Why would Dexxter's man call her by that name?

"She's not responding." The doctor sounded bored. "I think—"

"Matt, Matt," interrupted a strange voice. "I've been looking for you."

His hands released hers, leaving her chilled. Chafing noises like shirts brushing and clapping of backs followed. She ventured a quick peek and saw a strikingly handsome blond man bear-hugging the stranger whose name was Matt.

"I read your note," said the blond man as she snapped her eyes shut. "I waited for you to come back to Half Moon Bay, but—"

"I thought Shelly would regain consciousness sooner than she has."

"Shelly? You mean Rochelle Ralston?"

The way the blond man said the name made it sound like a four-letter word. Who on earth was Rochelle Ralston? Why did they think she was this woman? Could they be discussing the blonde driving the car?

"Yeah, it's Shelly," replied the husky voice of the dark-haired stranger. "I made a few phone calls. After she was fired from her job at the *National Reporter,* she went for months without work. She was offered a job with the *Key West Daily.* That's why she was driving down here."

"So? Let her family and friends look after her."

"She has no family. I spoke with the people who worked with her in New York this morning. Shelly has one friend, but the woman can't come down here for a few weeks. I'm—"

"All she's got."

There was something unnerving in both men's attitudes, but she didn't stop to wonder what it might be. Instead, she concentrated on the fact that the dark-haired stranger she'd initially confused with Trent Hastings wasn't a man to fear. For now Dexxter Foxx had no idea where she was.

Thank you, God.

With that comforting thought, the world tipped and slowly became fuzzy. Then darkness claimed her again, dragging her into the netherworld in a second.

By degrees she awoke, realizing someone was changing her bed or bandages or something. Someone rough and uncaring. Through the gauze she saw a male nurse looming over her. He snapped the sheet, then shoved it under the mattress.

A lightning bolt of pain racked her body, threatening to make her black out. Pinpricks of searing red dots danced before her eyes. Her head ached as if a rusty hatchet had hacked way and hacked away until her head . . . split open.

"You're hurting me!"

But her words were nothing more than a silent scream in her own brain. The man yanked a tube from her arm and jammed in a replacement. Nurses weren't supposed to treat patients like this, she told herself.

"I'm going on a break," called a soft female voice.

"Okay. I've got them handled," the male nurse replied.

Them? Dimly, she recalled there had been another person in the room with her. She cracked one eye a fraction of an inch and saw the bed across the room and the form of a woman lying flat, tubes and wires coming from every part of her body.

"That's what I look like," she silently told herself.

A wave of helplessness like nothing she'd ever known overwhelmed her. For her entire life a disfiguring birthmark had isolated her, making her a loner with no one to turn to, no one to call a friend. But this was much worse.

Like the woman in the other bed, all she had was a bank of machines to help her. Yet those machines weren't human. She couldn't tell them about the crippling pain or protest about the brute of a nurse.

Simple communication was impossible. She was a prisoner in her own body. She clenched her fist, fear and anger welling up inside her as her frustration mounted. She was alone, more alone than she'd been when the disfiguring birthmark branded her a freak.

"Oh, oh . . . oh," moaned the woman in the other bed.

The nurse left her and walked over to the woman. From a tray beside the bed, he picked up a syringe. He held it up and squirted a bit of fluid out of it before inserting it into the shunt in the woman's arm.

"What about me?" she silently asked. She could almost feel the wave of release as the painkilling medication flowed through the woman's veins. "Give me a shot too."

Her silent prayer went unanswered. Now her lungs burned with each breath as the pain continued to mount, weakening her with every second. Across the room, she saw the nurse toss the syringe onto the tray. For a moment he stood over the woman, who was now unconscious, a sullen look on his face.

He moved so his back was to her, blocking her view. She squinted, trying to see what was happening through the restrictive gauze. Evidently, the nurse was changing the woman's bedding or something.

She hoped he was being more gentle with the other patient. He must be, she decided; he was taking longer with her. The woman had received a shot of what had to be a painkiller. Why hadn't she been given one?

Unexpectedly, she heard her mother talking, but Amy couldn't quite make out what she was saying. Amy supposed she was going to die, or perhaps she was already dead. How else could she hear a dead woman's voice?

A few minutes later the nurse finally turned toward her, and she realized she was still alive. The strange look on his face sent a prickle of alarm across the back of her neck. He walked over to her and picked up the syringe from the tray beside her bed. Out of the corner of her eye, she saw a small plume of liquid shoot into the air.

"Yes . . . yes," she silently cried.

He hadn't once looked at her face and didn't see the desperate pleading in her eyes. "It's all right," she told herself. "He's going to give you a painkiller."

A hank of ginger-brown hair fell across his forehead, and he brushed it back with his sleeve. His face was average, but something odd in his almond-shaped eyes made her apprehensive. Maybe he wasn't preparing a painkiller.

Dexxter Foxx might have sent him.

"Matt, where are you?" she tried to scream, but her jaw remained locked shut. "Help me! Please, help me."

He inserted the needle.

A rush of relief like a tsunami wave hit her a second later. Her body seemed dangerously light, nearly weightless—the wrenching pain no longer torturing her. If she could have smiled at the male nurse, she would have.

Until she gazed up through the slits in the gauze.

He was lifting the sheet covering her body and didn't notice that she was still conscious. Watching. Suspicion mushroomed inside her as she realized what was happening.

She yelled for help, but no sound escaped her lips. Instead, the scream ricocheted through her brain, a desperate plea no one could hear. His hands slipped under the sheet just as her world faded to black.

CHAPTER

FOUR

The pink edge of dawn slowly reclaimed the night sky as Matt woke up. For a moment he didn't remember where he was. The rhythmic swish of the ceiling fan above his head reminded him that he was in one of Trevor's guest suites. He'd left Shelly early last evening and come home with Trevor. Matt had dropped into bed, and he was certain he'd fallen asleep before his head touched the down pillow.

Trevor hadn't questioned Matt about why he'd so unexpectedly decided to visit Key West for the first time in years. Typical. Trevor had a relaxed, easygoing attitude toward life. He let people tell him about themselves in their own time and in their own way.

Matt threw back the sheet and climbed out of bed naked. The limestone floor beneath his bare feet was cool as he crossed the room to watch the sunrise. He closed the plantation shutters and folded them back so the morning light could fill the room.

"Awesome," he said out loud, realizing that in all his thirty-four years he had never watched a sunrise or a sunset. "Life's too short not to take the time to enjoy it. Too damn short."

Roused from its cradle in the ocean, the amber sun chased away a ribbon of low-lying mist. The soothing indigo of the sea gradually became a breathtaking turquoise as the sun rose. Dazzling in the morning light, the sand was as white as new fallen snow. It was easy to understand why Trevor had come to Half Moon Bay, fell under its spell. And stayed.

Matt showered and put on shorts and a T-shirt, not bothering with a belt or shoes. It was early, and he was sure no one would be up yet. He took his time walking from his suite to the kitchen. The open-plan interior of the home featured a sculpture gallery. He'd been too exhausted last night to inspect Trevor's latest acquisitions.

He was examining a contemporary bronze piece, trying to decide if it was a man in some weird position or a bird, when he heard a woman singing quietly in the kitchen. Trevor had told him that he had several people staying with him, but it was surprising someone was up already. He didn't feel like meeting anyone and being forced to make small talk, but the smell of coffee lured him into the kitchen.

Like the rest of the house, the spacious kitchen had an airy feel with light woods and creamy ivory granite counters. The French doors were open to the exterior, where wicker chairs surrounded a glass-topped table. The morning breeze gently ruffled the palms shading the house.

Two of Trevor's cats were lounging on a plush wicker chaise facing the beach, while another was inside eating from one of the eight bowls lined up against the pantry wall. Trevor had a thing for stray cats. And stray people.

" 'Mornin'," a young redhead greeted him with a southern drawl. "Coffee?"

"Sure. I'll get it." He went over to the Brewmatic and poured himself a mug of coffee while she flitted around the kitchen like a hummingbird on uppers.

She sported a diamond stud in one nostril, a gold safety pin pierced the edge of her eyebrow, and a series of studs and gold hoops paraded up her earlobe to the top of her ear. She smiled at him and revealed yet another stud in the tip of her tongue.

Yuck!

Okay, so piercing was the rage with kids these days. What bothered him was her outtie belly button peeking over the top of her hip-hugger shorts. From it dangled some damn gold charm. It made him wonder what else she'd pierced.

Without saying a word, he took his coffee outside and sat in a chair facing the water, hoping she wouldn't join him. No such luck. A second later she plopped down in the chair beside him.

He could feel her eyes on him, but he didn't turn toward her. He'd begun his career in journalism as a cub reporter on the police beat and had developed his observational skills. One look and he'd memorized her face and come to some conclusions about her.

She looked young. Seventeen or eighteen max, but she was probably twenty-five. Her red hair contrasted vividly with her pale gray eyes, making them appear even lighter. A clan of freckles gathered on the bridge of a nose surgically snipped a bit too short.

"I'm Bubbles. Bubbles McGee, and you're Matthew Jensen, right?" She spoke with a pronounced drawl, the stud in her tongue flashing at him. "Trevor told me all about you."

Matt doubted Trevor had told her much. It wasn't his style.

"You two were roommates at Yale, right?"

"Uh-huh." Could Bubbles possibly be her real name, he wondered. But he didn't ask. He just wanted to be alone. He'd slept the sleep of the dead last night, yet he had the disturbing feeling he'd dreamed about Shelly.

He was convinced she was close to regaining consciousness. What would he do when she did? He didn't want to be involved with her, but he couldn't desert her either.

Bubbles rattled on and on and on about how Trevor's cats were descended from Hemingway's six-toed cats. It wasn't true, of course. Trevor had rescued them from various places, but Bubbles sounded sincere, proof positive that a southern accent could make BS convincing.

"Well, gotta go," Bubbles informed him. "I have to catch the first commuter launch to town. If I don't get there real early, some twit, like, takes my spot in front of Margaritaville. Do you know what she's trying to sell?"

"I'll bite. What?"

Bubbles leaned close and whispered as if imparting top secret information. "The twit is selling *The Mother Teresa Sex Diaries* and charging ten dollars."

"Sounds like fascinating reading."

"I wouldn't know. I don't, like, spend my hard-earned money on erotica. I'm a legitimate businesswoman."

Standing on the sidewalk in front of Margaritaville? Yeah, right.

"I'm saving money to open my own shop."

"I'm relieved to hear it." Only a fool would have asked what kind of shop.

"Right now I sell insurance."

God forbid.

"Wanna see?" From the paisley tote she'd brought with her, she whipped out a scroll of parchment paper secured with a curly red ribbon. She untied it and shoved it between his nose and his coffee cup.

The bold black letters at the top read ALIEN ABDUCTION IN-SURANCE.

Only in Key West. Okay, okay, it worked in L.A. too.

"Matthew, you're just the type aliens love to kidnap. You need my UFO insurance."

"Really? Well, I'll be damned. I've always wanted aliens to beam me up to their spaceship and have their way with me."

Bubbles rolled her eyes as she stood up. "You're no fun. I'm outta here."

She flitted away and left Matt alone to watch a great blue heron fishing in the surf. Matt was certain he'd seen one the last time he visited, but he hadn't bothered to notice what a fine coloring job Mother Nature had done. The bird was a pale blue gray with darker blue wings. Its tail and breast feathers were startling blue like a rare sapphire. His upper legs contrasted sharply with the rest of his body, a vivid orange like its bill.

"Good morning," Trevor called from the kitchen. "How'd you sleep?"

"Great, thanks." Matt stood and went into the kitchen.

Trevor was barefoot too, and wearing shorts and a tropical-print shirt. While Matt looked like an unmade bed, Trevor could have stepped off a page in *GQ*. Not only was Trevor the kind of man that women drooled over, he had a certain flair. It was something you were born with, not something you could acquire.

Matt had grown up on the mean streets of Chicago, a scrappy kid who always got into fights. If fate hadn't kicked in, sending him to Yale on a scholarship, Matt would probably be in prison right now. Trevor had come from the opposite end of the spectrum. He'd grown up on an estate in Connecticut and prepped at Choate before coming to Yale.

A street fighter from Chicago and a silver spoon, yet they'd become best friends, a relationship that had withstood the test of time and distance. Next to his sister, Emily, the only person Matt was close to was Trevor.

He slowly walked into the kitchen, careful to avoid a number of cats who'd appeared out of nowhere at the sound of Trevor's voice. They darted across the room and positioned themselves at the bowls lined up along the far wall.

"I'm going to whip up an omelet," Trevor told him as yet another cat appeared and jumped up onto the counter to watch. "Let me make one for you."

"Now you're talking. I haven't eaten since—" He tried to remember the last time he'd eaten. He'd been cleaning out his apartment in Manhattan so he could sublease it, when the call about Shelly came. He must have had lunch earlier that day. Maybe not. He'd lost his appetite the day he'd quit his job.

Trevor cracked egg after egg, never once missing the bowl or dropping a bit of the shell into it. "Can you stay for a while, or do you have to rush back to *Exposé?*"

"I want to see what I can do for Shelly, then I'd like to stay down here until I decide what I want to do." Matt leaned against the center island where Trevor was working and tried to appear casual. "I've left *Exposé.*"

He saw the questions in Trevor's green eyes, but his friend didn't ask them. After a moment's hesitation, he added the last egg to the bowl. Matt had planned to explain the situation to Trevor, but he wasn't ready yet. Telling Emily had been hard enough.

"Stay here as long as you like, Matt. I'm renovating a house on Angela Street. If you want, you might be able to help us with the house history."

"Sure."

Trevor owned a very profitable gallery on Duval Street, the main drag, but his passion in life was the Old Island Restoration Association. Key West had more houses on the historical register than any other city. Trevor had been involved in preserving these historic homes since he'd come to the Keys.

"How's Emily?" Trevor asked as he beat the eggs with a whisk.

"Great. I spent last weekend in Nantucket with them. She's still trying to have a baby."

"Hey, that's wonderful. You'll be an uncle soon."

An uncustomary note of regret colored Trevor's voice, and Matt knew he still took his family situation hard. His father was a domineering man who controlled the family. When Trevor's father disowned him, the rest of Trevor's relatives had been too intimidated to ignore Graham Adams's wishes.

Trevor took out an omelet pan from a drawer in the island, then walked over to the commercial style Viking range and turned on a burner. Matt sat on a barstool and watched. "That's Bingo," Trevor said as the enormous one-eyed cat who'd been on the island plopped down on Matt's lap like a bag of cement. "Bingo rules."

The apricot-colored cat rubbed against Matt, purring for all he was worth, scrutinizing him with one big green eye. The big cat was cute, but Matt had always preferred dogs. Suddenly, he remembered Shelly had a dog. "Where would the police have taken Shelly's dog?"

Trevor tilted his blond head to the side so he could see Matt and still keep his eye on the omelet. "The Humane Society has a facility not far from the house we're renovating. Do you want me to check on her dog?"

"If you have the time."

Trevor took a bowl of sliced mushrooms and shredded cheddar out of the refrigerator. He artfully arranged the mushrooms in the omelet pan. Then he asked, "What do you hear from Kelly Taylor?"

Matt ran his hand over Bingo's sleek coat, thinking about Kelly. She had attended Yale with Trevor and Matt. Later Matt and Kelly had worked together as journalists. They had been inseparable once and he'd thought Kelly was "the one," but it hadn't worked out.

He'd assigned her the best-selling story *Exposé* had run last year. Logan McCord, who had been kidnapped as a child and disappeared for twenty-one years, had suddenly reappeared, working with the elite Cobra Force Antiterrorist Unit. His story had fascinated the nation.*

And Kelly Taylor.

"The little boy Kelly and Logan adopted"—Matt had to think for a minute to come up with the kid's name—"Rafi, is doing great. He's learned to ride his own pony, and stuff like that."

Like a Cordon Bleu chef, Trevor flipped the omelet over, then smiled at Matt. Something inside Matt's chest tightened. Telling Trevor about his problems was going to be hell. Emily was Matt's sister by blood, but Trevor was his best friend. And Matt was reminded of an old saying: Friends are the family we pick for ourselves.

Amy awoke by degrees, sensing rather than seeing her surroundings. She heard the low hum of the machines and the almost inaudible drip-drip of the IV. There was a slight bustle of movement in the ICU.

She allowed one eye to drift open slowly. A woman in a white uniform was tending the other ICU patient. The disgusting male nurse was nowhere in sight. She opened the other eye and tried to clear her drug-fogged brain.

---

* See *Tempting Fate*, Zebra Books, May, 1998.

Matt—whoever he was—did not know Dexxter Foxx. Her life was not in danger from Matt, but what had that hideous man done to her last night? The shot he'd given her had kicked in just as he'd lifted the sheet.

She thought her body might give her a clue about what had happened, but pain numbed every muscle, rendering her motionless. A film of sweat crusted her body, yet she was chilled. It was nearly impossible to concentrate on anything with the white-hot pain searing through her.

The gauze restricted her vision, but she managed to watch the female nurse tending to the other woman. The nurse treated her gently, a stark contrast to the male nurse on the night shift.

"I've got to make her understand . . . somehow," whispered a voice inside her head. She did not want to spend another night at the mercy of the male nurse. Imagining what he might have done brought the bile up in her throat.

Suspended in hell, unable to speak or make anyone understand her, was like being trapped in the twilight zone. There had to be a way to help herself. She thought a moment and realized there was a way to communicate using her left hand.

There was no point in pretending to be unconscious now. Matt was no threat to her; if anything, he might help her. Where was he?

The nurse walked over to her bed and picked up the chart. Holding her breath to keep the pain at bay, she raised her left hand. "Take my hand, please," the little voice inside her head begged.

The nurse dropped the chart, clearly astonished at what she was seeing. "Glory be! You're—you're"—she peered intently at her gauze-shrouded eyes—"awake."

She lifted her hand higher. *Hold my hand, please. Touch me.*

The nurse spun around, saying, "I'll get the doctor."

Exhausted from the effort of lifting her hand, she closed her eyes and rested her good arm. Surely, she would have better luck with the doctor.

A few minutes later the doctor she'd seen yesterday walked into the room. She opened her eyes, telling herself to find the strength to lift her hand again. It took all her power, but she managed to raise her hand and wiggle her fingers.

"We're better today, aren't we?"

We? Why did doctors always use that word? There was no we in this. *She* was all alone with her pain, trapped with the nurse from hell.

She waved her hand again, sending a bolt of pain through her chest. Ignore it, she told herself. She had lived with mental pain her entire life. She could endure this.

She had to touch the doctor to be able to have a prayer of explaining what was happening. He studied her chart, then scribbled a few notes, either not seeing her hand or not realizing it was important.

"Keep your head on the pillow. Your jaw was badly broken. It's been wired shut. It'll heal faster if you keep your head level and don't move."

So that's why she couldn't talk. He rattled on about her other injuries, and she listened, praying for an opportunity to use her hand to communicate. She mustered the strength to lift it again and crook her forefinger, signaling for him to come closer.

He checked his watch, missing the sign. "It's not quite eight. Matthew Jensen probably isn't awake yet. I'll wait until nine, then tell him you're conscious. He's been worried about you."

Pain raging through her like wildfire, she waved her hand. Too late. The doctor was already turning away.

Matthew Jensen. The man in the blonde's journal. *He thinks I'm the woman he loves so much.* What had happened to the woman? She must have died in the crash, she decided.

The journal had detailed the perfume, sexy lingerie, and other gifts he had given her. They had been so very much in love. From what she'd read in the journal, their sex life would have made Satan blush.

She didn't dwell on what it would be like to have a man—especially a man like Matthew Jensen—in love with her. She had learned that ugly lesson years ago. But she did pray for him to return and take her hand again.

It was her only chance.

The nurse came in and out several times, changing IV bags and consulting the chart. She struggled to get the woman to take her hand, but her efforts with the doctor had depleted her reserves of strength. Now all she could do was raise her hand a scant inch above the sheet and flex her fingers.

The woman never noticed.

Minutes lapsed into an hour, then at least two hours passed. There was no clock she could see, so it was hard to tell. She waited and waited for Matthew to come.

"Here's a little something to make you feel better."

She looked up, realizing she had drifted off. The nurse was preparing to give her a shot. Oh, no. She'd miss Matt. The attempt to wave off the syringe produced nothing more than a flop of the wrist. The needle entered the shunt and the room disappeared seconds later.

When she opened her eyes again, the shift had changed and a new female nurse was tending the other patient. Had Matt come, then left? It didn't seem likely that he would leave before he spoke to her.

A shaft of sunlight caught her attention, and she slowly turned her head toward it. The room was on the ground floor near two palm trees. Judging by their shadows, it was late afternoon. In a few hours the night shift would take over. The revolting male nurse would return.

"Matt, please come soon," she silently pleaded. "Hold my hand again, please. I need you. Oh, how I need you."

CHAPTER

FIVE

"How's she doing?" Matt asked the nurse.

"Shelly seems a little agitated. She keeps waving her hand."

He'd stopped at the ICU nurses' station on his way to see Shelly. It was dinnertime at the hospital, and trays were being delivered to rooms adjacent to the ICU. From outside the building he heard the high-pitched yodel of an ambulance arriving.

Since receiving the doctor's call that morning, Matt had spent hours trying to determine if Shelly had health insurance. Under Cobra, she had coverage from her previous employer for her accident injuries, but it did not cover the reconstructive surgery necessary to make her face look normal again. Matt had tracked down the owner of the *Key West Daily,* Shelly's new employer.

The man flat refused to advance Shelly any money for plastic surgery. Worse, he wouldn't hold her job for her, insisting he needed someone immediately. Matt couldn't blame him. The paper was a two-bit operation and probably could not afford it.

How was he going to break this news to Shelly, then leave her alone to face life with a disfigurement? He was all kinds of pissed. With himself. With Shelly. With the whole damn situation.

When she had been stalking him, Matt had tried to reason with her and convince her that he wasn't interested. Shelly kept insisting he loved her and just wouldn't admit it. He'd consulted a psychiatrist who specialized in such cases. *Have no contact with the stalker. Interaction—of any kind—only reinforces the behavior because the stalker craves your attention. Any way they can get it.*

Still, he had to talk to her this one last time.

He walked up to her bed, half hoping she was sedated, but he could see her blue eyes were open. They seemed different than he'd remembered, a color so rich, so intense, it caused a catch in his breath. It had to be the contrast between the blue of her eyes and the stark white gauze.

"Shelly, you're awake. Good. You had the doctor worried."

He smiled—or tried to—and she responded with a pathetic flutter of her left hand. There was a spark of some indefinable emotion in her eyes.

Be dead honest, he told himself as he swung a chair around backward and straddled it. But don't give Shelly any reason to think you care too much about her.

Shelly's hand trembled as it rose from the white sheet and shakily reached for him. Her body went rigid with the effort, and a frantic look glittered in her eyes. He was glad he'd turned the chair around. Touching Shelly would only encourage her.

"Have they explained about your injuries?" he asked, ignoring the way she was feebly reaching for him. He knew the doctor must have talked to her, but he needed a way to lead up to the bad news. "Your dislocated shoulder is better, so they've taken the pulley away."

The hand imploring him to hold it was trembling violently now.

"Your leg is broken, but it's not bad. The doctor says you'll have one of those walking casts for a few weeks, then a canvas cast with Velcro straps. You can take it off when you sleep."

Shelly's eyes conveyed something he interpreted as desperation. She squeezed them shut, and her arm hit the bed with a lifeless *thunk*. A second later she opened her eyes again. There was something so pathetic in them that he felt like a real shit for not taking her hand.

He steeled himself, remembering what she'd said the last time he'd seen her in New York—when the police were handcuffing Shelly after she'd threatened his sister. *I'll love you until you die, Matt.*

At the time he'd been too damn mad and worried about Emily to wonder what Shelly meant. Later the psychiatrist warned him that stalkers often resorted to murder when they were convinced they'd been rejected. *If I can't have you, no one else can.*

He hadn't been concerned about Shelly's threats. They had been vague. Stay away from Matt or you'll regret it. But what if she became violent? Emily or some other woman around him could be in danger.

The psychiatrist cautioned him that restraining orders often drove obsessive types over the edge. Court orders might be seen as proof of rejection. Each year many women were killed after taking out a restraining order.

After that incident she had disappeared from his life. Until now. Right this minute she didn't seem the least bit threatening. If anything, he pitied her. She crooked her index finger, beckoning him to come closer.

Shelly . . . oh, Shelly don't do this.

Now came the hard part. "Shelly, raise one finger if you understand me."

The finger twitched, nothing more. He imagined the effort she'd put into reaching for him had exhausted her. Jackass that he was, he felt sorry for her, sensing her utter frustration from the pleading look in her eyes.

He might have handled this another way, but after consulting the shrink on stalkers, he'd continued to research the subject. Stalkers are persistent and often make people feel sorry for them. Most people attempt to let them down gently, which only encourages them.

Exactly what he had done.

The way to end stalking is to stop contact, he reminded himself. Do what's right, then get the hell out of Dodge.

"You're lucky to have survived the crash. It's a miracle you don't have brain damage."

Her eyes no longer were blue. As he spoke, they had become bleak, turning as gray as the winter sky. She was no longer looking at him.

You schmuck! he cursed himself, then glanced down at her left hand, her good hand with the IV shunt, the hand he'd held while she'd been unconscious. Her fingers were splayed awkwardly on the white sheet. Why couldn't he just walk away?

Don't feel sorry for Shelly. Never forget, she's mentally unbalanced. Possibly dangerous.

The hell of it was, she didn't look the least bit dangerous now. *Pathetic* fit better. Pathetic and helpless.

Aw, hell, she was getting to him—big-time.

"Your jaw was badly broken," he continued to talk to her. "It's been wired shut. In about three weeks the wire will be removed," he told her, but wondered if she was listening. Her eyes had a glazed, faraway look. "Shelly, lift a finger if you still can hear me."

Her index finger rose a fraction of an inch, but she didn't look at him.

"The right side of your face was badly damaged, but luckily, not your eye." He exhaled a measured breath, then continued, his voice pitched low. "You're going to need expensive reconstructive surgery. It's not covered by your insurance. Do you have any money or know someone who could lend it to you? Wiggle your finger if you do."

The only movement was the drip-drip-drip of the fluid in the IV as it flowed into her hand. Exactly what he'd figured. He could lend her the money. Hell, he could *give* her the money. What did it matter to him?

But if he did, she would see it as an expression of love. Life was too damn short to get involved with a nutcase like Rochelle Ralston. Still, it was impossible to look at her and not want to do something.

"Matt?" Trevor's voice interrupted his thoughts.

Amy saw the blond man standing in the doorway and a flutter of hope replaced despair. She had counted on Matt taking her hand so she could tell him what was happening. But he had pointedly ignored her efforts.

Evidently, something had gone wrong in his affair with the woman who had been driving the car. She could tell by the way he talked to her that he no longer loved the woman. He refused to even touch her.

"Shelly," Matt said. "This is Trevor Adams."

The astonishingly handsome man walked up to her bed with a friendly, easygoing smile. His green eyes were full of unmistakable warmth, yet there was a poignant sadness in them too, as if he'd seen the dark side of life.

She immediately was drawn to Trevor. She was almost too exhausted from trying to communicate with Matt to lift her hand, but Trevor gave her hope, and she managed to reach toward him.

Please, Trevor, help me.

Trevor hesitated, then lightly brushed her fingertips. He pulled back his hand, saying, "I have good news for you. I picked up your dog at the shelter."

Miracle of miracles, Jiggs had survived. Thank you, God.

"He was a mess, so I took him to Groomingdale's. My friend there gave him a bath and an avocado/papaya moisturizing treatment to soften his fur."

He seemed so genuinely pleased he'd been able to do something to help her that tears pricked at her eyes with a hot sting. No man had ever shown her such kindness. Over the years she'd observed men like this, who were so knee-weakeningly handsome. They expected women to grovel.

She reached for him again, even though the movement caused pain to crackle up her spine and into her skull with blinding intensity. He gently squeezed her fingers, then released them.

"There's been a wreck," Trevor told Matt. "A motorcycle hit the Conch train and about two dozen tourists were injured. Nothing serious, cuts and bruises, but they've flooded the emergency room."

"That's what all the sirens were about."

"There's only one nurse at the station. Everyone else was called to the ER. I think we could sneak Jiggs in here." He turned to Shelly. "Would you like that?"

She knew better than to move her head, but she couldn't help nodding just a little. Jiggs, dear Jiggs. He'd saved her life. If she hadn't heard him whimpering and gone out to see what the brute had done to him this time, she would have been in the house with the federal marshal when Dexxter's man blew up the building.

Matt went outside with Trevor to get the dog. "It's a mistake for me to stay around Shelly much longer. She keeps reaching for me, trying to hold my hand. Everything I've learned about obsession warns against physical contact with the stalker."

"She kept reaching for me too. She seems frantic . . . or something. Does she understand the extent of her injuries?"

"Yes. The doctor explained, then I told her."

"It must be frightening though. She doesn't have any family or friends to see her through this."

It wasn't hard to miss the compassion in Trevor's voice. Even a wacko like Shelly could get Trevor's sympathy. If Matt didn't handle this situation right, Trevor would take over. When it came to saving birds with broken wings, Trevor was in a class by himself.

Then Shelly would fall for Trevor. Legions of women had chased Trevor and had broken hearts to prove it. Matt wondered what had happened to Trevor's latest relationship but respected Trevor's privacy enough not to ask.

Trevor opened the door to his sleek black Porsche. A little dog cowered in the passenger seat as if waiting to be kicked.

"Now, I ask you, have you ever seen an uglier dog?"

Trevor chuckled. "You should have seen it *before* I took it to Groomingdale's."

The dog was the size of a chihuahua, with coarse, shaggy fur the

color of sludge—not brown, not black. Its soulful eyes were chocolate brown, its only redeeming feature. The dog turned and Matt saw
part of one ear was missing, cut off at an odd, jagged angle.

Trevor asked, "What do you suppose happened to its ear?"

"Beats me."

Trevor scooped up the trembling animal and put it in a canvas
shopping bag. "This should get us past the nurses' station."

It did. They walked right by the station and into the deserted
ICU. The woman in the other bed appeared to be asleep, but even
from the door Matt could see Shelly's intense eyes expectantly
watching them through the slits in the gauze. Trevor placed the dog
between Shelly's body and her uninjured arm.

The little mutt stopped shaking the second its paws touched the
sheet. Its scrawny tail swished back and forth while the dog licked
Shelly's fingers. There was a smile in Shelly's eyes, then the sheen of
tears.

Man, oh, man. Don't cry. Matt had never been able to handle it
when a woman cried. He never knew what to do, what to say.

The tiny dog nuzzled her body. Tears silently slipped from her
eyes and seeped onto the gauze, dampening the bandage below her
eyes. She blinked hard, fighting back the tears, but they kept coming.

An odd twinge of something Matt couldn't quite name struck
him along with an unexpected thought. *I'll love you until you die,*
she'd told him many times. She claimed to love him, yet she hadn't
been nearly as glad to see him as she was this dog.

"I don't want you to worry about your dog," Trevor told her. "I'm
going to take care of him until you're well. You can see how great his
fur looks after the moisturizing treatment."

Trust Trevor to know what to say to a woman at a time like this.
The tears slowed and the happy glimmer returned to Shelly's eyes.
Damn, if she didn't have remarkably striking eyes.

"He wouldn't eat the dog food the groomer had, but don't
worry," Trevor continued. "We're going to dinner at La Te Da in a
few minutes. It's one of the best restaurants in town. Friends of mine
own it. They'll keep bringing food until we find something he likes to
eat."

"What's that dog doing here? It's not allowed."

Matt turned and saw a male nurse approaching the bed. Trevor
opened his mouth to explain, but didn't get the chance.

"Look at the patient. You've upset her. You'll have to leave immediately."

Shelly had stopped crying. She was looking at the man with an expression Matt would swear was pure hate.

The burly man glared at Matt with such an in-your-face attitude that he was tempted to deck the cocky little prick. The nurse grabbed for the dog. Without thinking, Matt thrust out his arm to stop him.

The man squared his stocky shoulders. "I'm calling the supervisor."

"Come on, Matt." Trevor picked up the dog. "We have a dinner reservation." To Shelly he said, "Don't worry about your dog. I'll take good care of him."

Shelly's eyes frantically flashed from the nurse to Matt. Something was disturbing her, but he couldn't tell what. It seemed to be more than just having her dog taken away. She lifted her head off the pillow and shook it, saying no the only way she could.

No what?

"You must keep your head on the pillow," said the male nurse as he pushed her shoulders down.

Panic glistened in Shelly's midnight-blue eyes now, making them almost feral in their intensity. Those eyes were locked on him, pleading.

For what?

She was a nut, Matt assured himself. Little she did made sense. How could she be so agitated about a dog that she had to know wasn't allowed in a hospital room?

It had to be the dog, didn't it? What else could it be?

Unless she didn't want him to leave. Just as this thought crossed his mind, Shelly lurched sideways, grabbing for his hand, something akin to terror in her eyes. Despite his better judgment, Matt would have taken her hand to reassure her, but the nurse blocked him with his body.

"Matt, we should go," Trevor said. "We're upsetting her."

"Shelly, I'll come by tomorrow," he said over his shoulder as he walked away.

At the door he looked back. The nurse was scribbling on the chart. Shelly was staring at Matt, her eyelashes fluttering in a rapid, frenzied way as if she were trying to tell him something.

Matt left the ICU and walked down the hall beside Trevor. "Is it my imagination, or did Shelly seem more than just a little weird to you?"

"I thought her reaction to the pooch was normal." Trevor grinned at the dog that only its mother could love. "She has no way of communicating with us, but she didn't need words with the dog. He loves her and missed her."

Matt shouldered his way through the swinging doors and walked out into the early evening heat. A warm breeze was blowing the clouds around a lopsided moon that was just visible in the darkening sky. The scent of the tropics invaded his nostrils, and he welcomed the change from the antiseptic smell of the hospital.

Trevor opened the Porsche's door and placed the dog on the ledge behind the seats. Matt went around to the passenger side and almost opened the door, but stopped.

"You know, I'm going to walk around the corner of the building and look into the ICU. I want to see if she's okay now."

"I'll come with you." Trevor shut the car door.

They walked in silence across the asphalt parking lot. Even though it was almost dark, heat still shimmered from the surface. They stood beneath the twin palms outside the brightly lit ICU. The nurse was bustling around the room, changing IV bags and checking monitors.

From this angle it was impossible to see much of Shelly's face. They were too far away to read any emotion in her eyes.

"She's settled down," Trevor said. "We should get over to La Te Da."

Matt's sixth sense kicked in. "Just a minute."

The nurse was preparing a syringe for the other patient now. He gave her the injection, then stood there. The peculiar half-smile on the jackass of a nurse kept Matt watching. The man reached under the sheet.

"Is he doing what I think he's doing?" Trevor asked.

The male nurse fondled the woman's breasts for a moment, then tucked the sheet into place.

"You dumb shit!" Matt cursed himself. "That's what Shelly was trying to tell you."

"From where she is, she can't see what he's doing."

"She saw something or he did something to her. That's why she was so frantic."

The man headed toward Shelly's bed. Matt sprinted around the corner, slammed aside the entrance doors, raced down the hall, and charged into the ICU. The nurse had a syringe in his hand. As he bent down, Shelly's arm shot upward to ward off the needle, ripping the IV from her skin. Blood spurted from Shelly's hand, splattering the nurse.

He spun around, obviously shocked to see Matt thundering into the room. Matt grabbed him and shoved him flush against the wall.

"You little shit!" Matt clamped his hand around the guy's throat just as he rammed his fist into his soft gut.

"L-let go," he whimpered.

Matt whacked the son of a bitch's head against the wall.

"Matt, stop!" yelled Trevor.

Behind Trevor, another voice distracted Matt. He took his hand away from the bastard's throat, but kept his fist solidly planted in his beefy belly.

"This man's been copping feels—maybe worse," Matt said. "Shelly didn't want to be put under because she was afraid of what this asshole was going to do."

"That's absurd," insisted a prim-looking older woman in a nurse's uniform. "Simon's been with us for years."

"On the night shift, right?" Matt asked. "That way there isn't anyone around to see what he does."

"Don't be ridiculous. We trust Simon implicitly."

"We were watching," Trevor informed her. "We saw him fondling the other patient's breasts. We're calling the police."

"Oh, goodness me. I'll get my supervisor."

The woman scurried away, and Matt took advantage of her absence to slam his knee into the prick's groin. The man's eyes crossed and he gagged as he crumpled to the floor. Matt cocked his fist, ready to let him have it again.

"Matt, wait . . . stop!" cried Trevor, then he yelled, "Shelly, you can't sit up."

Somehow Shelly had managed to lever herself upright, yanking the pulley to one side. The contraption snapped, releasing her. Matt lunged to catch Shelly before she pitched forward and injured herself more. A second later she was in his arms, her bandaged head resting against his shoulder.

He brought her closer, dodging the wires and tubes as well as the arm encased in a plaster cast. Her body seemed unbelievably light, yet it relaxed against him as if he were an old, trusted friend.

"You were trying to tell me, weren't you?" he asked as he stroked her back.

Her fingers were twined with his and blood from the tear made by the IV oozed, hot and sticky, onto his skin. She was touching his palm. Writing. What a fool he'd been. This was the only way she had of communicating.

He cradled her in his arms as Shelly stroked his palm with a very shaky finger. H-E-L— She paused, her hand trembling, then she began again. P-M-E. It took a split second for his brain to process the message. *Help me.*

He gathered her even closer, whispering, "Don't worry. I'm going to help you."

CHAPTER
SIX

Dexxter Foxx inspected the magazine photograph of himself in *Software Update,* the industry Bible. Shit! It didn't do him justice. His baby blues—those sexy bedroom eyes—looked squinty. He was handsome, he assured himself. Drop-dead handsome.

The buzzer on his desk trilled and he heard his secretary's voice. "There's a gentleman here to see you from the Federal Bureau of Investigation."

His secretary sounded rattled, and a thread of unease wound through Dexxter. "Send him right in."

Special Agent John Thomas walked in, flashed Dexx his identification, then said, "We're investigating the death of a federal marshal who was killed in Sacramento."

"California?" Dexx said as if it were some third world country no one gave a shit about.

"We have reason to believe Amy Conroy was involved. She worked here, didn't she?"

The man knew she did, probably knew everything about her, but Dexx played along. "She was my employee for nearly five years, but when her mother died, Amy went off the deep end. After the funeral, she disappeared."

"Did you suspect foul play?" The man asked the question with a poker face as if he didn't know exactly what had happened to her.

"We were worried when she didn't show up for work. Irene, one of my employees, went over to Amy's apartment. The landlord said Amy had moved out. She was going to L.A. We assumed that's what she did."

The FBI agent nodded slowly, and Dexx's guard went up even more. Why was he really here? He knew all of this. It must be some sort of a trap. Say as little as possible, he warned himself.

"She was living in Sacramento in a rental house. A federal marshal was visiting her when the place was bombed, and he was killed. She vanished."

"Why would she murder him?" Dexx asked, thinking this would be a logical question if a person did not know Amy had been in the witness protection program. Dexx gave himself a mental pat on the back for having Zane bribe an FBI employee to obtain the confidential dossier on Amy. Now they had an inside source.

"We're not certain she committed the crime, but we'd like to question her. Do you know the names of any of her friends?"

"She didn't have any friends that I know of. She had an ugly birthmark on her face. She was very sensitive about it, so she kept to herself." Dexx leaned back in his chair, doing a damn good job of appearing relaxed. "She didn't have time for friends either. Her mother had Parkinson's disease and required constant care, especially at the end."

"You won't mind if I question the other workers? Amy might have said something that will give us a lead."

"Sure, go ahead," Dexx replied with a smile. What choice did he have?

The agent left, and not two seconds later Irene rushed into his office, breathless. As usual, she wore a short dress that gloved her buns like a lover's hand.

"Are they on to us?" she asked.

"No, it's just a fishing expedition. They've lost their star witness. They're hoping someone around here can help them."

"Do you think anyone else—"

"No one else knows. Amy was smarter than all of them put together."

Irene hitched her skirt up and sat on the edge of his desk, exposing a lot of thigh. "Anyway, we've corrected the problem. No one can prove we're doing anything illegal, or that we've had anyone killed."

"Do you know what this visit tells me? The Feds don't have a clue where Amy is either. Otherwise they wouldn't be sniffing around here."

Irene stood, then came around his desk. "You're tense. I can see it in your neck. Let me give you a back rub while I tell about Zane's latest report."

Dexx almost told her to forget it, but the agent's questions had left him on edge. Even if he was one step ahead of them, no one wanted the Feds breathing down their neck.

Dexx had to turn sideways in his chair for her to give him a massage. Irene began as she always did, by raking her long fingernails up and down his back in slow, sweeping motions. He'd taken off his jacket earlier, so her nails felt sharper than usual. Almost sexy.

"Zane contacted all the plastic surgeons in the Sacramento area. None of them treated Amy."

Dexx leaned his head forward as she worked her way up his neck with her nails, then into the hair at the base of his skull. He released a long sigh, his blood feeling heavy and thick as it thrummed through his temples. Irene was good for something after all. "Tell him to check San Francisco. It's close. Amy might have gone there."

Irene was using her hands now, kneading the taut muscles at the top of his shoulders. Languid heat shimmied through his body.

He should have let Amy give him back rubs, he thought. If he'd paid more attention to her, Amy would still be here. He didn't like looking at her, but if she'd been behind him like Irene was now, Amy's face wouldn't have deflated the erection he was getting.

"Dexx, do you know how much this is costing us? Zane can't just walk into a doctor's office and expect to get confidential patient information. He and his men have been posing as reporters doing an article on the use of laser surgery to remove birthmarks and other scars."

"So?" He hadn't known how Zane was getting the info and didn't give a shit. Results were what counted.

"If a doctor doesn't cooperate, he has to break into the office to get the information." Irene was working on his upper back now, the base of her palms massaging the deep muscle tissue. The effort made her voice breathy and mildly arousing. "Zane charges us triple if he has to break in."

"It's worth it. If we don't find Amy, it's just a matter of time before the FBI does."

"I have an idea. I'm going to use the Internet to see if I can locate the bitch."

Her tone might have frightened some men, but Dexx had been around Irene for too long. She was full of herself, that's all.

"Do you know about animalnetwork.com?" she asked as she pummeled his muscles with the sides of her hands in short, choppy motions.

"Nope, never heard of it." He left surfing the Net to dumb fucks. The money was in microchips and software.

"Zane got a picture of the dog Amy was supposed to have stolen. One of the other neighbors took the picture to show to the Animal Rescue League." She pulled a photo out of her pocket, an amazing feat, considering how tight she wore her clothes.

He didn't like animals; they got fur all over his suits. This dog was less likable than most. It was butt ugly. "What happened to its ear?"

"According to the neighbor, the dog's owner cut half of it off to prove to his wife that she'd be sorry if she left him. He got drunk that night and his wife simply disappeared."

He cocked his head and gazed up at Irene. "Two women disappear from the same neighborhood. Maybe the connection's there."

"Perhaps, but I'm checking in at animalnetwork. If anyone has seen that dog, missing a piece of its ear, they aren't likely to forget it."

It sounded like a half-assed idea to him, but he kept his mouth shut and let her use her thumbs to ease the tension in his neck. He pretended it was Amy Conroy behind him, and was amazed at how erotic he found that thought.

As Irene's thumbs roved up and down, she leaned forward until her tits brushed his back. Casually yet provocatively. The hot nubs of her nipples pressed against him.

It was a little game Irene liked to play. She relaxed him, then she purposely aroused him. She changed position, deliberately dragging her huge tits with their bulging nipples across his back.

He imagined Amy's jiggling breasts as she'd walked across the office—her good side to him—and pretended those big jugs were against his back now. His body responded, heat turning his groin to iron and kicking his pulse into high gear. He closed his eyes, letting the fantasy take hold.

"So what do you think about my idea?" Irene asked, jolting him back to reality.

"I'll think of something myself," he snapped. "I always do."

He had a world-class hard-on that was begging for relief. He refused to give in to the urge to screw Irene. Instead, he would let her strut her stuff, then he would pick up the telephone and call Technical Assistants.

It was just a fancy name for a call girl service conveniently located just up the street. They would send over a real looker to take care of him. The techs cost a lot, sure, but it was worth it, because he could walk away.

If he became involved with Irene, there would be no escaping her. She'd been after him since they were kids. Once her claws were in him, she would never let go.

"You're right, Dexx," she whispered in his ear as she stroked his neck with her talented fingers, triggering the upward surge of his cock. "We have to get rid of Amy. I just wish we knew where she's gone, or who might be helping her."

His burgeoning erection made it difficult to think. The tip of Irene's tongue flicked his ear for just a second, a light but very erotic touch. It might have been accidental, but, of course, it wasn't. She was getting bolder all the time.

Soon he would give her exactly what she wanted. He'd throw her over the desk and screw her brains out. Then he'd leave her behind forever.

He was already making arrangements to sell Foxx Enterprises. Amy squealing to the Feds put a crimp in his style. It was time to start over—without Irene.

Amy awoke with a start, disoriented, not remembering for a moment where she was or what had happened. Then through the slits in the gauze she saw Matthew Jensen asleep in the chair beside her bed. In a dizzy rush everything came back to her.

Too vividly she recalled the blinding panic and hopeless frustration of reaching for Matt, attempting to communicate the only way she could. She had thought it was a lost cause, but somehow he'd sensed her distress and returned in time to save her.

Don't worry. I'm going to help you.

He'd been holding her in his arms when he'd said those words. She marveled at the thought, acutely aware he was the only man who'd ever taken her into his arms. And it had felt so . . . right. So unbelievably right.

She allowed herself a rare moment of self-indulgence and closed her eyes, reliving the experience. At the time, she'd experienced a gut-wrenching sense of relief, knowing Matt had saved her from the nurse. Then, her body, exhausted from fighting, realized a man was holding her.

A dizzying current had raced through her, and instead of pain, she had been filled with an emotion too intense, too precious, to be reduced to a single word. A savage need had gripped her, the need to be held, the need to be comforted. The need to have someone care.

She had been alone in the world for so long. Her whole life, actually. Only her mother had been there. Now that she was gone, the world seemed empty and lonely.

In the corner of her mind she realized Matt had believed he was comforting Shelly, but at that moment she was beyond caring. As weak as it seemed to someone who had been content in her insular world, she needed this man.

Kicking herself for giving in to her emotions, she raised her eyelids. She'd softened, opening herself up more than she'd ever allowed. Yet, she couldn't ignore the inexplicable sensations that made her feel alive with a wondrous sense of anticipation, a rare exhilaration that she had never before experienced.

"You're asking for trouble," whispered the ever-present little voice in her head as she gazed at Matt, who was still asleep in the chair beside her bed.

Evidently, he took his promise to help her seriously. He was in the same clothes, and whiskers shadowed his angular jaw. He hadn't left her side, hadn't taken the chance anything else would happen to her.

She was so touched that tears pricked at her eyes, then crested, dampening her lashes. "He didn't do it for Amy Conroy. He did it for Shelly Ralston."

Still, she knew she would remember being in his arms—forever. His chest had been so sturdy and warm, his arms strong yet gentle. He'd held her so close that she'd felt the rapid thud-thud of his heart against her breast.

Her body ached with the all-consuming need to be in his arms again. He'd been so gentle with her, and the feeling of tenderness lingered. Haunted.

Most women took a man's embrace for granted, but she knew better. She had plenty of experience with the bone-deep despair of being one of life's untouchables. *The Beast.* She shuddered inwardly, recalling years upon years of being alone and telling herself that she didn't mind. No wonder she remembered being in his arms with a surge of longing so intense, it bordered on physical pain.

When she took his hand again and explained who she was, he'd have no reason to stay. As he slept, she studied the masculine planes of his face, tempered by a sensual mouth and long, thick black eyelashes. He projected nonchalance that bordered on arrogance, but on another level lurked a compassionate, caring man.

What would it be like to have him kiss her?

"Stop it!" cried the voice in her head. "Your life is in danger. Don't daydream about Matt. Start thinking of a way to protect yourself."

If she revealed who she was, it might appear in the paper, or even on television. The moment Dexxter found out, he would have her killed. But what if she didn't confess? It would buy her time to come up with a plan.

She wouldn't have much time. When the bandages were removed, Matt would see enough of her face to realize that she was not the woman he loved.

Her stomach churned with anxiety and frustration as she recalled Matt discussing her injuries. Apparently, the hideous birthmark wasn't enough. Fate cursed her yet again. Her face needed reconstructive surgery, but she didn't have a penny to her name and had no hope of earning money until her injuries healed.

Matt's eyes drifted open, and he straightened up. "Are you okay?"

She managed a slight nod, thinking the brooding intensity of his gaze was enough to take any woman's breath away. Just looking at him sent a rush of longing through her aching body.

"Remember, don't move your head."

He leaned toward her and inspected her left hand. She'd forgotten all about the wound she'd caused when she'd swung at that creep and ripped out the IV shunt. It had been bandaged and a new IV inserted in another vein.

"Don't worry about the nurse. He's been arrested." His eyes were a tawny shade of brown in the morning light and seemed less intense than they had yesterday. "After they medicated you last night, the doctor examined you. Apparently, all the jerk did was touch you."

She was shocked at the impact of his words and could feel the heat rising to her cheeks. She told herself not to be embarrassed. After all, Matt thought he was discussing this with someone he knew quite well. He didn't realize she was a virgin, or have any idea how panic-stricken she'd been not knowing what that creep had done to her when she'd been unconscious.

"You're going to—"

"Jensen, I heard what happened." A policeman interrupted Matt, walking into the ICU in the khaki uniform of the tropics, starched shorts and a shortsleeve shirt with a badge gleaming on its breast pocket. "I was off duty, or I would have been the one to arrest the scumbag."

She wasn't certain how the policeman knew Matt and didn't dwell on it. The man was going to question her. She mentally weighed her options, then rolled the dice. She would pretend to be Rochelle Ralston for as long as possible.

Matt introduced the police officer, but the name didn't register. Her mind was too busy scrambling for a plausible way to dodge as many questions as she could.

"Forensics in Miami tell us that the other body is that of a woman," the officer told Matt.

Of course the other body was a woman's. It was Shelly's body, and they could quickly confirm this—if they knew to check. Any minute they were going to ask her who the dead woman was.

"They've positively IDed the truck driver, but they aren't sure if the woman was a hitchhiker he picked up or not. It's possible she was in the car with your friend."

"Shelly, did they tell you the details of the crash?" Matt asked. "Lift one finger for yes."

She kept her hand still and prayed he'd give her enough information to conjure up a story they would believe.

"It was a head-on collision. Everyone was thrown from the vehicles. That saved your life and your dog's. The others weren't so lucky. They were ejected but landed close to the truck. It exploded, burning them to death."

A twinge of guilt uncoiled in her chest as she thought of Shelly dying such a tragic death. Pretending to be the woman and allowing Matt to believe she was still alive was cruel. She started to reach for his hand and tell him the truth.

Dexxter Foxx's smug face flashed across her mind.

She vowed to make this up to Matt later. When she had recovered a bit more, she would explain, then pray he would forgive her.

"Shelly, lift your finger if the woman was a friend of yours. Her family will need to be told."

She didn't move, taking the additional precaution of closing her eyes, not wanting Matt to detect the truth.

"Just what we figured," the cop said. "That trucker picked up someone. We don't have any missing person reports in Key West. I'll check the state's computer and see what they've got."

He shook Matt's hand, then left, and she said a silent prayer. She hated herself for becoming a liar—like Dexxter Foxx—but she was like a turtle on its back in the desert sun. She was utterly helpless.

"Shelly, I've been thinking about your situation, and I've come up with a plan." Matt's voice was absolutely emotionless now, and it chilled her. "Despite what you did, I'm going to help you."

For a soul-searching moment the world froze. What had Shelly done?

"Without reconstructive surgery, you'll go through life badly disfigured. Do you know what that will be like?"

Of course she knew. Better than anyone, she knew to expect stares and whispers. And worse. You'd live a life never knowing the tenderness of a man's embrace.

Loneliness stabbed at her heart as she recalled Matt's arms around her. It had been so brief a moment that he might not remember, but she would never forget the compassion, the tenderness shown her by the only man who had ever held her. Yes, oh, yes, she knew what life would be like without the surgery.

"I'm going to pay for the surgery, if—and this is a very big if, so think carefully before answering. I want you to swear you won't come near me or call me or contact me in any way . . . ever again."

Was this the last time she would see him? An ache swelled upward from her heart, causing tears to pool in her eyes. Why? Why?

"Shelly, raise your hand if you agree."

She closed her eyes, reliving the moment when he'd cradled her in his arms. What she was feeling defied all logic. He didn't know who she was, and he certainly wasn't hers to keep. Yet something inside her did not want to let him go.

"Aw, Shelly, don't do this to yourself."

She had no choice, so she opened her eyes and raised her hand slowly.

He stood up. "This is the last time you'll ever see me. I don't want you to go through life a freak, but I don't want to become involved with you again. Do you understand?"

She didn't. Not for the life of her. Did he really mean that she was never going to see him again? Obviously. He turned and walked out the door.

She cried out for him to come back. But the words were locked in her heart.

CHAPTER
SEVEN

Trevor wheeled Amy from the MedVac van up the walk to the Bel Aire Clinic. The short drive from Key West to Paradise Key had exhausted Amy, and she struggled to remain upright in the wheelchair. The time she'd spent in the hospital had weakened her more than she'd realized.

It had been five days since she had seen Matt. Trevor had taken over, coming in each afternoon to see how she was progressing and giving her a report on Jiggs. He hadn't mentioned Matt, nor had she asked. After all, she'd given her word.

It made it much easier to pretend to be Shelly Ralston, since Trevor hadn't met the woman. She couldn't help wondering what Shelly had done to make Matt never want to see her again. It seemed to be an extreme reaction, considering how much in love they'd been.

She couldn't help missing Matt.

It was ridiculous, of course, a total waste of her time. Still, she couldn't stop it. During the day her thoughts often drifted to him. At night her dreams were filled with him.

"I understand Clive Burroughs is an extremely gifted surgeon," Trevor told her as he pushed her wheelchair toward what appeared to be a graceful southern mansion not a clinic. "Women fly in from across the country to have cosmetic surgery here."

Inside the mansion, clusters of baby pink rosebuds filled at least a dozen exquisite vases. The scent of the flowers and the hushed atmosphere reminded Amy of the funeral home where she'd made final arrangements for her mother. She tamped down the profoundly disturbing memory.

The antiques and original oil paintings on the walls left no doubt in her mind that Dr. Burroughs charged outrages fees. Criminy! How on earth was she going to earn enough money to pay back Matt? She *would* do it, she vowed, even if it took years.

The receptionist was seated at a French writing desk. The woman was so astonishingly beautiful that she had to be a freak of nature—or a cosmetic surgeon's masterpiece. She looked up and saw Trevor. The warmth of her smile echoed in her voice.

"Good morning," she said to Trevor. "You must be Rochelle Ralston."

"Actually, I'm Trevor Adams. This is my friend, Shelly Ralston."

If she could have moved her jaw, she would have giggled. Trevor had a devastating effect on women, even a breathtaking beauty like this one.

"Yes, of course. That's what I meant."

The receptionist hadn't given her more than a brief glance, which was fine. She wasn't accustomed to direct eye contact. All her life people had avoided looking her in the eye. It made her nervous when they did.

"The doctor's reviewed the file the hospital sent over," the receptionist informed him with a flirtatious flutter of her eyelashes. "I'll let him know you're here."

They were immediately led into a mahogany-paneled study lined with leather-bound books. Behind a highly polished desk sat a man about forty years old. Attractive, with close-cut brown hair, and wire-rimmed glasses that magnified no-nonsense brown eyes, Dr. Burroughs smiled eagerly at Trevor.

The doctor graced her with a quick glance, then directed his remarks to Trevor. "I've studied Rochelle's file, but I'll need to examine her myself. That hospital's third rate—at best. I need to assess what damage they've done."

As silent as a shadow, a nurse appeared from behind a paneled door and wheeled her into a chamber off the study. The woman made small talk while she cut the bandages off her face.

"Oh, my," the nurse inhaled sharply, then looked away.

Amy realized there wasn't a mirror anywhere in the room. She couldn't possibly look any more hideous than she had with the birthmark, could she?

Dr. Burroughs came into the room. His face devoid of expression, he examined her from several different angles. "They did one thing right at the hospital. The dressing on your face is cadaver skin. That prevented further deterioration."

Cadaver skin? Her stomach lurched, then took a sickening downward plunge. A dead person's skin was on her face. How much worse could things get?

"My nurse will apply another dressing, then we'll discuss the procedure with Trevor."

The nurse followed the doctor's directions and used a soft brush to apply a viscous gel he called Ryboten, then rebandaged her face. The woman wheeled her back into the study where Trevor was waiting.

"The underlying bone structure on the right side of her face will have to be repaired," the doctor told Trevor. "But the damage isn't as bad as I thought when I read the hospital's report. Most of the skin was sheared off, but the muscles are intact."

Did that mean the birthmark was gone? It must have been sheared off, because no one had mentioned the birthmark. If this doctor could repair the injured bones, she would look like an ordinary person.

What would it be like to walk into a room and not have your heart pound, anticipating averted eyes and stares? And even more humiliating—whispering. Dear Lord, she would give everything she had or ever hoped to have just to be normal.

"The challenge will be to replace the missing skin. I use DermaGraft, a new bioengineered product that's living skin tissue produced in the laboratory. Before it became available, we had to graft skin from another part of the patient's body."

She noticed Dr. Burroughs was speaking to Trevor as if she didn't exist. Trevor had a magnetic effect on people. When he was in a room, no one else existed.

"This way there won't be any scarring. She has one excellent cheekbone. By using a matching submalar implant, I can reconstruct the shattered cheekbone."

Trevor turned to her and took her hand, then gently squeezed. "Don't worry about a thing. You're going to be fine."

She held his slim hand, then traced a message on his palm. *Bless you.* Through the slits in the gauze her eyes locked with his, and he smiled with such sincerity and reassurance that tears stung her eyes.

* * *

Matt gazed up at Nantucket's blue sky and braced himself for Emily's next attempt to change his mind. He loved his sister more than anyone on earth, but he had already made his decision.

"You were born a fighter," Emily said, her voice pitched low and charged with emotion. "Mom didn't even get to the hospital. You fought your way into this world, bawling your head off, in the backseat of a police car. And you've been fighting ever since. It's not like you to give up."

Matt inhaled the briny scent of the sea and let his gaze drift to the bay, where a pair of sailboats had their rails in the water, racing into the harbor. He silently conceded Emily was right, but the tough kid on the mean streets of Chicago seemed to be another person. In another lifetime.

"I want to kick back for a while," he told her.

To make his point, he swung his bare feet up on the porch rail of his sister's summer home and pretended to enjoy the spectacular view. It was a flawless Indian summer day, warm, yet with long shadows cast by trees that had already changed colors.

"Oh, Matt, I'm so glad you're here. We haven't spent enough time together these last few years."

He ventured a look at her and saw love and concern etched on her pretty face. Although Emily was five years older and distinctly feminine, they'd inherited the same amber-brown eyes and dark, thick hair. They shared similar personalities too. Both of them were driven, determined to be successful. That's why it was difficult for Emily to understand his decision.

"I have an idea," she said. "Why don't you—"

He jumped up, knowing his sister well enough to realize she had some new plan—one he wouldn't like. He hated arguing with her when he'd already made up his mind. "Hold that thought. I need to make a phone call."

Key West had been on his mind all day. Okay, Shelly had been on his mind more than he cared to admit. She'd had reconstructive surgery three days ago and come through it without complications.

He dialed Half Moon Bay's number, hoping to catch Trevor at home. A feminine, southern-fried voice answered, and he asked Bubbles if Trevor was there.

"He's in the kitchen and trying to, like, persuade Jiggs to eat some filet mignon. I'll get him."

Jiggs was Shelly's half-eared mutt. Apparently, the dog was as nutty as his owner, refusing to eat much of anything. Of course, Trevor wasn't going to give up. Trevor Adams—friend, brother, vet. You name it and Trevor was there for you.

"Matt, how's it going?"

"Great, just great. I called to see how Shelly is doing."

"She's better every day. I know she's in pain, but she hasn't complained."

"When do you think they'll release her?"

"Clive says the bandages will come off in another two days. If everything's okay, she'll blow up like a balloon. She'll have to stay in bed another day or so to reduce the swelling."

"If everything is okay," Matt repeated. "Does the doctor think something is wrong?"

"Clive won't know until the bandages are removed if he correctly repaired the problem. I have some good news for you. He's going to waive his fee. Shelly's surgery isn't going to cost you a dime."

Clive? Apparently, Trevor had taken such an interest in Shelly's case that he was now on a first name basis with her doctor, and he would bet Trevor had persuaded the doctor to donate his services to help Shelly. Christ! Just what he didn't need—his best friend getting attached to that wacko.

"Great. Thanks."

"There's an outside chance that Shelly will reject the bioengineered skin. It's rare, but it happens. Clive will have to graft her own skin."

Matt hesitated, then said, "Has she asked about me?"

A beat of silence. "No, she's kept her promise."

Matt had forced Shelly's promise, half expecting her to break it. Yet, she hadn't even asked about him, which would have been a logical first step. Was he just a little disappointed? No way.

"I don't think Jiggs is eating the way he should," Trevor told her. "Don't be upset. He's fine, but he's . . . finicky."

It had been ten days since Dr. Burroughs had performed the surgery. Since then a series of nurses had pampered her, changing her dressings and making sure her head was elevated on a triangular pillow to lessen the swelling.

Trevor visited every day, spending a little time with Dr. Burroughs to get an update on her condition before coming to her suite. The nurse on duty would be ga-ga in seconds, but Trevor never noticed.

She took Trevor's hand to communicate with him. Drawing letters on palms was almost second nature to her now. P-O-P-C-O-R-N.

Trevor looked up from her palm, his green eyes puzzled. "Popcorn? You feed Jiggs popcorn?"

She raised her hand to say yes. The brute who owned Jiggs before she'd taken him spent his nights in front of the TV, eating popcorn and getting drunk. The next morning, he flung the leftover popcorn into the yard.

Jiggs had been traumatized since he'd been a puppy. He was accustomed to eating leftover popcorn and refused other food. On their cross-country trek, she had fed him popcorn, intending to wean him from it later.

"S'okay," Trevor said with a soft chuckle. "I'll try popcorn. Jiggs likes my cats. He even sleeps with Bingo."

Beneath her bandages, she almost smiled. Trevor seemed so proud of his work with Jiggs. She owed him, she reflected, every bit as much as she owed Matthew Jensen. Maybe more. He had been with her every step of the way through the excruciating pain of reconstructive surgery.

"They're taking off your bandages today, you know." Something dulled the warmth in his eyes, warning her.

What was wrong? Had Dr. Burroughs told him bad news? She wasn't worried; anything was better than a repulsive birthmark.

"I thought beauty and the beast were two people, not one."

Those hurtful words, uttered so many years ago, echoed through her mind. She could still feel the agonizing thrust of the knife in her heart, young love destroyed in seconds by cruel words.

She sat up in bed while Dr. Burroughs cut off the bandages, and Trevor stood nearby. Please God, she silently prayed. Let me be normal.

The doctor tossed the bandage in the trash, then closely inspected her face. "The DermaGraft took very nicely," he said to Trevor. "Smile for us, Shelly."

Her lips quivered, but nothing happened. Her jaw was too tight. She tried again, and this time her lips parted. She managed a shaky twist of her mouth.

"You can talk, Shelly," the doctor told her. "The wire they inserted has been removed."

She tried to open her mouth, but her jaw refused to budge. Finally, it gave a little and her lips parted just enough for her to feel air on the tip of her tongue. Her mouth was as dry as the dead palm fronds skirting the tree outside her window. Her parched throat worked up and down. No sound emerged.

Nothing.

"Have a little water." Trevor handed her a glass with a straw. She took a sip. Instantly her throat felt better, but her jaw was like a vise. Her vocal cords seemed to have been removed.

With mounting alarm she tried to recall the last time she'd spoken. True, she'd whispered to Jiggs and talked a little during their cross-country sojourn. But her last real conversation had taken place over two months ago on the fateful night of the federal marshal's visit.

Maybe her vocal cords had somehow been damaged by the accident or the operation on her jaw, or by medications she'd been given. *Please, please let me talk. There is something I have to say.*

Trevor encouraged her. "Try again."

She ran her tongue over her dry lips, then attempted to speak. All that emerged was a wheezing sound. Trevor and the doctor exchanged concerned glances.

"Take your time," Dr. Burroughs said.

Finally a sandpaper-like whisper came from her mouth. "H-how . . . can I . . . thank you? B-both of you."

Trevor shrugged, clearly embarrassed by the emotion that must have shown on her face. It certainly wasn't in her gravelly, three-pack-a-day voice.

"Thank Clive," Trevor responded. "He performed the surgery for nothing. Matt won't have to pay anything."

"Th-thanks so much." At least she didn't owe Matt money. Considering the way they had parted, this was for the best.

"Don't thank me yet," Dr. Burroughs said. "You have a little swelling, but now that the bandages are off, you'll be Miss Pumpkin Face just like my face-lift patients." He pressed the buzzer attached to her bed. "Let's get your head down and have the nurse put a Koldpak on you. Twenty minutes on, ten minutes off for the next forty-eight hours."

What do I look like, she wondered. Judging from their faces, she couldn't be too terrible, but she wanted to see for herself.

"May I have a mirror?" Her voice was louder now, but with a distinct croak.

The doctor glanced at Trevor, and Trevor nodded. She could see the two had become good friends during this process.

The doctor took a hand mirror out of a nearby cabinet, saying, "I don't want you to be upset. Your skin is very pink, but it will tone down in a few days."

"Clive was careful about getting an exact match with the bioengineered skin," Trevor added. "Until your own skin grows back, no one will notice."

"Don't be concerned about the bruises under your eyes. They're from working on your nose."

"My nose—"

"It was too long for your face. You were out of proportion, so as long as I was at it, I snipped a bit."

How arrogant of him, she thought, but she didn't complain. All her life she had wanted to wake up and be someone different. This doctor had granted her wish and he had waived his fee, which had to be enormous.

He handed her the mirror and she held it up. She gazed at the side of her face. It was pink, but the splotchy wine-colored birthmark was gone. She heard her own quick intake of breath that was actually a gasp of relief.

Then she looked more closely. Despite the raccoonlike bruises under her eyes, she instantly recognized the face. Oh, my God! Her mother was staring back at her.

She had inherited her mother's blond hair and blue eyes, but she'd gotten her father's nose. Fate had changed that. Now, as she looked in the mirror, she saw the one person who had always loved her.

Looking back over her life, she felt blessed, not cursed. The birthmark had made her miserable, true, but she had been given something of infinite value. Her mother's unqualified love.

From the time she was little and first sensed she was "different," her mother had made her feel special. Later as the birthmark made her more and more self-conscious, her mother encouraged her, praised her. Never let her down.

Her mother saw the beauty in Amy, not the hideous birthmark. She had been so unbelievably proud of her. Even now she remembered the thrilled smile on her mother's face when she had graduated summa cum laude. Standing up in front of all those people had been humiliating, but the joy she had given her mother made it worthwhile.

"Never a doubt," her mother had said. "You're as smart as you are beautiful. I'm just sorry your father isn't alive to see you."

It wasn't true, of course, but she *had* been beautiful in her mother's eyes. Oh, how she wished her mother could see her now. She missed her mother so terribly that tears sprang to her eyes, and she blinked hard to keep them from falling.

It didn't seem possible she would never hear her mother's loving voice again. Never see her fond smile. Never was an eternity, she reminded herself as tears tumbled down her cheeks. An eternity without the most gentle, caring person she could ever imagine.

Oh, Mom, thank you for loving me.

Trevor put his arm around her. "Shelly, don't cry. The pinkness and the bruises will go away."

She looked into his green eyes and realized Trevor possessed the same compassionate soul that had made her mother so special. She gave him a one-armed hug.

"I'm not worried. I miss my mother, that's all."

CHAPTER
EIGHT

The sky was a lovely shade of blue, a rich, deep hue with a single wispy cloud like a mare's tail visible just beyond the cluster of towering palms. The trees were leaning slightly, their fronds gently rippling. If she went for a walk, which she was allowed to do several times a day, she could visit the azure sea bordering the clinic's grounds.

A view to make anyone's spirits soar.

While the view lifted her spirits, Amy still wasn't accustomed to seeing her beloved mother when she looked in the mirror. Each time, her breath would stutter-step before she realized she was gazing at herself. No longer being a freak cheered her, yet poignant sadness assailed her as well. How she wished her mother were still with her.

She was slowly adjusting to being able to live her life without the hideous birthmark. The world's hard edges seemed softer now. With her new face, negative forces seemed to recede, allowing her personal universe to expand. The life she'd always dreamed about was within her grasp now, its possibilities limitless.

Except for Dexxter Foxx.

He was lurking out there somewhere. She knew the beady-eyed weasel too well to think he'd given up searching for her. It was only a matter of time before he found her.

She had survived the near-fatal crash, but she wasn't completely healed yet. She had a walking cast from the knee down, a new device that could be removed when she bathed or went to bed, but she needed a cane to walk. Her shoulder ached constantly, even though it was supposed to be all right. Her right forearm was still in a cast, and her entire hand was encased in something that looked like a catcher's mitt made out of plaster.

She was in no condition to go on the run now.

Trevor had dropped a comment or two in their conversations, and she knew Matt was no longer in Key West. From what she could gather, no one in the area knew Shelly Ralston. It only made sense to pretend to be this woman for as long as—

"Officer Marley is here to see you," a nurse interrupted her thoughts.

She'd been expecting another visit from the police. It had always been difficult for her to lie, but it was going to be even more so now that people looked her in the eye. Remember, she told herself, your life is at risk.

"Amazing!" the young officer said the moment he walked through the door. "I wouldn't have thought it possible. You were so badly injured."

"The doctors worked a miracle." She shifted the bag of frozen peas to the other side of her face. Three days with a Koldpak mask on her face had reduced the swelling, and now all she needed was to hold the bag of frozen peas against her face for fifteen minutes every hour.

"I have some good news for you."

She doubted it, but showed him her teeth, hoping he'd think she was smiling.

"Your things are at World Wide Movers."

Good Lord, no.

"I'll bring the boxes over here if you like."

He looked directly at her, obviously pleased at what he saw. She wasn't accustomed to men—willingly—looking directly at her, much less volunteering to do things for her. She managed to nod with what could be mistaken for a smile.

He reached into the pocket of his khaki shorts and pulled out a small notebook, then flipped it open. "First I need to ask you a few questions."

She put the bag of now mushy peas over her eyes to shield them from his gaze. "What do you want to know?"

"Tell me how the accident happened."

Having anticipated his question, she peeked one eye out from behind the bag of the Jolly Green Giant's finest and attempted to appear truthful.

"I've tried and tried to remember the crash, but the last thing I can recall is going into a Stop 'N Go about an hour north of Miami." She slid the bag over her eye. "After that, everything is a black hole."

"Don't worry about it," the Officer Marley responded. "I understand it's common in serious accidents like this for victims to blank out the incident. It may come back to you later. If it does, give me a call."

With a flirtatious grin he placed a card on her nightstand. She managed a weak smile in return and dropped the bag of peas as soon as he left. What was in those boxes, she wondered, all too aware that any little thing could blow her cover.

Just after lunch the officer returned with two large boxes. She pretended to be too exhausted to open them, which was close to the truth. Dr. Burroughs wanted her to walk the grounds twice a day, and she was eager to get out, but the effort left her muscles trembling from weakness.

She waited until the officer had left, then asked the nurse for a pair of scissors. Working with just her left hand, it took forever to open both boxes. One contained articles that Shelly had written, beginning with her stint on the high school yearbook up to a year-old article for a smarmy tabloid.

Shelly had put a yellow journalism spin on Logan McCord's story. It didn't offer a bit of evidence to support the allegations, but the article was the type of tabloid sensationalism that sold newspapers at the supermarket checkout counter.

That article Shelly had saved reflected a woman with average writing talent who worked for one of the sleaziest rag sheets in the country. Matt's photojournalism magazine, *Exposé*, was just the opposite; its pages were devoted to substantive issues that were important to all Americans. It was difficult to imagine Matt with someone like Shelly, but, of course, she was beautiful, sexy. And men were men.

The items in the first box were of some use, she decided. She now knew where and when Shelly had gone to school as well as a little about her job. She was prepared to field the simple questions anyone might ask.

The other box contained casual clothes that were larger than what she wore, but the size difference could be explained away as weight loss from the accident. Her shoes were two sizes too large.

At the bottom of the box she found matched sets of bras and panties. With her good hand she caressed the soft, filmy fabric edged in fine lace. Oh, my! She'd seen expensive lingerie like this, of course, but even if she'd had the money, she would never have spent it on seductive lingerie meant to be seen by a man.

Matthew Jensen's face appeared out of nowhere.

Her vision blurred, and suddenly she imagined wearing nothing but the black lace bra and matching bikini in her hand. He was gazing at her, not at her body, but at her face. And he was smiling.

A surge of purely feminine power swept through her, astonishing in its intensity. This is what it was like to be a woman who was proud of her body.

A woman with a pretty face.

"Go for it," she whispered as she held up a wispy black bra with one hand. "Oh, rats." The bra was far too small for her.

She shoved the enticing lingerie aside. "Character determines fate, and it's just not in your character to prance around in this kind of lingerie like a Penthouse Pet."

But it would have been fun, she silently conceded as she opened the last item in the box, a manila envelope. Inside she found a stack of black and white photographs. All the shots were of one person.

"Matthew Jensen," she said out loud.

The camera captured him in unguarded, intimate moments. A pensive Matt, reading a newspaper at a sidewalk cafe©. A smiling, happy Matt, laughing with friends as they jogged side by side. A serious Matt, talking with someone who appeared to be homeless.

Something tugged at her heart. These were sides of the man she had never seen. They revealed the inner depth and power she had glimpsed in the brief time she'd known him.

"What had happened between Matt and Shelly?"

The pictures didn't give a clue, and before she had the chance to give it another thought, Trevor knocked on the open door and poked his head into the room.

She shoved the photographs into the envelope and silently reminded herself to get rid of the shoes and the bras before someone discovered she wasn't Shelly.

"Are you feeling better?" Trevor asked as he walked into her room with his usual smile. "Ready to go for a walk?"

"I'm better every day," she responded, determined to sound upbeat.

Interestingly, Trevor put her at ease, but he seemed unaware of his devastating effect on women. There was something about him that made her certain he would have treated her the same even if the hideous birthmark still marred her face like a splash of scarlet paint.

"Some of my things came. I won't have to leave here in an open-back hospital gown."

Her attempt at a joke was met with an adorable grin. "I have good news. Clive says you're going to be released tomorrow."

Great, she muttered under her breath. She had no money, nowhere to go.

Trevor helped her into a robe, and she hobbled outside. Usually, the balmy air and the rhythmic lap of the sea on the sand cheered her. Not today. Her mind kept scrambling to come up with a plan, a way to stay one step ahead of Dexxter Foxx.

They were standing under the palm trees, watching an egret wading along the tide line, when Trevor asked, "Where will you go?"

She lifted her shoulders in what she hoped was a casual shrug. "I have friends who will help."

"Really? That's . . . wonderful."

There was such heartfelt hope in his eyes that she had to look away, embarrassed that she'd relied on the cocoon of his protection for so long. Even if she hadn't been hiding from Dexxter Foxx, she had no friends, nowhere to go. But she refused to burden Trevor any longer.

They watched the egret for a few minutes, but when the bird flew off, Trevor led her down the path toward the parking lot. "Someone's here to see you."

Ahead in a Porsche convertible she saw Jiggs peering out the open window at them. As they came closer, the little dog hopped up and down. He'd been groomed again, which had given his brown fur a lustrous gloss.

Even before she could set the cane aside, Jiggs scrambled toward her, wagging his fluffy tail. With her good arm she lifted him up and held him against her chest. A suffocating sensation tightened her throat as she realized that here was the only living being who knew her as The Beast.

And loved her anyway.

Trevor studied her a moment as she blinked away a rush of tears. "How are you going to take care of him, Shelly? How are you going to take care of yourself?"

She hadn't fooled him, not for a second. Jiggs had suffered enough. She had no idea where she would go or how she would support herself. It wasn't fair to drag him along with her.

"I'll manage, but if you could keep Jiggs, it will help. I'll come for him as soon as I can."

"You're not in any shape to take care of yourself. Come home with me. I have a big place. Bubbles will help take care of you."

"I—I can't. I promised Matt that I would stay away from him."

"Matt's gone." Trevor threw up his hands. "You know how Matt is. If and when he does come back, you'll be gone."

The archangel Michael. That's who Trevor reminded her of. He'd known she would refuse further help and had used Jiggs to convince her.

"Thanks, you have no idea how much I appreciate your offer."

"I want you to do one thing for me," he said quietly.

Too quietly. Uh-oh. She hugged Jiggs and looked directly into Trevor's troubled green eyes, bracing herself for unpleasant news.

"I have a friend who's a psychiatrist. He's worked with people with obsessions—"

"Obsessions?"

Trevor swallowed hard, and she knew this wasn't easy for him. He must truly believe Shelly needed psychiatric help. He took a moment to study the mirror-finish wax on his Porsche before continuing. "Shelly, you hounded Matt, following him everywhere. You deluded yourself into believing he loved you."

She started to tell him about the romantic trip to Bermuda and all the gifts Matt had given Shelly, facts she'd gleaned from the journal while she had been a stowaway in the trunk of the car. What woman wouldn't think Matt loved her?

Then she remembered the grainy photographs she'd found among Shelly's clothes. Taken with a telephoto lens. The light slowly dawned. Oh, my God. The woman must have been stalking him, shooting pictures when he wasn't looking.

"I'm sorry for what I did," she whispered.

"I can understand you falling in love with Matt, but it's hard to justify threatening his sister."

"I did?"

The odd look on Trevor's face told her that she might have tipped her hand, but the words were already out of her mouth. "Shelly, I know you're . . . troubled. I promise you won't regret consulting a psychiatrist."

He walked her back to the room in silence. She didn't know what he was thinking or why he would offer to help such a horrible person. She hated lying to him, but she didn't have any choice.

"Wait just a minute," she said as she shuffled into the room. Bending over was painful, but she managed to find the manila envelope with the photographs. "Take these. That's how obsessed I became. I swear, the accident changed me. I'll never bother Matthew Jensen again."

Trevor rifled through the photos, disappointment marring his handsome features. It was all she could do not to confess, to admit she wasn't crazy Shelly, but she remained silent, staring down into the box with the dead woman's things.

He dumped the photos back into the envelope, then gazed at her. "Please, Shelly, don't make me sorry I'm helping you."

CHAPTER
NINE

Matthew heaved his duffel out of the launch and onto the dock at Half Moon Bay. Lights sparkled from every door and every window while the sounds of chatter punctuated by laughter filled the warm night air. A party. Just his luck.

He secured the mooring lines around the cleats, then slowly made his way toward the house. Skirting the property, he walked along the sand so he could enter the side of the house without passing through the group gathered on the front terrace. He'd left his sister in Nantucket and returned to Key West because he intended to enjoy the laid-back lifestyle. And because Trevor wasn't going to prod him to change his mind the way Emily did.

The last time he'd spoken to Trevor, he had told Matt the doctor was releasing Shelly. Matt had assumed it would be safe to return, but he hadn't expected a party.

Under his breath he muttered, "You're one presumptuous jerk." He should have called first. What if Trevor had more guests than beds? Trevor would give up his own bed rather than turn anyone away, but Matt didn't want to put him on the spot. Trevor had already gone beyond the call of friendship by taking care of Shelly.

He spotted a Keys hammock floating in the breeze between two royal palms near the kitchen. The lightweight hammock was fringed with shells that tinkled as it swayed in the whisper of a breeze. Matt dropped his duffel and climbed into the hammock, deciding he could sleep there under the stars. In the morning he could talk with Trevor and see if there was any room at Half Moon Bay for him.

He relaxed, staring up at the whirlpool of stars overhead. The air was so warm, the night so clear, he felt he could reach up and touch the stars. Touch the stars. He mulled over the thought.

He'd been determined to touch the stars with his career. And he'd done it. He'd gone from next to zero, a street kid from Chicago, to a top-notch investigative reporter. He'd topped off his career—before his thirty-fourth birthday—by taking a nearly bankrupt rag sheet, *Exposé,* to a premier position as the most respected newsmagazine in the country.

But sometimes touching the stars wasn't enough. His personal life was a crock. Be careful what you ask for; you just might get it. He'd wanted the stars. Okay, he had touched the stars, but what did he *really* have?

Nothing.

Nothing that really counted except his sister, Emily. And Trevor.

A high-pitched shriek brought him bolt upright, and he nearly tumbled out of the hammock. Bubbles McGee was calling to someone.

"Shaw . . . lay." Shelly.

Son of a bitch. Shelly couldn't be here, could she? He gazed out at the rippling water, asking himself why in hell he was so surprised. There wasn't a lost soul who couldn't find shelter under Trevor's roof. No doubt, Shelly had appealed to Trevor's sympathetic nature.

He slipped out of the hammock and picked up his bag. Turning to leave, he glanced into the house and saw Trevor go into the kitchen alone. Matt dodged a pair of pygmy palms, then walked through the open door into the kitchen, nearly stumbling over one of Trevor's cats.

Startled by the noise, Trevor turned. "Matt, what are you doing here? I—I mean, I'm glad to see you, but I wasn't expecting you."

"Sorry to barge in like this." For the first time since Trevor had told him about his split with his family, Matt didn't know what to say. He valued Trevor's friendship too much to yell at him for taking in Shelly. "I'll find a place in town."

Trevor looked like a dog who'd just been kicked by a master he adored. "You've seen Shelly."

"No, but I heard Bubbles calling her name."

"Shelly's been through a lot. She isn't going to bother you, Matt." The quiet firmness in Trevor's voice startled him. He'd known Trevor had that take-charge attitude, but he'd never directed it at him. In a way it made Matt feel like an outsider despite their years of closeness. Matt cursed Shelly for coming between him and his best friend. "Talk to her, you'll see."

"Forget it." Matt turned to go. "I'm outta here."

Trevor caught his arm. "Matt . . . do it for me."

Matt opened his mouth to refuse, but a long-buried memory flashed into his mind. His first week at Yale. He'd been at home on the mean streets of Chicago, but he was totally unprepared for the snobs at Yale, whose first question was were you prepped. Except for Trevor. He'd befriended Matt when no one else would.

If it hadn't been for Trevor's help, Matt might have dropped out of Yale and missed the opportunity of a lifetime. He might never have enrolled in his first journalism class, which led to a career he loved as an investigative reporter. He might . . . aw, hell. There were too many *might-nevers* to count. Plain and simple, he owed Trevor—big-time.

"Okay . . . sure. Where is she?"

Trevor led him through the open air foyer toward the terrace facing the glistening sands of Half Moon Bay. Tables had been set up on the terrace and about two dozen people were standing around, sipping drinks and chatting. Off to one side stood a petite blonde with her back to them.

Shelly.

He wasn't quite prepared for the hitch in his chest. The last time he'd seen Shelly, she had been hooked up to machines, her face wrapped like a mummy. It didn't seem possible she would ever recover, he thought, his eyes skimming the near backless pale lavender sundress she was wearing.

Yet there she was, still with casts on her arm and lower leg and leaning on a cane, her blond hair shimmering across the back of her neck. Among the living again. He couldn't help being proud of his part in her recovery.

"She's talking to Clive Burroughs. I told you about him. He performed the reconstructive surgery." Trevor stopped and spoke in an undertone even though no one was close enough to hear them. "He used biogenetically engineered skin and a new type of surgical glue instead of stitches. She won't even have a scar."

He was thankful to the doctor who had made Shelly normal again—without charging him—but he doubted her mind-set had changed. According to the experts, intensive therapy was the only hope for obsession disorders.

Almost as if she sensed him staring at her, Shelly slowly turned, leaning on a cane. Their gazes collided, hitting him like a sucker punch in the gut.

Her eyes were the same vibrant blue, yet they seemed closer to violet than he remembered, with a smoky, almost sultry look to them. She wore no makeup and had made no attempt to style her hair. It hung in tousled waves to her shoulders, as if she'd just rolled out of the sack with some guy.

High cheekbones and a patrician nose offset lips that were—he kicked himself when he realized what he was thinking—kissable. Her lower lip was a little too full for perfection, but the hell of it was—that's what made her mouth so appealing.

"That's not Rochelle Ralston," he told Trevor. "I don't know who in hell she is, but that woman is not Shelly."

"Of course it's Shelly. Clive couldn't help himself. He trimmed her nose and gave her cheek implants to improve the contours of her face. All he does these days is cosmetic surgery. He's an expert at making women beautiful."

Beautiful wasn't the word for what the cosmetic surgeon had achieved. *Stunning* better described the woman with the lavender-blue eyes and a smile that seemed almost shy.

Her gaze shifted suddenly, veering away from him to Trevor, and her smile became radiant, no longer suggesting the least hint of shyness. Irritation surged through Matt as he saw Trevor return her smile with equal warmth.

Her effortless sensuality took him by surprise. The Shelly he remembered had tried too hard to be sexy; this woman didn't bother with makeup or fixing her hair, yet she was damn near irresistible.

For a second he'd imagined this babe chasing him around the way Shelly had, and letting her catch him. He'd have that sundress off her in no time. The sway of her breasts as she turned had told him that she wasn't wearing a bra. He hadn't detected a panty line either.

He gazed at the sandy beach glistening in the moonlight, and his pulse kicked up another notch. He wanted her naked body beneath his on the soft sand. He wanted her hot breasts in his palms. He wanted her mouth opening for him. He wanted . . .

Christ! When was the last time he'd been laid, he wondered. He hadn't thought about sex much—until now.

"That woman is not Rochelle Ralston."

Not only did this beauty look entirely different, his gut reaction was alarmingly intense. Not even the first time he'd met Shelly, when she'd been dressed in a slinky black number, had he experienced the emotional equivalent of an earthquake.

No way was this the same woman.

"Clive is a master with the scalpel," Trevor said with unmistakable pride. "He's made Shelly into a new person."

"Bullshit, look how—"

"No, Matt, you look." Trevor took his arm and led him to the side of the compound, where Trevor's private suite looked out on the starlit sea. He opened the middle drawer of his writing desk and pulled out a stack of photographs, then handed them to Matt.

"Where did you get these?" he asked as he began shuffling through them. By the time he'd hit the sixth picture, he knew what the rest would be like. They were candid shots of him taken with a telephoto lens. What kind of person did something like this?

Someone with a deranged mind, like Shelly's. He hadn't recognized her new face, but these photographs left no doubt about her true identity. Once he'd caught Shelly stalking him and shooting pictures. Now he knew there had been other times when he hadn't seen her.

He cursed himself for the depth charge of sexual attraction he'd felt a few minutes earlier. His usually infallible sixth sense had told him the gorgeous blonde wasn't Shelly. Obviously, he'd been mistaken.

"Shelly gave them to me. She's terribly sorry about the way she behaved." Emotion underscored Trevor's words in a way that deeply disturbed Matt. Trevor was much too involved with this psycho. "The accident has changed her. Shelly's a new person."

"Yeah, right."

His cynical response snuffed the light from Trevor's eyes, and he regarded Matt with searching gravity. "Shelly has more guts than a dozen men. Do you know what it's taken her to make it this far? Courage. Commitment. She swore to me she isn't going to bother you."

Like hell—Matt stopped before he could utter the words, sensing this was a defining moment in his relationship with Trevor. Why argue with a close friend over a woman like Shelly?

"I wanted to spend some time here . . . with you," Matt said. "If Shelly's around, that'll be impossible."

"You do? I—I mean, I assumed—" Trevor paused, confused. "I don't know what I thought, Matt. You quit your job so unexpectedly, saying you wanted to kick back. Then you left here—"

"I didn't want to go, but I needed to get away from Shelly."

Matt knew he should tell Trevor what was going on. He didn't want to discuss his problems. Right then he had a slight headache. He prayed it wouldn't become a migraine. He'd never had one, and he sure as hell didn't need one now.

"How long do you plan to stay?"

Matt shrugged, conscious of the unspoken questions in his friend's eyes. "I don't have any plans right now."

"You're welcome here. You know that." Trevor leaned against the counter, studying him intently. "It's too late tonight, but tomorrow I'll find someplace else for Shelly to recuperate."

Trevor deserved to know what was going on. He'd imposed on him enough, asking him to take care of Shelly, then disappearing, only to suddenly reappear.

"Let's walk along the shore," Matt suggested. "There's something I want to tell you, and I don't want to be interrupted."

They left the house and walked across the side terrace, away from the party. As they silently crossed through the sea oats, the wild grass rippling from the motion of their legs, music drifted over the water from Key West. The lights glittered in the distance, and Matt could see one of the big cruise ships docked at Pier A and lit up like a floating hotel.

When they reached the sand, Matt took off his shoes and left them near the band of sea oats lining the shore. Trevor was barefoot, and he waited silently. It wasn't an awkward silence; he and Trevor didn't need to talk. They understood each other, or they had until now. Matt wasn't positive Trevor would accept his decision.

Emily certainly hadn't.

They strolled along the tide line, gentle waves rushing over their bare feet until they came to a neighbor's dock. Matt swung up onto the wooden platform and sat with his legs dangling down, his toes skimming the water. Trevor positioned himself beside him.

"I've always been on the fast track," Matt hedged, backing into the disturbing truth. "Just recently I realized that the top of the ladder is really the end of the plank. Know what I mean?"

"Remember the night I was in the hospital and they had called my father?"

"Yes, I remember." They had been at Yale then. It seemed like a lifetime ago, but who could forget that night? Or Graham Adams— the heartless bastard.

"That night changed the direction of my life. I could have gone into the family business. Instead, I'm doing what *I* want to do."

It suddenly struck him that Trevor had a house full of misfits who counted on him. It didn't seem right to dump anything more on his friend. Instead of telling Trevor the whole truth about his troubles, he just said, "Now I'm going to do what I want to do."

"Like what?"

"Like . . . like . . ." What in hell was he going to do? Given his situation . . . chilling out for a while was his *only* plan.

"You don't have to decide right now. Take your time. Life's too short not to enjoy it."

"That's for damn sure."

CHAPTER

TEN

The timeless tryst of sugar-fine sand and moonlit water was more beautiful than she had ever imagined. Tranquil. Eternal. It made her problems seem small, insignificant. The retreating tide lapped at her toes as she stood leaning on her cane and gazing across the waterway at the lights of Key West. Fearful of the gentle surf, Jiggs waited at a safe distance.

"What's Matthew Jensen doing here?" she whispered to herself. "He didn't seem to realize I'm not Shelly. Did we look enough alike that he thinks cosmetic surgery accounts for the changes?"

The soft night closed in around her without bringing an answer. The only response was the sound of rock and roll drifting over the water from Key West's rowdy Duval Street, and it was almost lost in the night air.

The light-headed sensation had diminished—a little—but she still had to take a sustaining breath each time she thought about meeting Matt's eyes. Granted, he possessed a virility that she didn't quite know how to deal with, but there was so much . . . more to Matt.

He'd appeared in her dreams with an intensity that was haunting, bewildering. She knew better than to indulge in fantasies about him, but he invaded her thoughts with disturbing frequency. It wasn't a good sign, considering her need to concentrate on getting well and coming up with a plan for dealing with Dexxter Foxx.

Yet each time she'd gazed into the mirror, she wished she could see Matt again. What would he think of her now? she had often wondered.

Of course, he didn't know what she looked like before, so it was a ridiculous thought. Yet she couldn't help herself. She was positive that Matt wouldn't have been like most men. He would have met the gaze of a disfigured woman head-on.

He would not have thought her attractive. Now surgery had radically improved her looks. She was pretty, like her mother, but she was still unaccustomed to her new face. She'd been out of the clinic three days and living in a paradise called Half Moon Bay. Each night she'd awakened, sweating and trembling with dread from a dream she couldn't quite remember.

Was she still The Beast?

She would rush into the bathroom and flick on the light to check her new face. The horrid birthmark was truly gone. Yet The Beast would always be with her, trapped somewhere inside her head.

Tonight when she'd turned and had seen Matt she couldn't help noticing the slight narrowing of his eyes as he gazed at her. For one heart-stopping moment she thought the game was over, but he didn't walk up and accuse her of impersonating Shelly the way she'd expected.

According to the journal she'd read, their affair had lasted over a year, enough time for Shelly to fall hopelessly in love with the man. Her behavior was unforgivable, but on some level she understood. Matthew was the type of man who would break a woman's heart, driving her into a deep depression, or worse.

They had known each other intimately. Any little thing, something so insignificant she might not realize it, could expose her. If her face hadn't given her away, it would only be a matter of time before something did.

She had to leave. Tomorrow she must strike out on her own—despite her injuries.

"Shelly . . . Shelly." The name floated toward her on the breeze, so softly spoken that she might have imagined it except the sound came again, louder and closer this time. "Shelly."

Jiggs trotted up to her for protection as she turned around. Matthew Jensen emerged from the shadows of the terrace. Her body stiffened and she tried not to lean so heavily on the metal cane.

Had he called the police and told them she was an impostor?

She marshaled her thoughts as he approached. Barefoot, wearing khaki shorts and polo shirt open at the neck, he was bigger than she'd remembered, more powerfully built. He was taller than average, but not exceptionally so. It was something about the way he carried himself that made him seem taller, powerful.

Intimidating.

He stopped in front of her, towering over her and gazing at her with such intensity that she had to force herself to look him in the eye and try to appear calm. The pit of her stomach churned as she prayed he believed she was the new Rochelle Ralston. A cosmetic surgeon's miracle.

He analyzed every inch of her face with incisive blue eyes like shards of ice. Then his gaze scorched a trail across her bare shoulders, down to her breasts, then roved lower and lower until he reached her sandals. He inspected her body with the thoroughness of a man who had undressed more than his fair share of women. No doubt he was mentally picturing her stark naked.

It took all her self-control not to gasp. Men rarely looked at her, and certainly not like this. A rush of heat flooded the good side of her face, while the other side with the bioengineered skin felt chilled.

She told herself to be flattered, to be thrilled a man was looking at her in an unmistakably sexual way. To him she was not The Beast. On one level she was excited, yet there was something insulting and degrading about the way he was scrutinizing every inch of her body.

This was not the way she remembered Matt. This was not the way she'd expected him to behave. Perhaps he was suspicious and was checking to see if she was Rochelle Ralston.

The sensual line of his mouth tilted upward as he lifted his hand and brushed his fingertips across her cheek, tracing the curve of her face. Her heart hammered foolishly while her mind scrambled any coherent thought she might have had.

If Shelly and Matt were still in love—the way the journal had described them—he might try to kiss her . . . or something. Then what would she do? She had absolutely no sexual experience. She'd never trick him into believing—

"You're one hot number now, aren't you, Shelly?"

Sarcasm underscored each word, leaving her trembling inwardly. Hot number? No one had ever said such a thing. Deal with it, she mentally told herself. Be thankful he believes you're Shelly.

"What do you mean?" she heard herself ask in an unsteady voice.

His fingertips touched the fine wisps of hair at her temples, then sifted through the scraggly hair she'd been unable to properly brush. It was an alarmingly intimate gesture, a shattering reminder that no man had ever touched her like this. While the real Shelly would have known how to handle it, she was completely out of her league.

"Not only did you have the doctor repair the damage, you had him fix your nose and raise your cheekbones so you'd be drop-dead gorgeous."

Drop-dead gorgeous? His description should have thrilled her, but the words had such an offensive edge that it was all she could do not to tell him off.

"I didn't know until after the surgery that Clive had worked on my nose. I certainly didn't ask him to do it."

She'd managed to keep her rising anger out of her voice, but just barely. Granted, Matt had good reason to be upset with Shelly, yet she resented his attitude. Why didn't he just leave her alone? That's what he said he was going to do.

His fingers were still in her hair, and one brushed her earlobe. Her body quivered and she had to lean heavily against the cane to steady herself. He didn't seem to notice the devastating effect he had on her.

He pulled his hand away, saying, "Are you going to tell me silicone boobs were the doctor's idea?"

Her lips parted and she almost said her breasts were real, but stopped herself in time. He was the type of man who noticed women's breasts and could tell a bra size at a glance. Apparently, Shelly had a smaller chest. Denying she'd had breast implants would only give her away.

He took her silence for an affirmative answer. One brow angled upward, giving him an even more cynical expression than usual. Anger ticked away inside her like a time bomb.

"You're prancing around without a bra, jiggling. Your hair looks like you've just gotten out of bed. There won't be a man in Key West who won't want to hop in the sack with you."

Only a lifetime of controlling her emotional reaction to people's insults kept her silent. She glared at him and held up her right hand. It was a complex cast, each finger encased in plaster that covered her entire hand up to the wrist.

"It's hard to dress yourself properly or comb your hair when your right hand is useless. The last thing I want to do is attract men. I've got problems enough."

That got him. It was probably easier to back down a pit bull than get the best of Matthew Jensen, but she could see that she'd scored a small point.

"What about your voice?" he asked, a little of the edge gone from his tone. "Why are you deliberately trying to sound sexy?"

"My jaw was broken in two places, remember? It had to be wired shut. I can open my jaw only so far. I couldn't scream if my life depended upon it."

"I see."

She knew he couldn't possibly understand. Having Dexxter after her and not being able to scream terrified her. What would she do if Dexxter found her?

He seemed to hesitate before adding, "Trevor's the kind of person who tries to take care of everyone. Don't take advantage of him."

"Don't worry. I'm leaving on the commuter boat's last run," she informed him, knowing she had to get away from Matt tonight, before he realized she was an impostor. "I'd never hurt Trevor. He takes care of everyone. Stray cats, lost souls, you name it. But who's going to take care of Trevor?"

She nudged Jiggs with her cane, and the little dog hopped up. With as much dignity as she could manage, considering her halting gait, she moved around Matt.

"What in hell is that supposed to mean?"

"Do you seriously believe Trevor is happy?"

Shelly was halfway to the house, hobbling on her cane like an old lady, before Matt admitted to himself that the impossible had just occurred. Wacky Rochelle Ralston knew his best friend better than he did. Trevor had filled his life with all sorts of projects, from the cats he rescued, to the people he helped, to the homes he lovingly restored.

Trevor worked constantly, but did he have a life? No, of course not. Trevor wasn't happy, and Matt should have realized it before now.

"Thank God you had the sense not to unload on Trevor," he muttered to himself. "He has his own problems. He doesn't need to take on your troubles. Just handle it yourself."

When he'd come back to the house from walking on the beach with Trevor, the party had been over. He'd spotted Shelly down by the water and couldn't resist talking to her. He'd expected to prove to Trevor that she hadn't changed, but she'd outmaneuvered him.

Her ordeal had made her smarter. Different.

Just seeing her up close, her mane of blond hair tumbling wildly over her bare shoulders, and his pulse had skyrocketed. He'd wanted to throttle her for what she'd done to Emily, but instead he'd touched her face.

Caressed it, actually.

He hadn't stopped there, had he? Something had compelled him to stroke her hair. It was fine, far silkier than he'd remembered, but then, he'd never been tempted to touch Shelly's hair—until then.

God help him, he'd gazed into those sexy blue eyes and had been unable to resist touching her soft cheek. Man, oh, man, what had gotten into him? He'd saved himself by lashing out at her, trying to bait her into a fight.

If it had been anyone else but Shelly, he would have had her on her back in a minute. He knew how to handle women. He would have her writhing under him right now, his mouth tasting those pouty lips, his hands squeezing those lush breasts.

He dug his toe into the sand, trying to think with his head not his cock. "You want her. Admit it." His body already knew the truth. "What in hell have you got to lose? Not a damn thing. Your friggin' life is already a hopeless mess."

He sprinted across the beach and caught her just as she was entering the foyer. "Shelly, look . . ."

The way she gazed up at him, her head angled to one side, struck him as being shy, the way it had when he'd first seen her tonight. Or maybe she was sensitive about the side of her face that had needed reconstruction.

Anger shimmered in her eyes, making them even sexier. "Don't worry. I won't bother you ever again. I'm leaving."

Her sincere tone made something in his chest tighten. What kind of a jackass let a woman who could barely get around leave in the dead of night? He'd meant to protect Trevor from a nutcase, but now he realized he'd gone too far.

"If you're grateful to Trevor, you'll help him."

She gazed at him, baffled. "How can I help Trevor?"

He wasn't sure how anyone could help Trevor, but he was fairly certain he knew what the problem was. He couldn't discuss the situation with anyone without violating Trevor's trust.

"It's important for Trevor to see you're well before you leave."

Shelly blinked hard, lashes lowering quickly, shadowing her eyes. "I can't stay."

"Why not? Are you still so hot for my bod that you can't resist me?"

"Don't worry about me bothering you," she shot back, her eyes blazing. "For Trevor, I'll stay a few days, but I'm not going to have a thing to do with you."

CHAPTER
ELEVEN

Checking the Ashe Street address Trevor had given her, she saw this was her destination. Like many houses in Old Town, the psychiatrist's home was two stories with a white picket fence and a white-railed veranda that wrapped around the building. Pastel colors were typical of the area; this one was a creamy yellow with moss-green shutters.

This lovely old frame house was similar to others. It had wooden gingerbread scrollwork dripping from the eaves. Trevor had told her ships carpenters had built many of the homes and tried their best to show off their woodworking skills.

She leaned on her cane, admiring the beautifully restored house and saying a silent prayer. Could she possibly fool a professional who had treated others with this disorder?

"You have no choice," she mumbled to herself. "Pretend to be obsessed with Matt."

After her confrontation with Matt last night, she had committed herself to a course of action. Like it or not, she had to become Rochelle Ralston. And live in the same house with Matthew Jensen.

At least she didn't have to talk to him. Why would she want to? Her back went up every time she thought about the way he'd treated her. His behavior didn't square with the man who had stayed by her bedside. With a few words he'd destroyed the image she'd had of him.

"You got what you deserved," she muttered to herself. "White knights exist only in fairy tales." Still, she couldn't help being profoundly disappointed that he was nothing like the man she'd dreamed about so often.

She'd tried to justify his actions—after all, he had saved her from that lowlife—and the real Shelly had given him reason to despise her. Still, his reaction to her seemed a bit extreme. She wondered if something else was going on with Matt.

She would never find out. She'd vowed not to have anything to do with him. It was just as well, actually. The more he was around her, the less of a chance she had of deceiving him.

She took her cane off her arm and used it to walk up to the door. Taking a deep breath, her lungs were flooded with the rich, ripe scent of the tropics. God, she loved it here. She'd spent her whole life by the ocean in Seattle and was accustomed to briny sea air. But here the heat of the sun warmed the soil and brought forth the pungent scents of paradise, mingling them with the ocean air.

"Quit stalling," she told herself. "Go for it."

She automatically raised her right hand to knock on the doctor's door, then remembered it was useless. Earlier, she'd gone to the hospital and had the cast removed. Her hand might as well still be encased in plaster. She couldn't even draw her fingers together to knock on the door.

Looking around for a plaque with Dr. Holt's name on it, she saw nothing to indicate a doctor's office. She'd seen enough of Key West to know it was a place with little regard for the conventional. The town was a warren of narrow streets, tucked-away lanes, and dead-end alleys. Often a house was in front of a house in front of yet another house.

Lush, colorful tropical plants concealed hidden doorways and secret alleys. Birds sang exuberantly from the nooks and crannies of the buildings. An ever-present breeze ruffled the palms, the dried fronds rustling like tissue paper.

Key West reminded her of a cross between a village in the Caribbean and New Orleans's French Quarter. It was fascinatingly unpredictable, with its own unique charm. She'd fallen under the island's spell and planned to live here.

After she got her life sorted out.

Using the hand with the cane, she knocked. As she waited, she again silently prayed that she could fool the doctor.

An astonishingly beautiful woman opened the door. Tall and slender with shoulder-length black hair, the woman was dressed in a classic beige suit and high heels that showed off her legs. She assumed this elegant lady must be Dr. Holt's wife, because she was too expensively dressed to be a receptionist.

"I'm Rochelle Ralston," she said, now very aware of Shelly's sundress that hung on her like a choir robe. "I'm here to see Dr. Holt. Did Trevor Adams call about me?"

"Yes, I spoke with Trevor." The lady held the door open with a hand crowned by fingernails polished the same color of beige as her suit. "I'm Dr. Holt."

What? Trevor had distinctly said *Peter* Holt.

The doctor chuckled, a husky sound, then said, "I can see Trevor didn't tell you, did he?"

She shook her head and managed a weak smile.

The doctor gestured toward a bent-willow sofa with plump pillows in a lime-green pattern. "Don't let my sex concern you. I'm a psychiatrist and you have a problem. Let's sit down and talk about it."

She walked over to the sofa and slowly sat down, keeping the cane in her left hand. The doctor sat across from her in a chair that matched the sofa and crossed legs too gorgeous to be a man's. The doctor smiled, an engaging smile that made the situation less uncomfortable.

Leaning forward slightly, long-lashed brown eyes looking at her with interest, the doctor asked, "Rochelle, you go by Shelly, don't you?" When she nodded, Dr. Holt added, "Call me Peter. All my friends do."

She smiled—or tried to—then said, "All right . . . Peter. I don't know how much Trevor told you."

"Very little. He said you had been obsessed with a man, and I know you nearly died in an accident. Trevor thinks the trauma has changed you, but he wanted me to talk to you and see if I could help."

"Believe me, it was a terrible accident. You can see I still have a cast on my leg." She was rattling on, finding it easier to talk about her injuries than lie about an obsession she didn't have. "I just got the cast off my hand this morning."

She held up her right fist. The fingers were curved inward like an old crone's withered hand. If she flexed them more than a fraction of an inch, pain would shaft up her arm.

The doctor nodded sympathetically. "How has this helped you get over this man?"

"I'm lucky to be alive. Why waste my time on someone who no longer loves me?"

"What made you think he loved you?"

"We dated for a while, and he gave me beautiful gifts," she said, trying to remember what she'd read in the journal. She'd wanted to question Trevor, but didn't, fearing she'd expose herself. "He took me to Bermuda," she added, not mentioning the part about making love in the surf. "I thought we'd get married. Then he told me he didn't love me."

Again the doctor nodded sympathetically, but didn't comment.

"I should have accepted it. I couldn't . . . somehow. I followed him around and took pictures, using a telephoto lens." Criminy, she sounded like a total nut. "I thought he was going out with another woman." She took a deep breath and tried to appear contrite. "I threatened her, then discovered she was Matt's sister."

"When did you last see this man?"

"At breakfast."

"What?" To say the doctor was floored would have been a gross understatement. "You're both staying at Half Moon Bay?"

"Along with a few other people. But it isn't what you think. I'm not talking to Matt or having anything to do with him." After she'd finished breakfast this morning, Matt had walked out onto the terrace. She hadn't even looked up. She'd marched away. Well, as close to marching as she could with a cane. "I have no money. It'll take weeks of rehabilitation before I can use my hand again and get a job."

"What type of work do you do?"

"I was a reporter, but I'm thinking of a career change. I took some advanced computer courses. I think they're the wave of the future, don't you?"

The doctor nodded thoughtfully, and she had the disturbing feeling Peter saw right through her. Still, she had to lay the groundwork for the job she intended to get. Somewhere in Key West was a good-paying position as a computer systems analyst.

"How much do you know about obsession disorders?" the doctor asked.

Oh, boy, here it comes. "Not much. This person gets into your head. You want to see him, be near him . . . anything. It's pretty sick, really. I'm all over it—honest."

"It's possible, considering the trauma you've been through, but it would be unusual. Obsession disorders are difficult to overcome."

The doctor studied her intently for a moment before adding, "You're at risk of fixating on another person and beginning another cycle."

"I won't. I swear. I'm not going near a man."

She meant every word. While it was thrilling to be normal and have men look at her for a change, she had to remember that her life was in danger. Not only was Dexxter hunting for her, undoubtedly the FBI was searching for her. A federal marshal had died in the bombing. They would want to question her. She'd thought about this in the hospital but had shunted it aside. She could no longer allow herself that luxury.

"I'm concerned about you being around Matt. It might very well trigger your erotomania again."

"Erotomania?" It sounded pornographic, disgusting.

"That's the term for patients who delude themselves into believing someone loves them. The wisest course of action is to have no contact with the person."

For the life of him, Dexxter Foxx couldn't understand what had happened with Irene. First Amy Conroy, now Irene. Women—go figure.

Since the day she'd given him the back rub, Irene hadn't approached him, which was just as well. He was concluding his deal to sell Foxx Enterprises to an Asian consortium. He didn't want to break the news to her until the last minute.

He picked up the office telephone and punched the button for her extension. She answered immediately, "Irene Hanson, Foxx Enterprises."

"It's Dexx. Do you have Zane's latest report on Amy?"

"Check your computer for a memo." She slammed the receiver down.

He stared at the instrument for a full second before dropping it into its cradle. Shit! Irene was breathing fire. She must have noticed how aroused he'd been during the back rub, but he'd made no move to touch her.

Evidently, he'd profoundly insulted her. Why would he have sex with the likes of her? It was thinking of Amy that had given him the meanest erection he'd ever had.

"Let Irene sulk. She can't keep the sale from going through," he assured himself as he keyed in his password, then reviewed his private memos. Irene had lent him the start-up money to open his company. He'd paid her back; she didn't own any part of Foxx Enterprises.

Trouble was, she did know all about their illegal operation, and the people he'd killed to make his money. Just what he didn't need—two women who knew his secrets.

The memo consisted of the private eye's complete report. Checking plastic surgeons had not produced a trace of Amy. Same thing in L.A. She had vanished, which seemed impossible.

The FBI wasn't doing any better. Zane had received a message from his source in the regional FBI office. The FBI had lowered its priority on the case. They weren't looking so closely at Dexx. Agents were no longer searching for Amy, but they still had an alert status on her, meaning they still wanted to talk to her and agents were advised to be on the lookout.

Evidently, Irene hadn't had any luck with animalnetwork.com. The search for the abused mutt had proved futile, just as he knew it would.

It was late afternoon by the time she had finished discussing everything from obsession disorders to rare orchids with Dr. Holt—Peter. She'd never met a transvestite before and didn't know what to expect. She liked him, and what's more, the doctor accepted at face value her account of being obsessed with Matthew Jensen.

She left the doctor and went to meet Bubbles, aware she didn't have much experience with "scenes." Duval Street just before sunset was a scene to end all scenes. Middle-aged tourists wearing T-shirts and baggy bermudas with white socks and sandals paraded along the sidewalks beside teenagers wearing little more than suntan lotion.

No wonder the locals called it the "Duval crawl." Teeming humanity slogged its way past T-shirt shops, ice cream stands, more T-shirt shops, restaurants, croissant shops, another T-shirt shop, a swank gallery, jewelry shops selling items made from pieces of eight Mel Fisher had brought up from the shipwrecked *Atochia,* and yet another T-shirt shop. Between each shop was an open air-bar blaring live music.

It was a laid-back, anything-goes place, eccentric yet exhilarating.

"Yo, mama," one guy said as she tried to pass.

She kept her head turned to the side, the way she always did when men looked at her. It took a second to remember that she no longer had to look down.

He leered at her, blocking her way and blasting hundred-proof breath in her face as he brazenly rubbed his body against hers. "Babe, you're making my eyeballs sweat."

His friends hovered nearby, inspecting every inch of her body as they slurped from long-necked bottles of beer. She dodged the creep. The other guys howled and jabbed one another in the ribs.

Instantly, she remembered that day so many years ago when Trent Hastings had said: "I thought beauty and the beast were two people, not one." His buddies had laughed just the way these guys were laughing now.

"Some things never change—even if you do," she muttered to herself. The hair across the back of her neck prickled the way it had when her hideous birthmark had brought humiliating snickers and sneers.

You're still The Beast, cried the voice in her head, the echo in her soul. She still felt odd, different.

"Shel—lay!"

She looked up, startled to see Bubbles waving madly at her, a scroll of white paper in one hand.

"Is this where you're selling insurance?" She gazed at the coral building with the aqua writing: Jimmy Buffett's Margaritaville.

"Yeah. Ya okay? Fixin' to feel puny?"

Was she going to be sick? No, she didn't think so, but she was a little weak. Walking to Margaritaville from the doctor's office meant she'd been on her feet for longer than she had since the accident. "I'm fine . . . fine."

"I've made my quota," Bubbles said. "Let's get a drink."

She followed Bubbles to a sidewalk café nearby. Trevor was supposed to meet them at Mallory Dock to watch Key West's famous sunset show.

"Give us two Hog Snorts," Bubbles said as soon as the waiter came to their table.

"What did you order?"

"It's rum and blue curaçao. We're in the Hog's Breath Saloon. What else would we, like, drink?"

She'd thought they were in an open-air café, not a bar, but as she took a closer look around, her mistake was evident. From the looks of it, they were selling more T-shirts—HOG'S BREATH IS BETTER THAN NO BREATH AT ALL—than drinks.

She never drank, but tonight she felt so different. She might hate creeps like the guys who'd stopped her on the sidewalk, but going out in public was no longer the intensely degrading experience it once had been. The Beast still lurked inside her head, but the world saw a different person.

As dreadful as it was to be Rochelle Ralston, she was at last a normal person. It felt so good, so liberating. Something other women took for granted.

The drinks came and she sipped hers, savoring the languid feeling of the alcohol invading her bloodstream. Along with it came the hypnotic sensation of stately palms slowly casting shadows across the small patio. With the sun sinking into the sea, the breeze became gentle, almost nonexistent.

"Can we, like, have a talk?" Bubbles asked, breaking into her thoughts.

"Sure," she replied, unable to imagine what Bubbles could need to discuss with her.

"Do you have any shorts?"

She hesitated, wondering where this was going. There were a few pairs of shorts among Shelly's things, but they didn't fit. "Not really. A lot of my stuff burned in the accident."

"There's a shop in Bahama Village—that's just around the corner. Jo Mama's Duds sells T-shirts and shorts cheaper than anyplace around."

Obviously, Bubbles thought her clothes were a disaster, an insult coming from someone who believed body piercing was a fashion statement. "What I really need is a bra that fastens in front."

"Jo Mama's has undies too." Bubbles smiled, pleased with herself, and the stud in the tip of her tongue caught the light. "What ya really need is a sthaawlk."

"Sthalk?" Bubbles's vowels were like warm honey. It was often difficult to understand her.

Bubbles waved her hand. "An act that's all ya own, like selling alien abduction insurance or playing Tupperware with a wooden spoon in front of the Hard Rock Café."

"Aw, a schtick." An act. "Why?"

"How else are you going to make money?"

Make money? She almost laughed. If only she could use both hands and get on a computer, she wouldn't need a schtick. Before she could respond, Bubbles added, "And ya need an attitude."

"Attitude?"

Bubbles leaned closer, a brash smile on her freckled face. "I saw those guys hasslin' ya. Why didn't ya flip 'em off? If I had your looks, I'd have one bad-ass attitude."

She had to admit Bubbles was right. She needed an attitude if she planned to successfully deal with Matthew Jensen. She needed to be strong, tough like . . . Like who?

Jill on *The Young and the Restless* came to mind. So did Lucy on *General Hospital*. Those women weren't tough; they were ruthless.

During the last year of her mother's life, she could do little more than watch television. Each day she tuned in faithfully to see what cruel trick the bad girls would play next. She loved to hate them.

Character determines fate, she reminded herself. The Beast couldn't suddenly become a bad girl, but, maybe, if she modeled her new self after them, their toughness would give her more "character."

Bubbles tapped the rim of her nearly empty glass with the tip of her tongue, and the stud made a clicking sound, breaking into her thoughts. "Are you and Matt, like, still hot?"

"Still?" She tried to say it with an attitude like "mind your own business," but Bubbles didn't notice.

"Go on, Shelly. I'm no bimbo. I saw the way the two of you looked at each other last night. You two were an item, right?"

She tried to imagine what Bubbles knew about her supposed relationship with Matthew Jensen. "I guess . . . so."

"Matt looked at you like he was smokin'."

She decided to play along. "We split up some time ago."

"Yes!" Bubbles shrieked. "I knew it! Do I have good instincts, or what?"

Or what.

"Then you don't mind if I, like, go after Matt, do you?"

CHAPTER
TWELVE

"Come on. We're late." Bubbles rushed ahead of her. "Trevor must be wondering what happened to us."

What had gotten into her? Allowing Bubbles to drag her into the Bahama Village to buy a bra had turned into a minor shopping spree. Instead of just buying a bra, she'd gone overboard, using a little of the money Trevor had given her, to buy shorts and T-shirts as well as two bras and a bikini. They were such a bargain that the clothes would probably fall apart when she washed them.

How long could she mooch off Trevor? He'd helped her in so many ways. She was determined to pay back Trevor every cent. But it was going to be some time before she could use her right hand well enough to get a job using a computer.

Once again she considered contacting the FBI, and once again she discarded the idea. Dexxter must have a source inside the agency. She had been using her new identity, living in her little house for less than a week, when it had been firebombed.

She didn't trust the FBI to protect her. Until she could use her hand to defend herself, she was better off right where she was.

Maybe Bubbles was right. If she had a schtick, she could earn a little money to tide her over until she came up with a plan for dealing with Dexxter. But what could she do?

Computers had been her life, her sanity, since she discovered them in high school. An intelligent, entertaining companion, a computer didn't care what you looked like. It had been a way of avoiding contact with people, she reflected as she ambled along, everyone passing her by without the usual stares.

Duval Street's sidewalks had been packed, but that was nothing compared to Mallory Dock. It took all her strength to keep up with Bubbles as the redhead elbowed her way between people.

"Look," Bubbles cried. "There's Kyle."

"Who's Kyle?"

"Kyle Parker is, like, this awesome hunk. He's house-sitting next door to Half Moon Bay. He would have been there last night except he was training or something." Bubbles waved at a tall man with dark hair. "Don't ask Kyle about his job. It's top secret. He's a civilian, but he works at the naval station."

Kyle approached them, angling his wide shoulders to the side to work his way through the mob. He smiled, his deep blue eyes traveling from the new shorts and T-shirt she had purchased to the toes peeking out of her cast.

Suddenly, she was sorry she'd given Shelly's dress to the woman who'd sold her the new clothes. The baggy dress had concealed her body while the shorts and cropped T-shirt exposed quite a bit of skin.

She'd bought shorts and lightweight T-shirts because the price was right, and the warm, humid climate called for outfits like this. At least she had on a bra, she thought, recalling Matt's scathing remark about flaunting her breasts.

"Isn't Kyle, like, to die for?" whispered Bubbles.

She wasn't accustomed to men looking her in the eye, and she certainly wasn't used to men looking at her with such . . . interest. She mustered a smile as she gazed sideways at him. His nose was a bit too long, and his jaw was slightly angular, but there wasn't a woman on earth who wouldn't take a second look at him.

"Kyle, this is Shelly. She's staying at Half Moon Bay."

He stuck out his hand and uttered a single word, "Shelly."

He took her hand in his. A choking sigh rose from her throat before she could muffle it, but he didn't seem to notice. He didn't release her hand the way she expected. Instead, he held it, saying nothing, merely gazing at her for a moment.

Don't look at me, she silently cried. Something inside her shriveled when a man looked at her. Then she drew in a calming breath. Let go of The Beast. Get an attitude.

She stiffened her back and raised her eyes to look directly at Kyle. It took all her strength not to take a step back. Kyle's smile was charming, yet his eyes were wary, emotionless. Gypsy eyes.

Here was a man who carefully watched everyone, everything. She couldn't help wondering what he did that was top secret. Intuitively, she knew his work was very dangerous.

"You broke your leg," he commented.

Bubbles piped up. "Shelly was in an accident and almost died."

"It's a special cast," she explained. "I undo the Velcro and take it off to sleep."

She pulled her hand out of his and feigned interest in the carnival-like atmosphere around her. It wasn't hard. Ahead of them a golden retriever was doing a high-wire act, running along a narrow wooden plank suspended above the crowd by two tall ladders.

A melange of odors assailed her from every direction. Popcorn and cotton candy. Suntan oil on people who'd come directly from the beach without bothering to shower. Cloying incense wafting from a small basket where a snake charmer had a python swaying hypnotically.

"You'd better let me help you through this zoo." Kyle slipped his arm around her waist.

Bubbles rolled her eyes and winked. Oh, my, she thought, feeling Kyle's powerful arm, guiding her.

"Is this your first Mallory Dock sunset?" He negotiated a path around vendors selling woven palm hats, Key West *Sunset* T-shirts, visors with miniature fans on them, as well as all sorts of food.

"I've seen the town, but this is my first sunset on the dock. Trevor insisted I see the show."

"It's more like a pagan ritual," he said as they passed a man wearing nothing but a thong. He'd been spray-painted metallic silver and he was standing on the ball of one foot, his other leg gracefully pointing backward like a ballerina.

"He can hold that position for hours," Bubbles said as she tossed a coin in the cigar box at his feet.

"It's all about money," Kyle informed her. "The golden retriever is on the ground now, picking up dollar bills people have thrown down and putting them in a bucket. This is how most of these people make a living."

"Just like I told you," Bubbles said. "Everyone has a *sthaaulk*."

"I was expecting people to be standing around, watching the sunset," she said. The lingering rays of sunshine filtered through the crowd to warm her body. In a few minutes, another day in paradise would be over.

"The sunset is just an excuse to gather and see a bit of street the-ater," Kyle said. "I for one am sorry the police won't let the naked bagpiper perform."

Bubbles giggled, then waved. "There's Trevor. Matt's with him."

Matt. The blood froze in her veins, despite the warmth of Kyle's arm. Oh, God, could she pull this off? Remember your attitude.

Matt caught a glimpse of Shelly with some guy, who had his arm around her. A spark of some elusive emotion surprised him, but he tamped it down. On the beach last night, something about Shelly had appealed to him.

His reaction had kept him awake until the pink edge of dawn slowly reclaimed the night sky. Only then did he climb out of the hammock swinging between the palms and go to bed, deciding he'd been without a woman too long. Despite his better judgment, he couldn't keep his mind off a certain blonde.

"Who's the guy with Shelly?"

Trevor answered, "Kyle Parker. He works at Fleming Key."

"His hair's too long for the navy." Even from this distance, Matt picked up on a certain I-have-the-world-by-the-tail cockiness ema-nating from Kyle.

"I think Kyle may have been a SEAL once, but he's not in the ser-vice now. I'm not sure what he does out there."

"Could be with the DEA. Who actually knows what goes on at Fleming Key?" Matt commented. "SEAL training, for sure, but the DEA also has a unit there to stop the drugs coming in from the Caribbean."

"Kyle's a stand-up guy, and that's what counts."

A stand-up guy, someone you could count on in a crisis. Okay, maybe. The possessive way Kyle had his arm around Shelly almost irritated him.

"Who's going to tell Shelly the bad news? You or me?"

"I am," Matt said without thinking.

"Matt, how ya doin'?" Bubbles asked as she reached them before Kyle and Shelly.

"Great," Matt replied, watching Shelly. Even to his own ears, he sounded like a wounded bear.

"Kyle, meet my closest friend, Matthew Jensen," Trevor said.

Matt didn't catch what the guy said as he stuck out his big hand for Matt to shake. Shelly hadn't even glanced his way. She kept gaz-ing up at Kyle as if he'd hung the moon.

Kicking himself for noticing, Matt realized that nothing turned heads like a natural beauty. Shelly wasn't natural—not by a long shot. Still, in the amber light of the setting sun, no one could have guessed she was a cosmetic surgeon's creation.

There wasn't any makeup on her face and not a hint of lipstick on a generous mouth that curved up at the corners as if she were on the verge of a smile. Silky, tousled hair fluttered in the light breeze. A bod that was perfect for the swimsuit calendar. If her lower leg hadn't been in a cast, she could have been perfect.

On the outside.

"Thar she blows!" bellowed a man through a megaphone.

For a moment the crowd stopped watching the various acts and turned toward the setting sun. Only a thin ellipse of the light could be seen on the horizon. In front of it, the ocean was molten gold.

A drumroll sent the crowd into frenzied cheering, which reached a fever pitch when the ocean swallowed the sun in a kinetic bolt of color, representing the entire spectrum of light. Matt studied Shelly as she watched, awed. The childlike delight on her face was captivating.

The second the sun disappeared, most people turned to watch the various acts, the still beautiful spectacle taking a backseat to the human circus. Shelly kept watching, transfixed by the misty violets and rich ambers of the lingering sunset. He wanted to look away— look at anything but her—yet a supernatural force had seized him. He was powerless to take his eyes off her.

"Let's go see the cat show," Bubbles cried, breaking the moment.

Shelly turned, looked straight through Matt as if he were just another tourist, then smiled at Trevor. So what else was new? Every woman went for Trevor.

Matt followed the group, trailing behind as they made their way to where a man with green hair like plastic grass in an Easter basket was setting up hoops on boxes of various heights. Nearby, half a dozen cats where waiting in small cages.

"It's a big mystery how he trains them," Bubbles said.

He realized Bubbles had been at his side for some time. She was flirting with him for sure, but Shelly had yet to notice him. Obviously, she was keeping the promise she'd made last night. She'd ignored him at breakfast when they'd chanced upon each other just as she was ignoring him now.

The green-haired man with a GOD SAVE THE QUEEN tattoo on his biceps was now taking the cats out of their cages and placing them on stools. The alley cats docilely waited, alert, but unfazed by the throng around them.

"This is everyone's favorite act," Bubbles told him. "No one can figure out how he gets cats to jump through flaming hoops."

To his right on the other side of Bubbles stood Kyle. He was leaning down, whispering something to Shelly. She responded with a tentative smile.

"Shelly seems a little shy at times," Trevor said, his voice pitched too low for Bubbles to overhear.

"Looks can be deceiving," Matt replied, again troubled by how close his friend was to this woman. "Remember, she threatened Emily."

"Words spoken in the heat of the moment," Trevor said.

Matt cursed under his breath. Shelly had Trevor around her little finger. "Shelly swore she'd kill Emily. My sister was in tears. She honestly believed Shelly would hurt her."

"After that, Shelly left, didn't she? You never saw her again until the accident."

"True, but it took a restraining order to get rid of her."

The crowd watched as the hoops were set afire. Waving a magician's wand, the green-haired man chanted in what was supposed to be a foreign language, but sounded more like jibberish. He tapped one cat's stool with the wand and the saucer-eyed animal soared through the hoop and landed on the empty stool on the other side.

The crowd roared its approval and clapped frantically. The man continued to chant and tap, sending the rest of the alley cats off their stools and through the rings of fire.

"Amazin'!" Bubbles clapped her hands, totally delighted.

Shelly's reaction was quite different. Her eyes were narrow slits and a frown etched her brow. The same expression marred Trevor's face.

"Do you suppose those cats are drugged?" he asked Trevor.

"I have no idea. I've heard about this, but I haven't been to the dock show for some time."

Matt wasn't surprised. The sunset celebration at Mallory Dock was for tourists, not locals. Since the cruise ships had made Key West a port of call, the dock was as crowded as Times Square on New Year's Eve. No doubt, Trevor was here because he wanted Shelly to see the famous event.

Now the cats were all flying through the air at once, gliding through the burning hoops with amazing agility. Their glassy, wide eyes re-flected the fire, but they didn't seem afraid.

"Every animal has an instinctive fear of fire," Matt told Trevor.

Trevor nodded. "Let's go. I can't watch this."

"We're outta here," Bubbles informed Kyle and Shelly.

Matt and Trevor led the way, plowing through the fascinated crowd. He looked over his shoulder to make sure Shelly and Kyle were following. The big jerk had his arm around her shoulders as though he owned her.

They reached the far end of the dock, where the crowd was thin-ner, the air fresher. They walked down the street toward Mel Fisher's Maritime Museum. The noise from Duval Street filled the balmy night air. Reggae, jazz, the blues, rock—you name it.

The night scene in Key West. Matt remembered someone calling it a consensus hallucination. They weren't far from wrong. After sun-set Duval Street belonged to the tourists who'd come to party. And there were plenty of clubs—gay and straight—to do it in.

"There's Dr. Burroughs." Shelly's excited voice came from be-hind him.

"He's joining us for dinner," Trevor said.

A good-looking man with close-cut brown hair and wire-rimmed glasses was leaning against the fence in front of the Audubon House. Matt had met the doctor briefly last night. He seemed like a nice guy.

"Where are we goin' to dinner?" Bubbles asked.

"Margaritaville," Trevor said as they joined Clive Burroughs in front of the charming home that had once belonged to the famous bird-watcher.

"You're kidding," Kyle said, echoing Matt's own reaction. He gave the big lug credit. Locals usually had the good sense to get off Duval after sunset. There were a few good restaurants, but they were jammed with tourists.

Trevor smiled at Shelly. "I promised Shelly a cheeseburger in par-adise."

Shelly looked at Kyle, then at Clive, then at Trevor, and finally at Bubbles. What was he, Matt wondered. The human equivalent of a tarantula?

"We could have a cheeseburger at Jimmy Buffett's another time," she said.

"Babe, if that's what you want to do"—Kyle changed his tune—"I'm game."

Just what Matt thought. What a guy! He'd say anything to lure a woman into bed.

"No, really. I don't mind eating at Margaritaville another time."

"Shelly, I have a suggestion," Clive said. "Tomorrow, I'm off. Trevor and I will meet you for cheeseburgers in paradise. Margaritaville is less crowded then."

"Great, I'd like that." Obviously, Shelly was flustered at being the center of a very minor controversy.

"Let's take rickies over to Louie's Backyard," suggested the doctor. "It's fun and the food's good."

"Come on, yaw'l. Let's go for it."

Bubbles led the charge around the corner to where the rickshaws were lined up, waiting for customers. Buff guys in muscle shirts and biking shorts made their living pedaling the two-wheeled carts around the Old Town's crowded streets.

Clive, the take-charge type, negotiated like a rug merchant in a bazaar for a special rate for three rickies to take them out to Louie's and wait while they dined. Matt stepped directly in front of Shelly.

"You're riding with me. There's something private we need to discuss."

Matt put both hands around Shelly's bare waist and lifted her into the rickie. To the driver he said in a tone too low to carry, "I'll give you an extra twenty to take the scenic route to Louie's Backyard."

CHAPTER

THIRTEEN

Matt hopped into the rickie next to Shelly and made certain to take up more than his fair share of the small bench seat just to see how she would react. He didn't know quite what to make of her. He suspected the way she kept ignoring him was some sort of act.

She was clutching her cane, staring straight ahead with all the enthusiasm of someone facing a firing squad. The driver began pedaling and the rickie bumped over the cobblestones, then turned up Duval. The vehicle swayed as the driver swung to one side to avoid hitting a trio of drunks who'd stumbled out of Sloppy Joe's Bar and into the street.

Could he help it if his bare knee brushed against Shelly's leg? Still staring ahead, she didn't seem to notice. He seized the opportunity to take a close look at her. Her slim legs did wonders for the shorts she was wearing even though one leg was in a cast from the knee down.

The cropped T-shirt was kick-ass. Silicone or not, he couldn't help wondering what it would be like to put his hands around her waist, then slowly move upward until her breasts were cradled in the palms of his hands.

The narrow road was a slug fest, typical after sunset, but the rickie driver maneuvered the rickshaw between the taxis and cars, quickly passing them. From the open-air bars and clubs lining the street came raucous laughter and music. The driver, pumping the pedals for all he was worth, turned off noisy Duval onto Eaton Street.

Shelly had yet to spare him a single glance. She gazed off in a detached way he found damned irritating. He tried to sound casual and act as if her attitude didn't frost his cookies.

"Most of the historic houses around here are conch houses. It sounds like c-o-n-k but it's spelled c-o-n-c-h. The building to your right is one of Key West's most famous landmarks, The Donkey Milk House. Notice, it's a tropical Greek Revival different from the others—"

"I know. Trevor gave me the historical tour."

He resisted the urge to spin her around in the seat and force her to look at him. This wasn't the way Shelly usually behaved. Back in Manhattan, nothing he said or did could discourage her. She pursued him, following him everywhere he went.

She had deluded herself into believing he loved her even though they'd had only one date. At that point Matt had gone ballistic and let her know that he wasn't putting up with her bullshit. Being mean hadn't fazed Shelly. She'd continued to dog him relentlessly. No matter how brutal his words, she'd kept coming back for more.

Now she was playing another game. Hard to get. If she wanted to play games, he was in the mood. Why not pretend to be nice?

"Shelly, about last night . . . I don't know what got into me. I acted like a real jerk."

"You won't get any argument from me."

A little surprised, he waited a moment for her to say something more, but she just looked at the CLOTHING OPTIONAL sign posted in front of the Déjà Vu Bed and Breakfast. No clothes, tangled sheets. An image flashed across his mind: Shelly on top of the sheets, hair fanned across his pillow, wearing nothing but a smile.

"Shelly, look at me."

"I can't." She set her chin like an Arkansas mule ready to let the big one rip. "Doctor's orders."

"What in hell are you talking about?"

"Dr. Holt thinks looking at you or talking to you will make me obsessed with you again. I'll die before that happens."

He laughed—or tried to anyway. If nothing else, her traumatic experience had sharpened her tongue. "Okay, I'll bite. Who's Dr. Holt?"

"A psychiatrist friend of Trevor's," she responded without looking his way. "I told Dr. Holt I was completely over you. I have no idea what I ever saw in you."

"Methinks the lady doth protest too much. I'll bet if you even looked at me for one second, you'd start panting and try to jump on my bones."

Bull's-eye! Shelly pivoted in her seat, her expression bordering on a death threat. He put his arm across the back of the rickie, accidentally touching her shoulder. Then he zapped her with his killer grin and waited for her to blink.

Her remarkable blue eyes regarded him as if he were an insect that must be squashed immediately.

He kept smiling. "I'm God's gift to women, right?"

"Don't you wish." She sounded as if she meant it.

Damn, if she wasn't startlingly beautiful. Last night had not been a trick of moonlight and his libido. He had to remind himself that she'd been artificially enhanced by a cosmetic surgeon, but her eyes were all her own, blue as the water in the Keys and framed by long, wispy lashes.

Right now those blue eyes were frigid and making a valiant attempt to turn him to stone. He had half a mind to kiss her until she was begging him for more. He could almost feel the generous shape of her mouth opening under his. Aw, hell—

Sick of smiling relentlessly like a TV evangelist, but unwilling to admit he'd lost the pissing contest, he yelled to the driver, "Take the shortcut through the cemetery."

Of course, going through the cemetery was an even longer way to Louie's, but he doubted Shelly realized this. "Now that you've got me out of your system, tell me what about me attracted you in the first place."

Uncertainty flickered in her eyes as the rickie left the street and headed into the dark cemetery. "I thought you were a nice man, a good person who looked after those who couldn't help themselves. I thought you were perfect."

Something in her tone told him that he had profoundly disappointed her, which was ridiculous. She was the one with the psychological problem, not him.

"Perfect, huh?" he teased. "Maybe I should apply for sainthood."

"Ahead of Mother Teresa? I don't *think* so."

Okay, she had a sense of humor that he hadn't picked up on in New York. So what else was new? He'd been on the fast track—with blinders.

"All right, I'm not perfect, but close enough for government work."

Her expression said: Hopeless case. "How do you live with yourself, Jensen?"

"No one else will have me."

The corner of her mouth twitched. She might have been on the verge of a smile. Pale moonlight filtered down through the cemetery's tall trees from a hunter's moon, glinting off her blond hair, but she'd turned her head slightly, making it hard to see her face in the shadowy darkness.

He reminded himself that the road to hell was no place for a woman, even one as screwed up as Shelly. Still, he couldn't seem to stay away from her.

Why had he suggested going through the cemetery instead of taking another long route to Louie's? The crypts were aboveground due to the high water table. It was an eerie place by day, and at night it was spooky enough to give anyone the willies.

He'd been buying time, trying to loosen Shelly up before breaking the news to her. It was too dark and too depressing to tell her anything until the driver pedaled the rickie out of the cemetery.

"Tell me, your holiness, why did you insist I ride with you?"

Matt choked back a laugh. Just when he thought he'd been called every damn name in the book, Shelly came up with something new.

"I wanted to warn you," he said, stalling. They were almost out of the cemetery. Ahead he could see the spires of St. Mary, Star of the Seas, the Catholic church. "Don't fall for Trevor—"

"Get real, Jensen. Do you think I'm stupid?"

"Well, now that you mention it—"

"Trevor is gay. He and Clive are meant for each other. Trevor just doesn't know it yet."

He heard his own quick intake of breath. He'd pegged her as someone far less insightful. Not everyone realized Trevor was gay, and Matt certainly hadn't picked up on anything going on between Trevor and the doctor. Now that Shelly had called his attention to it, he realized it was possible.

Who's going to take care of Trevor, she'd asked last night. Well, I'll be damned, he thought. Compassion and Shelly had never been linked in his mind until last night, when she'd picked up on the subtle undercurrent in his friend's personality. A permanent state of loneliness.

"If I had a brother, I—I mean, if my brother, Shawn, were still alive. Well, I feel the same way about Trevor that I did about Shawn."

An unmistakable pang of sympathy shafted through him. Shelly had lost her brother and her parents in the ValuJet crash. She was alone in the world. She might be trying to play the sympathy card, he warned himself. He had absolutely no idea what she was trying to pull.

"Trevor's a wonderful person," she added. "I told him I was over whatever obsessive tendencies I'd had, but he asked me to see Dr. Holt. It was the least I could do after all Trevor's done for me."

Matt knew an opening when he heard one. They were out of the cemetery now, the lights of the historic Tree Top Inn allowed him to see Shelly as he told her what he'd learned.

"Trevor asked me to talk to you about something," he fibbed. Trevor had said Shelly needed to be warned; Matt had volunteered. "Simon Ambrose—"

"The creep from the hospital?" Something shifted in the depths of her eyes.

"Yes." He fought the urge to put his arm around her to break the news. "The D.A. plea-bargained the case. The judge let him off yesterday with time served."

A beat of silence. "Great. Another victory in the war on crime."

Her voice was barely above a whisper now. She wasn't like so many women he'd known in New York. They were forced to act strong or they wouldn't be taken as seriously as men. Shelly's personality seemed to be tempered by a vulnerability he'd never seen before now. She had an edge, but she wasn't as tough as she pretended.

"Ambrose is still in Key West. He's staying with friends in Bahama Village." He didn't add that he planned to find the little shit and do the court's work for it.

"I was in the village just before sunset. I bought this T-shirt and shorts at Jo Mama's Duds. I didn't see him—and believe me, I would know him anywhere."

"I don't want you in the village," he said without thinking.

"He won't recognize me. I'll be able to spot him though." She didn't sound as confident as she had. "Don't worry about me."

Trouble was, he found himself doing the damnedest thing—worrying about Shelly Ralston. Maybe that's exactly what she wanted him to do. This just might be a new ploy on Shelly's part.

The rickie pulled up to Louie's Backyard and stopped in front of the conch house built by one of Key West's original sea captains.

Matt jumped out and shoved money into the driver's hand, quickly thanking him. He turned to help Shelly, but she was already out of the rickie and heading into the café.

The cropped T-shirt exposed an enticingly soft skin at her waist. Moving up behind her, he put his hand on the small of her back to guide her. After all, she needed a cane. She could use the help, couldn't she?

"They'll be out on the terrace," he told her as they crossed the dining room. "Louie's is famous for his backyard—the Atlantic Ocean."

Shelly didn't bother to respond. They passed a cluster of tables. All of the men were gawking at her, all of them seeing her naked, all of them—

"Matt, over here." Bubbles waved madly at him. Her red hair bounced and the light glinted off the stud in her nose. "I saved you a seat next to me."

Just his luck.

Kyle smiled at her and gestured to the chair next to him. She turned her back on Matt without a word and hobbled over to Kyle. Now, how was that for an attitude?

She collapsed into the chair Kyle had pulled out for her, amazed that she had actually managed to bluff Matt. The whole time, she'd been nervous he would realize she was not Rochelle Ralston. Talking to him, being near him, was dangerous.

And exciting.

Her pulse skittered alarmingly as she thought about how near he'd been in the rickie. She'd been disturbingly aware of the masculine contours of his body—its heat, its raw power. He possessed a virility that demanded attention.

What if Matt and Shelly still had been lovers at the time of the crash and Matt wanted to continue the relationship? Where men were concerned, she was out of her depth in a mud puddle. No way could she have handled him under those circumstances.

She'd kept her wits by acting like a bad girl. Calling him by his last name, then joking even though she'd been nervous had paid off—she thought. But she couldn't be sure Matt wasn't suspicious.

Even now, without looking in his direction, she could feel his eyes on her with a gaze so penetrating it made her breath catch. She smiled at Kyle and said yes to something he said, then realized that she'd ordered a drink. Two drinks in one evening. Two men. Too much for The Beast.

She was courting trouble.

She inhaled a calming breath, winked at Kyle, then gazed out at the terraced rear deck, directly over the water. Silver ribbons of moonlight glinted off the sea, and a warm breeze ruffled the palms, bringing with it the heavy scent of night-blooming jasmine mixed with the salty tang of the ocean.

She couldn't believe she was here, living a real life, enjoying herself. If only her mother had lived to see her now. How proud she would have been.

If only she didn't have to worry about Dexxter Foxx.

CHAPTER

FOURTEEN

It was almost two o'clock in the morning when she returned with Kyle to Half Moon Bay. After dinner at Louie's, Trevor had gone over to Clive's Truman Annex home for coffee. Kyle had insisted that she see some of Key West's famous night life. Thankfully, Bubbles had tagged along.

Matt, who'd been disturbingly silent throughout dinner, had taken a water taxi back to Sunset Key. She'd released a long, deep breath when he'd left. All evening she'd dodged his penetrating stare, wondering how much he suspected.

When would he expose her?

"Next time it'll be even more fun," Kyle said, his voice low as they came up the walk to Half Moon Bay. "You'll be able to dance."

Next time? She was too startled to do more than nod. This was as close as any man had ever come to asking her for a date.

They stopped at the front door, which faced the center of the small private island. Kyle had been friendly all evening, putting his arm around her and helping her walk with the cast. It had taken a little time, but she had become accustomed to having him touch her.

Now, though, she was disturbingly aware that they were alone. At Barefoot Bob's, a Deadhead hangout, Bubbles had run into some guy she knew. They'd gone down the block to Tequila Flats to sample premium tequilas, leaving her alone with Kyle.

Well, not alone exactly. There had been plenty of people on the streets, and the Sunset Key launch was crowded because it was the last commercial boat run to the island until morning. But once they'd started down the brick path toward the far end of the key, no one else was around.

"I'm going to be gone for a few days on a special assignment," Kyle said, his alert eyes shifted, checking the shadows, the way he had all evening. "I'll call you when I get back."

His words sent her confidence spiraling upward. She was over her head with him, for sure. Once again she wished she had more experience with men. "Thanks, you have no idea how much fun I had tonight. It was great."

"Really?" he sounded surprised. "You seemed—I don't know—distracted. I thought you were involved with someone."

She shook her head and managed a smile. Involved? Of course not. She'd never been on a date, never been kissed. The list of nevers was endless.

Now all those nevers seemed possible.

Kyle's gaze was riveted on her lips, and she thought he was going to kiss her. The sensual light in his eyes confirmed her suspicions. A pulsing knot formed in her chest as she waited, senses on alert.

The minute he kissed her, Kyle would be disappointed. A man this sophisticated wouldn't be interested in kissing a woman who had less experience than the average fifteen-year-old.

"Hey, Shelly, you're looking at me like I'm from another planet. What's wrong?"

"Nothing's wrong. Bubbles sold me alien abduction insurance. I haven't got a care in the world."

Kyle stepped back and rolled his eyes heavenward. Unless she missed her bet, he didn't seem to be the praying type.

"I just remembered my dog, Jiggs. I've been gone for hours. He'll be frantic." She rose onto the ball of her good foot and smacked her lips against his cheek. "Call me when you get back."

Like a breeze through the palms, she was inside the house before she heard him say, "Good night, Shelly."

She leaned back against the closed door to catch her breath. Too bad she didn't have an instruction manual: Dating Men for Dummies. Other women grew into the role, learning from the first time a little boy chased them around the school yard, then graduating to more sophisticated interactions.

She wandered into the kitchen to find Jiggs, who usually hung out with the cats. Zeke and Zoe, an elderly couple whom Trevor had taken in, were filling Yohimbe packets. Bubbles had told her the powder was an aphrodisiac. She had her doubts, but people went for it.

The couple had been homeless when Trevor found them, living off the food in the Hard Rock Café's Dumpster. They had gotten a schtick, as Bubbles would say. They spent their time working the crowds waiting to tour Hemingway's house. The Yohimbe scam had netted them enough to rent a small loft over a garage. They were moving out in a few days.

"You two are up late," she said, glancing around the spacious kitchen for Jiggs.

"Tomorrow five buses of Japanese tourists are stopping at Hemingway's place," Zeke said.

She couldn't help returning Zeke's engaging smile that made his blue eyes twinkle. His long silver-white hair and turned-up mustache reminded her of Wild Bill Hickok—in a Hawaiian shirt.

"The sons of Nippon are into aphrodisiacs big-time," Zoe said as she spooned Kool-Aid powder into packets labeled YOHMB.

It was all she could do not to laugh. The older couple came from a small town in Wisconsin, but somewhere along the way to paradise they'd picked up a lot of teenage jargon. It sounded strange coming from grandparents.

She was getting used to them. To Key West. Nothing was too wild, too unusual, to be accepted. Maybe that's why she felt safe here. She could blend in without being noticed.

"Have you seen Jiggs?"

Zeke shook his head. "Poor thing—"

"He got into the catnip that Trevor keeps in the pantry," Zoe put in.

"Jiggs kept running in circles after his tail, then tried to climb the palm tree like Bingo."

Bingo was a one-eyed tom that Trevor had found wandering the grounds of the Little White House, once a favorite vacation spot of President Truman's. Trevor had no response from the cat-found posters he'd put up around the Truman Annex's cluster of posh homes. Small wonder.

Despite having only one eye, Bingo was the terror of Half Moon Bay. He stalked the egrets every morning as they tried to feed and fearlessly attempted to catch sand sharks basking in the shallow water near the shore. She had no doubt that Bingo had once again broken into the pantry and upended the jar of catnip.

But what would possess Jiggs, the world's finickiest dog, to eat catnip?

"Jiggs kept making awesome noises."

"Awesome?" Zeke scoffed at Zoe.

"Maybe Jiggs was trying to bark," she told the older couple. "I've never heard him bark. He whimpers sometimes, but he never barks."

Zeke shook his head. "I tell you, Jiggs was trying to meow. He thinks he's a cat."

"Like ta Oded, but Matt saved him."

Oh, Jiggs, no. The poor little guy had suffered so much already. Then a wave of anxiety swept through her. Matt had saved him. She needed to stay as far away from Matt as possible, but now she would have to thank him.

"It was way cool," Zeke added. "Matt poured cod liver oil down Jiggs's throat—"

"Jiggs started upchucking all over the place." Zoe shook her head. "But it got the catnip out of his stomach."

"Where's Jiggs now?"

Zoe crooked a tightly permed head of blue-white hair toward the terrace. "He's resting outside with Matt."

Unsteady after so many hours upright, she limped out onto the terrace. Coming out of the brightly lit kitchen into the darkness made it difficult to get her bearings. She paused a moment, glancing around.

Off to the side was a dark form on one of the chaises facing the ocean. Matt. With any luck, he would be asleep. Treading softly, she moved across the grass.

Matt's arms were crossed behind his head. There was just enough moonlight to see he was awake and staring up at the stars. At his feet Jiggs was curled into a ball, asleep.

"Thanks for helping Jiggs," she said. "I understand he was really sick."

"No big deal," Matt said without making an effort to look in her direction. "Someone should explain to him that he's not a cat."

"Right," she said. Jiggs had graduated from eating popcorn to Nine Lives. He was about the size of a cat and acted more like one than a dog. "It's an identity crisis. I'm sure he'll grow out of it."

She hooked the cane over her arm and reached for Jiggs. The poor little guy must have fought hard when Matt fed him the cod liver oil. His three sessions at Groomingdale's getting moisturizing treatments were wasted. He looked like a rat with long, greasy fur.

Jiggs scuttled out of her reach, dashing to Matt. Great! She'd saved Jiggs, and now he was kissing up to the man who had doused him with cod liver oil.

"There's probably an uglier dog . . . somewhere on the planet," Matt said.

"Beauty is more about what's on the inside than what's on the outside. He's a sweet dog. He—"

"You're right. He's grown on me." Matt stroked Jiggs's head, and the little dog's tail beat against the plush cushion. "In the morning I'll take him to the groomer while you have your cast removed."

"That would be great."

At dinner she'd told Kyle about seeing the doctor in the morning. She hadn't realized that Matt had been paying attention. All through the meal he'd seemed bored . . . or something. Now a charged silence filled the air between them like a tropical storm gearing up to unleash its fury.

In one lithe movement he swung his long legs to the ground and sat up, taking her by surprise. He tugged her arm and pulled her down beside him, saying, "You can quit pretending."

The heaviness in her chest intensified under his scathing gaze. There was no point in trying to fool Matthew Jensen any longer. He'd known Shelly intimately; he was bound to realize, sooner or later, that she wasn't the woman he had once loved. All through dinner she'd refused to look at him, but she'd sensed his skeptical gaze tracking her and knew he was suspicious.

"Ignoring me, pretending I don't exist, isn't going to cure your obsession."

Braced to be exposed, it took a full second for his words to register. Matt hadn't guessed the truth; he still thought she was Shelly.

"Jensen, give it a break, will you?" My, she sounded tough, didn't she? "I'm over you. Can't your ego accept that fact?"

"My ego has nothing to do with this." His brow creased and his moody eyes glinted in the darkness, but his voice was lethally calm.

"I'm not pretending. I'm over you."

Now, that was an out-and-out lie. There was something so compelling about him that she knew she would never be over Matthew Jensen. In her heart she would always remember the voice in the darkness, his encouraging words luring her back to the land of the living.

Some part of her still longed for that man. She was suddenly aware of how close they were, sitting shoulder to shoulder, his muscled thigh touching hers. A shiver of some inexplicable sensation crackled down her spine.

She told herself she wasn't really attracted to Matt. What captivated her was the image she'd formed. Now, she truly knew the meaning of reality check.

"Shelly, if you're not careful, you'll be in trouble . . . big-time."

Jiggs crawled into her lap and the putrid odor of cod liver oil wafted up as she asked, "What are you talking about?"

His large hand cupped her chin. Her skin prickled at his touch, then became warm except for the cool spot where the birthmark had been. Her heart beat in heavy, uneven lurches, and she had to force herself to look directly into his intense eyes.

"Kyle Parker is not your average guy," he informed her with perplexing hostility underscoring every word. "If you stalk him, you'll run into a bunch of military bastards."

"Stalk?" She pulled back so he was no longer touching her. "You think I'm going to stalk Kyle?"

"The experts say people with obsession disorders tend to transfer the obsession from one person to another."

She tried to concentrate on what he was saying, but the way he was studying her was even more disturbing than his words. Her senses were on full alert, anticipating. Expecting what?

"Kyle doesn't trust his own shadow. That tells me he's either a highly trained SEAL or he's with the CIA."

Handsome and blessed with the devil's own charm, Kyle Parker *was* wound a little too tight. Even though she had no experience with men, she understood this much.

"If you stalk Kyle, hiding in the bushes taking pictures, he'll shoot first—then ask questions."

"That's absurd. Kyle and I are just—"

He lowered his head, and his lips pressed against hers, smothering her response. Stunned, she clutched Jiggs's greasy body. Matt pulled her closer, slanting his mouth over hers, more insistent now. Aware of the strength of his arms and the restrained power in his body, she stiffened.

His moist, firm mouth demanded a response, and she released Jiggs, then tentatively wound her arms around his shoulders. A little bell went off in her brain—stop. She knew she shouldn't be doing this, but she didn't pull back.

She couldn't, she honestly couldn't. She clearly remembered how wonderful Matt's embrace had felt when she'd been in the hospital.

In spite of her better judgment, some part of her had longed to be in his arms again.

He raised his mouth from hers for a second and gazed into her eyes. In the shadowy darkness it was impossible to read his expression. She didn't have time to speculate on what he was thinking. His lips reclaimed hers, and he pulled her so close that her chest pillowed against his powerful torso, flattening her breasts.

She told herself to part her lips a little more, the way they did on the soap operas. The slow, drugging kiss sent heat spiraling through her as his tongue traced the soft fullness of her lower lip. Her breasts, already feeling flushed, swelled with pleasure.

Inhaling deeply, some elusive scent with a trace of citrus filled her lungs. Matt, she realized with a pang of intense emotion. It was the masculine smell she recalled from the dark abyss of unconsciousness. The scent brought back such potent memories.

Here was the white knight who had rescued her.

The man of her dreams.

But she wasn't dreaming now, she reminded herself as his tongue stole between her lips. She ventured forward, brushed his tongue with the tip of hers, then jerked it back. He was much more bold; his tongue invaded her mouth with startling aggression.

His lips did not become softer as he kissed her. Instead, his passion seemed to increase as his tongue cornered hers. Their tongues danced, darting little forays at first, then the cadence slowed, allowing their tongues to mate. Her pulse throbbed in her temples, gaining speed as she savored the kiss and the heat rising from his chest as his heart beat against her breast.

This was what she'd been waiting for all her life, wasn't it? Rational thought eluded her, but on some level she knew she hadn't wanted Kyle to kiss her because she had wanted Matt to be the first man she kissed.

Only Matt.

With a start she realized his hand had slipped under the cropped T-shirt. He was caressing the bare skin along her lower back. His fingers coasted upward a scant inch at a time, moving around toward her rib cage. Any second he would be touching her breasts.

The little alarm bell that had been tinkling in the back of her brain since the moment his lips met hers became a deafening GONG! She wasn't ready for this. She twisted hard in his arms and managed to free herself.

With as much dignity as she could muster, she reached for her cane, which was propped against the chaise. Jiggs had jumped down and was at her feet, his head cocked, watching them.

"You're still hot for me, Shelly. You'll love me until I die, remember?"

His voice had a husky, sensual quality like the rasp of a cat's tongue. In the aftershock of the kiss it took a minute for his words to register. Why would Shelly say she would love him until he died? How very odd.

"If you're going to fixate on anyone, obsess on me. I've been down that road with you before, babe. I can handle it."

White-hot anger arced through her, and for a moment she was incapable of speaking. She could have kissed another man tonight, but she hadn't. She had wanted Matt to be the first man to kiss her.

To her that single kiss had been worth all the suffering, the years of being The Beast. How many times had she watched lovers walking hand in hand . . . and secretly wished? She'd tried to steel herself against those dangerous longings, but it hadn't been possible.

At night, alone in her bed, she would pretend she was someone else. She never asked for too much. She'd just wanted to be ordinary—not The Beast. Tonight she thought her wishes had come true when he'd taken her into his arms.

She'd been transported back to the time in the hospital when he'd held her in his arms. The first man to ever hold her. The only man she'd ever wanted to hold her had finally kissed her. For a moment a single kiss had made up for a lifetime of loneliness and ridicule.

To him, it was nothing more than a way of proving a point.

Common sense said to march away, but then she realized that's what The Beast would have done. She wasn't Rochelle Ralston, and she wasn't The Beast either. She was a new person, someone who didn't have to take this.

She stabbed the air with the index finger of her left hand. "You know, Matt, if you dropped dead tomorrow, I'd dance on your grave."

His eyes narrowed, but he didn't say a word.

CHAPTER

FIFTEEN

Dexxter stood at the window, staring at the sign illuminated against the dark sky. FOXX ENTERPRISES. He should feel something, he reflected. He had just inked the deal with the Asians who were purchasing his company. Foxx Enterprises no longer existed.

He liked to gaze out of his office window at the sign, symbolizing his success. His practical side told him that it was time—past time—to go to ground. The FBI had been hot on his tail. Now they had cooled off, but you never knew. . . .

Time to reinvent himself.

Time to ditch good old Irene.

A soft knock sounded on his door, and he called, "It's open."

A blonde with a bombshell bod sashayed into his office, courtesy of Technical Assistants, the call girls he used. "Hi, there. I'm Camilla Cassidy."

His breath caught in his chest as she swanned across the room, her blond hair brushing her bare shoulders.

Amy Conroy.

Where had that thought come from, he wondered as the blonde strode toward him, her impossibly long legs hiking her skirt higher with each step. This woman was much more beautiful, much more sophisticated than Amy.

Camilla halted beside him as he stood by the window, her big tits brushing his arm. Her breathy voice sent a ripple of excitement down to his groin. "Monty up, Dexx. Monty up."

She reached between his legs and cradled his balls. Her index finger homed in on the pulse point between his thighs. And gently pressed.

White-hot heat flooded his cock.

The techs were worth the price; he was fully erect in a second. Quick as a snake, she had his zipper down and her hand in his pants.

"Dexx, you have quite the monty," she said as she freed his cock.

He grinned as she sank to her knees. Her silky hair brushed his shaft while she ran the tip of her tongue across his hot, aching flesh. He jutted his hips forward and she got the message. Hand cradling his balls, finger on the pressure point, she applied sweet suction.

All he could see was the top of her head. Amy, he thought, holding in his breath and trying not to come too quickly. Amy's face disgusted him. It promised perfection—then revolted.

What if he didn't have to look at her? Dexx imagined it was Amy on her knees before him, giving him the best blowjob he'd ever had.

When he found Amy—and he would find her eventually—he had plans for her. Then she had to die. He toyed with the idea of murdering her himself.

Death was messy and best left to professionals. He'd had several people killed, but he hadn't been present to enjoy it. This time he intended to relish every second.

His private line rang, interrupting his thoughts, and he realized that he'd zoned out somehow. He was still holding his breath and he hadn't come yet. The blonde—what the fuck was her name?—looked up at him with wide blue eyes.

He released his breath with a grunt. "Ignore the phone."

The phone continued to ring, the blinking light indicating it was an interoffice call. Since it was past seven, everyone had gone home. Except Irene. She'd probably seen the blond come into his office and waited, timing it just right to ruin his fun.

He stared at the blond head so attentively bent over him. In the next instant his body shuddered, then exploded in a rush of heat so intense that he saw blotchy stars like Rorschach dots. The shaft of pure pleasure reverberated up his spine into the base of his skull. He threw his head back and released a lusty groan.

The phone hadn't stopped ringing. He let the blonde take care of him while he answered it. "Yeah, Irene, what is it?"

"Am I interrupting anything?" Her voice was all honey.

"I don't have time to talk to you." He planned to make the blonde do him again. Pretending the woman was Amy turned out to be the hottest sex he'd ever had—bar none.

"I thought you might want to know what I picked up on the Internet about Amy Conroy, but I'll tell you later." She hung up on him.

He cradled the phone against his shoulder, punched the button for Irene's line, then he jammed his cock back, where it belonged, and zipped his pants. The phone rang and rang.

That bitch was deliberately not answering. She couldn't have left her office this quickly. He slammed down the receiver and sprinted out of his office. As he rounded the corner, he saw the elevator doors closing.

Dexxter tried to enjoy dinner with Camilla, but inside he was seething. He kept getting up to call Irene. Either she wasn't home or she wasn't answering.

He took the blonde home right after dinner and drove over to Irene's town house, but she wasn't home. He sat in the pitch dark in his Ferrari, freezing his ass off until she returned just after one o'clock.

He barged past her into the warm condo. "What did you find out?"

Irene yawned, then said in a sugar-coated tone, "Can't this wait until morning? I'm bushed."

"I want to know what you found out—now."

"You can't imagine the hits we had when we put out the word on the Web that we were from Hollywood—"

"Who's we?"

"Zane helped me. Who else?"

"He's a crappy excuse for a private eye."

She crossed her legs again and smiled. What was so damn funny?

"Zane didn't find Amy because you had him looking in the wrong place. We put that mutt's picture on the Internet, saying we wanted a dog like him for a commercial."

"Who's going to buy that bridge? A half-eared, butt-ugly dog."

"After the chihuahua on the Taco Bell commercial, weird-looking dogs are all the rage. We received thousands of responses. One seems particularly promising. Groomingdale's in Key West claims to have groomed a dog named Jiggs that looks exactly like the picture."

"Key West?"

"The southernmost place in the country. That's just about as far as you can get from Seattle, isn't it?"

She had a point, but he wasn't about to admit it. "What did they say about Amy?"

"That's the interesting part. The dog's owner was in a terrible car accident that required extensive reconstructive surgery. The groomer hasn't met the woman."

Dexx leaned back in the chair, his pulse beating erratically. This was as close to a lead as they'd come. Heat pooled in his groin just thinking about the plans he had for Amy.

"I've sent Zane to Key West to check it out."

Matt walked up Thomas Street with Jiggs wrapped in a towel under his arm, heading toward Groomingdale's. The main drag in Bahama Village, the street was lined with quaint churches and Cuban stores. Unlike touristy Old Town a few short blocks away, the village was just enough off the beaten path to give him a glimpse back in time.

"Aw, hell," he said out loud. His temples felt tight; he had the beginnings of a headache. Sometimes when he'd gone without sleep, working a big story, he developed a killer headache. The last thing he wanted now was a bad headache.

He reached a shady part of the sidewalk and decided that he didn't have a headache. It was just an unusually hot, humid day. He should have worn his Yankees ball cap.

The homes in Bahama Village were one story high and one room wide, shotgun style houses with tin roofs. They were packed together like cigars in a box, he decided as he looked around. Most of the residents were Bahamians and Cubans, many of African descent.

Simon Ambrose was living off Thomas Street with friends, Matt reminded himself. He'd have to pay him a visit while Groomingdale's washed Jiggs. No one touched Shelly like that and got away with it scot-free.

He stopped dead in his tracks. How had she managed that? She'd turned the tables on him. Now he was feeling protective of her.

Go on, admit it. You're feeling a helluva lot more than protective.

Since when had desire replaced hate, he wondered, starting to walk again. Why did he want to get closer to Shelly when he knew damn well he should run the other way?

Last night he'd sat in the restaurant, watching Shelly. Kyle Parker had made a real play for her. The man was proof positive that bullshit could be delivered with a macho spin. She went for it, never once slanting a look in his direction.

"I'm not jealous," he muttered under his breath.

Don't lie. Life is too damn short.

He *had* been jealous. Why? She hadn't appealed to him at all when they'd been in New York. So, what had changed?

Face it, schmuck, you've changed—big-time.

He knew better than to kiss her. Contact—of any kind—encouraged obsessive types. Shelly was a nutcase, of that he was positive, yet something about her called out to him. Long ago he'd learned to accept his physical needs. What guy wasn't horny more than half the time? But his reaction to a woman had never been this intense.

He could still feel her lips parting under his. There had been a tentativeness to her kiss, an unexpected innocence that reminded him of a sultry summer night and his first kiss. Suddenly, he'd been young again, unburdened by the cruel realities of life.

The kiss had aroused her as much as it had him. The feel of her body, the sweet, musky smell coming from her skin had gone to his head like a shot of tequila. In another minute he would have had her down on that chaise. She'd stopped him. Why?

She'd been mad as hell when he reminded her of how hot she'd been for him. Okay, okay. It wasn't a smart thing to say, yet something inside him forced him to antagonize her.

It had backfired. *If you dropped dead tomorrow, I'd dance on your grave.* Her words echoing in his ears, he'd gone to bed last night with the mutt in cod liver oil dogging his heels.

He'd lain there in the darkness, the half-eared dog curled up at his feet, the ceiling fan overhead swirling. Cod liver oil fumes wafted through the air, nearly gagging him, as he pictured Shelly.

Dancing on his grave.

She'd been furious with him when she'd said it. He understood her anger. After all, their entire relationship had been charged with anger and lies. Still, he couldn't help feeling something more was going on now.

She seemed to be using anger to disguise . . . hurt.

Could Shelly be hurt? It didn't seem possible, considering how she had behaved in Manhattan. Then she couldn't be hurt, but now . . . Who knew?

When it came to women, he was worthless except in the sack. This woman seemed to be hurt and disappointed in him. For the life of him, he couldn't understand why.

Sure as hell, he was missing something.

He told himself to let it go, let her go. He knew better than to hang around her, kissing her, angling for a chance to make love to her. He knew better, for chrissake. "Just leave her alone."

The promise sounded empty. Even Jiggs looked up and cocked his little head, not believing one damn word Matt had said.

Ahead, he saw the Groomingdale sign, a snow-white poodle with a pink bow in its hair. He shifted Jiggs to his other arm. "No bow, you hear? That's sissy stuff."

He walked past the offices of Vegetarians for Earth Consciousness, the kind of green movement that could exist only in Key West. Down a narrow walkway stood the grooming salon. He walked in and the bell on the door tinkled.

No one was at the counter, but a female voice yelled from the back room, "I'll be right there."

He put Jiggs on the counter, removed the towel, and tried not to gag. The cod liver oil was bad enough, but this morning Bingo had pushed Jiggs into a bowl of Nine Lives. Tuna and cod liver oil ripening in the tropical heat was worse than manure.

He looked at the wall behind the counter and read the sign: **As long as you see men as worthy of respect, we're going to have a problem.**

Great! Lesbians owned the place. He might have known. The gay community was extremely tight-knit. Trevor was bound to support his friends.

He reflected a minute, then decided that being a lesbian meant taking a lot of shit from macho types. It was a classic problem of stereotyping. Some men gave them a hard time, so all men were lumped together as the enemy.

"My stars!" cried a heavyset woman with buzz-cut black hair. "What happened to Jiggs?" From beneath grizzled brows she scowled at him as if he'd slithered out from beneath a dank rock.

"Conditioning fur is best left to professionals." She swept Jiggs into her arms, raised him to her nose, and took a deep whiff. "Tell me it's not cod liver oil."

Matt didn't bother to explain. "He needs a good bath. No prissy bows."

She headed toward the back room, then stopped. "Do you talk to the woman who owns Jiggs?"

"Sure, we're both staying at Half Moon Bay with Trevor."

"There's a picture of a dog like Jiggs on animalnetwork.com. A producer wants an unusual dog for a commercial. If she's interested, I'll let them know."

Jiggs in a commercial. Now, that was a stretch even for Hollywood. "I'll tell Shelly about it."

CHAPTER
SIXTEEN

She gazed into the mirror and decided that her leg didn't appear too withered. No doubt, having a removable cast that could be taken off at night had helped. She was pale by Key West standards, she thought, looking at herself in the Day-Glo orange bikini she'd bought for a dollar at Jo Mama's.

"It's the only body you've got. It'll have to do." She was never going to be tanned like burnt cinnamon, the way so many women around here were. And Clive had ordered her to stay out of the sun.

The doctor who had just removed the cast had told her to swim as much as possible to rebuild strength in her leg. She ventured out of her room and onto the terrace at Half Moon Bay. Thank goodness no one was around to see her pale body in the skimpy bikini.

When she'd gotten up that morning, no one had been awake except for Bingo, who had been patrolling the beach, dying to strike terror in the hearts of the birds who fed along the tide line. She had found a note at message central, the table in the foyer, indicating Bubbles had called to say she was "trying out a tequila sunrise" and not to expect her home.

Jiggs had been nowhere in sight. Last night the little stinker—reeking of cod liver oil—had insisted on staying with Matt. Feeling slightly betrayed, she'd let him.

She'd taken the first boat to Key West without seeing anyone who was staying at Trevor's. When she had returned, after having lunch at Margaritaville with Clive and Trevor, Half Moon Bay was deserted. She'd put on her new bikini, and now she was walking—using both legs fully—down to the beach.

She gingerly put one foot in the soft sand, then the other, taking care not to twist the leg that had been in the cast. She dabbed one toe in the water and found it was deliciously warm, inviting. She took a few more steps into the welcoming surf, then plunged headlong into the sea.

Beneath the aquamarine water, seashells were scattered across the crystal-white sand, and seaweed swayed like graceful ballerinas in the undulating surf. Gliding through the water, colorful fishes swam beside her as she floated along.

For the first time in weeks some part of her didn't ache painfully as she moved. True, the fingers on her right hand still curved inward like a catcher ready to field a fast ball, and her left leg was still weak, but she was whole again.

With a new face, a new life. Giddy with happiness, she shot to the surface. Laughter erupted from her throat as she treaded water and stared at the magnificent blue sky doming overhead.

"Oh, Mama, look at me now!"

She gazed up into the blinding sun, positive her mother was in heaven. Watching. It was oddly comforting to think of her mother looking down at her and sharing her life. It didn't make her feel so alone.

She couldn't help wishing her mother could have visited Half Moon Bay, paradise on earth. Her mother would have loved the majestic palms rimming the white sand beach. The egrets, kingfishers, and frigates would have delighted her mother with their antics.

But her mother wasn't with her to enjoy nature's treasure, and wishing things were different was futile. She had to channel the love and courage her mother had given her in the proper direction.

"Character determines fate, Mama. Don't worry about me."

A man on a Wave Runner whizzed by, snapping pictures of Half Moon Bay and sending a rogue wave in her direction. It slapped her in the face and washed over her head. She emerged, hair slicked back, blinking furiously to clear her blurred vision.

"What a jerk."

This was nothing new. Boaters cruised by all the time, fascinated with the compound Trevor had built at Half Moon Bay. The man aimed his camera at her and clicked. She dove under the water, wondering if The Beast would ever get used to people looking at her.

A disturbing thought hit her. Could the creep on the Wave Runner be one of Dexxter's men? She doubted he could find her. More likely the man was taking pictures of women in bikinis, a favorite pastime in Key West, she thought as she skimmed, weightless, through the water.

"Get used to it," she told herself. "People look you in the eye now. They talk to you. They take pictures. Amazing."

She blew out bubbles and inspected the sea life on the ocean floor. She could have stayed down forever, except her lungs were burning, crying out for oxygen. Surfacing, she blinked, the saltwater stinging her eyes.

"Oh, lordy, it can't be."

Matt was standing on the shore, watching her. After last night, she never wanted to see him again. *"You're still hot for me."*

Who did he think he was?

Actually, a better question would have been: What kind of person had Rochelle Ralston been? *"You'll love me until I die, remember?"* Matt's words had seemed chillingly strange last night. Even more so now that she'd had time to think about the comment.

No matter how weird Shelly had been, it was difficult to forgive Matt's conceited, arrogant attitude. She stopped herself, admitting this was really her problem, not his. He couldn't help it if he didn't live up to her expectations. If she'd had more experience with men, she wouldn't have been so . . . so thoroughly disillusioned.

She stood up and waded ashore through chest-level water that dropped to her waist, her hips, then her thighs as she emerged from the sea. Matt's sunglasses were pushed to the top of his head. He made no attempt to disguise the scorching gaze that slowly roamed from her wet hair to her ankles hidden in the foaming surf.

And back again.

The soft sand made her a little unsteady on her bad leg as she stepped out of the surf. She did her best to sear Matt with a bad girl's drop-dead-you-creep look.

"I see the doctor took your cast off."

Matt's voice had a hint of a truce in it. She tamped down the urge to make a sarcastic remark.

"Yes. I have to swim three times a day and go to a physical therapist, but I don't have to wear the cast any longer." She glanced around for her beach towel, then remembered dropping it onto a chair on the terrace, some distance away. The way Matt kept looking at her made her feel positively naked. The Beast would have run for cover, but she refused to allow him to intimidate her.

"Is that orange thing you're wearing scraps from a life jacket, or is it supposed to be a swimsuit?"

She bit down on her lip, determined not to take the bait. Obviously, she'd been mistaken about hearing a truce in his voice. He was as confrontational as usual.

"Must be one of Jo Mama's specials," he said with a grin some women might consider sexy. He tilted his head toward the man on the Wave Runner. "You're turning this place into a pornographer's paradise. That guy can't stop taking pictures of you."

The suit was more revealing than anything she had ever owned—including her underwear. Once she would never have dared to wear it and call attention to herself, but urged on by Bubbles and the ridiculously cheap price, she had bought the bikini.

"Check out Jiggs," he said lightly.

Ahead, she saw something maroon curled up on her beach towel. Couldn't be Jiggs. Usually, the little guy was the color of sludge.

"What can I say? The woman at Groomingdale's thought a henna rinse would make Jiggs distinctive."

She cocked her head toward Matt and saw the humor sparking his amber eyes. Maybe he had been teasing her about her bikini. She had so little knowledge of men and the way their minds worked that she could easily have mistaken a joke for criticism.

"Hold it." Matt's arm shot out in front of her, forcing her to halt. "Here comes Bingo."

The orange-colored alley cat sauntered up to the chair where Jiggs was snoozing and jumped up beside the little dog. Startled, Jiggs opened his eyes, saw it was Bingo, and scooted to the corner of the towel, making room for the cat. Bingo dropped down beside him, then began picking his teeth with his hind paw.

"Look at Bingo's tummy," said Matt. "It's the size of a football. God-only-knows-what he's digesting."

She couldn't help smiling even though Bingo had probably bagged one of the magnificent shore birds. Matt's tone was lighthearted, engaging. She ventured another look into his eyes.

"Matt, you're about as charming as a pit bull."

His adorable grin turned his lips up at the corners of his mouth as if he'd just received the ultimate compliment. She quickly looked away, telling herself not to be taken in by a heart-stopping smile. Or a powerful, inescapably masculine body. Remember, a good offense is a strong defense.

"You know, Jensen, I've been thinking—"

"Uh-oh. Naked women should not be allowed to think."

She looked down at Jiggs and Bingo, deciding against yanking the towel out from under them.

"Okay, I'll bite. What's going on behind those gorgeous baby blues."

It was a back-handed compliment, and she refused to allow it to soften her attitude.

"Jensen, I think you've got a problem. I—"

"No, honey"—he touched her arm, a light gesture that seemed surprisingly intimate—"people no longer have problems. They have 'issues.' So? What's the issue here?"

He was good, really good, at verbal sparring. She knew she was out of her element, but she had a point to make.

"Did you see *Indecent Proposal* or *Honeymoon in Las Vegas?*" she asked, boldly looking him in the eye.

"Sure." His reply was emphatic, but she could see she'd caught him off guard.

"The men persistently pursued those women. What happened? They get the girl."

He nodded slowly, his dark eyes narrowing—evidently he was trying to figure out where she was going with this.

"Now, take *Fatal Attraction* and *Play Misty for Me*. Women chased the men. Did they get the guys? No, sir. Did they get respect? Are you kidding? They got killed."

Matt took a half step back, saying, "I'm sure there's a point to this."

She indulged in a second to blister him with another glaring look. "What we have here is a double standard. Men pursue women and they're credited with being persistent—a good trait. Women chase men and society condemns them for being obsessed."

An astonished silence followed her heated comment. Matt's eyes never left hers, and she could almost hear his brain revving into gear, assimilating what she had said, then formulating a response.

He smiled, an arrogant half-lift of the corner of his mouth. "It's absurd to expect me to have an intellectual discussion with a nude woman."

"Jensen, get a life. Can't you be serious for once?"

Two beats of silence followed, the air filled by the staccato beat of her heart and the soulful call of a kingfisher circling overhead.

"I'm serious, Shelly, dead serious. Society probably does give men more credit than it should for persistence, but this is a matter of degree. You crossed over the line when you threatened my sister. You said you'd kill her if she didn't leave me alone."

She had tried to jam that disturbing incident to the far corner of her mind. She couldn't justify what Shelly had done. Yet, she had no choice except to pretend to be this terrible woman.

"You're right. What I did was unforgivable." The reply seemed forced even to her own ears. "I'm truly sorry."

He shrugged, then looked out over the water toward Key West. "Obsession is complicated and lasts a long time. There was a case, right here in Key West, in the 1930s."

The way he paused made her wonder. What now?

"A girl named . . . Elena died and was buried in the cemetery we rode through last night. A man by the name of Von Cosel was so obsessed with her that he retrieved her body and took it to his house. He mummified her, then made love to her every night. It took seven years before their grisly affair was uncovered."

She swallowed hard to fight down the bile rising in her throat. "Don't worry about me digging you up, Jensen. I won't bother you ever again, I promise."

Why in hell had he told Shelly that story? It was true, but gross. Even in Key West, a mecca for misfits, a man like Von Cosel was certifiable. He opened his mouth to tell Shelly something more upbeat. Jiggs could be a TV star. But the telephone rang and Shelly rushed off to answer it.

Watching her tight buns move beneath the bright orange bikini bottom, Matt cursed under his breath. She was so damn sexy. His unwilling response to her intensified every time he was around her.

He gazed down at Jiggs and Bingo—an orange and maroon eyesore if there ever was one—and tried to get his mind off Shelly. It was impossible. She appealed to him on several different levels.

Sure, she was a heart-stopper, but she was bright too. If she hadn't threatened Emily, he might have excused her obsessive behavior. That was how convincing her argument had been.

She was itching to take him on, which amused him. He was in a mean mood these days, and she'd borne the brunt of his temper. When he acted like this, he scared the shit out of most people. Not Shelly.

"I won't bother you ever again, I promise." Her words came back to him. *I promise.*

Kicking himself for not remembering sooner, the psychiatrist's warning replayed in his mind. "An unsolicited promise is a reliable indicator of a troubled person, demonstrating obsessive behavior."

Shelly had often promised to leave him alone if—and there was always an if attached to the promise. If he would see her one more time. If he would read the note she'd sent. If he would take this one last phone call.

The unsolicited promises had merely been attempts to manipulate him into *contact*. She would promise and promise, never intending to keep her word.

"Shelly just made another promise," he muttered under his breath as he walked to the far edge of the terrace and gazed out at Key West across the short expanse of water.

But this promise was different. There was no if attached. She had merely promised to leave him alone.

Friggin' weird.

It didn't fit the classic profile of an obsessed person. Okay, maybe she was playing a mind game with him. She promised not to bother him, then deliberately flaunted her sexy bod every chance she got. To attract him, luring him ever closer.

It was working. Even now . . . Aw, hell. He needed to go into town and find a woman who could take his mind off Shelly.

He turned and walked down the brick path to where Trevor kept Half Moon Bay's launch. The boat was bobbing in the water, its blue and white striped bimini shading the interior from the afternoon heat. He was untying the mooring line, when he heard Shelly call.

"Matt! Matt! Wait!"

Just what he expected. She had tried to lure him by promising not to bother him, but she'd secretly hoped seeing her in that bikini would make her irresistible. It damn near had.

Okay, Jensen, haul ass. He put one foot in the boat and glanced over his shoulder. Naturally, Shelly couldn't let him leave. She was running toward him through the sea oats growing along the high tide line.

Don't run! he silently called. You just got your cast off.

She hit the soft sand, and her injured leg buckled. Arms out flung, she pitched forward, landing facedown.

"Shelly," he yelled, jumping out of the boat. He raced up the dock and made it to the sand just as she was sitting up. "Are you okay?"

She gazed up at him, her eyes swimming with unshed tears. Aw, hell, she'd hurt herself. Again.

He dropped to his knees beside her and put his hand on her leg.

The skin beneath his fingers was smooth and surprisingly soft. "I don't think you've broken it again."

She wasn't making a sound, but tears were parading down her cheeks. He tried to lift her into his arms, intending to carry her to the terrace, but she pushed him away.

"I'm fine. My leg's a little weak. It gave out, but I'll be all right." She swiped at her tear-dampened cheek with the back of her hand. "Matt, I need you. Something terrible has happened."

Uh-oh. Here it comes. He braced himself for one of her tricks. She gazed at him, her beautiful eyes still luminous with tears. Her lower lip quivered as she tried to speak. One look was enough to break any man's heart. His, for sure.

"The telephone call. It was about Trevor."

CHAPTER
SEVENTEEN

Her words hit him like a sucker punch straight to the gut. "What happened to Trevor? Is he all right?"

"He's fine." Blinking away tears, she whispered, "It's his mother. She died."

Son of a bitch. This was going to be a blow to Trevor. A big time blow. Long ago Trevor had accepted that his family wanted nothing to do with him, but he had always hoped that one day his mother would change her mind.

Shelly rose to her feet, swaying slightly, favoring the leg that had been in the cast. He circled her with one arm, his hand on the small of her back for support, and guided her back to the terrace.

She stopped and gazed up at him, her face just inches from his. "We have to do something."

He gently eased her down onto a chaise. "Let's get some ice for your leg."

"I'm fine, honest. It's Trevor who needs help."

Matt ran his fingers through his hair, wondering how he was going to break the news to his friend. "Don't worry about it. I'll go back to the funeral with him."

Tears welled up in Shelly's eyes again. "It's too late. The funeral was held more than a week ago."

"What?" Matt sank down on the chaise near Shelly's feet, facing her.

"Trevor's mother had been diagnosed with terminal cancer several months ago—yet no one contacted Trevor."

Knowing his mother had chosen not to call would cut out Trevor's heart.

"Some older man phoned. He told me to tell Trevor. He said the family hadn't wanted Trevor at the funeral. That's why he waited until now to let Trevor know about her death." Tears spiked her long lashes, and she shook her head. "How could they be so cruel?"

He'd never understood Trevor's family. He shook his head, unable to offer any explanation.

"He spoke so fondly of his childhood. I know he loved his mother very much." Shelly's voice was low and charged with emotion. "It'll upset him terribly to have missed the opportunity to say good-bye."

"That man on the phone must have been Trevor's old man. He's a real bastard, trust me."

"Why? Trevor is wonderful—the perfect son."

Matt wasn't sure Trevor would want him to discuss this. Since the night Matt had been called to the hospital and met Graham Adams for the first—and last—time, Trevor had never again mentioned his ordeal.

"Trevor's father expected him to go into the Wall Street brokerage firm the family established at the turn of the century. Trevor was on track. Top grades at the best schools. There were other children, but Trevor was the shining star—"

"Until he announced he was gay."

"Right. His father was totally disgusted by the news," he hedged, telling half the story.

Shelly's gaze shifted to one side for a moment, then turned back to him. "There's got to be more to it than that."

Okay, Shelly was as perceptive as she was insightful. She recognized a half-truth when she heard one. She stared wordlessly at him, her blue eyes gently imploring him to tell her everything.

"I met Trevor at Yale and we became best friends. I never suspected he was gay. We were rooming together our junior year when Trevor became . . . different. Moody. Secretive. One day Trevor came to me and told me that he was gay."

"I hope you were supportive," she said as if she had her doubts.

"I was blown away, because we'd been so close and I never suspected. But it didn't change the way I felt about Trevor." He stared out at the horizon, where the cloudless blue sky blended with the sea. "I couldn't love him more if he were my own brother."

"Have you told him that?"

"I don't have to say it. Trevor knows."

"Does he?"

A suffocating sensation tightened his throat. "It's not the kind of thing men talk about."

"That's the problem with guys. They don't express themselves, so they never know what to say when it really counts."

She had a point, and he couldn't deny it. He had no idea how in hell he was going to break the news of his mother's death to Trevor.

"Go on," she prodded. "Tell me the rest."

"What makes you think there's more?" A movement near the corner of his eye caught his attention. "Look at that guy, will you? He's still shooting pictures. He's scaring the kingfisher away from her nest."

"The chicks will die if they're in the sun too long," Shelly said. "They need her to shade them."

Matt stood up and strode to the edge of the terrace, where the dichondra began. He raised his arm and gave the dumb-ass on the Wave Runner the Italian salute. "Here's a picture for you."

The man gunned the engine and shot off across the water, a rooster tail of water streaming out from the rear. Matt returned to the chaise and sat down a little closer this time.

"You were telling me about Trevor."

He began slowly, measuring his words. "Trevor had become involved with a man. He moved in with him, but pretended to be rooming with me to fool his family. For almost a year I rarely saw Trevor except when he came by for his mail."

"How did you feel about it?"

She *would* ask that question. Holding raw emotion in check, he took a breath, then continued. "I hated the bastard. He'd stolen my best friend. But I was busy, so, life went on. In retrospect, I should have known something was wrong."

"What?" she asked when he hesitated.

"I got a call in the middle of the night. Trevor was in the hospital."

Shelly turned her head just slightly, and her eyelashes cast forlorn shadows across her cheek. He wondered if she'd already guessed.

"He'd been beaten up pretty badly."

"His lover did it, didn't he?" she asked, her eyes wide with concern.

"Battering is more common among gays than most people realize."

"Why would Trevor stay in an abusive relationship?"

"He told me that he'd known for years he was gay and tried to deny it. Then he finally met someone he couldn't live without. Trouble was, the guy was jealous and had a hair-trigger temper." Even now Matt could feel his stomach clench the way it had back then. "I should have realized and done something. I'd noticed bruises. Once Trevor had a black eye."

"I hope Trevor pressed charges."

"Trevor's parents arrived at the hospital the next morning. It wasn't exactly the ideal way to find out your son prefers men. His father went ballistic."

"Didn't his mother—"

"She cried the entire time. They had to give her a sedative." Matt lifted his shoulders high, exaggerating a shrug. "Trevor agreed not to press charges and create a scandal. The next week Trevor's father disowned him, and his mother never spoke to him again."

"Just like that?" she asked, and he nodded. "How unbelievably heartless."

"It hit Trevor big-time. He was already down for the count, then his family deserted him."

"The creep got away with it." Her reproachful eyes bored into him.

He held up his hand, flexed his fingers, ignoring his skinned knuckles. "Not exactly. I paid him a little visit—just to teach him what it felt like to be a punching bag."

"Really?" A thoughtful smile curved her lips. "Good for you."

"It made me feel better, but a few punches didn't help Trevor. The ordeal changed him. Outwardly, he's perfect. Inside, he's still hurting."

"He needs to deal with his feelings."

Matt nodded his agreement as they sat there in the shade. A minute passed, then another, the only sound the whir of Jet Skis on the water in the channel between the Keys and the wind rustling the palms. It was a comfortable silence. For the first time, the tension between them was gone.

She reached for his hand, and her soft fingers brushed his bruised, skinned knuckles. "What happened?"

"I looked up Simon Ambrose. Don't worry about him. He's decided that job opportunities will be better in Key Largo. His nursing license has been revoked."

"You didn't," she said in a choked voice.

He laced his fingers through hers and gave her hand a squeeze. "There's nothing as satisfying as walloping someone who really deserves it. Trust me. It's a guy thing."

"Thank you. I—ah—don't know what to say."

He leaned forward, still holding her hand, and brushed his lips against hers. He knew he shouldn't, but after that kiss last night, something inside him kept gnawing away at him, urging him to kiss her again.

Her lips parted and the velvet warmth of her mouth welcomed him. Excitement rippled through his body at the unexpected sweetness of her response. He thrust his tongue forward and found hers waiting.

Christ! This woman had his number. He was so damn confused that he didn't know from minute to minute if he should strangle her or make love to her.

As he kissed her, Matt remembered how she'd looked earlier, emerging from the water like a siren from the sea. Just watching the water purling down her body had made heat rise in dangerous places.

Right now, his gut instinct told him not to put his arms around her, not to crave the lush softness of those breasts, not to run his hands over her silky skin.

He released her hand and pulled her into his arms, deepening the kiss. Her pebble-hard nipples pressed against him, the wet fabric of her suit dampening his shirt.

Who in hell listened to gut instincts anyway?

He kissed her, holding her close, yet giving himself enough room to work one hand between them. As he captured one breast in the palm of his hand, her body went rigid. She pulled her lips away from his.

"Matt!"

"That's the first time since the accident that you've used my name." His mouth was a fraction of an inch from hers. He cradled her breast in his hand, gently squeezing, testing its soft fullness while he caressed her nipple with his thumb. "I like Matt better than Jensen. When you say Jensen, it reminds me of a drill sergeant."

She might have giggled. He wasn't sure about the strange sound. Her lower lip was trembling now, and her eyes were wide with shock.

Or something.

He was too aroused to hold the thought. Instead, he bent down and took the nipple into his mouth. The bikini was slick and wet beneath his tongue, the nipple marble-hard. He suckled her, drawing the nub into his mouth.

Her startled little cry of pleasure made him smile inwardly. This was a numbers game. She had his number. He had hers.

Her nails sank into his shoulders as his tongue roved over the tightly spiraled nipple, urging him on. Not that he needed any encouragement. He was a man, right?

He nudged aside the damp fabric and coaxed her bare breast into his mouth. She made a soft, throaty sound that shot right through him. The iron heat of his sex jammed against his fly. Man, oh, man, what she could do to him without half trying.

She broke away, breathing hard. "Matt, Matt, don't you think we should . . ."

He could think of several things they should do right now. All of them in the horizontal.

She fumbled with her bikini top to cover herself. "Trevor . . . we've got to let him know what happened."

He threw his head back and took a big gulp of air. Who said women were the weaker sex? He had but one thing on his mind, but somehow she'd managed to keep focused.

"You're right," he said, although he dreaded breaking the news.

"I have an idea how to help Trevor get through this."

"Shelly, I know you mean well, but Trevor will want to be alone."

"He needs his friends. He was there for us. We need to be there for him. I'll round up Bubbles, Zeke and Zoe, then I'll find Clive."

"Clive? Not a good idea. Trevor hasn't had a relationship since Yale. Sure, he goes out, but it's just one-night-stands. He wouldn't want Clive involved in anything this personal."

"I believe you're wrong. Clive and Trevor are perfect for each other. Now, here's the plan."

Honest to God, how could he say no to her?

CHAPTER
EIGHTEEN

She hung her damp bikini on the shower door to dry, then changed into a T-shirt and shorts, another of the outfits purchased at Jo Mama's. As fast as her weak leg allowed, she hurried down to the dock and found Bubbles waiting for her.

"Matt told me what happened." Bubbles shook her head. "Poor Trevor."

"Where is Matt?"

"He took a water taxi to see Trevor. He said to meet him at the Sunset Key section of the Key West dock."

"Okay," she said as casually as she could. She felt the good side of her face warming as she thought about Matt. How could she have let him kiss her and . . . everything?

She carefully stepped into Trevor's boat and sat down while Bubbles cast off. The doctor had warned her to take it easy, slowly working her leg back to full strength. She should elevate her leg, but she couldn't take the time now.

"You go for the flowers while I run by Clive's," she told Bubbles.

"Right. Matt told me the plan, but I'm not coming out on the boat with you." Bubbles stared straight ahead, guiding the craft around a fishing trawler returning with its catch. Her red hair fluttered behind her like a banner, and the late afternoon sunlight glinted off the studs and hoops piercing her body. "I can't, like, stand anything that has to do with death."

Personally, she thought everyone at Half Moon Bay owed it to Trevor to be there for him, but she didn't voice her opinion. "Could you see if you can locate Zeke and Zoe? They may want to join us."

"Sure." Bubbles maneuvered the launch into one of Sunset Key's slips at Key West's main dock and secured the mooring lines.

"I'll meet you right here," she called as Bubbles headed off toward Duval Street.

She waved over the first rickie she saw and gave him Clive's Truman Annex address. She had tried to reach him by telephone, but, like most doctors, Clive had an unlisted personal number.

Truman Annex was a posh neighborhood adjacent to the Little White House, where Harry Truman had often stayed when he'd been president. It looked quaint, she thought as the driver pedaled by the white clapboard home.

"John Kennedy vacationed here," the driver yelled over his shoulder.

She couldn't imagine a president and his entourage staying in the small cottage. Before Kennedy had been assassinated, life had been simpler. Now a president needed much more security.

Beyond the Little White House, they entered an elegant neighborhood with white picket fences like petticoats around homes with large verandas and gingerbread dripping from the eaves. A large brass plaque with a star marked the Truman Annex as a National Register Historic District.

Stately trees shaded the homes along the waterfront. Unlike other parts of town, all these homes were either new or immaculately restored. It didn't have the patchwork look typical of the rest of the area, where only some of the homes were restored to prime condition.

"Wait for me," she told the driver when they arrived at Clive's home.

She hurried up to the door, taking care not to put too much weight on the leg that had recently come out of the cast. Ahead, the door to the large home was open. She rang the bell, and a moment later the doctor came down the stairs.

"Shelly, what are you doing here? I was trying to reach you." He swung open the screen door.

"Really? Why?"

"My office called. Some man came in asking questions about you."

Oh, my God. Dexxter. Or had the FBI tracked her down? It was all she could do not to shudder. As calmly as possible, she asked, "What kind of questions?"

Clive grinned and shook his head. "Someone at Groomingdale's told the man about Jiggs. He's a producer looking for an unusual dog for a commercial."

"Really?" She hoped she didn't sound too suspicious. Maybe it was nothing, but an unsettling prickle of alarm raised the hair on the back of her neck. "Jiggs is so shy. I can't imagine him in front of a camera."

"I told the receptionist to have the man leave his card. We never give out patients' names or phone numbers."

She nodded, thankful for his discretion, but still suspicious. "I came by to talk to you about Trevor."

Behind his wire-rim glasses, Clive's dark brown eyes brightened. "What about him?"

"His mother died a week ago, but his family didn't want him at the funeral. His father just called today to let him know."

"Jesus H. Christ. How could they?"

"Good question." She released a pent-up sigh. "We're going out on the boat now and have our own memorial service for his mother. We've got to help Trevor get through this."

"Trevor wants me to come?" Clive sounded surprised.

She hedged. "Yes. He needs you."

She wasn't certain how—or if—anyone could help Trevor, but she had to try.

Matt walked up the stairs to the house Trevor was renovating, taking care to avoid the third stair, where a plank was missing. Shutters were hanging by broken pegs or gone entirely, and the paint was peeling so badly that the building appeared to be molting. Still, he could see this house was the most stately home on Angela Street and had to be among the finest historic mansions on Key West.

He stood at the open front door, listening to the sound of hammering coming from somewhere inside the house and thinking about what Shelly had said. She was right—damn her sweet hide—men didn't express themselves enough. How in hell was he going to break the news to Trevor?

Unexpectedly, Trevor bounded down the stairs, a workman at his heels. He spotted Matt and greeted him with a wide grin.

"Hey, Matt. Let me give you the tour." Trevor turned to the man behind him. "Finish up the back porch, then I'll come show you what to do next."

White paint smudged Trevor's nose; his cutoff jeans were splattered with at least three colors of paint. For Trevor, this was unusual. He'd always looked as if he'd just stepped off the pages of *GQ*.

Right now, messy paint or not, Trevor was in his element, doing something he clearly loved. He was as happy as Matt could remember seeing him. Man, oh, man, he did not want to devastate Trevor.

"This is the best house I've ever had—and the biggest challenge." Trevor smiled again, his green eyes reflecting an excitement that was almost contagious.

Almost.

Matt was tempted to put off the news. What could one more day hurt? But he couldn't stall. Shelly would have everything ready and be waiting at the boat.

"There are more homes on the registry of historic homes here than anywhere else in the country," Trevor informed him with unmistakable pride. "I've renovated more of them than anyone else on Key West. This one is special. It's even more interesting than Calvin Klein's—"

Trevor halted mid-sentence, gazing at Matt, concern replacing his elation. "What's wrong? Is it Shelly?"

Matt sucked in a stabilizing breath. Shelly. What a head trip. He couldn't afford to think about her now.

"No. Shelly's fine. She's waiting for us down on the dock." He looked around, not sure where to have this conversation without risking being interrupted by workmen. "Let's go outside."

Trevor led him through a set of side doors that opened onto the side of the veranda. They leaned against a railing that had already been stripped and prepped for a fresh coat of paint.

"This afternoon someone called Half Moon Bay," Matt began, breaking the news as gently as he could. "They—ah, he, wanted to let you know that—" Suddenly, his throat locked up.

Worry marred the handsome planes of Trevor's face. "Know what?"

Bracing himself, Matt answered, "Trevor, it's about your, ah . . . your mother . . . she has passed away."

The words detonated on impact, leaching the blood from Trevor's face. He gripped the railing and gazed, unseeing, across what had once been a beautiful private garden but now was nothing more than a snare of weeds and vines growing unchecked in the tropics.

"It must have been a heart attack or a stroke. Mother was never sick a day in her life."

Matt studied his friend's bent head, then noted the way Trevor's hands clasped the railing as if he couldn't stand without support. No one ever promised life would be easy, Matt reminded himself. If your best friend couldn't tell you the whole truth, who could?

"Six months ago your mother was diagnosed with cancer. She died surrounded by her family." Matt gazed into Trevor's tear-sheened eyes and almost couldn't go on. He hesitated, then forced himself to deliver the final blow. "The funeral was last week."

For a moment Matt thought Trevor hadn't heard him, but then Trevor turned slowly, his back now to the railing. He slid down slowly, collapsing to the floor, his shoulders against the spindles. Matt had never seen a look like this on his friend's face, not even when Trevor had been in the hospital, physically and emotionally shattered by a beating.

Say something! Do something!

There were a thousand things he should say, creating a logjam in his mind. Coming over he'd rehearsed this a dozen times, but now he couldn't remember what he'd decided to tell Trevor. Instead, he sat on the floor beside Trevor and put his arm around his friend.

They stayed on the veranda, listening to the workmen hammering inside the house for almost ten minutes. Finally Trevor broke the silence.

"I should have known better than to expect Mother to forgive me."

Forgive! Matt bit back a curse. What was there to forgive? But Trevor's voice was so choked with emotion that he didn't want to interrupt.

"It's been years since she spoke to me. Do you know what the last thing she said to me was?"

Matt hoped Trevor was going to answer his own question, but he didn't. "It must have been at the hospital."

"Yes. I had a cut over my eye, remember. She said she hoped it wouldn't leave a scar."

Beneath Matt's arm, Trevor stiffened as if someone had struck him. Matt gave him a one-armed hug. How sad, Matt thought, recalling his own mother's death so vividly that it brought an ache of sadness too deep for tears. She'd lost her ability to speak, but her expressive eyes conveyed her deep love. A mother's love.

"There they are."

Ahead, Shelly was waiting in the boat with Clive as Matt and

Trevor made their way through the throng of tourists migrating to Mallory Dock for the sunset festivities. It had taken a little convincing before Trevor agreed to the memorial service.

What was he doing? Matt asked himself. Did he want to go out on the water and talk about death? No way.

But he was trapped.

He couldn't leave Trevor. So he stepped onto the boat, ducking beneath the navy and white striped bimini, shading the craft. While Clive spoke to Trevor, Matt whispered to Shelly, "This was your idea. You're in charge."

"No problem, Jensen." She pointed to the lavender roses standing upright in the ice chest. "We have the flowers. We're all set. Your job is to drive the boat out to a picturesque spot."

Jensen. So she was back to calling him Jensen. Just wait, he thought. Now was not the time to pull her into his arms and kiss her until she cried "Matt" in that breathy voice he found unbelievably erotic.

Matt motored the launch up the channel, dodging a bevy of wind surfers and a Jet Skier who insisted on crossing in front of them. The others were silent. He figured no one knew what to say. He sure hoped Shelly could pull this off.

He cut the engine and drifted into Fleming Key's shallow waters. The property belonged to the navy. SEALs usually trained there, but today the ellipse of crystal-white sand flanked by mangroves was deserted. He removed the "lunch hook" from its locker, then tossed the lightweight anchor into water so clear that he could see a crab burrowing into the sand.

To the west the sun was setting over the Gulf of Mexico, glazing the water with golden light. Herons and egrets were stalking dinner in the mangroves, while a mangrove cuckoo sang his heart out.

"It's perfect," Shelly told him as she lifted the roses out of the chest.

She handed each of them several lavender roses. He didn't know what in hell to do with them or what to say to Trevor that could possibly make up for the way his family had treated him.

"We're here to help Trevor say good-bye to his mother," Shelly began, her voice gentle and compassionate. "It's hard to realize someone who has been a very important part of your life since you can remember is no longer going to be around. When death comes slowly, it isn't easy, but when the news hits us suddenly, it's like a physical blow."

Trevor nodded, his expression somber. Clive muttered, "True. So true."

"I know how it feels," she said, her steady gaze on Trevor. "I lost my mother too. One moment she was here, the way I assumed she would always be"—tears misted her eyes and her voice dropped with each word—"suddenly, she was gone."

Matt recalled Shelly had lost her whole family in the ValuJet crash. Evidently, she had been closer to her mother than the other members of her family. They all were closer to their mothers, he decided. Mothers were special, no question about it.

"Oh, Shelly, that's terrible." Trevor's voice broke into a husky rasp. "I knew your family had been killed in the crash, but I never realized—"

"What an ordeal," Clive added.

"Please, don't feel sorry for me." Shelly managed a smile, but her lower lip trembled. "I just shared my experience with you so that you would know that I'm not winging this. I know how much you hurt. I could tell you that time will make it better, but it's not true. Time gives you the ability to cope, but the pain never goes away. You just learn to live with it."

The heartfelt emotion in her voice ripped him apart. Her tone conveyed the extent of her suffering and her deep mourning for the family she obviously loved and still missed. He'd thought of her as being not quite human, but the opposite was true.

She felt more than he'd ever suspected. And loved with astonishing intensity.

Matt saw her in a new light. This sensitive woman was capable of a depth of emotion that he could only imagine.

"On some level we can all share your grief because we've all lost a loved one," she continued, sympathy still lingering in her voice. "Didn't your mother die when you were young, Matt?"

She would ask.

He resisted the urge to shout: *Don't go there!* Everyone's eyes were on him, expecting a response. "My mother died shortly after my thirteenth birthday."

They waited for him to elaborate, but he left it at that.

Clive bailed him out. "It was a long time ago. Matt probably doesn't remember much."

"He has never dealt with it," Shelly interrupted. "If Matt had, he could talk about his mother's death."

Honest to God, he was going to put both hands around her sexy neck and strangle her. Then he reminded himself that Shelly couldn't possibly know about his problem. Discussing his mother would bring to the surface things he would much rather forget.

"Clive, what about your mother?" Trevor asked, taking him off the hook.

"My mother is still alive. I call her first thing every Sunday before she goes to church."

"You're lucky," Trevor said with uncharacteristic bitterness. "My mother turned her back on me. Even when she knew she was dying, she didn't send for me."

"She'd already given you what counted," Shelly said. "Character determines fate. That's what my mother always said. Character is developed at an early age, and it's strongly influenced by your mother."

"You're right," Clive responded. "My mother always encouraged me. She always told me I could do anything, and I believed her."

Shelly stared at him and arched one eyebrow. Matt knew she wanted him to say something. "Trevor, I know you're upset because your mother sided with your father, but Shelly is right. You're the best person I know. Let's give your mother some credit for that."

"Mother wanted me to be perfect," Trevor said in a broken whisper. "She couldn't accept it when I wasn't."

"It's time to let it go . . . let her go," Shelly said. "Your mother is buried in a grave miles from here, but I truly believe death releases your spirit. That's how we get to heaven. Your mother, my mom, as well as Matt's mother, have entered the spirit world.

"They are with us now in a way that they never were during their lives. They are part of nature now. Smell the roses." Shelly waited while they all sniffed the roses she'd given them. "The beauty of the rose and its unique scent embodies the spirits of our mothers. They are with us always now.

"Their spirits are part of the roses." She gestured with her good hand at the sun, half hidden by the sea—one of the postcard sunsets that had made Key West famous. "They're part of every magnificent sunset, and they're with us each morning as the sun rises.

"Our mothers haven't left us. They are with us every step of the way. They are a part of all the things we love, from a drop of dew on a blade of grass to the blue sky overhead. If we realize this, then we haven't lost our mothers. Instead, we are much closer to them than we ever were."

Clive nodded thoughtfully while Trevor's faint smile held a touch of sadness. Matt had to admit Shelly's words had moved him. It was comforting to think of his mother being a part of nature. Before, she'd been lost to him.

Memories fade, he reflected. He could barely recall the details of his mother's face, but the power of her love remained as strong as ever. He thanked God that he'd gotten the chance to sit with his mother when she was dying. Over and over he'd told her how much he loved her.

And how much he was going to miss her.

CHAPTER
NINETEEN

They all tossed the lavender roses into the sea just as the sun, a molten red, slipped into the sea, leaving the water glazed with golden light.

"To Trevor's mother," Clive said, taking up where she'd left off. "May she rest in peace."

"We thank her for giving us Trevor," Matt added. "A wonderful person and a true friend."

There might have been a hint of moisture in Matt's eyes—or maybe it was just her imagination. Clive was teary-eyed, and Trevor made no attempt to hide his tears of grief.

Tears dribbled down her cheeks and sluiced off her chin. "Good-bye, Mother," she whispered under her breath, realizing this service had brought her own feelings about death to the surface. "Character does determine fate. I'm going to get Dexxter just as soon as I can."

She held up her right hand. The fingers were still curved inward, and trying to straighten them only caused her to wince with pain. She couldn't scream and she couldn't use her right hand. Great. She had better come up with a doozy of a plan for getting Dexxter Foxx.

"Hey, Shelly." Matt put his arm around her and pulled her close. "Don't cry."

She wiped her face with the back of her hand and mustered a smile. "It went all right, didn't it?"

He gave her a quick hug and kissed her forehead. "You were great. Let's give them a chance to be alone."

Trevor and Clive sat at the back of the small boat, talking quietly. She sat on the bench behind the wheel, while Matt hoisted the anchor. The boat glided out of the shallow water and into the channel. A crescent moon rode high in a velvet black sky, and crystal-bright shards of stars glinted down at them.

How romantic, she thought with an inward sigh. Matt put his arm around her, a casual gesture, but to her it seemed intimate, seductive. Watch out, she warned herself.

Given the way he'd kissed her and caressed her breasts, Matt would be making love to her if she weren't very careful. Then he would discover she wasn't Rochelle Ralston. For a moment she toyed with the idea of confessing the truth.

An image flashed across her mind: The thunderous roar and the blast that knocked her to her knees. Dexxter hadn't hesitated to have a federal marshal killed. If she involved Matt and Trevor, no telling what might happen to them.

"You're awfully quiet," he said. "What are you thinking about?"

She said the first thing that popped into her mind. "Chocolate."

He smiled that adorable smile, telling her he was up to something. "Right. Chocolate body paint. I brush it on you, then lick it off, right?"

The powerful image of his mouth on her bare skin evoked the memory of the way he'd kissed her earlier that day. Suddenly, her knees seemed weak and she was glad to be sitting. Think like a bad girl, she told herself. "Yeah, right, Jensen. The last thing I need is body paint."

"Don't knock it until you've tried it."

"Don't forget I'm a psychopath," she reminded him.

"Yeah, right." He pulled her closer until the back of her head was resting against his sturdy shoulder. She was thankful for the noise of the engine. It kept Matt from hearing the rapid thud of her heart.

They were approaching the Key West dock where Sunset Key homeowners had moorings adjacent to the water shuttle that went out to the private island every hour. A throng of people jammed the dock. She assumed someone on the island must be having a party, and everyone was waiting to be ferried across the channel.

Key West was famous for its offbeat characters, and it seemed that every one of them had assembled on the dock. Now they were waving at them.

"What in hell is going on?" Matt wanted to know.

"I think they're singing," Clive said from the back of the boat. Matt turned off the motor, and she spotted Bubbles as well as

Zeke and Zoe among the group. A song swelled out from the crowd with a lilting note.

"I once was looost . . . but now I'm found."

"It's all of your friends," Matt said to Trevor. "They're singing 'Amazing Grace' for you."

Bubbles must have gathered them, she decided, instantly forgiving Bubbles for not coming with them.

" 'A-maz-ing Grace . . . how sweet the sound / That saved a wretch like meee / I once was looost . . . but now I'm found.' "

The song brought tears to her eyes, and she gazed at the group through blurry eyes. "There's no sweeter sound than a chorus of friends' voices."

"You're right," Trevor said, his voice choked with emotion. "I once was lost, but I found friends on Key West. I found myself actually."

That's what she intended to do, she thought. Just as soon as she took care of Dexxter, she was going to start a new life right here in paradise.

Matt turned on the motor and pulled the boat into the slip, then cut the engine. The group had finished the song, and everyone rushed up, offering Trevor condolences.

"We're throwing a wake at Pepe's," Bubbles informed them the minute they stepped onto the dock. "We've taken the whole place."

"Thanks for doing this," she said to Bubbles.

"It was the least I could do for Trevor," Bubbles said, her eyes on Matt. "If it weren't for him, I'd be in a flophouse in Bahama Village, turning tricks."

"That's Trevor, all right." Matt's tone echoed respect that bordered on reverence. "It's good for him to see that people appreciate him."

People were hugging Trevor. Many of them had tears in their eyes or were crying. It occurred to her that she didn't know this many people. She had never allowed herself to make friends.

"Friends are the family we choose for ourselves," Matt said. "Trevor's family deserted him, but there are plenty of people who care about him."

"Pepe is making margaritas and his special conch chowder," Bubbles told Matt.

It was clear that Bubbles intended to monopolize Matt, which was fine. She hung back as the group moved off the dock, heading toward the restaurant. Her leg was aching; she should take the next water shuttle back to Half Moon Bay and elevate her leg. Turning her back to the group, she leaned against a piling and waited for the shuttle.

"Hey, where do you think you're going?"

Matt had come back down the dock to find her. The pit of her stomach tingled, and she had to admit she found his attention flattering.

"My leg is bothering me. I'm going back to the house."

"Good idea. I'm coming with you. Just let me tell Trevor."

She would be all alone at romantic Half Moon Bay with Matt. I don't *think* so. Bad idea. "You go to the wake. I'll be all right. I'm tired. I'll probably go right to sleep."

"Well . . . if you're sure."

She dropped her lashes quickly to hide the hurt. A tiny part of her had hoped he'd insist on coming with her. "I'm positive. Go to the wake, and explain to Trevor why I'm not there."

He leaned down and kissed her, a swift brush of his closed lips against hers. It was a chaste kiss with no trace of the passion she'd seen that afternoon on the terrace. He turned and was up the dock in a few powerful strides.

She sensed that something had changed between them. His attitude toward her seemed different. She wasn't sure what this meant, but it worried her.

The shuttle motored up to the dock, and a few passengers disembarked. She was the only one to return to Sunset Key. The shuttle took her to the far end of the island, where there were guest cottages clustered around a pool. Rather than walk the distance—she was limping badly now—she took Trevor's golf cart to the opposite end of the island.

There had been a few lights at the cottages, but the stately homes around Half Moon Bay were dark. The only light came from the artful lanterns along the paths and from the sliver of a moon overhead. The faint sound of music usually drifted over the channel from Key West. But tonight the wind was blowing the other way. It was eerily quiet as she parked the golf cart and went into the pitch-black house.

"Why are you so jumpy?" she said out loud as she threw on the lights.

From behind the potted palms, from down the hall, from the open terrace door, cats padded up to her. Bingo greeted her with a gruff, "Meow." Others rubbed her legs or circled her. Jiggs stood off to one side, his henna fur glowing in the light.

"I'll bet you guys are hungry, right?"

Ignoring the ache in her leg, she made her way to the pantry, taking care not to trip over one of the cats. They hadn't been fed since morning, and with the wake, it wasn't likely anyone would return until after midnight.

She found their food in the pantry, noting the catnip was now on the top shelf in a glass jar with a lid. Feeding Bingo first seemed like the best idea. The orange terror would certainly take the others' food.

Once she had all eight bowls filled and the cats eating, she opened a can of dog food for Jiggs. The henna rinse had improved his appearance, she decided, but the fur on his sawed-off ear stood up like a doggy cowlick. He was hardly television material.

While Jiggs picked at his food, she called the clinic and got the producer's number. She doubted he would be in, but she wanted to satisfy her curiosity. Suspicion still niggled at her.

"Alley Cats Guest House," a female voice answered at the number the producer had given.

"I'm trying to reach John Rodgers," she told the woman.

"He checked out, but I think he'll be back next week. Isn't it a hoot? A producer staying at Alley Cats while he's looking for a dog to star in a commercial."

It was a hoot all right, she thought as she hung up. Bingo had finished his meal and was now devouring Jiggs's dog food. Maybe John Rodgers really was a producer, but it still bothered her.

Jiggs was her only link to the past, the only way Dexxter could trace her.

Suddenly, Jiggs's good ear went up and he cocked his head toward the door. They had all left Half Moon Bay in such a hurry that she must have forgotten to close the door. Considering Bingo's lust for blood, she thought she'd shut the door to keep him from dragging in a bird or something.

From the deep shadows, a shuffling sound alerted her. She dove for the lights. Darkness engulfed the kitchen. There was enough moonlight for her to make out the silhouette of a man coming across the terrace toward the open door.

She ducked into the pantry and closed the door. With luck the man would go into another part of the house and she could slip out. Where would she go then? What would she do?

The only people on the island were way across the key at the cottages. Getting that far on her bad leg would be miserable, but it seemed to be her only choice.

She heard the man walk into the kitchen. A strange *clack-clack* noise followed. Oh, no! Jiggs was scratching on the outside of the pantry door. The kitchen lights went on, seeping under the pantry door.

"Hey, dude, don't even *think* about getting into the catnip."

Matt's voice. Relief nearly knocked her to her knees. She swung open the door and found Matt standing near the center island, cuddling Jiggs.

"Shelly, what are you doing in there with all the lights off?"

"I heard someone coming. I didn't know it was you."

"This is Sunset Key, for christsake. No one bothers to lock their doors around here. What were you afraid of?"

"No one's around. I thought maybe Simon was sneaking around . . . or something." It was a lame excuse, but she couldn't think of a better explanation.

Matt put Jiggs down on the floor. "I told you not to worry about him. After our little chat, Simon left for Key Largo."

"I guess I'm just jumpy. Living so long in Manhattan makes you worry if you don't have a dozen locks on every door," she said, and the corner of his mouth hitched up a notch, then eased into an engaging smile. Uh-oh. "What are you doing here?"

"I brought you some of Pepe's conch chowder." He gestured toward the counter, where Bingo was circling a container, sniffing. "Why aren't you in bed with your leg up?"

"I had to feed the cats."

"Let me see your leg." He sank down on his haunches and examined her leg, running strong, cool fingers up her calf. "It looks swollen. Does it hurt?"

"Just a little."

He rose, his expression serious. "Let's get you to bed, then I'll bring you the chowder."

Before she could protest, he swept her into his arms. "You've got to take it easy for a few weeks."

"How did you get here?" she asked as he carried her across the deserted house.

"I have Trevor's launch. He won't be needing it. He's spending the night at Clive's."

Just what she suspected. They were alone.

He shouldered open the door to her room, then flicked on the light with his elbow. He gently placed her on the bed. "Get into your nightgown. I'll round up some pillows to elevate that leg."

"I'll be all right, honest. You don't have to fuss over me."

He leaned close. "Fussing over beautiful women is my specialty."

Great, she thought as he left the room. What was she going to do about him? She changed into the faded Sunset Key T-shirt Trevor had given her. It hung to her knees, and normally she slept only in it, but tonight she kept on her panties.

She propped the pillows up against the headboard and had just settled back, when Matt came in with more pillows. He gently lifted her sore leg by the heel and arranged pillows under it.

Thunk!

"What was that?" she asked.

"Conch chowder all over the kitchen floor." Both hands on his hips, Matt blew out his breath. It ruffled the hank of hair across his forehead. "I'm going to skin Bingo alive."

He left the room in a huff. No doubt it would take him a while to clean up the mess. Could she help it if she fell asleep?

Before she could close her eyes, he was back, a wicked smile on his face. She'd managed to pull the sheet over her body. Just her leg stuck out, propped up by the pillows.

"I'm leaving the cleanup to eight cats and one little dog. Most of the chowder was gone before I hit the kitchen. I'll mop the floor later. Do you want me to make you something else?"

"No, thanks. I'm not hungry."

He sat on the edge of the bed. She was pretty sure he wasn't thinking about food.

"What is conch anyway?" she asked, a little frightened by the dark desire she detected in his eyes. "I know it's pronounced *conk* but that's all."

He ran one finger along her bare leg, a light, teasing touch, while his heavy-lidded eyes remained locked on hers. "It's a huge sea snail. It crawls along the ocean floor like this."

His hand disappeared under the sheet just above her knee. Her heart fluttered to her throat but she grabbed his wrist. "Jensen, do you ever give up?"

"Sure. When I get what I want."

His sensual smile sent a heated rush of longing through her body.

He leaned forward, hands braced against the headboard on either side of her shoulders. As he lowered his head, she knew he was going to kiss her, but she was powerless to move.

His lips brushed against hers as he spoke with a pronounced drawl. "You know, darlin', if I didn't know better, I'd think you were afraid of me."

He couldn't possibly suspect how close to the truth he was. She forced a sassy smile. "Right, Jensen. I'm terrified."

His hands still braced against the headboard, he leaned down and kissed the pulsing hollow at the base of her throat. The touch of his lips on her sensitive skin sent shivers of desire coursing through her veins. He continued to explore with soft, moist kisses, searing a path around her neck and finding an even more sensitive spot behind her ear.

Her own passionate response to his kisses shocked her. If she didn't do something fast, she might as well confess she wasn't Shelly.

"Jensen, have you forgotten I'm a psychopath?"

Raising his head, he gazed into her eyes. "No, you're not. You're a little mixed up. That's all. Having your whole family die so suddenly probably accounts for the way you behaved."

The heartrending tenderness in his smoldering blue eyes startled her. Oh, my God. She had unwittingly given him a way to excuse Shelly's actions.

He stretched out beside her with a slow, sexy smile. His touch was light, teasing, as he brushed her lower lip with the pad of his thumb.

"Jensen, knock it off. I'm dangerous . . . honest."

"So am I."

His words were smothered against her lips as he kissed her, more hungrily this time. Parting her lips, she allowed herself to meet his kiss. She knew better, truly she did, but she couldn't help herself.

The forceful domination of his lips and the invasion of his thrusting tongue sent a shock wave of savage desire to every pore. A delicious shudder raked her when the hard length of his body pressed against hers. She had a fully aroused male on her hands.

She tried to whimper a protest, but he was kissing her so deeply that it was impossible. His tongue stroked hers in a parody of another more intimate sexual act. Tremors of passion cascaded through her, and she clamped her legs together against a shameless rush of heat between her thighs.

Before she realized what she was doing, her arms were around him, her fingers clutching his powerful shoulders. Somehow his hands had gotten under the T-shirt and were on her bare breasts. Slightly rough hands against smooth skin enflamed her even more.

He molded one breast with his hand, capturing its nipple and brushing it with his thumb. A low moan rumbled from his throat, and she experienced a surge of feminine power. While arousing her, he was also arousing himself.

He broke the kiss, but didn't stop caressing her breast. "You're dangerous all right. It's dangerous how much I want you."

She wanted to tell him that she felt the same, but she didn't dare.

"Don't deny you want me." His voice had a hard, ragged quality.

His hand left her breast and nudged her thighs apart. She tried to grab his arm. Too late. His hand was inside her panties. Touching her.

The instant his fingertip brushed her, pleasure thick and dark swept her into an erotic world where nothing existed except the sweet sensation of rising passion. It was torture, exquisite torture. She couldn't even muster a smart remark to wipe the conqueror's smile off Matt's face.

Panting slightly, she sank her nails into his shoulders as she arched her back and shamelessly pressed herself against his palm. He eased one strong finger inside her as he continued to stroke the taut bud.

A second later she heard herself cry out. Her entire body shuddered with pleasure in one devastating surge of ecstasy that left her limp and trembling. She closed her eyes.

After a few minutes her breathing became more normal, and she opened her eyes. Matt was stretched out beside her, watching her with a heavy-lidded gaze.

"Am I good, or what?" He flashed her a wicked smile. "Just wait for the main event."

He took her hand and clamped it around his penis. Through the thin material of his shorts and underwear she felt the hot, iron heat of his sex. Her foolish body wanted him . . . inside her.

But how could she possibly explain being a virgin?

"Do you have any life jackets in your nightstand?" he asked.

"Life jackets?"

"Condoms."

She shook her head. How stupid could she be?

With a groan, he sat up. "I'll get some."

Suddenly, she had a brilliant idea. If they made love in the surf, he might not notice that she was a virgin. "Why don't we go down to the beach," she called as he headed toward the door. "Let's make love on the beach, the way we did in Bermuda."

He stopped, his back to her, his hand on the doorknob. He stood there a moment, then slowly turned. "Forget it. This is a big mistake."

Before she could respond, he closed the door and turned out the lights. Overhead, the ceiling fan continued to purr in the darkness, stirring the musky, masculine smell he'd left on the sheets. What had gone wrong, she wondered.

CHAPTER
TWENTY

Dexxter finished cleaning out his desk, expecting Irene to burst through his office door any second. Some wise-ass reporter had gotten wind of the Foxx Enterprises sale and blared it across the morning paper's business section. Robbed of the element of surprise, the noon press conference he'd so carefully orchestrated would be anticlimactic.

"What a pissoff!" He'd counted on watching the stunned look on Irene's face when he made the announcement.

Get over it, he told himself. He was stinking rich now, thanks to a bunch of Asians who were too stupid to realize they'd purchased nothing more than a software shell game. He needed to start over. Maybe this time he'd go into something legit like, like . . . well, he'd think of something. He always did.

He heard his office door open and the *click-click* of high heels on the marble floor. Without looking up, he knew it was Irene.

"Look what a courier just brought from Key West."

Irene breezed up to his desk, all smiles. Obviously, Irene didn't ferret through the business section the way he did. He was going to blow her away after all.

"Zane managed to get photographs of that woman." Irene laid a stack of color photographs on his desk.

The top one was a picture of a blonde standing at the edge of the surf, daintily testing the water with her toe. Triangles of orange fabric, each no bigger than an eyepatch, barely concealed centerfold breasts. Showgirl legs dovetailed into slim hips and a narrow waist.

Her head was bent slightly, so it was impossible to decide if this woman was Amy Conroy. He doubted it. The conservative, shapeless clothing Amy had worn couldn't hide her killer tits. He prided himself on his powers of observation where women were concerned. He would have known if her waist had been so narrow, her legs so long and nicely shaped.

The next picture was a close-up taken just as the woman's head had emerged from the water. The blue eyes might have been Amy's, but the nose and shape of her face was all wrong.

"You're wasting my time."

"Keep looking."

By the time he was halfway through the photos, he was willing to show this babe the full monty—anytime. Too bad she was miles away, down in some bumfuck key.

"Remember, darling, she was in a terrible car crash, which required extensive cosmetic surgery."

Darling? Since when had she started talking to him like that? He couldn't wait for the press conference. He'd have the last laugh.

"Zane looked into the crash. A truck loaded with diesel fuel struck a car. Three victims were thrown from the vehicles. Two died, burned beyond recognition. A dead woman remains unidentified. According to the police report, she had been a passenger in the truck, but Zane suspects the two women were in the car together."

"Are you saying Amy assumed that woman's identity? I don't believe it. People have friends, relatives. Someone would know her well enough to realize Amy was an impostor."

He kept leafing through the photos, even though he'd already studied each one and was convinced this knockout was not Amy. He half listened to Irene giving him a rundown on the Ralston woman's family.

"The only person who knew her well enough to ID her was Matthew Jensen. He'd taken her out one time, then she began to stalk him."

"She's a stalker? A mental basket-case? Unfuckingbelievable."

She could stalk him anytime, he thought, studying the picture of her emerging from the surf, droplets of water beading her breathtaking body. Something about her was vaguely familiar, but he couldn't put his finger on just what it was. He'd screwed dozens of bombshell blondes, courtesy of Technical Assistants. Maybe she reminded him of one of the techs.

Suddenly, it clicked.

"Fucking A," he cried. "It is Amy." The way she tilted her head just slightly to one side clicked. Amy had often done that—to keep the gross side of her face from being seen.

He stared hard at the photo. This was the woman Amy Conroy had been meant to be. Heat shot through him with a jolting upward surge in his groin as he thought about the plans he had for her.

"Of course it is . . . darling. She has the dog, doesn't she? How else would that ugly little mutt get from Sacramento to Key West?"

Irene had called him darling again, but he ignored it. Whatever the bitch was up to wouldn't work. He was through with her, but his plans for Amy were just beginning.

"Take a look at these." Irene handed him a few grainy snapshots taken at a distance with a telephoto lens.

The photos were of Amy reclining on a chaise, letting some man kiss her. Another shot showed the man kissing her breasts. It didn't take a fucking rocket scientist to know what these two were going to do next.

A wave of red, like a swift-rising tide, swept away every rational thought. Amy Conroy belonged to him, not to some jerkoff who liked to strut around half naked so women could admire his pecs.

If Dexx had given Amy the attention she had craved, when she'd been working for him, he could be enjoying her himself. Now he was going to have to kill her.

Twice as many reporters than Dexxter had expected had gathered for the press conference. No doubt he could thank the article in the paper for the increased attendance. Off to one side stood the company's executives. Like Irene, none of them had a clue what was happening. They were chattering excitedly among themselves, probably anticipating the announcement of a new software program.

Irene looked over at him and gave him a discreet thumbs-up. It was all he could do not to hoot with laughter. Just wait, bitch.

After Irene had left his office, Dexxter had sat in his chair, facing Seattle's skyline. But in his mind's eye he kept seeing the new Amy, flat on her back, legs spread. The man in the picture was humping her, jack-hammering into her gorgeous body so savagely that Dexxter could actually feel each thrust in his own groin.

The vision had been so powerful, so all-consuming that Dexxter had unzipped his zipper and shoved his hand into his pants. "Just wait, Amy. Just wait."

Now, looking across the podium at the group assembled to hear his announcement, Dexxter experienced another, very different arousal. This one wasn't sexual, but it was just as powerful. The future of his employees hung in the balance.

The dumb shits didn't know it. He was on the verge of changing their lives forever. The Asians were moving the Foxx operation to Singapore. In exactly two minutes they would be unemployed.

Irene would be wiped out of his life.

He tapped on the microphone to get their attention, then delivered the announcement in a casual, offhand tone that didn't reveal the hours he'd spent in front of the mirror carefully rehearsing every word. Out of the corner of his eye he watched Irene, gauging her reaction.

At first her eyes widened, then she smiled with forced enthusiasm. Around her the other executives attempted to smile, but it was clear they were astonished. Irene kept staring at him, grinning, as he completed the announcement.

He fielded reporters' questions, inwardly pissed that Irene hadn't been more upset. What did he expect? She had too much pride to fall apart in front of the others. Everyone in the company knew she had advanced him the start-up money for the business.

"Who needs Seattle?" he said out loud when he returned to his office. "Key West is sunshine, sugar-white sand, and . . ." His cock tightened as he thought about Amy. "Sweet, sweet Amy."

"Well, darling. You took everyone by surprise, didn't you?"

While he'd been fantasizing, Irene had come up behind him. Her hands clutched his shoulders and her silicone boobs rammed against his back. He expelled a long breath, silently asking himself what Irene was up to now.

"It's over, Irene. Foxx Enterprises is no more."

Irene spun him around to face her before he realized what she was doing. The bitch must be working out with weights. Her dark eyes glittered with almost feral intensity. If he didn't know how much she loved him, he would be afraid of her.

"Do you know where we went wrong with Foxx Enterprises?" She didn't wait for an answer. "We had a building, employees. We were too visible. But if we'd set up in Asia to manufacture phony chips and pirated software, the government would have played hell finding us."

He nodded slowly, trying to appear thoughtful. Irene was not the brightest bulb in the chandelier. Obviously, she still thought of herself as his partner. He opened his mouth to tell her that she was history.

Then he stopped cold when he noticed her cunning smile.

Irene knew all his dirty secrets. She'd loved him for so long, he doubted she would turn on him, particularly since she would only implicate herself. But now he wasn't so sure.

Why take chances?

"That's what we need, darling. A money machine without the hassles that come with buildings and ungrateful employees like Amy Conroy."

He smiled, Amy's name giving him a brilliant idea. Why hadn't he thought of it sooner? It would give him as much pleasure to kill Irene as it would Amy—maybe more.

Don't tip your hand now, cautioned an inner voice. String Irene along, wait for the right time, then kill her. Now that he thought about it, he'd never be rid of Irene unless she was dead.

She slid her fingers under the lapels of his suit. "So, Dexx, do you want to hear my plan? It'll make the millions Foxx Enterprises produced look like chicken feed."

Any second she was going to kiss him, he thought, his stomach churning in disgust. But only a fool would refuse to hear Irene's idea. She wasn't much to look at, and she wasn't intelligent like Amy, yet Irene was incredibly devious and clever.

He slid his arms around her waist to encourage her. "This sounds interesting. Tell me more."

"What's the fastest-growing, highest-profit business in America? Gambling."

"Gambling?" He would have pushed her away, but her arms were now locked around his neck. "Casinos are a whole lot more visible than Foxx Enterprises."

"I'm talking about online gambling. It's simple really. Set up a Web site, then we're in business."

"It can't be that easy."

They were so close now that their breath mingled as they spoke. The feral glint had vanished from her eyes. Now her pupils were enlarged. He knew exactly what she had on her mind.

"I know just how to set up an online gambling operation. All we really need besides a Web site is an offshore bank to handle the money. That way government regulators can't touch us."

"They can't?"

He just managed to get out the words, when she angled her mouth across his and kissed him.

He pulled back, then asked, "You can operate the Web site from anywhere, right?"

"Sure. You can bask in the sun on a sandy beach in Key West while your Web site rakes in the dough."

What was she, a mind reader? "Key West?"

"I already have a place down there leased for six months."

Jesus H. Christ. She was light years ahead of him. In a way, though, it was better. He didn't have to do any work.

"I think we should both go down there, make certain that woman is Amy, then get rid of her. There's so much water in the Keys. A boating accident or a drowning. We'll think of something."

It wasn't exactly the plan he had for Amy, but an accident would be perfect for Irene. Too many murders in a small place like Key West would only attract attention. And Amy's murder was going to be . . . well, he hadn't made up his mind exactly how he wanted to kill her yet. But he knew exactly what he was going to do before he snuffed her.

"Admit it, Dexx, you need me."

One arm still around his neck, she unzipped his trousers with her free hand. Skillful fingers homed in on his cock. In an instant she had him as hot and hard as any of the technical assistants.

He hated her for it.

As she stroked him, a plan crystallized in his mind. Take advantage of the situation; don't give her any reason to be suspicious.

He grabbed her hand. "You're right. I do need you, and in more ways than one. Let's get married on Key West."

Her eyes smoldered like coals on the devil's hearth. "Really?"

"Yes, Irene." Christ. She was pathetically happy. "Since we've been kids, we've both known that we belonged together, true?"

"Yes, but sometimes I thought you wanted to get rid of me."

"Why would I want to get rid of you? You're smart and sexy. I just needed to sow a few wild oats. I always used pros because my heart belonged to you."

With that outrageously clever lie, he took her standing up. It was the best fuck he'd ever had. By now he'd mastered the technique. He closed his eyes and imagined it was Amy.

CHAPTER
TWENTY-ONE

"You have much more mobility in your fingers than you had at our first session," the physical therapist commented as he finished her latest treatment.

"Yes," she agreed.

She could flex her fingers slightly, but her hand wasn't usable yet. She thanked the therapist and left his office above the Gato Gordo Café. Matt was standing at the bottom of the stairs, his world-weary eyes studying her intently.

What was he doing here? Three nights ago he'd left her room abruptly, and she hadn't seen him since. He'd deliberately avoided her, which was just as well. Every time she thought about what had happened, her embarrassment grew.

A savage, dark tension sharpened the angular planes of his face as he asked, "How's your hand?"

"Better," she answered, a cottony dryness in her mouth. She reached the bottom step and paused. "What are you doing here?"

"We have an appointment with Dr. Holt."

"We? Why?"

He reached for her good hand and brought her down onto the sidewalk beside him. His eyes, so frighteningly intense, sought hers. Their gazes met and locked. A silence fraught with emotions too complex for her to understand stretched between them.

Finally he spoke. "I made the appointment because I'm as screwed up as you are. I tried for days, but I can't get you out of my mind."

The emotional aftershock of having him walk out hurt her much more than she cared to admit. At first she'd been stunned, then a gnawing emptiness had set in. She didn't know what he was up to now, but she wasn't playing any more games.

"Jensen, this sounds like a personal problem to me." She jerked her hand out of his. "See Peter. I'm sure he can help you."

Her voice cracked just slightly, undermining the words. She didn't want him to suspect how thrilled she was to know he'd been thinking about her, or how miserable she'd been.

"Let's be honest here. We're attracted to each other. Hell, more than attracted."

She tried to make her lips smile as she gave a careless little shrug as if his words didn't mean a thing to her. "Face it, Jensen. You're experiencing an overload of testosterone. That's all. Pick up a willing female at one of the bars along Duval. Or, better yet, check into one of the clothing optional guest houses."

"Can't you be serious? If I thought sex was the answer, I'd be happy." He raked his fingers through his dark hair. "But I find myself wanting to talk to you and take you places . . . and just be with you."

For a moment she wasn't certain she believed him. The fickle trade winds riffled through the nearby palms. The hollow rush of the wind echoed the yearning deep in her soul.

"What are you saying?" The words burst from her lips.

"I want to be with you, Shelly."

There was no mistaking the gruff affection in his voice. An invisible skein of tension wrapped around them, drawing them closer.

"You do?" she asked.

He slipped his arm around her shoulders. His gaze roved slowly across her face, unmistakable tenderness in his eyes. Her throat closed up, and she had to look away.

"I'm crazy about you."

"You're crazy about me?" she asked, testing him, half afraid he was teasing. "Jensen, you *do* have a problem."

"Matt or Matthew. Not Jensen."

"Okay . . . Matt."

Her voice creaked like a rusty hinge. How many times had lonesomeness built up inside her and she would yearn for something. For someone. But nothing was there for her except a vast emptiness that went on forever. God help her, this man was what she'd been missing during those long, lonely years when she'd been The Beast.

He cupped her jaw with his strong hand, and a shadow passed over his face, his eyes darkening. He lowered his mouth to hers. The instant their lips met, every inch of her body ached for more. She wrapped both arms around him, giving in to her own pent-up desire.

He broke the kiss, his eyes squeezed shut as if bracing himself for a blow. He opened his eyes, saying, "See what I mean? We need professional help."

She didn't protest when he led her to the corner and flagged down a rickie. She didn't have much time with him, she decided. Why not enjoy herself now?

Soon her hand would be better, and she would have to leave. During the last few days she'd come to the conclusion that her only alternative was to contact the FBI again. They hadn't been able to protect her before, but knowing how dangerous Dexxter Foxx was, they would surely be more careful now.

She wanted to see Dexxter punished for what he'd done. As much as she would like to stay on Key West and enjoy her new life, she had a responsibility. Justice would corner the shifty little weasel.

Matt pointed to the decorations going up on Duval Street. "Tomorrow begins the Fantasy Fest that's held each year the week before Halloween. It's like Mardi Gras with costume balls and a fantasy parade that's too far out to be described."

"I'd like to see it."

His adorable grin made her want to throw her arms around him again. "We're going to watch it together. Trevor booked the whole balcony at La-Te-Da. That way we can see everything without being crushed by the crowd."

Making plans to do things together seemed so . . . right. It was a feeling that she never would have experienced if her life hadn't taken an unexpected turn.

"Is this it?" Matt asked her when the rickie driver stopped.

"Yes. Dr. Holt practices out of his home." She couldn't wait until Matt met the doctor. She would bet anything that Trevor hadn't told Matt about Peter.

He helped her out of the rickie, and she braced herself. She wasn't certain why Matt insisted they both see the doctor, but his remark about her obsessive behavior being a result of having her entire family die made her suspect he was seeking an excuse to forgive her. Fine. She was sick of pretending she was a nutcase. She wanted a way out of this.

When Dr. Holt came to the door wearing a navy linen dress, she decided to spare Matt. "Peter, this is Matthew Jensen."

The doctor greeted them, holding the door open, and they went inside. If Matt was shocked, he didn't show it. They sat in the airy living room where she had talked with Peter on her first visit.

"On the phone you said the two of you have a problem," Peter told Matt. "Tell me about it."

They were sitting on the love seat opposite Peter. Matt gazed at her, and she realized he expected her to say something.

"I'm fine. Matt has the problem."

He flashed her a look she couldn't quite decipher, then patted her shoulder as if she were a young child. "Shelly is still in a delusional state."

"I am not! If you think I'm so nutty, why did you say you were crazy about me?"

Peter asked, "Did you say that?"

"Sure. I *am* crazy about Shelly." Matt held up his hands as if surrendering. "I'm not saying I don't have a problem too. That's why I wanted you to see us together."

"What do you think your problem is?" Peter asked Matt.

Two beats of silence, then Matt shrugged. "I can't stop thinking about Shelly no matter how hard I try. I know better. This is the woman who threatened my sister." He paused, leaning forward. "Still, I can't seem to help myself."

Yes! cheered The Beast. The man of her dreams did truly care about her. He was fighting it hard, but he couldn't resist her. They were meant for each other.

In a perfect world, things would have been different.

But she wasn't living a fairy-tale life. The FBI might snatch her away and leave her stowed somewhere for months and months while they made a case against Dexxter. All she had was here and now.

Dr. Holt seemed perplexed. "What's troubling you?"

"I don't want to be so . . . so attracted to a woman who threatened my sister. Emily took over when my mother died. I was just thirteen, and she raised me. If not for her, I probably would be in a prison somewhere."

It was obvious how much he loved his sister. She'd longed for a sibling, someone who would love her and not judge her by the horrid birthmark. How could she continue to pretend she'd threatened his sister?

"Shelly . . ."

Dr. Holt's voice hung in the air. She tried to play the part. "My family . . . they were all killed when the ValuJet crashed into the Everglades."

She thought about her mother's death for a moment, hoping it would help her strike the right emotional note. "Suddenly, everyone I loved was gone. I was all alone. Then Matt came along. I-I guess I needed someone to love so much that I got carried away."

Matt was gazing at her intently, as if weighing every word.

"The next thing I knew I was in the hospital, near death, unable to utter a single word. I had been blessed with a second chance at life. I promised myself that I would be a better person. If Matt didn't love me any longer, then I would just have to accept that fact."

Matt slowly shook his head, assailed by a terrible sense of defeat. Could anyone possibly help Shelly? Sometimes she seemed so sweet and innocent, then she would slip into her fantasy world again. All they'd had was one lousy date, then she'd deluded herself into believing he loved her.

It defied all logic, but he was drawn to her in a way that he had never been attracted to another woman. He'd walked out the other night, having come damn close to making love to her. She'd stopped him by saying they had once made love on the beach.

He'd never made love to her. Period. He'd kissed her a couple of times, and it hadn't been particularly memorable.

After Shelly had suddenly disappeared from his life, he had received very bad news that changed his world. His whole outlook changed overnight. He learned how devastating the prospect of death could be and how it altered your life.

Death.

It was final, irrevocable. The land of no more tomorrows. Facing death changed people. His own experience prompted him to give up the job he loved. Shelly could have made just as radical a change.

Could have.

Shelly claimed to have gotten over her obsession, but obviously she hadn't. She still clung to delusions about an affair with him. In a remarkably short time he'd come to care about her. Despite his gut-wrenching sense of frustration, he wanted to help her in any way he could.

"Shelly," he began. "What made you think I once loved you? Did I ever tell you that?"

Her shoulders hunched forward slightly as he spoke. She didn't respond. Instead, Shelly cast a furtive glance at the doctor.

Peter didn't say a thing. It was probably some technique shrinks used, but it made him uncomfortable. What a crock! The seconds ticked by.

Finally, he gave up on the transvestite doctor and said, "Shelly, we can't help you unless you cooperate. Don't you want to get well?"

The soulful look in her blue eyes could have melted the devil's heart. "Of course I do."

"Then admit the truth. I never said I loved you. We had one date. That's all. We never made love anywhere." He tried for a reassuring smile, then added, "Although the surf could be interesting."

The color leached from one side of her face, and for an instant he thought she was going to cry. She stared at him, transfixed. Then she threw back her head, sending her golden hair cascading over her shoulders, and burst out laughing.

Aw, hell. She was a hopeless mental case. "What's so funny?"

She was still laughing, although it was more of a choking sound now, and humor was not reflected in her eyes. "I'm laughing at myself for being such a fool," she said tentatively, as if testing the idea. "How could I manage to spin one lousy date into such an elaborate fantasy? I guess I must have wanted it to be true so badly that I made up things."

There is a God, he decided. Shelly was coming to grips with her problem.

"Elaborate delusions are typical of this type of obsession," the doctor told her. "Since the accident, have you experienced new delusions?"

"No, not at all."

"Now, Shelly," Matt said as gently as he could. After all, they were on the verge of a breakthrough here. "Just the other night you mentioned the beach and Bermuda."

"Trust me, it was a slip," she said with a smile that he interpreted as almost defiant. "I had that fantasy in New York when it was snowing, and I saw a travel poster."

He wasn't quite sure he believed her. There was something odd about her expression.

"Shelly, have you stalked Matt since the accident?" Dr. Holt asked.

"No, absolutely not."

The doctor adjusted his skirt, looking at Matt for verification.

"She's telling the truth." He thought for a moment, then added, "If anything, I've followed her around. I guess there are degrees of obsession."

"Right," Peter said. "Mental health is a journey, not a destination. All of us are a little bit off."

No one would dispute that.

"Do you think it's safe for us to spend time together?" he asked the doctor.

"I have absolutely no idea," Peter conceded. "I've never heard of a case like this." The doctor rose, signaling the session was over. "What I would like to do is stay in touch with you both. I'd like to document this case for *Mental Health Today*. It's one for the books."

No kidding.

Outside Dr. Holt's home, the late afternoon sun blazed across the deep blue sky with nothing more than scrims of clouds to break the heat. Amy's whole body was sheened by sweat, but not from the weather. From the instant she realized the true nature of Rochelle Ralston's relationship with Matt, she'd been scrambling to excuse her actions, her anxiety mounting until perspiration dripped from every pore.

Who would have thought Shelly had made up everything she'd written in the journal? The account had been so incredibly detailed. Granted, she had known Shelly was obsessed and had behaved outrageously, but the woman had been deranged.

When the light dawned, she hadn't known whether to laugh or cry with utter relief. She wasn't going to have to guard her every move. Matt didn't know Shelly nearly as well as she had assumed.

"Shelly, let's go back into town," Matt said. "There's something I want to get."

Matt took her hand and they walked down the block. He stopped under the shade of an enormous gumbo limbo tree. He took her face in both his hands. He pressed his lips to hers, caressing her mouth more than kissing it. He gazed into her eyes with the kind of compassion she never dreamed she would see in a man.

"I'm so proud of you. I know it took a lot to admit you'd been lying."

She almost laughed, but he was so adorably earnest and genuinely concerned about her. Trying to appear contrite, her enormous sense of relief blossomed into anticipation. Since he'd never made love to Shelly, there was no reason not to let him make love to her. At the thought, her pulse took a perilous leap.

Matt put his arm around her and headed toward the center of town, checking his long stride to match hers. As they went, they talked about the upcoming Fantasy Fest. Trevor and Clive were throwing a costume ball. Matt suggested they go as Antony and Cleopatra. She agreed, but then, she was so happy that she would have agreed to almost anything.

Duval Street was bustling with the lighthearted revelry that went on around the clock. Music blared from the bars that opened at breakfast. As sunset approached, the whoopla reached a fever pitch.

"We're going to have to do something about your T-shirts," Matt said.

"Go on. You can't mean you don't like this."

She pointed to her chest. The shirt read:

DON'T SWEAT THE PETTY STUFF
PET THE SWEATY STUFF

"I'll have you know this T-shirt was a real bargain. Twenty-five cents."

"What a ripoff. They should have paid you to take it." His tone was a little gruff. "Besides, it gives other guys the wrong idea."

Glory be. He sounded a little protective. After years of fending for herself, she liked being in a man's care.

Not just any man, she thought as they passed Huevos Grande. A man was sitting at one of the tables, his hairy spare tire of a belly lopping over his swim trunks. He was gobbling food like a bear foraging in a dump and leering at her.

She knew what his look meant. Even if he'd been a major hunk, she wouldn't have welcomed his stare, but she didn't avert her eyes either. Yes! cried a little voice inside her. She was slowly changing.

Matt stopped in front of Proud Mary's. "What do you think of that dress?"

A lime-green slip dress hung on the mannequin. The silk was covered by another layer of sheer lace. It was simple, yet dramatic.

"It's beautiful. I've never seen a dress quite like it."

He gave her a quick hug and smiled with boyish enthusiasm. "I walked by this shop a dozen times yesterday. I wandered from gallery to gallery, trying to get you out of my mind. Each time I came by here, I spotted it and thought about you." He started toward the door. "Come on, let's get it."

She hung back. "Matt, no. I already owe Trevor money for clothes."

"I want to buy it for you as a gift."

"I appreciate the thought. You'll never know how much, but I can't let you. I don't have anyplace to wear it." She couldn't tell him how soon she planned to leave. Life in the Witness Protection Program hardly called for fancy clothes. "In Key West, women don't wear much more than shorts and T-shirts."

"Trevor's having a cocktail party tomorrow night for the couple who just leased a home on the other side of Sunset Key."

"Bubbles told me. Trevor did the same thing when I came to live at Half Moon Bay, but it wasn't a dressy affair."

"This is going to be a little more formal. Clive thought a sit-down dinner on the terrace would be fun."

"They've really hit it off, haven't they?"

He guided her into Proud Mary's. "Yes, thanks to you. Getting Clive to come out on the water was a start."

The clerk smiled at Matt and was only too pleased to show her to a dressing room. The woman hung the green dress on the hook beside the mirror. She shrugged out of her T-shirt, then pulled off her shorts.

Reaching for the dress, she recalled how she had always picked out clothes to make her disappear into the woodwork. She gazed into the mirror, studying herself. Even though she knew to expect to see her mother's reflection, it took a moment for her mind to adjust. She looked people in the eye now. She could wear pretty clothes.

The Beast only existed inside her head.

She slipped into the dress and gave a little shake to align the two layers. The silk whispered when she moved, incredibly soft and sensual against her skin. She twirled around to look from another angle.

Oh, my. The woman in the mirror was everything she had never imagined she could be. Daring. Sexy.

"What's going on in there?" Matt called. "Let's see what it looks like."

She took a deep breath and opened the door.

"Holy sh—"

The glint of wonder in his eyes made something in her chest seize up and alter her heartbeat. No man had ever gazed at her with such frank admiration. Until recently, they had looked away, avoided eye contact whenever possible. The way Matt was staring at her brought the hot sting of tears to her eyes. She fluttered her eyelashes to keep the tears at bay.

"Shelly, am I a genius, or what? That dress was made for you."

CHAPTER
TWENTY-TWO

Matt couldn't help grinning as he rode beside Shelly on the water shuttle back to Sunset Key. He'd never made anyone this happy. He hadn't anticipated buying shoes and earrings as well as a purse to go with the dress, but he didn't mind one bit.

Shelly had been so delighted with everything, confirming his decision. It had taken days for him to come to grips with his feelings. He had no business getting involved with a woman—any woman, but Shelly needed him. Okay, okay, maybe he was justifying his actions, yet he truly believed he could help her.

"You know, Jensen, you're not half bad," Shelly said. "Thanks for the outfit. It's awesome."

His arm was already around her, and he pulled her closer. "If you really appreciate it, then stop calling me Jensen. I like the way you say Matt."

She smiled with a depth that had been missing when she'd smiled at him before. "Thanks, Matt. I can hardly wait for tomorrow night to wear it."

"I can hardly wait for tonight."

"It's almost dark now. If we hurry, we can watch the sunset from the terrace with everyone."

"Everyone? Bubbles is going to the grand opening of Martiniville. Clive is helping Trevor decorate his galleries for Fantasy Fest. Nobody will be back until waaay after midnight."

"Oh."

She didn't sound too excited.

"I thought we could watch the sunset, then barbecue. Trevor usually has chicken and steaks in the fridge. What sounds good?"

"Anything."

He wasn't certain what she was thinking. She sounded detached. Almost too detached.

The shuttle pulled up to the main dock at Sunset Key, and he helped her off the boat. Carrying the shopping bag with the outfit, he walked beside her down the brick path that led across the small island to Half Moon Bay.

Shelly pointed to a Cape Cod–style home not far from the cottages and main dock. "Look. There's a couple on the rooftop deck, watching the sunset. No one's ever been at home before this. Don't you ever wonder why people build such beautiful places, then leave them empty?"

"What can I tell you? The rich are different."

They were too far from the house to see the man and woman clearly, but they appeared to be young.

"That must be the new couple who leased the house, the ones Trevor invited for dinner tomorrow evening," Matt added.

They hurried to Half Moon Bay, where the bevy of cats greeted them. Jiggs danced at his feet, then put his front paws on Matt's legs, begging to be picked up.

"Jiggs likes you better than he does me." She sounded slightly hurt. "After all we've gone through together, you'd think he'd be crazy about me."

Matt picked up the scrawny, henna-colored mutt. "You're going to find this hard to believe, but dogs like me almost as much as women do."

She rolled those sexy baby blues heavenward. "Go on. You can't mean it."

"Damn straight." He handed her the bag. "Hang up your clothes while I open some wine. If we don't hurry, we'll miss the sunset."

He carried Jiggs under one arm like a football and walked into the kitchen, feeling like the Pied Piper. All eight cats were at his heels. He opened the wine cooler and helped himself to a bottle of chardonnay. He set Jiggs on the floor beside Bingo. The orange cat glared at him with his one green eye, pissed off.

"Hey, dude. Din-din will have to wait until after sunset."

Matt opened the wine, then took the glasses off the shelf. He headed toward the open door that led to the terrace. Bingo hurled himself between Matt and the door, throwing a body block. Jiggs was right behind the fearless feline. Matt lurched to one side, stumbled over yet another cat, and banged against the doorjamb.

"Did you invent that move yourself?" Shelly said with a laugh as she came up behind him. "Or are you imitating Beavis and Butt-head?"

"Honey, you should see some of my other moves."

"Be still my heart."

"Come on, smart mouth. We're missing the sunset."

They walked out across the terrace followed by Jiggs and the cats. Matt poured Shelly a glass of wine and handed it to her. The light of the setting sun glazed her blue eyes as she looked at him with such . . . such what?

A complex woman, he thought, pouring himself wine. Unpredictable in many ways. She seemed almost nervous to be alone with him. He sensed she was trying to hide her anxiety with wisecracks.

Take it slow and easy, he told himself.

"Awesome," Shelly said, her tone reverent.

Brushstroke clouds painted the horizon, muting the sunset. The burnished-gold orb slowly slipped out of sight. Lingering pinwheels of russet and crimson fired the sky. The sapphire ocean, robbed of the light, turned a dark indigo. From across the channel at Mallory Dock a rousing cheer sounded.

Another sunset in paradise.

"Nature's beautiful," she said, her eyes still on the horizon, "and all-powerful. It makes you realize how small and insignificant we are."

He moved closer, and she turned to him. She had the damnedest eyes. Expressive yet mysterious. She seemed a little sad, which was the last thing he wanted.

"I don't know. I'm feeling mighty important right now."

All the cats except Bingo were either circling them or rubbing against their ankles. Off to one side sat Bingo, licking his privates while malevolently staring at them with one angry eye. As usual, Jiggs was watching Bingo with adoration. Go figure.

"I should feed them," she said, moving away from him.

"Yeah, probably." He tried not to sound too disappointed. This was not going the way he'd planned. What was wrong?

"Sit down, Matt. Enjoy your wine."

She dawdled as long as she possibly could, waiting until the very last cat, Morty, had finished licking his bowl clean. When she walked outside, the sky was dark; only the soft light from the nightscaping lit the terrace. Matt was standing down at the water's edge, his back to her.

The other night she had been caught up in the moment and ready to let him make love to her. Now she felt more than a little self-conscious. How did other women act when they knew a man intended to make love to them?

The sweet scent of plumeria floated on the warm breeze that stirred the banks of ferns and rippled through the palm trees as she wandered down to the shore. She opted to brazen it out and play her hand the way she imagined a bad girl would. She gave him a little swat on his tight buns, then said, "We've got the place to ourselves. Let's go skinny-dipping."

Slack-jawed, he turned toward her. It took a moment for a glint of humor to fire his blue eyes. "You're on. I mean, you're off. Take your clothes off."

She masked her nervousness with a saucy flounce of her head that sent her hair back over one shoulder. "I wasn't suggesting a striptease. I meant an *au naturel* swim like the French do." Not that she'd ever been in France.

"Right. What's stopping you from taking off your clothes, then?"

"I thought we could go behind the bushes—"

"What bushes? The ones clear back at the house?"

That was too far to make sense. "What about the palms over there?" She hitched her head toward the cluster of palms that marked the end of the beach. "We could get out of our clothes and put on towels, then leave them on the—"

"You're a real expert at skinny-dipping, aren't you?"

"Sure, towels are a must." She tugged his arm. "I'll take the palm nearest the water—"

He refused to budge. "We don't have towels."

"Good point. I'll get towels."

She streaked across the sand, hit the dichondra at full speed, heading for the terrace hamper, where Trevor kept a supply of beach towels. So much for brazening it out. She'd been flustered and not thinking clearly. Only a complete imbecile could believe one of those tall but skinny trees could conceal Matt's body.

And she'd totally forgotten they didn't have towels.

She grabbed two fluffy beach towels, positive Matt was down at the shore, howling with laughter. Refusing to let this little snafu throw her, she sprinted toward the water. She came to a stop beside Matt and gave him what she hoped was a naughty smile.

Before she got cold feet, she tossed the towels onto the sand behind them. She peeled off her T-shirt and flung it over her shoulder.

"What happened to the bushes?" Matt asked, his eyes coasting over her bra.

"Come on, Jensen, are you hiding a beer belly, or what?"

She unzipped her shorts, experiencing a momentary flutter in her chest. If she stopped now, she'd never go through with it. She yanked the shorts down, then kicked them aside. She stood beside him in her bra and bikini panties, the surf purling around her toes.

Matt cleared his throat, and she forced herself to look at him. After all, the bikini she bought was more revealing than her underwear. Still, the idea of being so exposed in front of a man unnerved The Beast.

Matt showed no sign he intended to undress. "Keep going. This *could* get interesting."

Her heartbeat throbbed in her ears, and she felt a little lightheaded. "Don't tell me you can't swim."

"I was captain of the water polo team at Yale," he said, but she decided his mind was not on water sports.

His eyes held hers for a moment, and something sparked between them, tension crackling like summer lightning. His gaze dropped to her shoulders and down to her breasts. He took his sweet time, examining their size and shape. Despite the warm, balmy air, she shivered, and her nipples peaked.

A wave of self-consciousness that was only too familiar to The Beast hit her. "I'm getting in the water."

"We're already in the water."

She looked down; the advancing tide washed against her ankles. She ventured another glance at him. The smoldering flame she saw in his eyes heightened her sense of anticipation and made her even more nervous.

"Skinny-dipping usually means no clothes." His voice had become a husky rasp. "Unless things are different . . . in France."

She refused to let him bait her. There was a bulge in his cutoffs that hadn't been there earlier. He could make a joke of this, but she was getting to him.

A-maz-ing.

She unhooked her bra, then flung it over her shoulder. Her

breasts swung free. In a half second she had her panties off and pitched them backward. With courage she never knew she had, she faced him.

"That's more like it, Shelly."

"You can stand there if you want. I'm going for a swim."

Before she could turn, he grabbed her wrist and hauled her into his arms. One hand gripped her bare buttocks, pressing her against his lower body. He rocked his hips just slightly in case she had somehow missed his hard, jutting shaft. Her breath stalled in her throat, and her body was warm, flushed.

She couldn't help herself. "Is that a mouse in your pocket, or are you glad to see me?"

His hooded gaze became strangely arrested. Then he laughed, a gruff, masculine sound that vibrated through her body as he held her. What she'd said had been incredibly silly, considering everyone used it so much, it had become a joke. She started to giggle, which only made him laugh harder.

They shared a gratifying laugh. Their chuckling tapered off, drifting into the balmy air as they stood nose to nose. His erection probed intimately at her. A delicious shudder shook her body.

Make love to me was all she could think.

Now.

His hand stroked her bare bottom, then his fingers roamed lower until he found the smooth curve of her inner thigh. The feather-light touch ignited currents of desire, radiating outward.

"Your skin is softer than a baby's."

Her arms slid up his shoulders and twined around his neck as she instinctively moved against his bulging erection. A low groan verging on a growl erupted from his throat. The combination of his sheer masculine power and being naked while he was clothed heightened the dark desire coursing through her veins like wildfire.

"The French don't know squat about skinny-dipping. Towels? Get real. But the French kiss, now, there's a helluva idea. Don't you think so?"

She couldn't manage a response. While he spoke—calm as you please—his hand had found its way between her legs. She'd felt the moist heat building from the moment she had stood before him clad only in her underwear.

Now she was slick, and the whole core of her being seemed to be centered at the pleasure point he was now stroking. She braced her head against his sturdy shoulder and surrendered to the moment.

"I guess we've had just about all the fun we can have."

"No," she cried. She wanted more. He wasn't going to do this to her again.

He swung her into his arms and carried her out of the water. "I meant all the fun we can have right here. In case you haven't noticed, the water is above your knees. There's no need to drown, is there?"

He took her across the sand and lowered her to the lush carpet of dichondra that separated the terrace from the sandy beach. She gazed up at him as he unbuttoned his shirt, his eyes on the cluster of pale blond curls between her legs. He dropped the shirt and paused.

A horned moon shone down from a whirlpool of stars, giving her enough light to see the contours of his powerful chest. Feathered with dark hair, his torso dipped and curved, the shadows highlighting his muscles.

She clutched the grass with her good hand, anticipating his next move. He unbuckled the belt, then used one thumb to unhook the top button on the cutoffs. The zipper came down slowly, a fraction of an inch at a time, while he grimaced.

No wonder. His cutoffs were wa–a–ay too tight. A thin strip of hair at the waistband unfurled into a dense thicket as the zipper opened more and more. She meant to look away, she honestly did, but she must have been thrown, because Matt didn't have anything on under his cutoff jeans.

"It's not polite to stare."

"Uh-huh," was all she could manage.

His sex proudly jutted out from between powerful thighs, aiming right at her. He was all male and so heart-stoppingly virile that her throat constricted.

This isn't going to work was her first thought. He was much larger, thicker, than she had anticipated. Suddenly, her mouth felt like parchment.

He lowered himself to the grass beside her. "Honey, I wish I could take my time. I will later, I promise, but since that night in your bedroom, I've had a hard-on that won't quit."

He hovered over her for a moment, desire glittering in his eyes, then he covered her body with his. His weight drove her bare skin into the grass, but it was a delightful sensation. She inhaled a deep breath, and his rich, musky scent mingled with citrus aftershave filled her lungs.

Like a powerful narcotic, the smell enthralled her. Blazing a trail of moist kisses over her bare skin, he slid lower and lower. The faint prickling of his emerging beard tickled her sensitive skin. She writhed beneath him, a velvety purr rising from her throat.

His warm breath ruffled the tangle of curls. Oh, my. She had absolutely no experience, but she was well-read enough to know what he was going to do. He nuzzled her with his lips, then his tongue found the sweet spot. Her whole body began to quiver, and in a second she was on the verge of going over the edge.

That would be two orgasms with her virginity intact. She couldn't let that happen. Arching her hips, she said, "Come on."

"Hold your horses. This time I have protection."

He fumbled with his cutoffs and pulled out a foil packet. With a chuckle bordering on a groan he waved it under her nose. "See what it says? This is a French Tickler."

"Very funny." Do *something* quick!

Before she could draw a breath, he had on the condom. She didn't have a moment to think too much about all the other times he must have used protection to be so fast. He nudged her knees apart and positioned himself between her legs.

He guided the velvet-smooth tip of his penis into her soft opening. She was slick, ready, but it hurt more than she had expected.

"You're a little tight, honey."

"I'm built that way," she hedged. "Don't stop."

"Actually, that thought hadn't crossed my mind."

CHAPTER
TWENTY-THREE

Matt drew back a little, desire at a flash point now, almost out of control. The way she was built? What a crock.

"You're a virgin?"

"Sorta."

Man, oh, man, what had he gotten himself into? This was no way to have a first experience. Gritting his teeth, determined to hold back and make this good for her, Matt struggled to control his body.

All day he'd driven himself half crazy anticipating this moment. He'd imagined hot sex, some of it X-rated and bordering on kinky. Never in his wildest dreams had he considered Shelly might be a virgin.

When she'd stripped and turned to him, wearing nothing but a seductive smile, his pulse had gone berserk. Not to mention what it had done to the rest of him. Her behavior had been a bit odd, he'd thought at the time. Probably because she had forced herself to take off her clothes.

"Don't stop," she pleaded.

He realized his eyes were squeezed shut. Letting out his breath, he opened them. Moonlight flickered over her hair, gleaming softly on her moist lips and dancing in her eyes.

"I'm not stopping. I'm just trying to figure this out."

"You've never had sex before?" she teased.

"Not with a virgin. They're a dying breed. We don't get many in these parts."

What he wanted to say was that this was a big responsibility. Was he up to the challenge? He eased forward with little rocking movements, allowing her body time to stretch to accommodate him.

"I liked it better when you didn't know I was a virgin."

"You're probably a backseat driver too."

He gave her what she wanted. Thrusting forward, he tested the barrier. He pushed harder and harder. Nothing. Cocking his hips, he pulled back a little, then drove into her. He felt her body give.

She gasped.

"Does it hurt?"

"A little, but I don't mind."

He kissed her forehead as he burrowed his way inside her. "You're so tight."

"I'm sorry."

"Don't be. You're perfect." He meant it; her body was slick and ready, fitting him like a glove that was a size too small. He'd never been this aroused in his whole damn life. It was a miracle his heart was withstanding the adrenaline rush.

"You feel . . . wonderful. So big."

He wasn't that big, but she was incredibly small and inexperienced. He lifted her hips to deepen the angle of his thrusts. She gave a soft moaning sound that shot right through him.

"Now I know what I've been missing," she whispered.

"A talker. I had to get a talker and virgin yet." He tried to joke, hoping to distract himself. The last thing he wanted was to come before she did.

His movements were easier now. He drew back, then came forward with renewed momentum. She clung to him, her nails biting into the skin on his back, then raking downward.

"Great! A virgin and a talker and a scratcher."

"Sorry, I can't help myself. You feel *so* good."

"You ain't seen nothin' yet."

She began moving beneath him, arching her hips to meet his thrusts.

"That's it, darlin'. You're getting the hang of it."

"I wa-watched a naughty movie in a hotel once." Her voice was a soft rasp in his ear, her breath coming in warm little pants.

"Don't let anybody find out. You could get arrested."

Talking helped, he found. He'd had sex too many times to count, none of them memorable. But he was never going to forget this.

It wasn't just that Shelly was a virgin. He'd been resisting her for so long that he seemed to have driven himself to the brink of frustration. Just by wedging his way inside her, he had nearly lost it like some horny kid in the backseat of an old Chevy.

With each movement now he buried himself to the hilt, her hot, tight body compressing around his penis. He couldn't help groaning with pleasure.

"Are you all right?"

No, he wanted to yell. He was so close to ejaculating that he couldn't talk any longer. Her lips were parted and her eyes brimming with passion, but she showed no signs of being close to an orgasm.

He adjusted his position so his hand could touch the soft folds of skin between her thighs. Spreading them apart. He made certain his shaft was up against her tight bud. Then he began to pump, slowly at first.

She rewarded his efforts with a sweet moan. "Oh, God."

He increased the tempo, hammering into her. "No, not God. He's busy. I'm Matt, remember?"

She moaned again, louder than before. "This is heaven."

Together they found the right cadence and moved together like dancers, hearing a silent tune. He permitted himself the luxury of losing himself in her, in this unique experience. All that existed was this moment, this special woman.

For now, at least, he could ignore the future.

His thrusts became heavier as he pounded furiously toward release. Beneath him, she was on fire, moving upward to meet him each time he lunged into her. She shuddered violently, then gave a gasping cry of pure delight.

He pummeled, faster and faster, on the brink himself. The coil of tension, wound so tight, exploded in a white-hot rush of pleasure. A guttural groan rumbled out of his throat as he flung his head back.

The orgasm lanced through him like a bolt of lightning, leaving him suddenly weak. He pitched forward, catching the brunt of his weight with his forearms on either side of her head and gasping for air.

She looked up at him, her eyes wide with wonder. "Did I do okay for a first-timer?"

He couldn't seem to get his breath, but he managed to nod. He gathered her in his arms and rolled onto his side, afraid he'd collapse on her. "If you get any better, you'll kill me."

She snuggled against him and planted a little kiss on his shoulder.

He was still inside her, and he didn't want to let her go. What had happened just now was powerful, all-consuming. He'd had sex before, but it had never been this intense.

This satisfying.

"It was much better than I ever dreamed," she whispered to him. "No wonder people like sex so much."

Matt chuckled.

"Hel-lo! Anybody home?"

Shelly jerked upright. "It's Bubbles. She's in the kitchen."

"Head for the water." He pulled out of her, yanked off the condom and tossed it onto his cutoffs.

When he reached the shore, Shelly was bobbing in water so deep, it covered her breasts. He dove in and surfaced beside her. "Come here, honey."

She glided into his arms as if she knew she belonged there. The gentle surge of the sea swayed them back and forth.

"Shelly. Matt." Bubbles and some guy were standing on the grass near the spot where they had just made love. "What are you doing?"

"Swimming."

"Let's hope they don't decide to join us," Shelly whispered to him.

"Why not? This is Key West. Anything goes. We might try group sex," he said, but he wasn't serious. No way in hell was he sharing her.

She tried to hold on to the elusive dream, not remembering what it was exactly, but knowing it had been pleasant. A smell had brought her out of the dream. Without opening her eyes and not wanting to wake up just yet, she sniffed. Coffee. She cracked one eyelid, then the other.

"It's about time you woke up, sleepyhead."

Matt was sitting beside the bed, dressed in shorts and a T-shirt and drinking a cup of coffee. Last night. Oh, my God.

After Bubbles and her friend left, Matt had carried her to his room. How many times had they made love? She didn't want to count, and she certainly didn't need to remember how wantonly she'd behaved.

Over the rim of his cup, he smiled at her. "You're blushing."

He was grinning at her now, a proud, masculine grin. She realized she was sprawled across his bed without a stitch of clothing on. She reached for the sheet.

"Aw, Shelly. I've seen every inch of your body. Hell, I've had my tongue on every inch." He put down his cup, then sat beside her on the bed. He grabbed her foot and planted a kiss on the bottom of it. "I missed that spot."

The imprint of his lips on her sole tickled and reminded her of all the other places his lips had been. He was right, of course. He had explored every inch of her body. Being modest was for The Beast—not for her.

"Thanks for last night," she said as she sat up.

His arm slipped around her bare shoulders with a casual intimacy. "No, angel, I should thank you."

"We're quite a team, aren't we?"

"Yeah, we are." The devilish glint in his eye told her he was up to something. "Tell me, have you ever been to France?"

She shook her head.

"So much for the skinny-dipping French." He chuckled. "You know, I never use the word *cute*, but that was just about the cutest thing that ever happened to me. You started babbling, then you took off your clothes at warp speed."

She gave him a playful punch on his thigh. "What did you expect?"

He kissed the tip of her nose, his expression serious now. "You keep surprising me. It blew me away to find out you were a virgin. In New York—"

"Matt, please. Forget that woman. Let's start over."

"Okay, sure. It's just that—"

"I should hop in the shower." She jumped up, then winced, discovering she was a little sore. "What time is it anyway?"

"It's almost noon."

He had a strange look on his face, and she wondered if he realized she was deliberately trying to distract him. She couldn't afford to talk too much about Rochelle Ralston. She trotted into the bathroom and glanced at the mirror. Before she could stop herself, a small cry escaped her lips.

Matt was standing beside her in a second. "What's wrong?"

She pointed at her reflection. "I could haunt a house and charge by the room."

"Bedroom hair is sexy as hell. A few dozen love bites." He pulled up the back of his T-shirt. "Check this."

Angry red scratch marks, some long, others short, covered his back.

"Oh, I'm so sorry."

He pulled down the shirt. "Don't be. It was the hottest, best sex I've ever had. If you don't get in the shower, I'm going to drag you back to bed."

"I should go to my room. I don't have anything to put on after I shower."

"Your bra washed up on the beach this morning. Bingo and Jiggs were playing with it when I was getting coffee. It's a goner."

She shook her head, imagining everyone having breakfast as Bingo and Jiggs dragged her bra up from the beach.

"I have a great idea," Matt said. "We should take one of Trevor's Wave Runners and go find a deserted key."

"Let's have a picnic," she said.

"Okay, but I was thinking we should see if the French have anything with this *au naturel* stuff."

CHAPTER
TWENTY-FOUR

Matt drove the Wave Runner up onto the ramp and turned off the engine. The sun was dropping behind Sunset Key. He hated to see the day end. Shelly's arms were around his waist, the way they had been all during the ride back from Pirate Key.

"I'm sorry the day's over," Shelly echoed his thoughts as he helped her off the Wave Runner onto the dock.

He gazed into her gorgeous blue eyes, half tempted to tell her he loved her. Where in hell had that thought come from? He couldn't commit himself.

The fact was he could never be there for Shelly—not in that happy ever after way she deserved. She was a sensitive woman. Telling her that he loved her would make parting even more difficult.

When he was gone, Matt wanted Shelly to find someone else. She had so much to give. Hour by hour she seemed to be changing, opening up more and more. Becoming a different woman. He wished he could stay around to see it. Stop being maudlin, he told himself. Get a grip.

"The day's not over until midnight," he said as he gave her a playful swat on her cute fanny. "We haven't had all the fun we can have yet."

"Did you forget about Trevor's dinner party?"

He stopped and slammed the heel of his hand against his forehead. "I totally forgot. I said I would get the table out of the storage room and set it up. I'm supposed to take care of the cats too."

"Run along. I've got major repairs." She pointed to her head; her hair was a windblown tangle that looked just as sexy as it had this morning. "I want to do the dress justice."

"You're beautiful just the way you are."

He bent his head to give her a quick kiss. Once, he would have had to pull her into his arms, but not now. She automatically closed the space between them and tilted her head up for the kiss. Their lips met and the heat of desire ignited a wildfire.

In a heartbeat, pressure was building in his groin. So what else was new? They'd made love just before they'd left Pirate Key, yet his body wanted her again. "I can't get enough of you. I don't know what's wrong with me."

"I think you got more than your fair share of testosterone." She winked at him. "Works for me."

She scampered off toward the far side of the house, where her room was. He watched her go, asking himself why he'd found her now. Why hadn't it been years ago?

He walked up to the kitchen door and paused. Inside, Trevor and Clive had their heads together, arranging hors d'oeuvres on a platter. He could tell by the smile on Trevor's face that his friend was happy being with Clive. Now, if Trevor would only trust his instincts enough to know he could have a lasting relationship with Clive.

"Sorry, I'm late," Matt said as he walked into the kitchen. "Shelly wanted to go on a picnic. I lost track of the time."

"I hope she had on sunblock. Bioengineered skin can't take the sun."

"Don't worry, Clive. We used up an entire tube."

He didn't say what they'd done with most of it. He couldn't let Shelly's bare breasts burn, could he? When he'd seen how much fun rubbing lotion on her was, he'd smoothed it on the rest of her.

"Are you going to admit I was right?" Trevor asked. "The accident changed Shelly. She isn't crazy."

"You were right. She's special."

"I'm going to take some credit here," Clive said. "She was attractive before. I saved her face, then nipped a bit off her nose. Now she's perfect."

Matt didn't give a rat's ass about Shelly's improved nose. She had a power and a depth to her that fascinated him. It had nothing to do with her face, and everything to do with what went on inside that head of hers.

"She didn't need her breasts enlarged," Matt said. "She was sexy the way she was."

Clive waved a carrot stick at him. "I don't do breasts. I leave that to the hacks in the clinics on every corner."

I'll be damned, he thought. He could have sworn Shelly had much smaller breasts. Not that he judged a woman by her bra size, but he was a man. He noticed these things.

He recalled the one date he'd had with Shelly when he'd been in New York. It took a second to picture her in the low-cut black dress she'd worn. No, she'd been smaller.

During the year she'd chased him around, leaving notes, she must have had her breasts enlarged. Women did it all the time. At least, he supposed they did. There were certainly enough newspaper ads to indicate some doctors were making big bucks from silicone.

Aw, shit. A twinge too strong to be just a pang arced through his head. It couldn't be a headache, could it? Not now, not today, when he was so happy. He rubbed his temples, praying his headache was just a result of spending too much time in the brutal sun.

"Earth to Matt," Trevor called. "Are you going to stand there day dreaming, or will you get the big round table out of the storage shed?"

He hurried to the side of the house where the shed was located. Behind him, he heard Trevor and Clive sharing a laugh.

That's what life is all about, he told himself. Sharing laughs and sunsets and quiet moments. Why had it taken him so long to discover what was really important?

"The Beast is gone," she told her reflection.

For the first time in her life she felt . . . whole. Matt had as much to do with her transformation as the surgery. There was something indefinably special about being with a man, making love to him, and enjoying his company.

Today Matt had taken her to a deserted key, where they'd gone snorkeling and had a picnic. With no one around, they'd taken off their suits. The Beast would have been too shy to do this, but Matt made her feel comfortable with herself and her body.

Yes, they'd made love. She was a little sore from all the sex, but she wouldn't have missed one second of it. She was having the time of her life.

"Yes?" she called when she heard a knock on the door.

"It's me," Matt's voice came from the other side of the door. "Everyone's at the party but you."

She walked across the room, a little unsteady on the vampy heels that went with the outfit. When she opened the door, Matt stared at her for a moment, then gave a low whistle of appreciation.

"Do you like it? Bubbles did my makeup and hair for me. Is it too much?"

He closed the door behind him. "I should have a gun to head off the guys."

"Be serious."

"I am serious. You're drop dead gorgeous." The look in his eye was as intimate as a caress. "Kyle's back. No doubt, I'll have to take care of him first."

She looped her arms around his neck. He looked incredibly handsome in a navy shirt and white slacks. He was every woman's dream come true.

"What about me? Bubbles has the hots for you. No doubt, the other women out there will be all over you."

"Bubbles is no competition for you, babe, and neither is Irene."

A chill skipped down her spine. "Who's Irene?"

"The new couple, remember?"

"Oh, sure, the couple we saw yesterday. What are they like?"

"Irene's okay, if you like cheap brunettes. But Dexx is a piece of work."

Dexx.

The word hit her full force, and she let out a startled gasp. She dropped her arms, mind-numbing fear engulfing her.

"Honey, what's wrong?"

She hurried toward the bed, trying to marshal her thoughts. "It's a cramp in my arch. I don't think I should be wearing heels so soon after getting out of the cast."

She collapsed on the bed, and Matt sat beside her while she took off the lovely shoes. She fiddled with the clasp, wondering how they knew where she was. Did it matter?

She had to leave before they killed her.

If she could get to Key West, she could call the FBI, then hide until they came for her. It would mean leaving Matt. Just the thought of not seeing him—for what?—months, or even a year, made a cold knot form in her chest.

"Are you sure you're all right?"

The heartfelt concern in his voice brought tears to her eyes. How could she leave him after waiting a lifetime to find him? He put his finger under her chin and brought her head to the side to face him.

"You're crying. Sweetheart, what's wrong?"

"I'm not crying," she protested in a shaky voice, tears cresting in her eyes but not falling. "I'm just upset that I'll have to wear thongs and ruin the pretty outfit you bought me."

She stood up, the sandals in one hand, and marched over to the closet. It was about as ditzy an excuse as she could imagine, but she couldn't tell him the truth. She needed to be in flat sandals so she could run if necessary.

As she opened the louvered door, a thought hit her. Why would Dexxter come here? The sneaky little weasel always sent henchmen to do his work.

Maybe they didn't know for certain that she was Amy Conroy. They must have come to see for themselves whether or not she was the right woman. It was the only explanation that made sense.

Buying time, she made a big deal out of choosing between the two pairs of sandals. With luck, she could fool them into believing she was Shelly. The Witness Protection Program had wiped all her records clean. There was no way —she knew of—that Dexxter could prove she was Amy Conroy.

Matt could be very helpful in deceiving Dexx. After all, Matt had known her in New York. If he believed she was Shelly, it might convince Dexxter.

What good would it do? Even if she fooled Dexx, there was Irene. Dexxter was a sniveling little weasel. In her opinion, Irene was the one to watch. Even if Irene didn't realize she was Amy Conroy, Irene might kill her just to cover her bases.

Kicking herself for not having anticipated this and having an escape plan, she decided she didn't want to call her contact in the FBI. Last time, there had been a leak somewhere, and she had nearly lost her life. There had to be a field office in Miami. If she went there and explained the situation, they might arrange better protection.

She slipped into a pair of thongs, then turned to face Matt. He was still sitting on the bed, studying her with a puzzled expression. Oh, Lord. She didn't want him to think she was so goofy.

"I just wanted you to be proud of me."

He stood up and walked toward her, his arms outstretched. Gathering her close, he whispered, "I *am* proud of you. Proud of the way you look. The way you've changed."

Changed? Oh, God. She didn't want him saying that in front of Dexxter. "I haven't changed. You didn't really know me. That's all."

"Okay," he responded.

His eyes bored into hers, and she wondered what he was really thinking. This night would be the last time she might ever be with him. She desperately wanted him to remember *her* and not think of crazy Shelly.

"I was just being silly," she tried to joke. "In those heels, I didn't have to look up to you all the time."

"Women." He rolled his eyeballs. "Go figure."

His arms tightened around her. She sighed at the feel of his powerful, male body. All she'd asked for was a little time to be with him and get to know him. But once again, fate had dealt her a crummy hand. She had to make the most of their last night together.

The precious memories might very well have to last her a lifetime.

Dexxter Foxx stood on the terrace, sipping a martini. This was *some* place. Half Moon Bay made the Cape Cod cottage he rented look like a log cabin. Well, what could he expect? Irene had handled the lease.

She was nearby, talking to Trevor, the fudge-packer who owned Half Moon Bay. His fruity doctor friend was serving miniature quiches. Matthew Jensen had disappeared over ten minutes ago to get the woman who called herself Shelly. Of course, he knew she was really Amy Conroy.

Since then Dexx had been waiting, anticipation building, eating his nerves raw. He'd screwed Irene more times than he cared to count, imagining he was driving into Amy Conroy's sexy body. Why hadn't she shown up yet?

Jensen probably had her flat on her back. If there was one thing Dexx hated, it was sloppy seconds. He'd make her pay and pay and pay.

"Isn't the view, like, awesome?"

The red-haired creature who called herself Bubbles walked up to him, expecting a response. Every visible orifice sported a pierced object. He didn't want to know what was under her panties.

"Great view," he said, wondering how he could ask about Amy. "What happened to Matt?"

"He's with Shelly." The airhead ran her tongue over her lower lip, revealing yet another disgusting stud. It was hard enough to understand an accent laced with molasses. Why pierce her tongue? "It's on again."

"What's on?"

"Their affair. They were, like, red hot lovers last year in New York.

Then something happened. Now . . . well, you can't, like, get a laser beam between the two of them."

"I see."

His so-called detective was as worthless as tits on a bull. Dexx had been led to believe Jensen hadn't had a relationship with the woman. She'd stalked him. The blonde in the pictures couldn't be Amy if she was involved with Jensen—again.

He'd done a background check on Matthew Jensen. He was a savvy reporter who'd parlayed a rag sheet into a respected newsmagazine. Then he'd shocked the publishing world by quitting.

Why?

It didn't make sense, but he didn't give a flying fuck. Dexx was interested in the woman. Surely Jensen would have detected an impostor.

He turned his back on the redhead and signaled to Irene. She sashayed over to him, tits jiggling in a black dress that left zilch to the imagination. Been there; done that.

Jesus H. Christ. How he despised her. He could hardly wait for her "accident."

"Kyle was just telling me the most interesting story."

Kyle Parker, the guy built like a storm trooper. Something about him suggested the military even though he was in khaki slacks and a shortsleeve shirt. Dexx couldn't decide who he'd instantly disliked more, Jensen or Parker.

"The words *Key West* come from the Spanish words *Cayo Hueso*. It means Island of the Bones. *Hueso* took on the English pronunciation that sounded like west."

"So?" Sometimes Irene had shit for brains.

"Island of the Bones. Don't you get it? We kill Amy right here. She's bones like the mysterious bones the first Spaniards found."

"Zane is a chicken-shit excuse for a private detective. The blonde he took pictures of is *not* Amy Conroy. The woman's been involved with Jensen for more than a year. They're hot and heavy again. Jensen would know if—"

Before he could finish, a striking blonde walked onto the terrace, her hand on Matthew Jensen's arm. The woman was beautiful, built like a Vegas showgirl. Legs. Tits. A body that wouldn't quit.

This woman oozed class from every pore. She was wearing a wispy layered dress in a bold shade of green, but the gown wasn't so tight that every man knew exactly what was beneath it the way

Irene's did. No, this dress was subtly provocative. It fueled a man's imagination.

The upward surge of heat in his groin made it hard to think. The only thought he could hold for more than a second told him that he wanted this woman under him and moaning.

"Of course, that's Amy," Irene whispered. "How else did she get the dog?"

Dexx didn't have an explanation. He watched the woman greet Kyle with an engaging smile. They were too far away to hear what was being said, but the blonde's low, throaty laugh carried across the terrace.

The shy gesture that he had noticed in the picture must have been a fluke. This woman moved with the self-assurance of a woman who knew she was the object of every man's desire.

From the looks of it, Jensen and Parker were both after her. Jensen seemed to have the inside track, but Kyle had a certain macho appeal that women flipped over. Take–a–number time.

Dexx wasn't worried. Not only was he handsome, he had money up the ying-yang. That made him irresistible.

CHAPTER
TWENTY-FIVE

Pinpricks of sweat beaded Dexxter's brow as he watched the blonde chatting up Kyle. Dexx swiped at his forehead with the back of his hand, aware of Irene logging every move. He didn't care what she thought. He had already concocted a plan for her "accident."

Trevor led the group in their direction, and Dexx's hand went up to straighten a tie that wasn't there. He was in a lightweight madras blazer and an open neck shirt. He'd selected the outfit especially for the blonde in the pictures, assuming she was Amy.

He'd never given Amy more than a passing glance, but he'd known she had a thing for him. This woman was different; he couldn't count on her falling for him immediately. From the looks of it, she already had Jensen and Kyle after her. He would have to finesse this one.

"These are our new neighbors," Trevor said by way of introduction. "Irene Hanson and Dexxter Foxx. Irene, Dexx, this is Rochelle Ralston."

Dexx stuck out his hand, itching to touch her. "Call me Dexx. That's Dexxter with two Xs and Foxx with a double X."

She looked him directly in the eye, then giggled. "Oh, my, it sounds like a chromosome check, not a real name."

Everyone chuckled, even Irene, as Dexx stood, hand extended. Unfuckingbelievable! The blonde was having a laugh at his expense.

Shelly held up her hand, the fingers curled inward. "I can't shake, sorry. I was in an accident and my hand hasn't healed." She gazed at him as he withdrew his hand. "I'm sorry. I didn't mean to make fun of your name. I think it's . . . interesting."

Liar. *Interesting* was what people said just to be polite.

"I say the strangest things sometimes," Shelly went on. "They just pop into my head. It's a habit I've had for years. Right, Matt?"

"She's a troublemaker with a capital T. Always has been."

From the look on Jensen's face, Dexx could just imagine what kind of trouble. Dexxter's sense of embarrassment eased a bit. Close-up, Shelly was even better looking than he'd thought. The sound of her voice fascinated him. It was like raw silk, low-pitched and soft, yet with a slight rasp to it.

Nothing like Amy Conroy.

"Your parents probably, like, spent months to come up with your name, Dexx," commented the redhead. "Parents do weird stuff like that. Bubbles is my real name. Now, I ask you, is Bubbles, like, any kind of name to put on a birth certificate?"

Who gave a shit about her? Everyone, it seemed. The group sympathized, discussing names and their experiences. Even Irene jumped in, saying her name made her sound old, and it had been hard to live with as a child.

The fruity doctor, who had spent years wishing his name weren't Clive, brought Shelly a glass of wine. Kyle grabbed her attention with a story about how Kyle rhymed with bile and kids used to tease him.

Shelly leaned toward him, saying, "All my *friends* call me Shelly."

He decided she was coming on to him. Jensen's arm was still around her, but he was talking to Trevor and Kyle. This is more like it, Dexx thought, grinning at her.

Irene, sensing competition, no doubt, chimed in, "We're going to be married soon."

"That's wonderful," Shelly responded.

How humiliating, Dexx thought, outraged to have this beautiful woman think he'd want to marry the likes of Irene. Comparing Shelly to Irene was like trying to make a Thoroughbred out of horse shit. Irene's nails bit into his arm, and he knew she expected a response.

"We came down here to start a new business," he told Shelly.

"Matt and I are reporters."

"*Really?* Have you worked on some exciting cases?" Dexxter moved a little closer as he asked the question.

Shelly shook her head, a sexy gesture that sent her blond hair fluttering over her bare shoulders. "I've worked for tabloids mostly. You know, sex lives of movie stars and Elvis sightings. Matt was with *Exposé*."

"The newsmagazine?" Irene asked.

"That's right." Shelly turned her head toward Jensen, who was talking to Kyle. "Matt's covered lots of really interesting cases."

"Like, what case was your favorite, Matt?" asked the Bubbles creature.

Matt gazed at Shelly for a moment, an intimate look that fried Dexx, then Matt responded, "My favorite case was the one in Hawaii. Remember the woman who was discovered by a man out training a search-and-rescue dog? She'd been in a terrible accident. If he hadn't found her, she would have died."

"I remember that story," Irene said with uncharacteristic enthusiasm. "The woman had a head injury and lost her memory. She never recovered it. They couldn't identify her."

"I saw her story on television. *Missing!* did a segment on her, trying to get someone to come forward and identify her," Clive added. "The awesome part was that one of the shoes she was wearing belonged to a woman who had been murdered a year earlier."*

"I went to Hawaii," Matt said. "My article and pictures on Lucky's story got *Exposé* out of the red."

"Hello." A policeman dressed in khaki bermudas and a short-sleeve khaki shirt came out from the kitchen, an envelope in his hand. "No one answered the bell, but I could hear voices, so I came in."

Dexxter quickly looked at Irene. The police didn't make him nervous, but Irene had been jumpy since the FBI had come to the office. Irene lifted one dark brow and winked at Dexx.

Trevor walked toward the man. "You're not one of our regular officers. You must be one of the recruits from Key Largo."

"That's right, sir. They brought us down for the Fantasy Fest."

"Things get rowdy around here during Fantasy Fest," Clive told Irene and Dexx. "It's a lot like Mardi Gras where too many tourists get drunk and fight."

"What can we do for you?" Trevor asked.

"Chief Obermeyer sent me. He called this afternoon, but your phone was out of order."

"I knocked it off the hook and didn't notice for hours."

*See *Unforgettable*, Zebra Books, January, 1997.

"He wanted to let you know that the woman who was killed in the crash has been identified."

He extended the envelope, but didn't seem sure whom to give it to. Irene nudged Dexx, but his eyes were on Shelly. Chin tilted upward, Shelly looked expectantly at the officer.

Trevor took the envelope, opened it, and read its contents. "The forensic team in Miami has identified the victim as Amy Joyce Conroy of Seattle, Washington."

Dexxter watched Shelly's face remain impassive. Obviously, the name meant nothing to her. Irene poked him in the ribs again, and he was forced to take his eyes off Shelly. He whispered, "I guess Zane made a mistake."

"I don't know. This is weird." Irene shrugged.

"I'm supposed to bring in Miss Ralston for questioning," said the officer.

"Why?" Shelly's voice rose an octave. "I haven't done anything."

"The chief said something about the Conroy woman being in the Witness Protection Program. She might have told you something before she died."

Uh-oh.

The officer grinned, excited. "I'll bet it was a mob deal. A hit, maybe."

What if Amy had blabbed everything to the knockout blond, Dexx wondered. It didn't seem likely. Shelly hadn't batted a lash when they'd been introduced. She hadn't recognized his name.

Trevor said, "We're having a dinner party. Can't she come in tomorrow?"

"That woman didn't tell me anything," Shelly said. "She barely said two words."

"I thought you didn't remember the crash," Jensen said with a frown.

"I didn't until recently. Now I vaguely recall being at a Stop 'N Go, then I woke up in the hospital and you were there." The way she looked at Matt as she spoke made Dexx want to kick the jerk in the balls—hard. "A little has come back to me, but not much."

"Let's go call the chief," suggested the officer. "I'll ask him if it's okay to come in tomorrow instead."

A warning voice whispered in her head as she followed the officer into the house. The FBI had to be behind this. All her prints had been removed from databases and her dental records pulled. The only way Amy Joyce Conroy had died was because they had wanted it that way.

As soon as he had her inside, the officer said, "I'm Scott Phillips, special agent with the Federal Bureau of Investigation. I'm bringing you in."

"In where?"

"Into protective custody."

"Why? Dexxter Foxx thinks I'm dead."

"Maybe he bought it, and maybe not. We're close to making a case on him, but we need your testimony to cinch it."

"The Bureau knew where I was all along, didn't they?"

"Yes. When Dr. Burroughs requested bioengineered skin from DermaGraft, the company notified us. The technology is still experimental. They monitor its use. We checked and found Clive Burroughs was doing reconstructive surgery on an accident victim." The agent shrugged. "We figured you were as safe here as anywhere."

A dead federal marshal and two other murders could be attributed to Dexxter Foxx. She should have known the FBI would relentlessly pursue the one woman who could link him with the crimes.

"How did you find me?"

"Through the Miami office. They tried—unsuccessfully—to ID the other accident victim. One of our agents looked into the accident and discovered you. We were going to take you to a safe house again and start over. Instead, we took the precaution of altering the records. Prints, dental charts, vital stats. You are now Rochelle Ralston. Just don't forget your mother's maiden name was Merriman."

Scary. After pretending to be Shelly, now she *was* Shelly as far as the world was concerned.

"Come on. We're outta here."

"Wait. Think about this. If I suddenly disappear, isn't Dexxter going to smell a rat? We're so close to Mexico. He could run, and you'd never get him."

He hesitated. "I was told to bring you in."

In a split second she made a decision that she hoped wouldn't cost her life. But in her mind she heard Matt calling her back from the near death. She loved him with all her heart, and she had no intention of leaving him.

She had looked directly into Dexxter's eyes, behaving like a bad girl. Okay, her version of one. The wimp hadn't shown a flicker of recognition. If anyone suspected the truth, it was Irene. They had never known each other well. Irene had been too busy prancing around, trying in vain to get Dexxter's attention, to notice a disfigured woman glued to her computer terminal.

"I'm not coming with you. Your protection stinks."

"We had a leak, but it's been fixed."

"Why didn't you warn me that he was coming? They've been here for at least two days."

The guy shook his head. "Irene Hanson made the arrangements. We didn't have Irene under surveillance. When Dexxter disappeared, it took us a while to locate him."

"Great. Another few hours and I might have been murdered in my sleep."

"I don't think so. We had our profiler work on this case. She says Dexxter has a personality disorder. He believes he's handsome and invincible. But he's not brave enough to kill anyone himself."

"Handsome, Dexxter? Now, that's a stretch." He was short and average-looking, not terrible, but nothing like Matt. "I've always wondered what Irene saw in him."

"They've been together since they were kids. We haven't studied her too closely because until now Dexxter hadn't shown much interest in her."

"They're engaged."

"Really? That'll throw the profiler for a loop. According to her, Dexxter doesn't have relationships with women. He uses prostitutes. He may not realize it, but he does this because he doesn't want to be turned down by a woman."

"Irene will never turn him down. I swear, she behaved like a lovesick puppy the whole time I worked for him. If he paid any attention to a woman in the office, Irene saw that she was fired. There was even a rumor that she pushed one woman down a flight of stairs just because she worked late one night with Dexxter."

"He's suddenly decided to marry Irene. It doesn't fit the profile."

"Coming to kill me doesn't fit either. He had the whistle-blowers in Asia taken care of, didn't he?" Scott nodded thoughtfully, and she continued. "He had someone fire-bomb the house where I was living. It doesn't make sense that he would come here and take care of me personally."

"Something else is going on, but what?"

"I'll try to find out."

"No, stay away from him. It's too dangerous. We've been feeding him false information, so he doesn't realize how close we are to arresting him."

"Hurry up. When you need me to testify, I'll be here."

"I could get a court order and have you held in the protection program as a material witness."

"You could, but if you guys are smart, you'll see that I'm right. Don't tip your hand now. Let me handle Dexx."

He studied her a moment, then said, "You're going to have to explain the dog. That's how they located you."

She gave herself a mental pat on the back. A producer looking for an "unusual" dog had been very suspicious. "I'll make up something."

He made her memorize his phone number, then reluctantly left. She decided the simplest explanation about Jiggs would be the best. Less to trip up on. She manufactured a smile and walked back to the group.

"What took so long?" Kyle asked.

"I answered the chief's questions over the telephone."

"Let's sit down," Trevor said, making shooing motions with his hands. "Clive has made Coquilles Saint-Jacques. They're no good if they're overdone."

Matt pulled out a chair for her, and she sat down, still smiling like the village idiot. Dexxter grabbed the seat next to her. Irene had to clear her throat twice before he stood up and pulled out the chair for her.

The scalding look Irene threw her would have made the devil shudder, but she had more on her mind than a jealous woman. She had to convince Dexx that she really was Rochelle Ralston.

Kyle and Bubbles sat opposite her, laughing and joking. Trevor helped Clive serve the first course, oysters on the half-shell, then they sat down. She didn't know how to begin, but Kyle saved her by asking a question.

"Were you able to help the police chief?"

Everyone was eating the oysters, but their eyes were on her—especially Matt's. She should be more worried about Dexxter, but Matt was the one who knew her best. He might detect something the others couldn't and know she was lying. If he gave her away, no telling what Dexx would do.

"I'm afraid I wasn't much help. A few details have come back to me, but not much."

She forced herself to look Dexx in the eye. It wasn't suspicion she saw, but something more like lust. From the tight set of Irene's thin lips, it was evident she noticed it too.

"Like what details?" Bubbles wanted to know.

"We don't want to bore Dexx and Irene—"

"We're not bored," Irene assured her. "While you were on the phone, they told us all about the crash and Clive's remarkable work when half your face was sheared off in that horrible accident."

"What did the police chief have to say?" Kyle asked again.

She leaned forward slightly as if this was just so *intriguing*. "It seems the woman had information on some important case. They wanted to know if she had told me anything."

"Had she?" Clive asked.

"No, she hardly said a thing. She didn't even tell me her name."

"Now, let me get this straight. She was in your car, not the diesel truck, the way we originally thought."

She didn't like the challenging tone in Matt's voice. Dexx was slurping down the oysters as if he were listening only to be polite. Irene's eye had a gleam of something she didn't care to examine too closely.

"That's right. Somewhere north of Miami I stopped at a gas station. She asked for a ride—"

"You should never pick up hitchhikers," Dexx said, leaning a little too close to her as he spoke.

Irene chimed in, "*Anything* can happen."

She gazed at Trevor because she knew he would understand. "The woman had a little dog in her arms. The two of them looked so pathetic. Half the dog's ear was missing, and the woman had this horrid birthmark on her face. She said she'd been traveling for days and wanted to know if I would give her a ride to Miami."

The sympathy in Trevor's eyes was unmistakable. He would have seen the beauty in The Beast. Had they met under different circumstances, they still would have been friends.

"I thought she was homeless. I said to myself: There but for the grace of God go I."

"Oh, Shelly, that's, like, so sweet."

She smiled at Bubbles but didn't venture a glance in Matt's direction. Was something in her voice giving her away?

"Did you talk to her?" Kyle asked.

"It's all pretty vague. I didn't remember any of it until the last day or so."

Clive asked, "Why didn't you go to the police?"

"What good would it have done?" Trevor asked. "The woman was already dead. Shelly didn't recall anything helpful."

"I was waiting to see if I remembered more." She might have jumped in a little too quickly. There was a distinct quaver in her voice. "But I don't think there's much more to remember. The woman said she was exhausted. She got in the backseat and went to sleep."

"Why didn't you let her off in Miami?" Matt asked.

She ventured a look at him and lifted her shoulders in a perplexed shrug. "I have absolutely no idea."

"Maybe the woman, like, told you this awesome secret. That's why you brought her to Key West with you."

Oh, no, Bubbles, please.

"One day you'll remember everything about the accident." Irene's voice was just a shade too calculating.

How stupid could she be? She'd painted herself into a corner.

CHAPTER
TWENTY-SIX

Somehow, she made it through dinner. The scallops Clive had prepared were nothing short of a work of art, but she had to force herself to eat them. In her lame attempt to explain why she had Jiggs, she'd made her plight even worse. She had given Dexxter every reason to believe she might recall something that could be dangerous to him.

Not that Dexxter acted as if it bothered him. He kept flirting with her and ignoring Irene. All through the meal and the fabulous mango crème brûlé that was Clive's specialty, Matt had been quiet. He chatted with others, seldom talking to her.

But he wasn't himself.

She suspected that he hadn't bought her story about Jiggs. She tried to think how to handle the situation. It was difficult to concentrate with everyone talking to her and Dexxter tracking her every move with his reptilian eyes.

"We really must go," Irene said when the group had finished their coffee.

Dexxter opened his mouth to protest, but the look Irene shot at him would have buckled steel. Everyone else stood to leave and complimented Clive and Trevor on the meal.

"It was great meeting all of you," Dexxter said, but his eyes were on her. "I'm looking forward to getting to know you better."

What she was looking forward to was seeing him in handcuffs.

They left with Kyle, who was house-sitting next door to Half Moon Bay. Bubbles wandered off. She went into the kitchen to help clean up.

"Run along," Clive said. "We've got this handled."

She turned, expecting to find Matt at her elbow, the way he'd been all evening. He was nowhere in sight. Something was wrong, and she dreaded finding out what it was.

She had told so many lies.

If Matt confronted her, she was half tempted to tell him the truth. But Dexxter was right there on the island. She refused to jeopardize the people who had helped her—especially Matt.

Until tonight, when she was faced with leaving him, she hadn't allowed herself to admit that she had fallen head over heels in love with him. She'd led an insular life, and now, having found such a wonderful man, she didn't want anything to happen to him.

She'd rather die herself.

Walking out to the terrace, she saw Matt standing down by the water, where he liked to go. She slowed her pace, reluctant to face him, yet knowing she had no other choice. Putting it off wasn't going to make it any easier. She walked across the grass and left her thongs beside Matt's shoes.

"When are you going to tell me what's going on?" he asked as she stopped beside him. His eyes were sharp and assessing; unbridled anger punctuated every word.

"What do you mean?"

"You know exactly what I'm talking about. I saw how you acted when you were in the hospital. You cried when we brought you Jiggs. Don't expect me to believe that bullshit about him being someone else's dog."

He put his hands lightly on her waist, then let them drift upward. Through the sheer dress, she felt his warm fingers skimming her rib cage. When he reached her breasts, he cradled them, one in each hand, and squeezed gently.

"This isn't Clive's work. He told me so. These babies are the real thing." He leaned a little closer until they were almost nose to nose and said, "Who are you? Why in hell are you pretending to be Shelly?"

Torn by conflicting emotions, she hesitated. You can't tell him, cautioned an inner voice. Get away from him before you drag him into this.

She turned and sprinted across the sand, hit the grass full speed, and kept going without stopping for her shoes. Scott Phillips had given her an emergency number. If she called him now, he could get her out of here tonight.

She reached the terrace. Matt thundered up behind her. His powerful hands grabbed her shoulders and whirled her around, bringing her flush against the muscular length of him.

"Don't even *think* of running away from me, babe."

She'd seen that look in his eyes before and knew exactly what it meant. He backed her up against one of the limestone pillars, supporting the lattice overhang that shaded the terrace. The stone was cold and hard against her back, his body hot and unyielding against her front side.

"You have a way of getting to me even when I'm pissed at you big-time." He pressed a burgeoning erection against her, just in case she misunderstood. "Then my brain goes below my belt."

"Surprise, surprise."

"Don't tell me, whoever you are, that you're not hot for me."

She struggled to get away, but his body was too strong. In a way, it was exciting to be trapped like this. Savoring the heat rising from his chest and the pounding of his heart against hers, she waited.

He captured one breast with his hand and tested the nipple with his thumb. "See? You can't help yourself."

There was no use denying it. The needs of her body, so long denied, eagerly responded to him. It had been that way from the first. Now that she had experienced the height of sensual pleasure, her body yearned for him all the time.

"Even without knowing your name, I want you so much I hate myself."

He kneed her legs apart and settled his erection between her thighs. Moist heat seeped into her loins, and she couldn't resist arching her hips just a little to get closer.

He lowered his head, his lips seeking hers. There was nothing artistic about the bruising kiss. With a savage thrust of his tongue, he was inside her mouth. She couldn't help curling her own tongue around his as she clung to his shoulders.

He cupped her bottom in his hands, moving her up and down against the iron heat of his sex. The silky fabric of the dress slid back and forth in a way that was even more erotic than if they had been undressed.

Any second he was going to take her, standing up on the terrace. She wrenched her head away from the wildly carnal kiss. "L-let's go inside."

His answer was to hoist up her dress and yank down her panty hose. The sheer nylons ripped apart before they cleared her thighs.

"What's, like, going on out there?" Bubbles called from inside the house.

"Mind your own damn business," Matt snarled.

"Well, I, like never . . ." Bubble's voice trailed off.

"My room is closest," she managed to gasp as Matt kissed the sensitive curve of her neck just below her ear.

"I won't make it."

His voice was a low rasp with a slight tremor to it. She believed him; she was remarkably close to an orgasm herself, considering he'd just kissed her once.

He unzipped his trousers, freeing himself with a low moan and shoving the trousers to his knees. Protruding from a dark tuft of hair, his stiff erection jutted outward. He guided it forward, probing at the delicate folds between her legs, searching for the right spot. She clung to his shoulders as the velvet-smooth tip of his sex found its target.

His breath coming in heavy, uneven pants, he grabbed her buttocks with both hands and buried himself to the hilt. "Aw, hell, there's nothing better than being inside you. Nothing."

She could tell he was angry with himself, but she couldn't stop being just a little proud. She loved this man and couldn't resist him even when he was making love to her out of anger. It was only fair that she have the same power over him.

He'd filled her completely, stretching her until she was positive she would rip apart. He began to move, pummeling her with hard, demanding thrusts.

"Yes, yes," she heard herself moan softly.

He pounded away, lancing her body with pleasure each time he drove into her. Seconds later, a series of small contractions became one overpowering sensation. The orgasm lasted and lasted as her own body shattered around her with unimaginable pleasure.

She opened her eyes, not realizing she had squeezed them shut. He was still working, his face a mask of pain. Then his whole body convulsed. He let out a curse that could have been heard in Key West. And stopped.

He released her and she sagged against the cool pillar. With as much dignity as she could muster, she removed the torn panty hose and straightened her dress. She hurried to her room and locked the door.

Somehow Bingo and Jiggs had gotten in and were on her bed,

sleeping. "Change your clothes and make that call," she said out loud.

An angry fist pounded on the door. Bingo and Jiggs jumped off the bed and raced for the bathroom. She didn't have to ask who it was.

"Go away. We'll talk in the morning." Of course, she didn't plan to be here then.

"Let me in or I'll break down the door."

A moment later a *thunk* rattled the door's hinges. Matt meant it. He was going to break down Trevor's beautiful door. She flipped the latch, and he exploded into the room.

He stood before her, breathing like a long distance runner. A trickle of sweat ran down the side of his temple.

"You didn't let me finish talking to you."

"Conversation wasn't on your mind."

"Back at the beach it was."

"All right, I'm listening." She closed the door, then turned to him.

"You know, I thought we had something going . . . something special. But you don't trust me. What's a relationship without trust? Nothing."

There was an edge to his voice that some might have mistaken for anger. But she'd seen him angry and had been the object of his fury. This wasn't anger; it was hurt.

A lump rose in her throat and tears pricked hotly at the back of her eyes. No man had ever *cared* about her—ever. If she didn't do something, she would destroy their relationship.

"You're wrong, Matt. I do trust you—with my life. What's more, I love you with all my heart."

Evidently, he hadn't expected this. His expression stilled and became even more serious. "Oh, angel," he said as he pulled her into his arms. "You know I'm crazy about you. Tell me who you really are. I'll do anything to help you."

That was what she was afraid of. He was the kind of man who would die trying to protect her. She opted to tell him part of the truth. "You can help me most if you don't let anyone know I'm not Shelly. She died in the crash. I'm Amy Joyce Conroy, and I'm in terrible danger if certain people know I'm alive."

"I don't get it. The cop just said—"

"Scott Phillips is an FBI agent. He was only posing as a police officer. He really came to take me back into the Witness Protection Program, but I wouldn't go. Now that I found you, I didn't want to leave you."

He hugged her so tight that she could barely draw a breath, then he kissed the top of her head. He gazed down at her, asking, "I don't want anything to happen to you. Are you safe here?"

"Yes," she hedged, "as long as everyone believes I'm Shelly, then it's just as good as being in the Witness Protection Program. Much, much better, actually, because I'm with you."

The even, whiteness of his thrilled smile dazzled her. She was glad she'd told him she loved him. Granted, he was only "crazy" about her, but after a lifetime of loneliness, it was enough.

"Why are you in the program?"

"If I tell you, they might kill you." She caressed his cheek with her hand. "For your own protection, that's all I can say. Trust me."

He frowned, but reluctantly nodded, seeming to accept her decision.

CHAPTER
TWENTY-SEVEN

Stealing its way between the shutters, a slanting bar of moonlight played across Shelly's face as she slept.

No. Not Shelly.

"Amy," he whispered. "Amy Joyce Conroy."

They had agreed that it was too risky to use her real name, but Matt couldn't resist trying it. "Amy." Her name sounded so . . . right.

"You idiot," he cursed himself. He should have figured out sooner that she wasn't the woman he'd known in New York.

The chemistry between them had been too powerful. Even before she was able to speak to him, he'd been drawn to her, and despite his best efforts, he couldn't break free. There had been other subtle clues as well. Something about her had struck him as being slightly shy and innocent. He'd been proven right when they'd made love.

After he realized she was impersonating Shelly, a thousand scenarios had run through his mind, but being in the Witness Protection Program hadn't been among them. The FBI must think she was in some sort of danger, or they wouldn't have sent an agent to get her. She hadn't gone because she loved him.

"Amy," he muttered under his breath again. Watching her sleep, her injured hand curled near her cheek, he marveled at the miracle that had come so unexpectedly into his life. "Amy Conroy."

After she'd told him who she was, they'd made love again. This time they'd taken it slowly, and it had been even more pleasurable than the primitive mating on the terrace. He'd crossed an invisible line into some uncharted realm of emotion that was more intense—and satisfying—than anything he'd ever experienced.

"It isn't fair to her," he said to himself, thinking about his own terrible secret. In the end, he would hurt her, but he couldn't help himself. He loved her more deeply than he could have ever imagined. Leaving her now was out of the question.

Still, one day soon it would be time to face his problems. That would mean turning his back on this special woman who loved him more than he could possibly be worthy of.

She shifted position, and he resisted the urge to touch her. If he did they would be making love again. He couldn't help her until he found out more about her troubles.

Taking care not to wake her, Matt eased out of bed. He found his trousers in a heap on the floor. Bingo and Jiggs were snoozing on top of them. He roused the animals and pulled on his pants.

Not bothering with his shirt, he slipped out of the room barefoot, Jiggs and Bingo at his heels. The house was dark, his only guide was the moonlight filtering through the plantation shutters.

He walked into his room and flipped on the lights. He suddenly realized the nagging headache had vanished. With luck it had just been too much sun. Hell, he hoped so. She needed him, and he didn't want the headaches to begin now.

"If only you could talk," he said to Jiggs. "You could tell me all about her."

He found his laptop in the closet under his duffel bag. He hadn't touched it since he'd left New York. He sat on the bed and Bingo hopped up beside him. Naturally, Jiggs followed.

Waiting for the machine to boot up, he plugged into the phone line, then said, "Are you two going to watch?"

They settled at his elbow, seemingly fascinated by the now-lit screen. Years of training as an investigative reporter kicked-in. Despite resigning, Matt hadn't canceled an Internet service called Information Unlimited. For a monthly fee plus search charges, you could locate anyone.

Most of the time, the service found the person and could tell you their last known address, phone number, credit status, and a helluva lot more. He typed in her name and Seattle, otherwise he ran the risk of bringing up every Amy Joyce Conroy in the whole damn country.

"Deceased" flashed on the screen along with the date, and Key West, Florida. Okay, the FBI had entered the bogus death, but they hadn't reentered the information that the Witness Protection Program deleted when she went into hiding. IU had nothing else on her.

Next, he switched to Lifestyles America, an organization that tracked buying habits of Americans. Logging credit card purchases, recording warranty cards, the service advised big corporations—or anyone who could afford it—about what America was buying.

Nothing.

"The Feebies were thorough," he told Bingo who was washing his ears with his hind paw. Jiggs had fallen asleep. "That's it for the legal route."

He looked up the code that he kept in his Filofax under "D" for "desperate." When he'd been desperate for information as a reporter, he knew how to tap in to the supposedly secure social security database. It was a federal crime to hack in to it, but anyone with half a brain could. It just might be the only database that the Witness Protection Program hadn't wiped out.

He typed in her name. His entire screen filled with Amy Joyce Conroys. He scrolled down, searching for Seattle. "Bingo!" he said with a laugh as the cat peered up at him with his one eye.

Then he took a closer look at the information, reading out loud. "Employer: Foxx Enterprises. Holy shit!"

"That's why the FBI came for her tonight. Dexxter Foxx is involved."

Dexx—the double XX—had shifty little eyes and oozed phony sincerity like a TV evangelist. Matt had written him off the minute he'd met him. He tried to recall everything the little prick had said.

Small talk, mostly as he flirted with "Shelly." Lounge-lizard stuff that wasn't very intelligent or sophisticated. But his fiancée, Irene, had been pissed off big-time by all the attention Dexx paid to Shelly.

"This doesn't make sense," he said out loud. "If Dexxter knows her, why didn't he say something when the FBI agent said Amy had been killed in an accident?"

His gut instinct told him that she was in danger. He went back to her room and found her still sleeping at an angle across the bed, her body half-covered by the sheet. As he sat on the bed, the springs gave and she opened her eyes.

"Tell me about Dexxter Foxx."

She scrambled to a sitting position. "What about him?"

"Come on, honey. I'm a reporter. It didn't take me two minutes to find out you worked for him."

"Matt, stay out of this. I—"

"Why doesn't Dexxter recognize you?"

She hesitated a moment, measuring him with a worried frown, then seemed to decide she wasn't going to avoid telling him the rest of the story. "No, apparently Dexxter didn't know it was me."

"Did surgery change your face that much?"

She hesitated, longer this time. "It's a long story. I—ah . . ."

"Tell me about it. I love you. I want to help, but this doesn't make a damn bit of sense."

"Love?" she whispered as if it were a foreign word.

"Of course, I told you I was crazy about you." He didn't understand women. She seemed genuinely stunned as if she didn't realize how he felt about her.

"Being crazy is . . . different than love."

To him it wasn't but he didn't want to argue. He brushed a wisp of hair off her cheek. "It's hard for a man to say 'I love you' to a woman. I do love you—more than you'll ever know."

She put her hands on his cheeks and gazed into his eyes. There was no need for words. He could see the depth of her love. With every fiber of his being, he wished he could live for years and years to love her. If only he could make up for the way she had suffered before fate had brought them together.

"If you want to help, play along. Pretend I'm Rochelle Ralston."

"I can't blindly play along." He pulled her into his arms, saying, "Trust me."

"It isn't a matter of trust. It's . . ." She moved away with a troubled shrug. "You don't know me." She pointed to her face. "This isn't me. Surgery has made me look exactly like my mother. For years I was someone else. The Beast."

"The Beast? Yeah, sure."

"It's true. I had a horrid birthmark covering the side of my face. It was so bad that people looked the other way when I came into a room."

He was momentarily speechless, trying to imagine this beautiful woman revolting people. From the tone of her voice, he knew the experience had scarred her emotionally as well as physically.

"I wouldn't have looked away."

"Yes, you would have. It's a normal reaction. Kind, actually. The rude people stare. The cruel ones make nasty remarks."

"Honey, I'm so sorry." He recalled something she'd said, and the depth of her misery hit him. "When you were talking about the pathetic woman and the half-eared dog, you were talking about yourself, weren't you?"

"Yes, I *was* pathetic. The birthmark turned me into a loner without much self-esteem. I told myself I didn't care because I didn't want to admit how much it hurt. The accident gave me a new life. It brought me to you.

"I'm not running and I'm not hiding. That's what The Beast would have done. We deserve a lifetime together, but we're not going to get it. Let's enjoy the time we do have."

She spoke with quiet yet determined firmness. He knew he would never change her mind. She had sacrificed her safety because she truly loved him. Raw emotion swelled in his chest, and his heart actually ached.

"What about Dexxter?" he asked, anxious to fully understand the situation.

"I'm certain he doesn't know who I am. He must have come here to check." She thought a moment, then added, "He never does the dirty work himself, at least he hasn't before."

"You'd better start at the beginning. When did you first meet the double X?"

"After I completed my master's at the University of Washington, I went job hunting. Despite glowing references from my professors, no one hired me." She was making a valiant attempt to check the emotion filtering into her voice, but he picked up on it. "The birthmark made people uncomfortable."

He wanted to hug her tight, but he was afraid if he did, he would break down. She had endured a lifetime of suffering. Now, her love for him had opened a trap door. Without knowing it, she was falling into a pit where even more pain and misery awaited her—when he told her about his problem.

"I had to earn a living. My mother was ill with Parkinson's. When Dexxter offered me a job, I immediately accepted."

"What was your relationship with Dexx like?"

"I rarely saw him. I reported to the head of the computer department. A few times I caught him watching my good side." She patted her left cheek. "From one side I wasn't half bad. My nose was a little long before Clive fixed it, but I was passable. When you saw my full face, well, one guy called me Beauty and The Beast."

The tautness in her voice told him how much that cruel remark had hurt her. The realization unleashed a tenderness, a protective-ness that he hadn't experienced before. If he could find the dumb-ass who'd callously called her that name, he'd deck the bastard.

"Dexxter was notorious around Foxx Enterprises for having pros-titutes service him in his office. When I worked there, Dexx never had a girlfriend, even though Irene made it clear she was available."

Matt listened while she explained the FBI profiler's valuation of Dexxter. What it boiled down to was the man was a coward who didn't have relationships with women because that would dash his version of reality.

"Maybe Dexx sees Irene as someone *safe* because he's known her since they were kids," he suggested.

"Possibly, but why isn't she wearing an engagement ring?"

"Trust a woman to notice," he said. "I picked up on something you might not have. Dexxter is hot for you."

"You're kidding," she said, wide–eyed. "Well, I did realize each time he talked to me that Irene's claws itched to draw blood."

"Okay, so his love life is screwed up. Why does the FBI want him? That's the key to the puzzle."

"I became suspicious when I realized the Research and Development Department had only two people in it. If you know anything about software companies, you would find this odd. R and D can take up half the building. You have to invest a lot in develop-ment to stay ahead."

"Did you ask Dexxter about it?"

"Yes, he said most of the R and D was in Singapore, which isn't unusual. The computer business has grown so rapidly that we don't have the manpower to handle it all in this country.

"Out of curiosity, I e–mailed R and D in our Singapore office where the software is actually manufactured. There were four people in that unit, but all they were designing was packaging."

"Dexxter was pirating software and selling it as his own," Matt guessed.

"Exactly and it gets worse. He reproduced the software under less than ideal conditions. The failure rate was bound to be astronomical. Some of the phony software went into planes. Private jets, mostly, but the Pacific Rim airliner that crashed in Malaysia was using his software."

"I remember that crash. A reporter from the *Post* was on it."

"The accident made me even more suspicious. I e-mailed my contact in Singapore R and D that there were only two R and D people in Seattle. He started asking a lot of questions, and Dexxter had him killed. A week later, another man in the Singapore office was murdered."

"Dexxter was in Seattle when all this went on?"

"Yes. I knew if Dexx thought to check their e-mail, he would find out about me. My mother was near death, so I couldn't run. I didn't want to go to the authorities and be dragged in for questioning. I needed to stay at my mother's side. I loved her so much. I wanted to be with her . . . until the end."

With a rush of tenderness, he imagined a lonely young woman waiting those final hours at her mother's side. He remembered the feeling from his own youth. Her situation must have been even worse. He'd had his sister to share his grief and comfort him.

She had been all alone.

"After my mother's funeral, I went to the authorities. They took me to a safe house where I stayed until they could arrange a new identity. Dexxter found me. You see, The Beast was easy to spot with that livid birthmark."

"Couldn't it be removed with a laser?"

"Yes, and they had an appointment set up. Dexxter's man found me first."

"What a run of bad luck," he said, unable to imagine a life on the run, a killer dogging every step. "After the accident, Clive changed your face enough to fool Dexxter, right?"

Her arms slid around his waist and she burrowed against him, saying, "Yes, and the accident brought us together. I've never been so happy."

"I don't deserve you," he said, and he meant it. There had been other women in his life but no one who had been through so much yet loved him unselfishly. Another woman would turn her back and leap at the opportunity to enjoy a new life after being The Beast for so long.

He owed it to her to tell her the truth about himself.

This wasn't a discussion he planned to have with her until it was time for him to leave—months from now. But her confession changed things radically. There was no easy segue into this, so he opted for the direct approach.

"Remember me telling you about my mother?"

"She died when you were thirteen, right?"

"Yes. My mother had a brain tumor. I had no idea Mom's condition was"—Matt let out an audible breath—"hereditary."

She became utterly still. Only her eyes moved, searching his face in disbelief. "Oh, my God! Darling, you can't mean . . ."

He clenched his jaw hard to keep the lump in his throat where it belonged. "I'm going to die."

She threw her arms around him, currents of emotion deepening the blue of her eyes. "There must be a mistake. You seem so healthy."

"I am—now." He decided not to mention the headaches that would soon intensify into debilitating migraines. "I wouldn't even know I had a problem if I hadn't had an MRI after I was in a fender-bender. This type of tumor grows very slowly. I have a year, maybe longer."

He didn't add his mother had died a slow, agonizing death. Her speech slurred, then became too garbled to understand. Writing was impossible. She lost control of her muscles, and near the end she became blind.

It had been long ago, in another lifetime. Still, his mother's death remained one of the most vivid memories from his youth. He'd watched her suffer, unable to do a damn thing to relieve her pain. Before he became incapacitated, he planned to disappear and die alone. He couldn't put those he loved—especially this woman—through that kind of heartbreak.

"Have you had a second opinion?" she asked.

"Three of them. Surgery will leave me a vegetable."

"Oh, Matt, this isn't fair."

She hugged him tighter. He put his arms around her, loving her so much that his eyes blurred with tears as he tried to imagine leaving her behind. He thought of all the things he would miss. He'd always counted on tomorrow.

He'd wanted a big family, probably because he'd raised himself. Yes, he wanted to experience fatherhood. He almost heard his children's high-pitched laughter. And the lower, feminine laughter of this woman, their mother.

Almost.

Like it or not, he had to face reality. His tomorrows were numbered. All he had was the present. It had taken him so long to find love, and now that he had, he was going to enjoy it.

Until it was time for him to say good-bye.

"I have nothing left to lose except you," he told her, gazing into the beautiful blue eyes he loved so much. "You're in danger here. Go into the protection program again. I'll come with you."

She shook her head and tousled hair brushed over her bare shoulders. "No. We need the freedom to go wherever you want and do the th–things"—biting her lip, she looked away, eyes brimming with tears.

"Aw, honey, don't cry." He held her snugly against his chest. "It doesn't help. Crying only makes me feel worse."

"I'm not crying." A soft little sob escaped her lips as she blinked away the tears. "I'm not taking you into the program. We would have to live in some podunk town. You need to travel or do whatever you want."

"All I want is to be with you—anywhere. But I'm afraid for you. You're in danger."

CHAPTER
TWENTY-EIGHT

She dressed quickly after Matt left to shower and shave. Then she raced across the house to find Trevor. Matt had sworn her to secrecy about his illness. No way was she going to stand by and watch him die. There had to be something a doctor—somewhere—could do.

In the kitchen she found Trevor feeding the cats. "I've got to talk to you."

"Sure. What's up?" Trevor filled the last cat's bowl, then turned to her.

"It's Matt. He's, he's . . . very, very ill. He—"

"Call 911." Trevor headed for the telephone on the counter.

"Wait. He's not ill right now, but he's going to be."

Trevor took her arm and led her out onto the terrace. "You're not making sense. Let's sit down and talk about it."

She dropped into one of the chairs at the table where they usually had breakfast and blurted out, "Matt told me last night that he has a brain tumor."

The color leached from Trevor's face. "Like his mother?"

"It's a rare condition that's hereditary, it seems."

"What about his sister?"

"Emily shows no signs of having it yet. They're monitoring her." She gazed into Trevor's green eyes, his concern mirroring hers. "He doesn't want anyone to know he's dying."

Trevor covered his mouth with his hand, muffling a gasp. "Is he sure?"

"He's had three opinions. They all agree. Removing it would leave him a vegetable."

Muffin, one of Trevor's cats, jumped into his lap. He absentmind-edly petted it, saying, "Now I understand why Matt quit his job."

"I have an idea," she said, touching his shoulder. "Would you ask Clive to request Matt's medical records from Sloan-Kettering?"

"What good will that do?"

"Clive can contact clinics around the country, around the world if necessary, and see if anyone can help Matt." Panic like nothing she'd ever known tightened her throat until she could hardly speak. What if no one could help him? "I don't know what else to do."

Trevor shook his head slowly. "Neither do I."

"Remember, act upbeat around him. Don't let him know I told you."

"One of the first things they teach you in the Witness Protection Program is to use a public telephone, then you don't have to be con-cerned about anyone listening to your conversation," she told him.

Matt was walking beside "Shelly," as they approached Planet Hollywood. A public telephone was located near the thatched roof where they sold T-shirts. Even though it wasn't yet ten o'clock, it looked as if they were having an after Christmas sale.

He watched her dial the Miami number the agent had given her. She cocked the receiver so he could hear. He bent down and put his arm around her while the number rang. Scott Phillips answered.

Matt listened while she explained that he knew what was going on. The agent sounded pissed, but there wasn't a damn thing he could do about it.

"While Dexxter was at the party, Barry, another agent assigned to the case, bugged the home where Dexxter is staying. He also put a tracking device on the Boston Whaler that came with the house. We're watching Dexxter's every move."

"From Miami?" Matt asked.

"You're calling my cell phone, which has the Miami field office number. I'm right here at the Pier House with Barry. We're monitor-ing the bugs at Foxx's place."

Matt asked, "Do they buy her cover story?"

"From their conversation, they do not suspect Amy Conroy is still alive. Irene was suspicious, but Dexx convinced her. Then Irene pitched a fit over all the attention Dexxter paid to Shelly. The fight ended up in a knock-down-drag-out round of sex that blistered our ears."

"Do you know why they're here?" she asked.

"They're setting up a gambling operation on the Internet and use a bank in Grand Cayman. Key West is just a short hop from there."

"At least he isn't putting people's lives at risk this time," she told the agent.

His derisive snort shot out of the receiver. "He's responsible for a federal marshal's death as well as two men in Singapore. Then there's the hundred and eighty-five people who died in the airliner crash. I'd say he—" A muffled brushing sound of a hand being clamped over the telephone. Then, "Barry's picking up something."

It sounded as if the Feebies had things under control, but his sixth sense kicked in. Suddenly, he was sweating as if the sun were blistering down on him even though they were under the shady canopy of a gumbo limbo tree.

"Dexx and Irene are coming into Key West," the agent told them. "Barry will tail them."

"What if they split up?" Matt asked.

"Barry will stay with Dexxter."

Matt didn't like it one damn bit. Irene had cunning eyes filled with ruthlessness. Call it reporter's intuition, but he felt Irene was just as dangerous as the little double X jackass. Maybe more dangerous.

Dexxter mulled over his new plan as he rode with Irene on the water shuttle from Sunset Key to Key West. The plan had come to him in the middle of the night. He'd awakened, tangled in sheets that reeked of sex and sweat, and found Irene sharing his pillow. He'd almost puked.

Fucking her brains out was one thing because he could pretend she was another woman. Sleeping in the same bed was revolting. In his mind the stunning blonde that he'd once believed was Amy Conroy had morphed into Rochelle Ralston, the woman he wanted to share his pillow.

Rochelle. What a classy name.

Irene Hanson. That name sounded like a blue-haired old lady with dentures.

Last night he'd decided on her "accident." What he needed to do now was ditch her for an hour so he could buy what he needed. Trouble was, she stuck to him like a stink on shit.

"Irene, why don't you buy a new outfit? I'll meet you at Karumba! for lunch at one."

"Where are you going?"

"I want to surprise you."

"I don't like surprises."

"This one, you will."

She was suspicious, but ducked into Fast Buck Freddie's to shop. He rounded the corner and walked several blocks. Bahama Village. It sounded quaint in the guides, but you'd have to be dumber than dirt not to realize this was the wrong side of the tracks. He'd bet anything could be had—for a price—in Bahama Village.

Houses jammed together. Chickens scratching in the dirt front yards where grass should have been. Cuban grocery stores and African fabric shops. Caribbean voodoo shops. The place was culturally challenged.

He found the gun shop he was looking for up an alley near the Blue Heaven restaurant. The guidebook had touted the café as "authentic, fabulous." He wouldn't eat there on a bet. Friggin' roosters were running all over the place.

He bought the Tazer and listened carefully while a three-hundred-pound black man gave him instructions on how to use the stun gun.

"Doncha know, mon, the power of de Tazer is in its battery. Ya gotta keep her charged."

Dexxter could hardly understand the thick Bahamian accent, but he needed to verify the intriguing information he'd picked up on the National Rifle Association Web site.

"If I use this on full power, it'll leave a bruise, right?"

The man's eyes narrowed. "Dat's right. Could break de bone."

"If I let the battery drain to half power, then there wouldn't be any bruising. The person is still helpless, unable to move or breathe for about a minute, true?"

The man rocked back on his heels, hands on the counter, and studied Dexx with eyes that were now just slits in folds of fat. Way to go, meathead. Dexx had aroused the man's suspicions.

"I'm just checking. My girlfriend goes in for kinky sex, but I wouldn't want to hurt her."

A blazing flash of big white teeth in a very dark face. The knowing smile told Dexx that he'd erased those suspicions. Was he good, or what?

"Mon, ya need some poppers. S'true?" He reached under the counter and came up with a handful of capsules.

Dexxter hadn't a clue what you did with a popper, but he bought a dozen anyway to show the man Dexxter Foxx was cool. He paid for everything, then found the nearest T-shirt shop. He couldn't very well carry the small leather pouch under his arm and have Irene ask questions. He quickly bought several things he didn't need just to get the shopping bag where he could hide the Tazer.

He was running late, but his next stop was a must. Tourists were six deep at the counter of the Crown Jewels. Shit! He elbowed his way to the front, got the cheapest price, and was out of there in under five minutes.

Irene was waiting for him at Café Karumba! She looked slightly annoyed. He bit back a smile as he wended his way to the table. Her accident was going to be such fun.

Then he could turn his attention to Shelly.

"What took so long?" she asked as he sat down.

He treated her to one of his sexy smiles, then pulled the small jewelry box out of the shopping bag. "It took me forever to find just the right one."

"Oooh," she crooned as he opened the small box and showed her the diamond engagement ring. "I-I don't know what to say."

Say good-bye to this world.

"The last house Trevor restored has a gold star plaque, the highest honor the Old Island Restoration Association gives. It means the house has been flawlessly restored. It's like taking a step back in time to when the house was originally built."

She nodded, her mind on Matt's health, not on the old buildings that he was telling her about. After they'd spoken to the special agent, they'd gone to Mangia Mangia, where they were making fresh pasta in the sidewalk café's window. They'd both decided on penne with fresh pesto sauce.

When they finished, she asked Matt to take her to the house Trevor was restoring. By now, Trevor must have contacted Clive and have some news. She tried to be happy and upbeat, knowing the FBI had Dexxter under control, but at the back of her mind worry lurked.

There had to be some way to help Matt.

Hammers pounding, saws buzzing inside the house, they climbed the stairs to the front door of the house he was restoring.

"Trevor," Matt called.

"Back here."

They found Clive and Trevor in the pantry, examining a door hinge. "What we need to do is count the number of hinges like this,"

Trevor was telling Clive. "Then I'll have them made exactly like the originals."

"Hey, Matt, Shelly."

Clive's voice was a shade too bright. She knew he and Trevor must have been discussing Matt's problem when they had unexpectedly appeared.

"We came to check the progress," Matt told them. "Looks like you've done a lot since I was last here."

"We're making progress," Trevor agreed with unmistakable pride.

"Shelly, instead of coming out to the clinic tomorrow for your checkup, why don't I examine you now?" Clive asked, then he looked at Matt. "It'll take only a minute. I need to see her in the light."

She didn't have an appointment. Clive had something to tell her, she thought, following him into the sun room.

"Trevor told me what's happening." His dark brows drew together in a concerned frown. "It's, it's . . . unbelievable. I've already talked to Sloan-Kettering. I had to forge Matt's name on the consent form, but I did it, then faxed it to them. I should have his records this evening."

"Do you think there's any hope?"

"Even when I look at the records, I won't know. Reconstructive surgery is my specialty, but"—he held up one finger—"there is something online called MedLink. As soon as I get his file, I'll put the facts into cyberspace. We might have some information as early as midnight."

"That fast?"

"The information revolution has changed the world even more profoundly than did the Industrial Revolution. If there's info out there, we'll get it within minutes. Then I'll have to filter through it and decide what applies to this case."

She expelled a long sigh. "Great. I knew we could—"

"Look, I'm not going to give you false hope. Matt's had three opinions, including Sloan-Kettering, one of the leading medical centers. If there's someone who can help, it'll be an experimental procedure. Their work is usually on the Web."

"Hello there. Anybody home?"

She peered around the corner to the front door, the man's voice causing a sour feeling in the pit of her stomach.

Dexxter and Irene were standing there, holding shopping bags. A diamond sparkled on Irene's left hand while a smug smile tilted her thin lips upward.

This was his lucky day, thought Dexxter. He'd hoped to find Shelly at the house Trevor had told him all about last night, and here she was. For a moment she didn't appear to be too thrilled to see him.

Then she smiled at him.

Irene was smiling as well, a gloating grin. Amazing what the cheapest ring in the store could do. The stupid bitch actually believed he loved her and wanted to marry her.

What he really wanted was the knockout blonde standing next to the fag doctor. He jiggled his shopping bag, and the weight of the Tazer reassured him. He was going to get exactly what he wanted.

He always did, right? Oh, yeah.

C H A P T E R
TWENTY-NINE

"I think that's Dexxter and Irene," Trevor said to Matt. "Last night I invited them to see my latest project."

Matt's first instinct was to get Amy—no, Shelly—out of there. He must remember to keep thinking of her as Shelly. Using her real name would only put her in danger.

No doubt, the FBI agent was tailing Dexxter, but he couldn't just waltz into the house. He could protect her, Matt decided. He seriously doubted Dexxter would try anything with so many people around. If Dexx was actually planning to try anything at all.

They walked down the hall into the sun room where Clive and Shelly were talking to Dexxter. Irene had her hand extended, showing off her engagement ring. She was so proud of it that she kept her hand under Shelly's nose way too long.

"Congratulations," Matt said with all the enthusiasm of an undertaker.

Everyone else chimed in as he moved to Shelly's side and took her injured hand. Her fingers couldn't quite grip his yet, but she moved her thumb across his palm.

"It looks a lot like the Tiffany ring I wanted to give you," Matt said to Shelly. "Remember?"

"Yes, of course. It was stunning."

She smiled up at him, and he knew she'd gotten the message. He was doing his part to convince Dexxter that they'd had a long term relationship. But comparing this quarter-carat trinket to anything at Tiffany's was a joke.

Questions flickered in Trevor's eyes. No doubt, his friend was wondering why Matt would say this when his relationship with Shelly in New York was light years away from shopping for engagement rings. But he didn't contradict Matt.

"Let me take you on a tour," Trevor said.

Matt decided to tag along. His reporter's instincts had kicked into high gear. He wanted to know what Dexxter was up to, and he didn't trust the FBI to find out.

"Hello, Trevor."

Peter Holt came through the front door wearing a lightweight designer suit with a short, tight skirt and stiletto heels. Matt had to admit the transvestite was strikingly beautiful. He was no competition for Shelly, but chunky Irene with her piano legs and porn star boobs finished a distant third.

Dexxter's appreciative gaze swept over the doctor. Irene scowled, evidently sensing more competition. They hadn't figured it out yet. Not surprising. The only telltale sign was a slightly large Adam's apple, which most people didn't notice at first.

"Dexxter, Irene, this is Dr. Holt," Matt said, omitting Peter's first name to prolong the moment. He turned to the doctor. "They're leasing a place on Sunset Key."

"I know. I'm sorry I missed the party for them last night, but I had to lead a sexual addiction group."

The doctor shook Irene's hand, then reached for Dexxter's eagerly extended hand. "Call me Peter. All my friends do."

Matt could have picked Dexxter up with a spatula. Dexx stared, slack-jawed, then gasped.

Trevor stepped forward to ease the awkward moment. "Come on, everyone. Let's start the tour." He shooed the group up the stairs.

Matt released Shelly's hand, whispering to her, "Talk to Dexxter. I want to see how he reacts."

Matt hung back and let the others ascend to the second floor where carpenters were busy. Irene had a death grip on Dexxter's arm, but he glanced over his shoulder at Shelly, who was just behind him.

"This home was originally built by a ship's carpenter for William Otto, a cigar maker who had bribed his way out of a Cuban prison and came here."

"What year was that?" Dexx asked Trevor, managing to sound interested, but Matt noted he was watching Shelly.

"Just after the Civil War." Trevor pointed to a peg being hammered into place by a carpenter. "Ship's carpenters didn't use nails. To be true to their techniques, no nails will be used in this house."

"Restoration is very detail oriented, isn't it?" Shelly asked.

"That's the first thing I noticed too," Dexx eagerly told Shelly. "The details."

"Ship's carpenters built many of the fine homes in Key West," Trevor continued. "That's why there's gingerbread dripping from the eaves and some of the most beautiful shutters ever made. They didn't know what to do with themselves, so they just kept adding to the homes."

When Trevor was on a roll about Key West's history, nothing could stop him. Not that Matt minded. It gave him an opportunity to observe. The proud smile Clive wore told Matt how far their relationship had come. Trevor seemed to have found the right person.

Irene had not. Despite the ring on her finger, Irene was not a happy camper. He couldn't blame her. Dexxter's IQ couldn't hit double digits. How could he be so obvious about his attraction to Shelly?

Last night Dexx had struck him as being more full of himself than intelligent. His observations today confirmed it. Why was he engaged to Irene if he found other women including a transvestite so appealing?

His reporter's instincts went on alert. Things didn't square. Maybe they were just pretending to be engaged.

Why anyone would devote so much time and money to restore a crappy old house was beyond Dexxter's comprehension. Key West was beyond him. All the bars. All the fags. All the weirdos, like the doctor who was as hot as any of the techies who used to come to Dexx's office.

After touring the second floor, they went down the narrow back stairs, the servants' route. They had to go single file, and he was finally able to get away from Irene. He'd thought the ring would appease Irene until he could take care of her.

It had made her even more jealous and possessive.

Let Irene eat her heart out. He had bigger game to hunt. As they walked outside to check out the weeds in what had once been a garden, he moved closer to Shelly.

"Have you been to the Audubon House?" he asked.

"No, I haven't," she replied in that low, breathy voice he'd heard in his dreams last night.

"Audubon is such an interesting man, known worldwide as a conservationist," Dexx said, trying to think how to make intelligent conversation with this beautiful woman. "I'd like to see his home, wouldn't you?"

She beamed a smile at him that made his blood thick and hot. "Audubon didn't build the house. Captain Greiger did. John Audubon never even lived there."

"Really?" Dexx wasn't sure if she was making fun of him or playing hard to get. He'd spent too much time with hookers, he decided. He needed practice with a real woman. "Even if it's not his home exactly, I understand many of his drawings are on display there."

"True. Do you realize the man was famous in his time for killing birds?" she asked as he took a half step closer to her.

"It's absolutely a fact," Peter said, coming up to them. "Audubon considered it a bad day if he didn't shoot a hundred birds."

"It's amazing that his name has become synonymous with conservation," Shelly said to the cross-dressing doctor.

Dexx cursed Peter under his breath. Why didn't he stay with the others and leave him alone with Shelly? Dexx wanted to ask the doctor what he did with his dick when he wore such a tight skirt. But Shelly was a lady, and he didn't want to seem crude around her.

"We're going to Audubon House next," he told her as Irene's hand clamped around his arm like a vise. "Why don't you come with us?"

Before she could respond, Jensen stepped up beside her. "We're outta here. It's time for your therapy."

Shelly held up her hand, the only part of her that wasn't absolute perfection. "I still can't use my hand. I have therapy everyday. Have fun at the Audubon House."

Jensen guided her out of the garden, saying good-bye to everyone. The way Matt curved his arm around her was protective and possessive at the same time. It wasn't Irene's insecure clinging. This was a self-confident man who assumed Shelly loved him.

For the first time, Dexx considered that he might have to eliminate Jensen to get to Shelly. That presented a little problem, but not for a man of Dexxter's talent. He'd think of something. He always did.

"Therapy. That was a great excuse to get away," she said.

He smiled at Shelly as they crossed the living room on their way out of the house. "Actually, it isn't an excuse. I could use a little sex therapy."

She tried for a shocked expression. "Then make an appointment with Peter."

Matt chuckled, then pulled her into his arms for a kiss. As she closed her eyes, wondering if she'd ever become accustomed to the thrill of being in his arms, she looked over his shoulder.

At the back of the house, several rooms away, stood Dexxter, watching them. Every muscle in her body went rigid.

"What's the matter?"

"Let's go." She led him to the front door. When they were outside, she said, "Dexxter was watching. He gives me the willies."

"That's because he is a little creep." Matt looked up and down the street. "I don't see anyone who looks like they're tailing Dexx, do you?"

The area was deserted except for a woman pushing a stroller down the sidewalk. The late afternoon sun cast deep shadows along the tree-lined street. The houses were close together with banks of dense ferns between many of them.

"He could be hiding somewhere," she said.

"Maybe, but I'm not counting on it. Remember Waco and Ruby Ridge. Anything can go wrong. We may have to deal with Dexxter ourselves."

They headed toward the water shuttle, Matt's arm around her shoulders. She asked, "What do you think Dexx is up to?"

"I'm not positive, but I think he came down here to see if you were Amy. Now he's wa-a-y too interested in you—as a woman. Mark my words, Dexx wants to get you in the sack."

The idea was as shocking as it was sickening. The thought of Dexxter touching her made her stomach heave.

The shuttle to Sunset Key was just loading as they arrived at the pier. Matt helped her in, then sat beside her. She asked, "I can't figure why Dexxter suddenly gave Irene a ring."

"A very cheap ring at that. Last night he was bragging about all his dough. Then he gives her a chintzy ring. Why?" Matt pushed his sunglasses to the top of his head as the puzzle fell into place. "He doesn't care what she thinks, and he doesn't expect their relationship to last."

"That makes sense. This is some sort of temporary arrangement. Except—"

"Except that Irene is hopelessly in love with him."

* * *

"Okay, now this is therapy," Matt told her.

They were back at Half Moon Bay in his room. The shutters were closed, but light from a crimson sunset cast an amber glow across the bed. He was applying lotion to her back, soothing her tired muscles.

They'd already made love, stripping the minute they'd closed the door. Now they would make love again. It was just a matter of time.

"You know," Matt said, his palms fanning out across her back, spreading the lotion. "You're a fast learner. I swear, if I didn't know it for a fact, I'd never believe you were a virgin. Course, you did have a life master as a teacher."

"That's bridge, Jensen, not the sexual Olympics."

"Go on. You can't mean it."

She was relaxing so quickly now that it was hard to think, let alone talk. With the lotion now spread over her back, he began to smooth his hands over her shoulders. His fingers glided over her skin, exerting just enough pressure to take the tension out of her muscles. He worked down one arm, using his thumb to tease the sensitive skin.

When he reached her hand, he added two drops of lotion to her palm, then went to work on her injured hand. He tenderly coaxed each finger to straighten just a little more. Massaging her palm and between her fingers, he urged the taut muscles to open a bit more than they ever had.

He planted a kiss squarely in the middle of her palm, and slowly ran his tongue in a circle. She released a soft moan of utter pleasure.

"That feels s–o–o–o good."

"Hey, we aim to please."

Next, he placed his hands at her waist, using the heels of his palms to press into the muscles and force the tightness out of them. She was limp by the time he reached the back of her neck. Straddling her, he kneaded the tired flesh at the back of her neck with his thumbs.

At the base of her back she felt the hot, hard length of him pressing against her. She knew what was coming next and wondered if she had the strength to respond.

Well, maybe. Just once more.

She gripped the pillow with both hands as he focused his attention on her thighs, removing the tantalizing pressure of his arousal from the small of her back. Before a protest could leave her lips, he was applying lotion to the backs of her legs down to her feet. Moist heat was building rapidly now, desire replacing languid relaxation.

Only too well she knew what pleasure those talented hands could bring. Right now, though, he concentrated on smoothing the lotion into the arch of her foot. He continued upward, massaging her calves until they relaxed, then working his way up to her thighs.

By now the sun had set, cloaking the room in the deepening shadows of night. Somewhere in the distance a bird called to its mate, and through the open window she heard the surf rushing up to the shore. The scent of lavender came from the lotion, swirled through the air by the ceiling fan overhead.

She tightened her hold on the pillow and released a ragged sigh into the soft down as he stroked her, moving closer and closer to her inner thighs. He paid extra attention to the already soft muscles there, caressing them with exquisite skill.

"You're hired," she managed to say.

"I'm expensive."

"Worth it, trust me."

"Then I can count on a *big* tip?"

He shoved a powerful arm under her hips and levered her upward to a kneeling position. With an aggressive thrust of his hips, he entered her from behind.

In a few strokes he had her quivering beneath him—on the brink. Then a bolt of something akin to lightning hit her with blinding force. She barely heard herself cry out with pleasure. In a moment he joined her, collapsing sideways onto the bed.

How long she remained in his arms, she wasn't sure. When she awoke, she was cuddled against him and the room was pitch black. Something had awakened her, she groggily realized.

"Shelly, Shelly." The voice came from the other side of the bedroom door.

"Trevor?"

"Yes, Clive wants you to call a patient out at the clinic. She's having a bad time. He wants you to talk to her."

"What?" Matt asked from the pillow beside her.

"I'll be right back," she told him, diving into the heap of clothes beside the bed. She was positive there wasn't any woman at the clinic. There had to be news about a treatment for Matt. Oh, please, God, let it be good news.

CHAPTER
THIRTY

"What's up?" she asked Trevor once she closed the door behind her, leaving Matt.

"Clive's been on the Internet for hours."

She glanced down at her watch and saw that it was nearly midnight. A wave of guilt kept her silent as they crossed the house. While she'd been making love, Trevor and Clive had been working hard to help Matt. She should have been with them.

"We've found something, but we need to talk about it."

Trevor led her into his room. It was a suite facing the ocean on the other side of Half Moon Bay, which was a vast sweep of water with a thin ribbon of a beach. Off to one side of this private retreat was an alcove with a desk and a computer.

Clive was sitting at the desk, scrolling through notes on the computer's screen. He looked up when they came in. Trevor pulled out a chair for her next to Clive, then brought one up for himself.

"What have you found?" she asked, mentally keeping her fingers crossed.

"As I suspected, the tumor Matt has is inoperable," Clive said, "because it's growing between the coils of the hippocampus."

"I had just basic biology. I don't remember too much about the brain."

"The hippocampus is the enfolding of the cerebral cortex deep in the center of the brain. Its shape reminds many people of a sea horse. That's how it got the name, hippocampus. Think of it as a switching station buried deep in your skull. If a surgeon is off a millimeter, the body ceases to function normally."

The knowledge that Matt was so at risk twisted inside her. It was a moment before she found her voice. "Is there any hope?"

"Clive found one experimental laser procedure called micro-surgery," Trevor said. "It's a long shot at best."

"Has Matt mentioned having migraines to you?" Clive asked.

"No, he hasn't, but maybe he wouldn't say he had a headache."

"It would be more than a simple headache. A killer headache accompanied by nausea or vomiting or hypersensitivity to light and sound."

"No, he hasn't complained of anything like that. Why?"

Clive and Trevor exchanged a look that made her uneasy, then Clive said, "What Sloan-Kettering sent were tests almost a month old now. The absence of migraines may mean the tumor hasn't grown. If the tumor has grown, even the long-shot laser surgery will be out of the question."

"Matt must get a new MRI to see if the procedure is possible," Trevor added.

"What we're really going to need is a miracle to convince Matt to undergo yet another test. When he told me about his situation, he insisted he was through with doctors. That's why he doesn't want anyone to know. He doesn't want to be nagged."

Trevor touched her shoulder, saying, "You won't be nagging him. You'll be persuading him."

She had her doubts. There was a moody, brooding side to Matt as well as a certain stubbornness. *Character determines fate,* she suddenly thought. It fit this situation. Her character wasn't ruled by The Beast any longer; she was a much stronger person now. She would find a way to convince Matt.

"Tell me about the procedure and the doctor performing it," she said.

Matt peered into the refrigerator and spotted a platter of cold chicken. He took a piece and wandered out onto the terrace overlooking Half Moon Bay, Jiggs and Bingo at his bare feet.

"What's keeping Shelly?" he muttered to himself.

He ate the chicken, sharing a bite or two with the animals as he sat on the chaise. Across the water, the lights of Key West sparkled and the sound of reggae drifted toward him on a light breeze. He wondered if he'd ever been this happy, then quickly decided he hadn't.

Where had she been all his life?

Beyond his reach. Only an odd twist of fate had brought them to-gether, when he needed her the most. He didn't have long to live, and what he wanted was someone special to share the final months until he became ill.

Then he would have to go away.

He was determined that she remember him the way he was now. No chance he was going to allow her to see him slowly deteriorate the way he'd seen his mother. He intended to go through the suffer-ing and the pain.

Alone.

"Matt? Matt? Oh, there you are." Shelly walked out onto the ter-race. "Could you come inside? We need to talk."

Something in her tone put him on alert. He went inside, tossed the chicken bones into the trash compactor, and washed his hands. She was seated on a barstool at the island. He pulled out the stool beside her, curious about what she wanted.

"My mother had a saying," she began, looking directly at him, two deep lines of worry between her eyes. "Character determines fate."

"Been there, done that."

"Matt, do *not* joke. I'm serious."

He'd been testing her, and now he knew he was not going to like what he would hear next. She was going to badger him, the way Emily had. Unlike his sister, he had no intention of walking out on this woman.

He loved her too much.

"About your problem . . ." She hesitated.

"People don't have problems anymore. They have issues. I don't have either. I have an inoperable tumor."

Her eyes had a burning, faraway look to them. It was a minute be-fore she said, "If you don't want to listen to me, then there's no point in spending any more time together."

"Sounds like blackmail to me."

She was off her stool and heading toward the interior of the house before the words were out of his mouth. He watched her go. Women. They couldn't accept the world the way it was. They had to go around trying to make things better.

"Let her sulk," he told Bingo, who was now perched on the island near his elbow. "She'll change her mind."

He lasted three, maybe four minutes; then he went after her. "Might as well get it over with."

Afraid he'd wake Bubbles in the room down the hall, he knocked softly. Nothing. He tried again, louder this time. Nothing.

"Come on, now. You don't want me to bust down the door, do you?" His threat had worked before, but not this time.

He went outside and walked around to her bedroom windows. The trade winds and ceiling fans cooled Half Moon Bay, and he knew her window would be partway open. He hoisted it up and climbed through.

Lounging on her bed, she greeted him with a scalding glare in a silence so thick, it was suffocating. Aw, hell, he had no idea she could become this pissed off just because he'd tried to joke when she wanted to be serious.

"Okay, you win, babe. Let's talk." He sat down beside her at a safe distance, so she wouldn't get the idea that he had anything on his mind except their discussion.

"If you're not completely serious—leave."

Like it or not, he was going to have to hear her out. "I'm serious. You were saying character determines fate. Go on."

She crossed her arms over her chest. "When I went into the Witness Protection Program, I had to have a plan in case Dexxter found me. My birthmark was like a neon light flashing. Everyone noticed me. I had to take risks to get from California to Key West unnoticed."

There was a lethal calmness to her voice that told him her cross-country trek had been a terrible ordeal. Until now he hadn't thought much about how she'd managed to find her way to Key West.

"I'd seen a television show about a boy who stole a ride in the trunk of a car. While I was in an FBI safe house, waiting for my new identification and relocation in the Witness Protection Program, I studied car trunks. I learned which ones could be opened from inside, how to make an air vent, and how to get out.

"I was placed in the program, but I was still nervous about Dexxter finding me. I hid a small backpack near the house. When the firebomb hit, I grabbed the pack and ran, carrying Jiggs. I worked my way across this country, never once staying in a motel, never once eating even in a fast food place . . . doing my best to leave no trail Dexxter could find."

He struggled to imagine her running for her life. With no one to help or comfort her. Being brave for a moment, a day, was one thing. This kind of courage took an inner strength few possessed.

"I'm claustrophobic, and I'm not fond of the dark. I had to force myself into countless trunks, never knowing if I could actually get out. Twice locks jammed and I had to work at them until I finally got them open. I never gave up."

"I'm so proud of you. I can't imagine—"

"Matt, I believe in destiny. Being a stowaway, the accident, even having that creep Simon touch me—all the misery—was for a reason. It brought us together. I love you. We deserve a lifetime of happiness."

"I know, darling. I know." He reached for her, but she pulled back. "I love you so much, it hurts when I think all we have is a year—at most."

"Then why don't you do something about it? I was willing to take any risk to get here, even climb into strangers' trunks. Won't you do something for us?"

He'd known all along it was coming to this. "You're going to tell me to see another doctor."

She shook her head. "I'm going to ask you to go to Miami and have another MRI."

"What good will that do?"

"It'll tell us if it's . . . too late or not."

"Too late?"

"There's a doctor from Germany that we lo-cated—"

"Who's we?" Aw, hell, what had she gotten him into now?

"Trevor and Clive helped me."

"You promised you wouldn't—"

"I love you too much to give up. They *care* about what happens to you. Clive went on the Internet and found a doctor who is in this country demonstrating a new laser machine for neurosurgery."

He groaned and sagged back against the headboard. "Doctors and their toys."

"It isn't a toy, Matt. I'm not going to tell you it's without risk, but it is your only chance. You need to have a current MRI. If the tumor has grown too much, it will be impossible to perform this laser procedure."

He gathered her in his arms. This time she didn't resist. Resting his brow against hers, he whispered, "I hate to give you false hope."

"Every time I climbed into the trunk of a car, I took a chance. All I had was hope. I can deal with this. If the scan is negative, I can deal with that. But I can't deal with giving up."

"I'm not giving up."

"Thank you," she murmured.

He tilted her head up for a kiss and discovered her eyes were brimming with tears. "Sweetheart, don't cry."

"I'm not crying."

"Coulda fooled me." He thought for a moment. "Why are we going to Miami for the MRI? There's a hospital right here."

"Cl-Clive thinks the doctors who interpret the test results are more skilled there."

"I'm not leaving you here unprotected," he told her as he wiped away the tears that had not fell with the pad of his thumb.

"We'll call Scott Phillips from the airport. I'm not letting the FBI stop me from coming with you."

He knew better than to argue with this woman. Still, a sense of apprehension, a strange foreboding, gripped him. Not for himself—he'd faced his situation some time ago and had come to terms with it. He sensed danger to her, although he could not say exactly what would happen. Or when.

CHAPTER
THIRTY-ONE

Dexxter waited for a cloud to pass over the moon before he tiptoed out of the shadows and placed a piece of fish on the edge of the terrace. It was after two in the morning, and everyone at Half Moon Bay was asleep, but he didn't want anyone to catch him testing the Tazer. He slipped back into the shadows and waited, certain one of Trevor's cats would pick up the scent and come out through the open door to investigate.

"Here, kitty, kitty," he called under his breath, mentally luring the fat orange cat outside. What was his name? Bingo. He wanted the one-eyed cat.

He waited a few minutes and out trotted the orange cat followed by the half-eared mutt. Perfect. According to his calculations, Bingo was the biggest animal on the island at twenty pounds or so. The mutt was smaller, the same size as the other lap dogs on Sunset Key. Why no one had a big dog, a real man's dog like a Doberman was beyond him.

He'd like to test the Tazer on a large dog, but the cat was just going to have to do. Bingo was munching on the fish, head down. He needed a full body shot.

"Be patient," he told himself.

Bingo finished and sat back to lick his paws. Dexx aimed for the cat's chest and slowly squeezed the trigger. Zap. The jolt of electricity slammed into the cat, knocking him backward several feet.

Dexx held his watch up to the moon. He needed to see exactly how long the cat would be down, too stunned to move. Granted, a grown woman would recover more quickly, but he'd been itching to test the stun gun.

The maroon-colored mutt scampered to the cat's side and nudged the limp animal with his nose. Nothing. Bingo was out cold. Interesting, very interesting. The dog nosed the cat again, harder this time.

No response. Good, thought Dexxter. Half a minute and counting. The info on the National Rifle Association Web site said a Tazer at half power would stun a person, immobilizing the victim for over a minute.

Just long enough.

The mutt was circling the cat now, whimpering frantically. The dog halted, threw back his head, and howled like a coyote. Shit! Who would have thought the little dog could make a noise like that?

He had to get out of here before someone came. He slipped out of the bushes, intent on making his way back to the brick trail that wound through Sunset Key. A blast of light seared across the yard. He drew back and hunkered down, concealed by the dense ferns and night shadows.

He heard Trevor call, "Jiggs, is that you?"

The ugly mutt was still howling, but his cries weren't as powerful now.

"Bingo, are you all right, boy?" Trevor asked.

The doctor came outside with him—surprise, surprise—wearing a silk robe. A second later Matthew Jensen rushed outside, shirtless, wearing unbuttoned cutoffs.

"What's wrong with Bingo?" Shelly asked as she dashed up to the group.

His Shelly—he always thought of her as "his" now—wore nothing but an extra-extra large T-shirt that must belong to Jensen. Her flushed cheeks and tousled hair told him just what "his" woman had been doing.

Just wait, Shelly. Just wait.

Clive was kneeling beside Bingo, making a show of examining him for Trevor, no doubt. "He's still alive."

The faggy doctor tried to revive Bingo without any luck. Dexx checked his Rolex and saw almost three minutes had passed.

Watching the group, Dexx saw Matt put his arm around Shelly. She leaned into him as if it was the most natural thing in the world. Raw anger like a corrosive acid ate at Dexxter's stomach.

He was going to have to get rid of Matt. An accident wouldn't do.

A rash of the same type of accidents in the area would only arouse suspicion. He could pay Zane to kill Matt, the way he'd had the snitches in Singapore killed. But he wanted to take care of this asshole himself.

"He's coming to," Clive announced.

Dexx tilted his watch sideways to catch the light. Four minutes give or take a few seconds. He figured the National Rifle Association knew their business. The stun gun would render a woman helpless for just long enough.

"Yeee—ooow!" shrieked the cat as it tried to stand up. He collapsed on the flagstones. The stupid mutt began to lick its face.

Clive was feeling the animal. "Bingo has a strange break. He's broken a bone that's equivalent to a human sternum."

Dexx chuckled to himself. The black ape who had sold him the Tazer warned him that it could break bones. He didn't want her bones broken. No sir, that would only make the police suspicious. It was important the cause of death be listed as accidental.

"How could Bingo get such an injury out here on the terrace?" Shelly wanted to know.

"Revenge of the ospreys," Matt said. "Bingo has bagged enough of them."

"Matt, this isn't funny," Shelly said.

"I know. I feel terrible for Bingo. He's in a lot of pain."

"That's odd," Clive commented, still examining the cat. "There's a burn mark of some kind on his fur."

"Hey, like, what's happening?" Bubbles emerged from the house, yawning.

"Bingo has been hurt," Trevor said. "I'm going to call the vet."

"It's the middle of the night," Clive pointed out.

"Preston's a friend of mine." Trevor disappeared into the house.

Clive gathered the cat up in a towel that Matt had gotten and went into the house, followed by the others. Once they were inside, Dexxter slipped out of the bushes, patting the Tazer in his waistband. He'd never had this much fun.

And it was only going to get better.

"How's Bingo?"

She was sitting near Clive in the waiting area of Miami General Hospital, and Trevor had just returned from using the public phone. They'd taken the first flight that morning from Key West to Miami and had come directly to the hospital so Matt could have an

MRI. It had been the middle of the night when they'd rushed Bingo to Paws 'N Claws Veterinary Clinic. Trevor hadn't gotten a report until now.

Trevor's smile fired his green eyes with an inner light. "Preston had to make a special cast for the upper half of Bingo's body, but he'll recover. What happened is a mystery. Preston says the bone was shattered, not just broken."

"Strange," Clive said as Trevor sat down beside him. "How could that have happened?"

"I'm glad he's going to be okay," she said, but her mind was on Matt. He'd been gone for over two hours.

She leaned back and closed her eyes, saying a silent prayer for Matt. She must have dozed off. Trevor was nudging her. Looking up, she saw Matt coming down the hall.

"We might as well go to lunch," he said. "They won't have the results for an hour or so."

He sounded casual, and he was wearing a smile, but he didn't fool her. He had an aversion to hospitals and doctors that went back to when his own mother had been hospitalized with the same condition. They'd been up last night talking about it when the howls had gotten their attention.

"I'm your doctor of record," Clive said as Matt gave her a bear hug. "They'll page me as soon as they have the results."

The group wandered down the hall to the cafeteria and bought lunches that were one cut above airline food. They cleared a table on the patio.

"I have Dr. Dietz standing by," Clive told Matt when they were seated.

"I haven't had a chance to tell Matt much about Dr. Dietz," she said.

Under the table, Matt squeezed her knee. "Do I even want to know? If the tumor's grown, then surgery is out of the question."

"It hasn't grown," she said. Fate couldn't be that cruel.

"You haven't had any headaches," Trevor said. "That's a good sign."

Matt kept eating his turkey-on-rye sandwich.

"Oscar Dietz lives in Germany. He developed a laser that's attached to a special digital computer. He's been working at the NYU Medical Center with a team there that has invented a similar machine," Clive said. "It's pretty amazing really. He maps the brain with a functional MRI that outlines the brain on the computer, pinpointing not only the tumor, but also the blood vessels. That way Dietz knows exactly where to direct the laser."

"There's less margin for error," she told Matt who looked only mildly interested in this revolutionary procedure.

"The recovery time is remarkable. You leave the hospital the next day," Trevor added. "They shave just a patch of hair, not your whole head."

"Right now, Dr. Dietz is in Atlanta demonstrating his procedure at a clinic there," Clive said. "He's planning to return to Dusseldorf tomorrow unless we need him. Then he'll fly to Key West."

"Really?" Matt asked. "His equipment is that portable?"

Clive nodded enthusiastically. "A laptop, a small MRI unit and a laser."

"Have gun, will travel." Her attempt at a joke earned a weak smile from Trevor. Nothing from Matt.

"If the microsurgery is possible," Clive continued, "I'll have Dr. Dietz perform it at my clinic. I have the best medical team in the state."

"Maybe I should have a face lift while I'm at it."

She shook her head. "Very funny, Matt."

"I want you all to promise me something." Matt looked at each one of them in turn, first Clive, then Trevor, and finally her. "I know you want to help me, but if this doesn't work, you'll never mention doctors again. Let me enjoy what time I have left."

"Of course, Matt," Trevor said.

Clive slapped his hand on his hip. "There's my beeper. Looks like they have the results in record time."

Bracing himself for the worst, yet trying to be upbeat, Matt leaned over and gave Shelly a quick kiss. "Wish me luck."

Misty-eyed, she looked at him for a long moment. "It's going to be okay."

He left her with Trevor and followed Clive to the radiologist's office. One wall of the room was covered by MRI frames, slice after slice after slice of his brain. Having had three MRIs before this one, Matt knew what to look for.

He checked the sea horse-shaped hippocampus highlighted in each frame. He'd be damned if he could tell any difference from the earlier MRIs. But what did he know?

He and Clive sat opposite the doctor's desk. As a reporter, Matt had learned to read people fairly well. Doctors were tough. There must be a course in medical school: Mastering the Impassive Expression. The doctor began by sharing some medical mumbo-jumbo with Clive.

Matt cut him off. "Has the tumor grown?"

The doctor blinked, and Matt *knew*.

"Your tumor has grown." The doctor rose from his desk and went over to the wall where the MRIs were. He pointed to one. "Less than a millimeter, but I think it's too close to the hippocampus to operate even with a laser."

Matt didn't allow himself to be disappointed. All along, in his heart of hearts he'd never believed he had a chance. If he hadn't been so much in love, he never would have let them put him through this.

"Did you send the MRIs to Dr. Dietz?" Clive asked.

"Yes. We have a high-resolution fax. They went out to Atlanta right after they were taken." The doctor checked his watch. "He should be calling any minute now."

Clive leaned toward Matt. "Dr. Dietz may have a different opinion."

Matt tuned out the doctors, wondering how he was going to break the news to Shelly. Strange, he called her Shelly so often that the name seemed to fit. With the news he'd just received, he might not live long enough to be comfortable calling her Amy.

The telephone rang, and it was Dr. Dietz. They put him on the speaker phone, so they all could hear what he had to say. His English was excellent Matt decided as he listened to the doctor.

"Am I a candidate for your laser surgery?" Matt interrupted.

"Marginal," the German doctor conceded. "I can remove the tumor, but the heat from the laser *might* damage surrounding tissue."

The doctor lapsed into medical jargon, going into detail with the other doctors. Matt sat there, refusing to feel sorry for himself. Not quite making it. If she hadn't come into his life, he would have gone on his merry way and had fun—with a capital F—until the end was near.

But she had come into his life, bringing with her so much joy that leaving her behind gave him a crippling sense of defeat. Why me? Why now when I'm so happy? So much in love.

"Matt," Clive said to get his attention. "Do you understand the risk?"

"You have a forty percent chance of walking out of the hospital," the doctor said with just a trace of a German accent, "the day after surgery. If there's damage, you may never regain consciousness."

He would be a vegetable, a burden to those he loved.

"You could lead a normal life," Clive said, "but there is a huge risk."

"The decision has to be made immediately," the doctor said. "If the tumor grows any more, surgery will be out of the question."

It's now or never. Once he would have said never and walked out the door, but now he carefully considered his options. If he took this chance, he might be with her forever. A home. A family—a big family. Even without asking he knew that's what she wanted, too.

Forever.

They both wanted to be together forever and live a full life. Still, if the surgery failed—and it was experimental—they wouldn't even have the present to enjoy. He was gambling with his life.

Inwardly, he smiled, knowing some women were worth the risk. He'd found the love of his life. Why settle for a short time together when he could give them forever?

With luck.

"Let's go for it. Just promise me that you won't tell Shelly the odds. Act as if there's no risk. She's been through so much. I don't want her worrying."

CHAPTER
THIRTY-TWO

"The first night of the rest of my life."

Dexxter said the words out loud, but so softly that Irene, standing nearby in her bikini, couldn't hear him. Actually, it had been the longest day of his life. Waiting was a bitch, but it was almost over. In another hour he'd be rid of Irene.

And ready for sweet, sweet Shelly.

"Is that the champagne?" Irene asked, meaning the Kooler bag he had in one hand.

"Sure is. Three bottles of Cristal. Nothing but the best." He held up his other hand and showed her two champagne flutes. He'd hidden the Tazer beneath the champagne at the bottom of the bag.

They walked down to the pier where the Boston Whaler was moored. The small boat had come with the house, and they'd taken it out several times for harbor cruises. Tonight he needed to putt-putt around Key West, Stock Island, and Cow Key, then he would circle Sunset Key. When it was dark, he could get rid of Irene without anyone seeing him.

"Just think," Irene said as she climbed into the boat. "While we're on the water, sipping champagne and enjoying the sunset, we're making a fortune."

He cast off, tossing the mooring line onto the dock. "Right. Real Deal is a winner."

As much as he hated to admit it, Real Deal, his on-line gambling Web site, was a brilliant idea—Irene's brain child. Not that there weren't other on-line gambling sites, but Irene had found site designers who had come up with new, interesting interactive games.

Best of all, she'd set up a bank account in the Caymans to handle the money.

They'd never have the mess they had pirating software in Asia. What they were doing was legit, borderline, but legit. Irene had discovered a loophole in the law. On-line gambling was not regulated the way other casinos were.

Too bad he wasn't in love with her, he thought as he looked at her sitting nearby in her gold lamé bikini. Life would be so much easier if he were, but he had a thing for blondes. One blonde in particular.

"Ahoy! Hello, Dexx . . . Irene!"

"Shit!" It was the redhead from Half Moon Bay. Bubbles was coming toward them, driving Trevor's boat. He cut back the engine and let it idle while she pulled alongside them.

"Yaw'l out cruisin'?" Bubbles asked.

"Yes," Irene answered. "We're celebrating our new Web site. Do you want to come with us?"

Christ! Just what he didn't need. A witness.

"Thanks, but I can't. I have to, like, feed the cats and take care of things at the house. I'm the only one there."

"Where is everyone?" he asked, more than just a little curious about Shelly.

"They're in Miami, seeing a doctor."

"They're all sick?" Funny, everyone seemed all right last night— except the cat.

"No. Trevor called a little while ago and said Matt is going to have surgery tomorrow."

"Tomorrow! Why so fast?"

"I'm not sure," Bubbles said. "I picked up the message on the machine. Trevor did say that the surgery would be performed at Clive's clinic."

"Matt's probably having a tummy tuck," Irene said with a laugh.

"That's, like, not very funny." Bubbles revved the engine. "I've gotta run. Bingo, like, fell out of a tree or something last night."

"Really? Is he all right?" he asked, managing not to flash a shit-eating grin.

"Yes, he's at the vet's. It's Jiggs I'm worried about. He keeps, like, prowling the shore, looking for Bingo. He's even waded into the water, which is a first for him. He won't eat. At this rate, he'll starve before Bingo comes home."

A tragedy, I'm sure.

The light of the setting sun caught the stud in Bubble's tongue as she smiled and backed the boat away. Bubbles was an airhead, but she had given him a brilliant idea, he decided as he watched her wave good-bye.

Some people went into surgery and never came out alive.

It would be an accident, but nothing like Irene's. He'd have to hurry though. If Matt's surgery was scheduled for tomorrow, Dexx would have to come up with a plan fast. He'd think of something; he always did.

Irene asked, "Do you want me to open the champagne?"

"No, no. I've got it." How in hell was he going to open champagne and drive the boat? He couldn't let her open the Kooler bag and find the Tazer. "You take the wheel, Irene. It's time you learned to drive the Whaler."

She smiled that dippy little grin of hers and moved across the boat. "This is fun," she said, the moment her hands touched the wheel.

He popped the cork on the champagne and poured them each a glass. He wanted her blood alcohol level elevated. Drinking often contributed to "accidents." He handed her the champagne.

As she took the glass, he happened to look down and notice she was wearing gold lamé thongs that matched her bikini. He had to get her out of the shoes. How could he do that without making her suspicious?

"Dexx, darling, don't you think we should start planning the wedding?"

He almost gagged on his champagne. "Of course, plan away. The sooner, the better."

He tuned her out as they motored around Key West and she babbled on and on about their wedding. Dexx was feeling a little tipsy himself by the time the sun had set and they were heading home, passing Half Moon Bay on their cruise around Sunset Key.

"Look, there's that stupid little dog."

Irene pointed to the shore at Half Moon Bay. Jiggs was swimming just offshore, dragging an orange life vest that must have fallen off a passing boat.

"Poor little guy," Irene said. "I'll bet he thought the life jacket was the orange cat that he follows everywhere."

"Dogs are color-blind, but maybe orange reflects light differently than other colors. Who knows? Who cares?"

"I kind of feel sorry for him."

"Let me drive," he said.

They changed places, and he pulled the Kooler bag to his side. He'd put all three empty Cristal bottles back in the bag to hide the gun, which was on the bottom. He pulled it to the top so he could get to it quickly.

They were coming close to home now, and Dexx gave himself a mental pat on the back for timing this just right. It was dark, and the shuttle from Sunset Key's main dock was departing. It would be an hour before it returned.

No one would be around to see anything.

He put the boat in neutral and let it idle about one hundred yards off the beach. Irene was half in the bag from all the champagne she'd guzzled. She didn't notice they were no longer moving. Staring dreamily at the moonlit water, she was smiling to herself. No doubt she was planning the wedding.

He pulled out the Tazer and aimed it at Irene. "Take off your shoes."

"What?" Irene turned to him.

The small light on the boat's stern was bright enough for him to see the unfocused look in her eyes. Perfect. The coroner would say alcohol contributed to her "accident."

"Dexx, what's going on?" As she spoke, she automatically followed his instructions and kicked off her thongs. "What kind of game is this?"

"Sit on the rail."

"Why?" she asked, but she did it. "Is that a real gun?"

She was balanced precariously on the edge of the boat. With his dumb luck she would fall overboard. "Hold on to the rail."

Wide-eyed, she gripped the edge of the boat with both hands. "Tell me what's going on."

He couldn't hold back a smile. "I'm going to kill you."

It took a minute for the words to register in her alcohol soaked brain, then she asked, "Why?"

"Because I want you out of my life—forever."

"But, Dexx—"

"You've hounded me since grade school."

"I made you what you are. I found the deal in Singapore that launched Foxx Enterprises. I even found Zane to get rid of those troublemakers."

Her voice had such a hysterical edge to it that he almost laughed. He loved seeing her squirm.

"I set up your gambling Web site." She teetered to one side, then righted herself, adding, "I love you. I always have."

"Too bad. I've never loved you. I—"

"Why did you ask me to marry you?"

"To shut you up."

Irene blinked several times as if she couldn't believe what she was hearing. Finally, she said, "You've flipped over Shelly, haven't you? Don't think I haven't noticed how you act when she's around. Forget it. She's in love with Matt. She makes fun of you every chance she gets."

"She's flirting. That's just her way. She's classy, something you know nothing about."

"Pul-leeze. You're short and nerdy with beady little eyes. I don't know what I see in you. Shelly is never going to be interested."

"I have a way with women."

"Don't kid yourself, Dexx. You pay prostitutes. You've never had a relationship except for me."

He trained the gun on her sternum, just as the instructions on the NRA Web site had suggested. "You're about to have a terrible accident. You went out for a swim and drowned."

"Get real. I was on the swim team, remember?"

"This is a Tazer"—he waved the gun—"it will zap you. When you hit the water, you'll be stunned. Your muscles—especially your lungs—won't be able to function for a few seconds. I don't care how good a swimmer you are, when your body recovers from the jolt of electricity, your lungs will be filled with water. You're going to drown. The police will think it's an accident, and I'll get away with murder."

He squeezed the trigger. Zap. The impact sent her flying backward with an expression on her face as if she'd been flash-frozen. For a moment she bobbed on the surface, then the dark water sucked her under.

He waited, but she didn't resurface. He put the boat in gear and motored the short distance to his dock. Perfect. Flawless, really.

To the authorities it would appear that she'd left her home for a swim and drowned. A tragic end for such a talented woman. No one would suspect murder.

Whistling to himself, he tied up the Whaler, then walked up to the dark house. The only thing remaining was reporting Irene missing. It could wait until morning, he decided.

He would get on his computer and find some clever way of killing Matt, then he would go to sleep. The authorities would be told he worked late, then went to bed. The last time he'd seen his beloved fiancée was when she went for a swim in the early evening. He hadn't missed Irene until morning.

He went upstairs, so happy that he took two stairs at a time, shouting, "Free. Free at last."

Up in his office, overlooking the water, he turned on his computer. After surfing through cyberspace for a few minutes, Dexx decided he was too keyed up to work. He walked out onto the large rooftop deck where he and Irene had watched the sunset.

At the bar he poured himself a tumbler of Glenlivet. Champagne was for pussies. Real men drank single malt scotch. Sipping the scotch, he strolled around the deck.

Half Moon Bay had a much better view, and it was much more private. The crescent beach was guarded on one side by a cluster of palms. On the other side, mangroves created a natural barrier.

Shelly belonged at Half Moon Bay.

With all the money Real Deal was going to make, he could give her anything her heart desired. He wanted to pamper her. Irene could rot in hell. He knew that Shelly was attracted to him.

With Jensen out of the way—

A scraping sound behind him caught his attention. He turned, his heart slammed against his chest, and the drink slipped from his hand. It crashed to the deck, splashing all over his bare legs.

"Irene? How—how'd—"

"The gun did knock me for a loop, but I managed to clear my lungs. Then I swam to shore. I was suspicious, Dexx. The cheesy ring. Letting me plan the wedding. I smelled a rat and dumped my champagne over the side when you weren't looking."

"Shit!"

She advanced on him, a revolver in her hand. "You know, Dexx, I wasted half my life on you." She tossed her head, and a strand of wet black hair fell over one eye. "And what do I get?"

"It was just a game," he muttered.

"No, it wasn't. You wanted me out of the way so you could have Shelly. I knew what you did in Singapore, and you couldn't afford to have me go to the FBI. Now I'm taking what's rightfully mine—Real Deal. I'm going to be filthy rich and you're going to be six feet under."

The feral glint in her dark eyes was more chilling than her words.

She loved him; he couldn't believe she would actually kill him. She was just giving him a dose of his own medicine. Scaring him.

"Irene baby—"

"Shut up. You're worthless." She prodded his bare chest with the muzzle of the gun. "Well, not quite worthless. I like your idea of getting rid of people with an accident. I'm going to see that Shelly has the same accident you planned for me.

"I'll stun her with your Tazer and make sure she falls in the water. That way she'll drown, the way I was supposed to die. But first I'm going to kill you."

"Me?" Fear liquefied in his bowels. He was going to die. "Remember, you love me."

"Loved. Past tense."

She poked him with the gun, and he backed up a step. Then another and another. His butt hit the rail surrounding the rooftop deck.

"We drank a lot of champagne on the harbor cruise, then you came up here and continued to drink," she said with a satanic smile. "I was down in the kitchen when I heard this terrible noise. You'd slipped and fallen off the deck."

She lowered one shoulder and slammed into his chest and shoved him, putting all her weight into the sudden movement. He grabbed for the rail, but the force of their weight snapped the wooden railing.

He was airborne for a second, one hand brushing the side of the house. The last thing he saw was Irene waving good-bye.

CHAPTER
THIRTY-THREE

"Matt, do you think Bubbles is having a party?" Even though it was nearly midnight as they were returning to Half Moon Bay, she noticed the lights inside the house.

"Could be."

They were alone in Trevor's launch, having left Dr. Dietz and Trevor to spend the night at Clive's home. It was closer to the airport where Trevor would meet Emily's plane. Matt had called his sister, and she was flying in on the first flight the following morning. That was the excuse they gave, but she suspected they wanted to give them time alone. Apparently, they'd forgotten Bubbles.

As they pulled up to the dock, she spotted Jiggs standing nearby, forlornly staring out at the water. "He's lost without Bingo."

"Uh-huh," Matt responded.

He'd been preoccupied since they'd received the news that his tumor was operable if they used Dr. Dietz's new laser technique. She'd been jubilant, hardly able to contain her joy, but something was troubling Matt, and she was fairly certain she knew what it was.

"You're afraid of what Emily's going to say when she finds out you've taken up with Rochelle Ralston again, aren't you?"

"Not really."

"Well, I say we whisper in her ear and tell her the truth. She's going to be worried about the surgery. Let's not give her anything else to be concerned about."

"No. I explained to Emily how much you mean to me. Let's leave it at that until the FBI arrests Dexxter. Emily's bound to be a little hostile to you, but ignore it. Em can be a hothead sometimes."

"I guess the apple doesn't fall very far from the tree, does it? You have a temper too."

She didn't want to argue with him, so she walked up to the house at his side. The lights were on, but there was no sign of Bubbles except for a half-eaten bowl of ice cream that had melted into a puddle of chocolate.

"What do you suppose happened to Bubbles?"

Matt shrugged. Again, indifference, not concern, played across his face. He was dead tired, she realized. Bingo's accident and the early flight to Miami meant they hadn't gotten much sleep.

He hadn't even been that excited when they'd met Dr. Dietz's plane. Everyone else had been very impressed with the German doctor, but Matt had seemed much quieter than usual—almost preoccupied.

"Let's turn out some of these lights and get some rest."

She began snapping off lights in the kitchen, then in the foyer. She checked "message central" to see if Bubbles had left a note. Nothing. There were no messages on the answering machine either. The only lights in their wing of the house was in Bubbles's room, but she wasn't there.

Then she realized Matt hadn't followed her. She returned to the kitchen and saw him standing just outside on the terrace, holding Jiggs. He was talking to the little dog, and even though she couldn't hear him, she knew what he was saying.

He could be tough sometimes, but he had a soft spot. He was going to be a fabulous father. Not that he'd asked her to marry him, but she was certain he would.

"Matt." She walked up and he turned to her, the odd expression still on his face. "Let's get some rest."

He put Jiggs down and the little dog scampered off toward the water. "I don't want to sleep. I—"

"You're ba–a–ack!" Bubbles called from the kitchen. She flounced out to them, saying, "You're not going to believe this. There was, like, a terrible accident."

"How terrible could it be?" Matt asked. "You're smiling."

"That's because I just met the most awesome guy. He's down at the cottages where they're taking everyone's statement." She ran her tongue over her lower lip suggestively, and the stud caught the light. "Dexxter Foxx is dead."

"What?" Matt's voice echoed hers.

"He fell off the rooftop deck and broke his neck. Irene called 911 right away, but it was too late. He was dead the minute he hit the ground."

Dexxter dead. It didn't seem possible; her mind had trouble absorbing the facts. An oddly primitive warning sounded in her brain. Something wasn't right.

She stole a glance at Matt. The minute their eyes met, she knew he was thinking the same thing. There were certain people in the world who deserved to die, but they were never the ones who had fatal accidents.

"Why were the police interviewing you?" Matt was using his reporter's voice now, emotionless, yet asking probing questions.

"I saw Dexx and Irene just before sunset. They were, like, cruisin' and drinking champagne. Later, at dark, I noticed Jiggs swimming—"

"Jiggs was swimming?" She couldn't help but interrupt. "He never barked until Bingo's accident, and now he's swimming. Weird."

"He keeps looking for Bingo," Matt said. "It makes him brave."

"Like I was sayin', I spotted Jiggs towing this life jacket to shore. That's when I saw Dexx and Irene driving by. I was, like, the last person to see him alive—except for Irene, of course."

"Were there any witnesses?" Matt asked.

Bubbles shook her head. "Irene said they'd come home after finishing three bottles of, like, this outrageously expensive champagne. They went up to the rooftop deck to watch the lights of Key West. Dexx began to drink scotch. Irene thought he was drinking too much and went down to get some food. That's when she heard the crash. Dexx landed—splat—on the front lawn."

Matt grabbed her arm. "Let's go into town. It's too depressing around here." He led her off the terrace toward the dock.

"What about me?"

"Stay right here, Bubbles," Matt said over his shoulder. "That cute guy might come by."

"What's happening?" she whispered to Matt.

They were in the launch, casting off before he answered. "I'm not buying Irene's story. Let's talk to the FBI. They bugged the place. They'll know the truth."

"I agree, but does it matter? Dead is dead. I don't have to be Shelly any longer." She thought a moment, realizing she didn't feel like Amy either. So much had happened. The Beast was gone, but she wasn't positive who had taken her place.

"Let's wait until we speak with the FBI."

They used the public telephone at Sunset Pier. After a dozen rings, they began to be concerned, then Scott Phillips answered.

"What in hell's going on over there?" Matt asked without introducing himself.

"Jensen, you weren't supposed to take Amy away without telling us."

"Just a quick trip to Miami. We meant to call you from the airport, but things got hectic," she explained. "Do you know about Dexxter?"

"Yeah, we heard. I guess it saved the taxpayers a lot of money."

"You're closing your investigation? I can be Amy Conroy again?"

"Not so fast. We may have a case against Irene. I won't know for a few days."

"What about Dexxter's death?" Matt asked. "I suspect she killed him."

"We're going to review the disks and let the police know if we've got anything."

"You weren't listening when it happened?"

"No. Didn't you hear? The Pier House received a bomb threat and the whole place was evacuated. We just got back to the room. It'll take some time to review the disks. First we're going over to the house to see if the scene is consistent with Irene Hanson's story."

"Yeah, the local police don't get many murders. They may have overlooked something," Matt told him. "We'll call you first thing in the morning—like five o'clock—to see if there's a problem."

"Hey, that's early."

She broke in and explained Matt had to be at the clinic by six.

"All right, call me. I should have an answer."

Even though Amy Conroy seemed to have become a stranger, she wanted the FBI to give her back her real identity. When she met Matt's sister, she needed to explain that she was not the woman who had threatened to kill her.

Matt put his arm around Shelly and used his free hand to guide the boat toward the pier at Half Moon Bay. He cocked his wrist, checking the time. After midnight.

He had to report to the hospital at six for pre-op lab work. By the time that was finished, Emily would have arrived. He could talk to her and the others before surgery.

These next few hours might be all he had left of this life. At least he was with the woman he loved. If only he could be sure she was safe. She couldn't scream, and she still didn't have full use of her right hand.

"What's the matter?"

When she looked up at him like that with those big blue eyes, it was hard not to get choked up. Dying didn't seem fair, but then, he reminded himself that life was never fair.

"When I was working the crime beat, the cops used to say they had a 'hinky' feeling. That's me. Dexxter's death doesn't *feel* right." He couldn't tell her what was really bothering him. The risky surgery had him worried.

"Irene was so in love with Dexx. It's hard to imagine her killing him."

"I don't agree. She's one of those women that you don't cross. If Dexx made her angry enough . . . Who knows?"

He drove the boat up to the pier and secured the lines around the cleats. It was breezy tonight. The last thing he needed was for the boat to chaff through a line and float out across the Gulf of Mexico.

"Oh, my gosh! Bubbles was right. There's Jiggs. He's swimming out to something. I can't believe how he's changed. He's barking and swimming."

Matt peered at the dark water near the mangroves. Bingo used to stalk birds in the shallow water there, but Jiggs was out a lot farther than the cat went. "Looks like Jiggs is after a piece of wood or something."

"I guess he keeps hoping to find Bingo," she said as they climbed out of the boat.

"Here, Jiggs," he called softly. "Here, boy."

The dog gave up on the piece of wood bobbing in the sea and paddled his way toward the shore. The little mutt had a lot more guts than Matt had originally thought. They waited for him at the water's edge. Jiggs hopped out of the surf and greeted them by shaking hard and spraying them with water.

"Come on, Jiggs. Follow us. We're going for a walk in the moonlight."

"Matt, shouldn't you get some rest?"

"Nope." He still had his arm around her, and he gave her a little hug. "I won't be able to sleep."

They strolled down the beach, Jiggs trotting along behind. Matt had a thousand things he wanted to say, but couldn't find the words. They reached the far end of the beach, where the mangroves began. Jiggs darted into the dense bushes.

"Jiggs, don't do that. You'll get lost." She looked up at him for help.

"What can I say? The dog has a screw loose."

In silence they walked back the way they'd come. The lights were all off in the house, and the timer had turned off the yard lights as well. The only light came from the sliver of moon.

"Let's sit on the grass and count the stars . . . or something."

"Oh, Matt, don't tell me that you've got sex on your mind."

"Hey, it's been twenty-four hours. That's a record for us."

They stretched out on the dichondra, her head resting on his chest. The balmy air closed in softly around them, bringing with it the sweet scent of the tropics. Overhead the stars winked at them as if sharing the intimacy of the moment. Matt couldn't help wishing he could freeze time.

She turned her head toward him. "I love you so much."

"You're the best thing that ever happened to me," he responded, emotion choking his voice.

He kissed her, because if he didn't, he might break down. Before he had time to catch his breath, her tongue slipped into his mouth. Swift and sure desire welled up inside him the way it always did when their lips met. She pressed her body to his, rubbing herself against him.

"Hey, if you're not careful, you're going to lose your amateur status."

"I was just a helpless virgin until you waltzed into my life."

She took charge, kissing him and showing him all that she had learned. Within a minute she had wiggled out of her clothes and had his pants unzipped.

"I get to be on top this time," she informed him.

He didn't mind. It wasn't the first time they'd made love this way. It was fun to watch her. She tugged off his pants and underwear.

"So much for foreplay," he teased.

"Why waste time?"

True, time was something he didn't have to waste, but he would have enjoyed a more leisurely pace. He could see that she needed something different. She mounted him, impaling herself on him with a moan of delight.

She closed her eyes and threw her head back, obviously enjoying the sensation. Her breasts swayed slightly, the nipples jutting outward. He stored the memory, cataloguing the arch of her throat, the softness of her skin, her wild hair streaming down her back.

Every detail went into his memory bank.

Then she began to move, rocking back and forth with excruciating slowness. He let her take her time and find her own tempo. She increased the pace, then kicked into high gear.

His pulse skyrocketed, and he could feel himself close to going over the edge. A shudder ripped through his body just as she pitched forward and collapsed on his chest, panting.

"How was that?" she asked a little later.

"You were on warp speed."

"I hurried. The way I figure it, you're good for about two more rounds before it's time to shower and get ready."

He chuckled, holding her on his chest. That was just about how he saw it, too. But first he needed to talk to her seriously.

He waited until their bodies relaxed and naturally pulled apart. Rolling onto one side, he faced her, supporting his head with a bent arm.

"Tomorrow it's going to be crazy," he began. "They'll be prepping me and my sister will be here as well as Trevor and Clive. I won't be able to talk to you privately."

"I know." She leaned over and kissed his cheek. "I'm going to wish you luck now. Not that you need it, but I want to say it. Anyway, character determines fate. Your true character showed when you didn't desert a helpless woman even though she had threatened your sister. Everything is going to be fine."

"Probably," he said, refusing to worry her by telling her what a long shot this surgery was. "Just in case, I want you to promise me something."

"Don't talk like this. You're scaring me."

"Honey, listen. No surgery is one hundred percent safe. If something should happen, I want you to promise me that you won't waste a lot of time mourning me. You haven't had much of a life. I want you to live and have fun."

"Without you?"

"There are lots of great men out there." Right now, he'd like to kill the man who would take his place. "Promise me that you'll enjoy life. Let another man love you the way I love you. Don't hold back, thinking of me and remembering what we had together. Let yourself love someone else."

He trembled when she reached over and touched his face with her fingertips. Slowly her hand spread across his cheek, brushing the emerging whiskers. She moved closer, her lips hovering near his. The depth of love shining in her eyes staggered him with its intensity.

"Matt, without you, life won't be worth living. From the first moment that I heard your voice, I loved you. Nothing. Not time or distance or even death will change the way I feel. Can't you understand how special you are?"

He put his arms around her, his throat working hard to keep his emotions in check. "If anything does happen, just remember how much I love you. Death won't change that. I'll be with you in spirit always."

C H A P T E R
THIRTY-FOUR

Even the gulls were still asleep when they moored Trevor's launch at the Sunset Key pier next to Mallory Dock. She glanced at Matt and thought how healthy he looked. Freshly shaven, his hair still damp from his shower, he appeared to be so strong that nothing could bother him. Yet, last night he had been worried.

About her.

The depth of his love was amazing. They had known each other for such a short time, but in many ways, it seemed as if they'd been together forever. She couldn't imagine life without him and didn't want to think about it. Instead, she was looking forward to the future—their future.

"Let's see what the FBI found out," Matt told her as they walked up the gangway toward the pay phone.

"With luck, I can tell your sister the truth. I'll be Amy Conroy again."

They both shared the receiver as the phone rang. A very sleepy Scott Phillips answered, and Matt asked what he'd found out.

"We checked the rooftop deck. The only thing inconsistent with an accidental fall is that Dexxter dropped a glass full of scotch in the middle of the deck, not near the edge, where you'd expect."

"Do you think Irene pushed him?" she asked.

"It's a possibility. All it would have taken is a good shove."

"Does the disk show them fighting?" Matt asked.

"Not what we can hear. We're using an infinity system. Are you familiar with it?"

She had no idea what it was, but Matt said he knew how it worked.

"We're picking up conversation on the deck, but it's garbled. The next thing is a very frantic 911 call. We sent the garbled portion to Miami, where the field office has an enhancer. The results should be in this evening."

"Do I still have to pretend to be Shelly?"

"Absolutely. We may be able to make a case against Irene. Hang in there. It won't be long now. You'll be our star witness. We need you."

They hung up, then hailed a taxi to take them out to the Bel Aire Clinic.

"Explain the infinity system," she said once they were settled in the backseat.

"It's a sophisticated listening system that uses telephones. It records phone conversations, but it also picks up any conversation in the area through the receiver. Apparently, there wasn't a phone on the deck, so the nearest telephone, which must have been downstairs, recorded the conversation. That's why it needs to be enhanced."

"How do you know all this?"

"Being a reporter," he said with a smile. "In the old days we would have hours of blank tape because recorders ran full-time. Now they use laser disks that are voice-activated. Conversation is sent along the phone lines to a monitoring station. That's where the laser disks are."

"Can't people tell if they're being tracked?"

"Sure. If you're smart, you'd have a line checker that alerts you to the presence of an electronic listening device. I guess Dexxter wasn't concerned about an FBI sting."

"Things aren't always what they seem," she said. "Maybe something else went on up on that deck."

"You're right. I went with the *Exposé* team that covered Max Bassinger's death."

"I remember reading the Exposé article." She couldn't help being proud of all he'd accomplished, taking a nothing magazine and turning it into the nation's finest newsmagazine. "A filthy-rich oilman dies while watching a famous actress make love to another man."

"That's the spin they tried to put on it," Matt said with a frown. "Turned out that his death was linked to another case. Only the sheriff, Zach Coulter suspected the truth. After interviewing him, we dug deeper and came up •with a sensational story."*

"I'll bet that's what happens this time. There's more behind Dexx's fall."

The car pulled up to the clinic's front door. After paying the driver, they walked hand in hand into the flower-filled lobby. Like the first time she was here, she was struck by the way the clinic's lobby appeared to be the living room of a southern mansion.

"There must be a lot more money in face-lifts than I thought," Matt commented, his voice low.

"Wait until you see the patients' rooms. They're like hotel suites."

The same stunningly beautiful receptionist greeted them. This time the woman looked her over as she gave directions to the waiting room. Then she turned her attention to Matt, telling him that they were waiting for him down the hall in the laboratory.

She walked with him part way, then stopped. "I'll see you again, won't I? Before they operate, we'll have a chance to talk."

"We won't be alone. Let's say good-bye now."

"We said it all last night, didn't we?" She wanted to be upbeat even though she was on the verge of tears. "We love each other. You're doing this to give us a chance at a real future, not just a few months."

Gazing into his eyes, she saw the anguish and wished she could absorb his pain. Memories of his mother's ordeal made him hate hospitals and doctors. She tried to say something comforting, but the words lodged in her throat.

He bent his head to give her a quick kiss, but she couldn't resist throwing her arms around him and hugging him. Oh, how she wished he didn't have to go through with this operation.

Pulling back, he looked at her, misery etching the masculine planes of his face. "Darling, you'll never know how much I love you."

The words sounded mangled, as if they'd been ripped from his throat. He turned and walked away from her without looking back. She watched this man, her love, until he disappeared around the turn in the hall.

Rooted to the spot, she stood there, whispering to herself. "It's going to be all right. There's nothing to worry about."

* See *The Hideaway*, Zebra Books, November, 1997.

With slow, measured steps she went down the corridor to the waiting room. Like the rest of the clinic, the waiting room seemed more like a wealthy person's home than a hospital. The scent of roses filled the air, coming from large vases of cheery yellow blossoms. Comfy overstuffed chintz furniture was arranged so that visitors could watch the big-screen television or look at the view of the palm-lined shore.

She stood at the window, gazing at the waves as they gently tumbled across the golden sand. Matt's surgery was scheduled for eleven and would last about three hours. It would be another two to three hours before he was out of recovery. It might as well be a thousand years.

"Shelly, we're here."

Hearing Trevor's voice, she turned and saw him coming into the room with Emily. Even if she hadn't known Trevor had planned to meet Emily's plane, she would have realized this woman was Matt's sister. They both had the same brown eyes flecked with amber and thick, dark hair.

They shared the same type of nose and square jaw, but Emily's features were softer than Matt's. Her gloss-brown hair fell to her shoulders with a slight wave that added to her feminine appeal.

As their eyes met, she recognized Matt's inquisitive expression. She knew instantly that Emily despised her.

"It's not too late to change your mind," Clive told Matt.

He was in a bed, prepped for surgery. They had even shaven part of his head and painted it with iodine. He was one step from the operating room, but he could still back out.

"I'm going through with it. I just need to see my sister and Trevor first."

Clive nodded. "Okay, I'll get them."

A few minutes later Emily rushed through the door. "Oh, Matt. I'm in shock. I can't believe you're doing this."

"Em, stay calm." He patted the bed. "Sit here a minute."

She plopped down, tears misting her eyes. "You have a year . . . maybe longer. Enjoy life. Why take this chance? Why?"

"Did you talk to her?"

"To Shelly? Yes, a little. She seems different, but then all I had was one ugly encounter with her. I'll never forget her saying she would kill me."

"There's a lot about her you don't know."

He wished he could tell his sister, but didn't want to risk putting Amy in danger. A small slip, an unintentional one, could turn out to be a disaster. One of his worst fears about this surgery was that he wouldn't be around to protect her, should something happen.

"On the phone you said you were in love with her. Then why not spend the next few months with her instead of having this dangerous operation?"

He took his sister's hand in his and gently squeezed. "I want to spend the rest of my life with her, not just a few months. Can't you understand that? This is the only chance I have. It's a long shot, sure, but it is a chance. I have to take it."

Emily slowly nodded as a tear seeped from one eye and dribbled down her cheek. "I guess I understand. Why didn't you tell Shelly? Shouldn't she have some say in this?"

"No. It's my life. She would only try to talk me out of it."

"There's something I want to tell you." Emily managed a smile even though her eyes were filled with tears. "I—I . . . we're going to have a baby."

"Hey, that's great." Emily had been trying for years to get pregnant. He knew how much she wanted a family. "I'm going to be an uncle."

Then it hit him. He might never see the baby. The child would grow up, but he wouldn't be around to see it. Oh, how he longed to see his sister with the child she had wanted for years.

"One day you will have kids and we'll spend the summer at our place in Nantucket," Em said, and he noticed she didn't mention that they would be Shelly's children.

"Right," he said, praying that it would come true. "Look, I want to tell you—just in case—how much you mean to me. You raised me."

"You raised yourself."

"Okay, okay. The point is, I appreciate your steering me in the right direction. Without your encouragement I would never have applied to Yale."

"You were so incredibly bright. I was barely eighteen, old enough to have custody, but not experienced enough to handle a wild teen-age boy."

Matt's throat began to close up. "You sacrificed, going to a community college and working two jobs to support us. Thank you." He leaned forward and kissed her cheek. "God bless you and the baby."

It was hard to accept the fact that he might never see his sister or the baby she'd wanted for so long. His niece or nephew. Life isn't fair, he tried to remind himself, but there was a cold knot in his chest.

He heard Trevor's voice and looked up. His friend was hesitating in the doorway. "Run along, Em," he said, his voice cracking. "I'll see you this evening."

His sister gave him a big hug. "I'm not saying good-bye. You're going to make it." She muffled a sob. "You have to."

Trevor walked in, and from the expression on his face, Matt knew Clive had told him just how risky this operation was. Trevor stood beside the bed.

"Matt, you're the only family I have. I don't want anything to happen to you."

"Nothing is going to go wrong, but I'll feel a lot better if I know you're happy."

"Happy?" One eyebrow tilted upward. "You mean with Clive?"

"Who else?"

"Yes. I am very happy. As soon as we get a chance, we're having rings made."

"That's great. I'm happy for you." He mustered a smile, telling himself the first thing he was going to buy—if he ever got out of here—was a ring. "Would you do something for me?"

"Name it." Trevor sat in the spot where Emily had been.

"If something . . . happens and I don't come out of this, I need to know that someone is taking care of Shelly."

"Sure, sure." A hint of moisture glistened in Trevor's eyes. "I'll take care of her. Don't worry."

"Thanks. There's one other thing I need to say. You're like a brother to me. I want to thank you for all you've done for me over the years."

"Oh, Matt." Tears filled his friend's green eyes. "I was blessed to have known you. After my family deserted me, you were the one who kept me from killing myself. I owe *you*—big-time."

The nurse appeared, holding a syringe. "After this injection, we're going to wheel you into the operating room."

He held up his arm and she gave him the shot, then left. A second later, he felt woozy.

"Don't you want to talk to Shelly?"

"We already said good-bye."

Trevor bear-hugged him and thumped him on the back. He heard his friend sniffing, fighting the tears. Man, oh, man, he never knew how hard this would be.

"Tell Shelly how much I love her. I had no idea what love was until she came into my life."

Emily had come back from Matt's room several minutes ago, but she was still crying. Other than flash Shelly a hostile glare, Emily hadn't said one word to her. Matt's sister had taken a seat as far away as she could possibly get.

Trevor staggered in, fighting tears. He collapsed in the chair opposite Shelly. Boy, was she glad that they had said good-bye earlier. Trevor dabbed his eyes dry with a soggy tissue, then stared up at the ceiling.

"Why are you so upset? If Matt doesn't have this surgery, he's going to die soon. You should be glad he had this option."

Trevor turned his head to look at her. For a moment, she thought he was going to cry. Finally he said, "True. It's his only chance."

"We should be upbeat. Tomorrow he's going to walk out of here."

Emily's sobs grew louder with each word. Why were they both so upset? A disturbing thought hit her. Surely Matt hadn't lied to her.

"Trevor, there isn't much risk to this surgery, is there?"

He didn't look at her.

"Oh, my God! Matt didn't—he wouldn't lie to me."

"H-he did it for you." The venom in Emily's voice was unmistakable despite the tears.

"Did what? Trevor, tell me, please."

Emily cried, "Tell the troublemaker what she's done, Trevor."

"The tumor is too large to be sure this operation will be successful. Matt didn't want to worry you, but chances are he won't make it."

Darling, you'll never know how much I love you.

Oh, my God. What had she done?

"He could have had a whole year," Emily said. "But he wanted a lifetime—with you. Don't ask me how you managed—"

She didn't hear the rest of the sentence. Hoping she wasn't too late, she raced down the hall toward the operating area. Why? Why? Why?

No wonder Matt's sister hated her. She hated herself. How could she have been so selfish?

Matt had wanted to enjoy the time they had left, the final months of his life. But no she pressed him to undergo an experimental procedure. She was so stupid. The word "experimental" should have given her a clue to how dangerous this operation really was. Instead of having another year or more of life, Matt was risking death.

For her.

As she approached surgery, she saw Clive coming out of the swinging doors.

"Stop the doctor. Don't—"

"I'm afraid it's too late for that. Dr. Dietz has already begun."

"Clive, he didn't tell me how risky this is. I would never have let him."

Clive put his arm around her. "It was Matt's choice. There's nothing you can do now but pray."

CHAPTER
THIRTY-FIVE

"It can't be too late," she cried.

"Don't assume the worst," Clive said. "The surgery may be successful."

"But it's a real risk, isn't it?"

"That's true, Shelly."

She charged down the hall, to the waiting room and shouldered open the door. Why? Why? Why?

She should have guessed. Matt had been behaving strangely, but she'd chalked it up to the terrible experience he'd had when his mother had died in the hospital. How could he gamble with his own life?

Darling, you'll never know how much I love you.

He loved her enough to sacrifice what was left of his life. Unbelievable. She'd done nothing to deserve to be loved with such devotion.

Inside the waiting room, Trevor and Emily were sitting side by side on the sofa, talking. They looked up and saw her.

"Dr. Dietz has begun operating," she told them.

"If Matt dies, it'll be your fault," Emily said, hatred underscoring each syllable.

"Now, Emily. This was Matt's choice, not—"

"I don't know how she did it, but Shelly managed to get some hold over my brother. When he left New York, he despised her. Now, he's hopelessly in love. She's convinced him to have experimental surgery."

The rancor in Emily's words were like a physical blow. The Beast had lived her life avoiding people. She had no experience with ugly confrontations. Right now, she was in a weakened state, too stricken with what she'd done to argue with this woman.

"Shelly is a good person," Trevor said.

They were talking as if she were in another room.

"I'll bet the conniving bitch convinced Matt to change his insurance policy."

"He never mentioned a policy," she interjected.

"He never mentioned the risk he was taking either, did he?"

She refused to take this woman's scathing attack. If Matt's life was in such grave danger, what did it matter if she told them the truth?

"Blame me for convincing Matt to have this surgery, but don't accuse me of plotting to make a profit from his death." She dropped into the chair opposite the sofa where they were sitting. "My name isn't Rochelle Ralston. I'm Amy Conroy. I've been in the Witness Protection Program. That's why—"

"Oh, puleeze!" Emily jumped to her feet and crossed the room. "Don't expect me to buy *that* bridge. You're a nut. You had one date with Matt, then went around telling everyone the two of you were having an affair. You made up the most outrageous stories about things that *never* happened."

"I never met Matt until there was confusion after the accident. He mistook me for Shelly."

Emily whirled around to face her. "If that were true, Matt would have told me. We talked about you. He never mentioned one thing about you being someone else. You're lying."

"He wanted to protect me. There are people out there who might kill me—if they suspected I wasn't Shelly."

"You're insane. Next you'll be claiming aliens forced you to do things. I should call—"

"Emily, calm down." Trevor stood up and put his hand on her arm. "Let's take a walk."

He guided her into the hall, saying, "Look, Emily is a little overwrought. You see, she had custody of Matt after their mother died. She raised him, so she's like a mother bear, protecting her cub."

"I am telling the truth, Trevor. My name is Amy Joyce Conroy. I switched places with Shelly. She's the one who really died in the crash."

Trevor's earnest expression became confused. "The police positively IDed the woman as—"

"You didn't recognize the policeman, remember? It was Scott

Phillips, an FBI agent in disguise. He wanted me to have a foolproof cover."

Trevor slowly nodded. "Matt knew all about it, didn't he? That's why he said all that stuff about shopping at Tiffany's with you for a ring."

"You're right. He was protecting me. That's why he didn't tell Emily the truth."

"Are you in danger?"

"No. I don't think so. But keep this to yourself."

"I will. Funny, I had this feeling about you all along. In no way did you fit Matt's original description of Shelly."

"Oh, Trevor, I love him so much. I—"

"I know. I meant what I said. You're a good person, the best. You helped me deal with my mother's death." Trevor stopped; they were in the flower-filled reception area now. "Let me handle Emily. Why don't you go home and get some rest, then—"

"I can't leave Matt."

"The surgery will take several hours. If you don't mind me saying so, you look like hell. Do you want Matt to wake up and see you like this?"

It had been almost forty-eight hours since she'd slept, but she didn't feel like sleeping. "I don't care what I look like. I just want Matt to be okay."

"Give me some time alone with Emily. I'll make her understand that you're telling the truth. I'll take care of it."

"I can't leave. I want to wait—"

"With Emily going ballistic? Wouldn't it be better if you went home, then came back after I talked to her?"

"All right," she reluctantly agreed. "I'll check on Jiggs. He's been behaving very oddly, then I'll come right back."

"There's no hurry. Dr. Dietz told us he has to work slowly, remember? Why don't you call me a little later and I'll give you an update on Matt's condition?"

"I'll call you soon," she promised. "Please, make Emily understand."

She left Trevor and slowly walked outside. The morning sunlight washed over her, bringing with it the sweet, earthy smell of the tropics. The warm breeze moaned through the dried palm fronds, whispering Matt's name.

She was surrounded by the Key West that Matt loved, a profusion of blue. The sky, the water. And the freedom to be yourself.

If there was one thing she had learned since her mother's death, it was how to find herself and leave The Beast behind. There were many roads in life, but hers had zigzagged across the entire country to bring her to a place she could call home.

Key West.

Here she'd met the man she loved. Matt was her destiny. She couldn't imagine what her life would have been like if fate hadn't brought them together.

She ambled across the clinic's manicured lawn to the sugar-fine sand beach. A kingfisher prowled the shore, stalking some fish that she couldn't see. In the channel, kids on Jet Skies and Wave Runners were racing by.

Just another day in paradise.

But this wasn't simply another day. This might be Matt's last hours on this earth. Why hadn't he given her the chance to truly say good-bye?

She stood, watching the kingfisher eat his catch, then decided Trevor was right. She did not want to face Emily until Trevor had convinced Matt's sister that she was really Amy Conroy.

Praying the whole way, she walked back into town. Trevor's launch was still at the dock where Matt had left it. Thinking Trevor might need it, she waited for the Sunset Key's hourly water shuttle.

Thankfully she was the only one on the small boat. She didn't have it in her to make meaningless conversation today.

She got off the shuttle and looked for the golf cart that Trevor usually kept nearby, but it was gone. She set off on the brick path, anxious to get home and call Trevor for an update on Matt's condition. To the side was the house Irene and Dexxter had rented.

The place appeared to be deserted. The mangled railing on the upper level deck hadn't been fixed. Drawn by morbid curiosity, she moved closer. On the lush grass facing the sea was the chalk outline of a body.

What had Bubbles said? Splat! Well, that did describe it. Dexx had landed with each arm and leg pointed in a different direction, like a human starfish.

"Could Irene have killed him?" she mumbled to herself, staring at the chalk outline.

It didn't seem possible. The woman had been head-over-heels crazy about Dexxter, and they'd been together since they were kids. Still, people did strange things sometimes. She would never have suspected Matt would deliberately deceive her about the seriousness of the surgery.

She turned to go. Out of the corner of her eye, she thought one of the blades of the plantation shutters moved. The fine hair across the back of her neck stood at attention.

Having already been to hell—and back—she wasn't afraid of Irene, but she didn't want any trouble right now. She had to concentrate on Matt. Maybe she should let the FBI know she had returned to Half Moon Bay.

She hurried across the island and found the front door, which faced the center of the island, unlocked as usual. "Bubbles? Are you here?"

No one answered, so she walked to the message center. No one had left a note, and there weren't any messages on the machine. She called the hospital.

"I'm working on Emily," Trevor said when he came to the telephone. "She's every bit as stubborn as her brother. She thinks you've conned me. I'm going to need a little more time."

She agreed to call him again before returning to the hospital. If Emily wasn't convinced then, well, too bad. She was going to go back any way.

Even though the line might not be secure, she dialed Scott Phillips's room at the Pier Hotel. No one answered.

Out on the terrace she saw Jiggs swimming offshore. "Jiggs. Jiggs. Here, boy."

It appeared that he'd caught himself a Styrofoam cooler. He was swimming for all he was worth, towing the darn thing.

"You have to wonder what goes through his mind."

She sat on the grass where she and Matt had made love the first time and where they'd spent the previous night. "Please, God, spare him. I'll do anything. I would even become The Beast again, if you'll let him live."

She drew in a sharp breath of air that was thick with sunshine and the loaminess of the tropics. Who needed nature intruding right now? She wanted to caress his rough cheeks and savor the prickles of his emerging beard. She wanted him back, where he belonged, with her.

But he wasn't here. All she might ever have of him was a memory.

She'd been alone for so long that she honestly believed she knew the depths of despair. How wrong she'd been. Nothing could have prepared her for this moment. The fierce, heartbreaking emptiness of life without Matt spoke to what was already hollow and empty and lonely within her soul. She had suffered before, but this time, having known love, it was going to be unimaginably worse.

On her back now, she gazed up at the sun. Clive had said there was nothing she could do except pray. "Please, God, spare Matthew, please."

Like a mantra, she said the words over and over. She wasn't sure how much time had passed when the sound of the telephone broke into her thoughts. As she raced for the house, she saw Jiggs had wrestled the cooler onto the sand and was out in the water again.

By the time she reached the telephone, the answering machine was taking a very frantic message. "This is Paws 'N Claws. Bingo must be picked up immediately."

"Hello. Is Bingo giving you a problem?"

The woman released an exasperated sigh. "He will not shut up. He keeps hissing and spitting and throwing himself against the side of the cage."

"No one can come get him right now. Maybe—"

"Someone *has* to get him. Unless he calms down, the doctor says he'll injure himself even more."

"Can't you give him a shot of something?"

"Bingo is so full of medication that the doctor is concerned about an overdose. Can't someone take him home? Cats are much more comfortable in familiar surroundings."

Inwardly she groaned as she checked her watch. It would be a long time before Matt came out of surgery. She could get Bingo and be back at the hospital before the surgery was over. Bingo was Trevor's favorite. Bringing the big tom home was the least she could do.

"I'll be right over."

After she'd brought Bingo home, she would immediately return to the hospital. By then Trevor should have talked to Emily, and Matt would be close to coming out of surgery.

Why did people sit at the hospital—waiting? she asked herself. People knew surgery would take hours, yet they waited and waited. She supposed it was a way of being with someone in spirit, even if they didn't know you were there.

Feeling guilty for deserting Matt, she rushed down to the beach. This was something constructive she could do, she told herself. She owed it to Trevor. Still, she didn't like not being near Matt.

What if something happened and she wasn't there?

She rushed across the island to catch the shuttle. The boat was pulling away, but the captain saw her coming and waited.

"Hey, Shelly."

She looked up, realizing her thoughts had drifted. They were across the channel, pulling into the Sunset Dock. Kyle was standing on the platform, waiting for the water shuttle.

"Kyle, hi there."

He didn't know about Matt, and she wasn't certain she could explain the situation without bursting into tears. He helped her off the boat.

"Where are you going?"

"I'm picking up Bingo for Trevor. The cat had an accident, but now he's driving them nuts at the vet's."

"I'll help you." He took her elbow and guided her up the ramp. "What happened to Bingo?"

"We think he fell out of the palm tree. In the middle of the night, Jiggs started howling and we found Bingo on the terrace. His sternum had been shattered, not broken, but shattered."

"Shattered? That's weird." Kyle flagged down a rickie and they got in. "Cats are so agile, especially Bingo. He's a born hunter."

"There was an odd mark on his fur too. Like a burn."

Kyle studied her in that intent way of his. "It sounds like someone hit him with a stun gun."

"There wasn't anyone around except Jiggs."

"You may not have seen the person."

"How do you know so much about weapons? I wouldn't know a stun gun if I saw one."

Kyle shrugged and she knew he wasn't going to divulge any information about his job. "A stun gun looks like a regular gun except it has a fatter barrel. It delivers a jolt of electricity that immobilizes a person."

"Why would anyone on Sunset Key have a stun gun?"

The darkness seemed never ending, but it was a comforting darkness, like being inside a cocoon. The pitch blackness was warm, not hot, just pleasantly warm. He heard voices, but they seemed to be coming through water or layers of thick fabric.

Not one word made sense.

Don't fight it, said some inner voice. He let himself drift along. Minutes, hours, or, maybe, days slipped by as he hovered in the darkness, suspended in time.

"Matt, can you hear me?"

Inwardly, he smiled. That was his mother's voice. No, of course, it wasn't his mother. Unless he was in heaven.

The thought jolted him, and he tried to open his eyes, but his lids seemed to be sealed shut. He was trapped in a dark void that couldn't possibly be heaven.

The operation!

The last thing he remembered was hugging Trevor. Had he made it through the surgery? Could he possibly be so lucky?

"Matt, listen to me."

Ah, not his mother. His sister, Emily was talking to him, and although the words were softly spoken, her voice had an edge to it.

Something was wrong.

He tried to speak, but couldn't find his voice. His tongue was thick and as dry as old newsprint. He gave up and drifted off into Never–Never Land again.

Time blurred as he coasted along, aware of voices, but not quite hearing what was being said. Slowly, he awoke by degrees, realizing . . .

HE HAD SURVIVED!

He had a mild headache, but he was blissfully alive. Thank you, God.

"Matthew, do you hear me?"

A slight German accent. The voice must belong to Dr. Dietz. Matt struggled, finally managing to crack one lid, then the other. The light blinded him, and he snapped his eyes shut for a moment. When he ventured to open them again, he saw Clive and Dr. Dietz hovering over him.

"Do you understand what we're saying?" Clive asked.

He croaked out, "Yes."

"It looks as if you're fine," the doctor said with undisguised pride.

"We're going to test your reactions," Clive said. "Just to be sure you're functioning normally."

They pinched his toe and tapped his knee. Then they had him count backward from twenty-five. Yes, he knew the capital of Finland. Helsinki.

"Good, very good," said the doctor.

"I can't believe it," Clive said. "I wasn't sure."

Matt raised his hand. "That makes two of us, buddy."

"You're going to be able to go home tomorrow," Clive added with a smile.

"If we were in Germany, he could go home today," the doctor informed them.

"Hey, I'm ready," Matt said.

"Hold it. This is my clinic." Clive looked very concerned. "You've just had surgery. The medication hasn't worn off yet."

"We didn't use much medication. It wasn't necessary. I performed the surgery with the patient in the upright position." The doctor was getting a little huffy with Clive. "There is no swelling the way there would be with conventional surgery."

"I know. I know," Clive said, "but Matt is a good friend of mine. Let's be cautious." He turned to Matt. "I want to get you up and walking. Then we'll give you a light meal. After a good night's sleep, I'll release you first thing in the morning."

"Okay," Matt agreed. "I want to see Shelly now."

"I have a plane to catch," Dr. Dietz said.

"Doctor, how can I thank you?" To his chagrin, his voice had a slight rasp, and he had to swallow twice to get rid of the damn lump in his throat. "You gave me back my life."

"You're living proof that my method works. Digital computer images of the brain—during microsurgery—will become standard in the future. It's less invasive, less damaging. Tomorrow you won't even know you had an operation."

"Great. Thanks again," Matt said, realizing just how inadequate words were.

"What time is it?" he asked, noticing dusk was falling outside the fancy room.

"It's six-thirty," Clive told him. "Trevor and Emily are getting coffee. We tried to wake you earlier, but you weren't ready. I'll get them."

"Where's Shelly?"

Clive shrugged and waited while Dr. Dietz left the room before answering. "She realized you'd lied to her, and she was terribly upset. Then Emily accused her of . . . killing you by persuading you to undergo this procedure. Trevor sent Shelly back to Half Moon Bay. She called to check on you. She should be here soon."

He didn't like Shelly being out there all alone. Until they knew what the transmitter had picked up, they couldn't be sure Irene wasn't dangerous.

C H A P T E R
THIRTY-SIX

The sun was setting on paradise as Kyle paid the private water taxi to drive them directly to Half Moon Bay rather than taking the island's shuttle to Sunset Key's main dock. Getting Bingo had taken much longer than she'd anticipated, but then, she had never encountered a mob scene like the Fantasy Fest, which was in full swing.

Key West's streets had been clogged with people—most of them well on their way to being drunk—dressed in costumes. The Fantasy Fest was said to rival Mardi Gras, but she wasn't in the mood for it. There wasn't a rickie available coming or going. They had to walk the entire length of the island, dodging hordes of revelers.

Getting Bingo had taken twice as long as she'd anticipated. She should have been at the hospital waiting for news. She'd called the clinic and learned he was still in the recovery room but hadn't regained consciousness. They wouldn't know if the operation was a success until he was awake. No matter what Emily thought, she had to get back there right away. She'd already wasted too much time.

"Jee-zus! Let that cat out," Kyle said the moment they were on the dock.

Bingo had howled nonstop since they put him in the carrier at Paws 'N Claws. It had taken two trained techs to do it, and both of them had gotten scratched in the process.

"Jiggs, Jiggs," she called as she unlatched the cat carrier. "Look who's here."

Like a vest, a thick plaster cast encased the top part of Bingo's body. His legs were free as was his head, but his chest was encased.

He lumbered out of the carrier, staggering like a drunk at the Fantasy Fest.

"At least he's shut up," Kyle said.

Jiggs hit the decking full speed and scampered up to the cat. He slammed to a stop, almost skidding into Bingo. Jiggs gave Bingo a sloppy drubbing with his tongue. The two of them ambled off together.

"Doesn't that beat all?" Kyle said.

"It's just plain weird." She had to get to a telephone and check Matt's condition. She'd been so heartsick that she hadn't mentioned it to Kyle. She rushed toward the house and he followed her.

"Where is everyone?" Kyle asked.

"Bubbles met some new guy," she hedged, still not feeling like discussing Matt. "I'd offer you a drink, but I've got to run."

Kyle gave her a strange look. "You're not going back into Key West, are you? It gets pretty rowdy after dark during Fantasy Fest."

"No. I'm going out to the Bel Aire Clinic."

"Okay," he said as he paused at the fork in the brick path. "Catch you later."

"Thanks for helping me," she called over her shoulder, not breaking her stride. She had to find out Matt's condition. She'd been gone much longer than she had anticipated. "I don't know what I would have done without you, Kyle."

She raced into the house and went right to the message center to see if Trevor had called. The light wasn't blinking. There was a folded piece of paper with her name on it. She didn't recognize the writing. Unfolding it, she read the message.

Matthew Jensen died without regaining consciousness.

"Oh, my God! No! Tell me it isn't true."

She grabbed the phone, then realized she didn't know the clinic's number to verify the message. A few moments later, information gave her the number. The line was busy.

She dropped the receiver into the cradle. Why bother? The hospital would only reconfirm the message. The odds had been heavily against Matt. Only a miracle could have saved him.

It's all your fault.

She didn't know the tears were coming until they streamed down her cheeks. Choking back sobs, she wandered out to the terrace and stared at the deepening shadows. The sun had already set—no doubt, in a blaze of glory—and the breeze was nothing more than a cat's paw of wind, gusting through the palms.

Sadness too deep for tears pierced her soul. Suddenly, paradise didn't seem so beautiful. Instead, it was nothing more than a boundless sweep of blue water and blue sky. A vast, empty world.

Lonely.

There was no turning back the hands of time, but locked in her memory was an image of Matt, the way he'd been the first time she'd seen him, sitting beside her bed. Strange, she'd been a little frightened of him. He'd saved her, and she had repaid him by encouraging him to undergo an operation that ended his life even sooner than necessary.

How was she going to live with herself?

She stood there, silently crying, sad and frustrated and angry with herself. In the house she heard the telephone ringing. She didn't even consider answering it. What was left to say?

If you dropped dead tomorrow, I'd dance on your grave.

Her heartless words returned to haunt her. How could she have been so cruel? Matt had known he was dying when she'd carelessly taunted him. How could she live with herself?

She wandered the beach until the tears finally stopped. Her whole body seemed drained, a hollow, empty shell. She wasn't sure she had the strength to walk back up to the house.

Did it matter where she went or what she did?

She sat down on the grass where she and Matt had made love. Raucous music, a mixture of reggae, country, and heavy metal, blasted across the water. Duval Street's clubs were noisier than usual, celebrating the Fantasy Fest with live bands, each of them trying to out do the other.

Life went on, but she couldn't imagine it going on for her. The future had seemed so bright, but now . . .

"Yip! Yip-yip!"

Jiggs barked frantically, the way he had the night of Bingo's accident. She heaved herself to her feet and walked up to the house. Hungry cats bounded up to her, rubbing against her legs. When she flipped on the lights, Jiggs was standing by the pantry door, barking.

"Hush. I'm here. What's wrong?"

A quick peek inside the pantry revealed Bingo wedged between a huge bag of kibble and the wall. He'd evidently underestimated his new size with the plaster cast on his torso. She moved the bag, then picked him up.

"Raiding the pantry is out of the question, big guy."

She held him with both arms, realizing just how much weight the cast added. Thank heavens Kyle had carried him across the island. Nearly stumbling over the circling cats, she noticed a piece of paper on the center island.

Had it been there earlier? She didn't think so. Still holding Bingo, she walked over and read the computer printed message.

```
With Matthew gone, life is no longer worth
living. Thank you, Trevor, for all you've done
for me. Don't be sad. I'm leaving this world
to join him.
Shelly
```

"What on earth?"

"Your suicide note."

She whirled around and saw Irene Hanson aiming a gun at her. "I-I don't understand," she said, stalling, desperately trying to think what to do.

"I thought about arranging an accident. Then I found out about Matt's surgery. His death has left you distraught. You walked right off the end of the pier . . . and drowned."

"You'll never get away with it."

"Of course I will. They won't be suspicious about the computer note. No one expects you to write with your bad hand."

Something rose up inside her, a feeling so fierce and intense that she trembled from its force. Matt would have died in vain if she allowed this woman to kill her. She had nothing left to lose. The future Matt had wanted so much that he gambled with his life was nothing more than a pipe dream.

The Beast was gone. The new woman refused to die without a valiant fight.

"Move!" Irene yelled.

She parted her lips to scream, then remembered that her mouth didn't open wide enough for a full-blown yell that might get Kyle's attention in the nearest house to Half Moon Bay. All she had was her own wits.

And a right hand incapable of assisting her.

"Move!" Irene screeched.

"Where?" She tried to sound terrified, when actually a lethal calmness had settled over her.

"To the end of the pier."

Clutching Bingo, she slowly walked in front of Irene who had the muzzle of her gun pressed into the small of her back. Out of the corner of her eye, she saw the cats remained in the kitchen, waiting to be fed. Jiggs trotted along beside her.

"Irene, why are you doing this? It doesn't make any sense."

"You may have fooled Dexxter. He wasn't very bright, but I know you're Amy Conroy. With you out of the way, the authorities will never be able to make a case against me."

"If you shoot me, they'll get you for murder."

"I'm not using this gun. I have a Tazer in my pocket. It'll look like suicide."

She remembered what Kyle had told her about stun guns. One zap and she would be immobilized. If she fell in the water, she would drown.

They had crossed the terrace and were on the path down to the dock now. Time was running out fast, and she didn't have a plan.

"By the way," Irene said, a smirk in her voice, "Matthew Jensen's surgery was a success. He didn't die."

Alive! Matt was still alive! Thank you, God.

Her heart lurched madly at the news. If Matt was alive, she had to outwit Irene. The future she'd always dreamed about was at stake.

She halted and Irene bumped into her, ramming the gun into her back. She turned her head to look at Irene. "You left the note saying he died. Why?"

"I wanted you to suffer the way I suffered every time Dexx threw himself at you."

"It wasn't my fault. I—"

"It doesn't matter. I loved him with all my heart, but it wasn't enough."

"Did you kill him?"

"Of course." Irene smiled and nudged her with the gun. "Keep moving."

She slowly started to walk, Bingo a dead weight in her arms. Jiggs merrily skipped along at her side, keeping his hero in sight at all times. She walked out to the end of the long pier, then stopped.

"Face me."

As she turned, she saw Irene pulling the Tazer out of her pocket. She still had the revolver aimed at her. Time was up.

Acting on instinct, she flung Bingo at Irene's face.

"Yee-oowl," screeched the cat as he crashed into Irene, scratching like a wildcat. She dove off the pier, but just as she hit the water, a bolt of something akin to lightning struck her lower back.

Numb all over, unable to move, the gunshots that followed barely registered in her dazed brain.

"Shelly was with Kyle when she called from the vet's," Trevor told Matt.

Emily added, "Maybe they stopped for a drink somewhere."

"No, something's wrong."

At first he'd been so damn glad to have survived that he couldn't think of anything else. Now, he was more frightened than he'd been going into the surgery.

Something had happened to Shelly.

"I called Half Moon Bay. No one answered," Trevor told him. "Kyle didn't answer either. Do you want me to go out there?"

Before Matt could respond, Clive stuck his head in the room. "There's a Scott Phillips here to see you."

The FBI agent marched in. "Where's Shelly?"

"She's not here," Matt said. "We're not sure where she is."

"Son of a bitch!" The agent whacked his forehead with the palm of his hand.

Trevor said, "She called, but that was several hours ago."

"What was on the disk?" Matt asked although he already knew it was bad.

"Apparently, Dexxter tried to kill Irene. That's why she shoved him off the deck," the agent said to the group. "But first she told him she was going to kill Shelly with a stun gun and make it look like an accidental drowning."

The pit of his stomach churned. This was exactly what he'd feared. All along he'd sensed she was in danger. He swung his legs out of the bed.

"What are you doing?" Emily cried.

"I'm going to find Shelly."

Clive checked his move to the closet where his clothes were hanging, and Trevor stepped up beside him, saying, "Matt, you've just had major surgery. You can't go running around."

"In Germany, I would have gone home today," he informed them.

"That's premature," Clive insisted. "We must keep you under observation to make certain you're all right."

"Let me take care of Shelly," Scott Phillips said, blocking his way.

"Matthew, please." Tears were streaming down Emily's face as she clung to his arm. "You've just had surgery."

He couldn't fight them all, he decided, especially not his sister's tears. "All right." He climbed into bed again.

Scott Phillips left immediately, but Matt had a hell of a time getting rid of the others.

"What's going on?" Trevor asked. "Why would Irene want to kill Shelly?"

Matt used up precious time, explaining who Amy really was and her involvement with Dexxter Foxx.

"Now it makes sense," Emily said. "I'm sorry I was so mean to Shelly. I didn't believe her story."

"Matt understands," Trevor said when he didn't answer.

"I'm a little tired," he said. "I want to rest, but wake me up the minute you find out anything about her."

The second the door closed, Matt was out of bed. A little unsteady on his feet, he grabbed his trousers from the closet and pulled them on. Tucking the hospital gown into his pants, he didn't care how silly it would look. He peeked out the door; two nurses were chatting at the end of the hall. Seconds seeming like days, but finally, they left.

For once luck was with him. No one was around. He thought he might have to waste more time hot-wiring Trevor's Porsche, but a taxi was just dropping off a woman.

"I'll give you a hundred bucks to get me to Sunset Pier as fast as you can," he said, feeling more light-headed than he'd anticipated. "It's an emergency."

The Bahamian cabdriver sped south, making good time until they hit Old Town. "It's de Fantasy Fest, mon. De snails, dey be faster than my taxi, mon."

"I'll walk from here."

Matt tossed him a few bills, then jumped out of the taxi. For a moment, he stood there, swaying slightly as he watched throngs of people in costumes. Some of the outfits were authentic period pieces with unbelievable detail. Others were just plain outrageous like the man wearing an outhouse covered with graffiti.

He'd never been to Key West during this celebration, but he had been to Mardi Gras. It seemed to be pretty much the same, he decided as he shouldered his way through the mob, realizing he was weaker than he'd anticipated. No one paid any attention to a man in a hospital gown with a patch of his head shaved.

It was less crowded at Sunset Pier, and luck was still with him. Trevor's boat was there. He jumped in the launch and started the engine. Flooring the accelerator, the boat shot out from the dock. Halfway across the water, he could see lights and people at Half Moon Bay's pier.

"Please," he prayed out loud. "Let Shelly be with them."

As he pulled into the slip, Matt saw a policeman talking to Irene and Kyle. "Where's Shelly?"

"I don't know. She said she was going out to the clinic," Kyle answered.

Another boat zoomed up with Scott Phillips and another man in it. "What are you doing here?" the agent asked Matt.

"Where in hell have you been?"

"We had engine problems." The agent jumped out of the small boat and flashed his ID at the policeman. "What's going on?"

"Mr. Parker called us."

"I heard gunshots, and when I got here I found Irene," Kyle Parker said. "I called the police on my cell phone."

"That one-eyed cat attacked me. I shot at him, that's all." Irene had a jagged scratch mark down the side of her face and claw marks on her arms.

Matt grabbed Irene by the throat. "Where is she?"

It took both the policeman and Phillips to pull Matt off Irene. The conniving bitch never uttered a single word. Before, Matt had felt weak. Now a surge of fury made every muscle tighten.

"We have a recording of you killing Dexxter Foxx and threatening to kill Shelly. You might as well tell us where she is," Phillips said. "You're under arrest."

"I know my rights. I want my lawyer."

Matt raced off the pier, Kyle at his heels. Ahead, on the terrace, was Bingo, rubbing against the side of the house, trying to pry off the cast.

"I'll search inside," Kyle said.

Matt ran along the shore, calling Shelly's name. The silvery sand was deserted, a fickle breeze riffled the palms. There was no sign of her anywhere.

An accidental drowning.

That's what Irene had said on the disk. Shelly must be out in the water, by the pier where Kyle had found Irene. He needed to get flashlights from the house and go out in the boat.

He spun around, then stopped, not certain if he heard something or not. Driven by the trade winds, loud noise floated across the channel. There was so damn much commotion from Key West's Fantasy Fest that it was hard to hear.

"Yip. Yip-yip!"

It was just Jiggs. He was out in the mangroves that flanked the far side of the beach. Matt rushed toward the house and noticed Bingo again. Jiggs never left Bingo's side. What was he doing in the mangroves?

Matt charged over the sand toward the cluster of low-growing trees and kicked off his shoes. He waded through knee-high water, making his way to the barking dog. He shoved aside a prickly branch, then another and another. Ahead, on a sandbar, he saw Jiggs standing beside a prone body that was half in, half out of the water.

"Shelly! Shelly!" He waded closer.

She lifted her head slowly as if it were a dead weight. Her hair was soaked, a livid bruise marred one cheek, and she was frighteningly pale. She was the most beautiful thing he'd ever seen.

"Matt? What are you doing out of the hospital?"

He collapsed to the sand beside her. "I had to help." He touched her wet head. "Are you okay?"

She groaned as she pulled herself into a sitting position. "I'm fine—honest. How are you? Why aren't you in the hospital?"

"I was worried about you," he said, suddenly feeling the strength leave his body. "I was going home tomorrow anyway. I just left a bit early—to see if you were all right."

She reached over to pet Jiggs. "This little guy saved me. Irene zapped me with a stun gun. I was in the water and couldn't breathe. Irene was shooting at me. I was barely floating when Jiggs jumped in. He towed me by my hair under the pier, where Irene couldn't see me. When I could move again, I swam underwater and came here to hide."

Matt gathered her into his arms. "Didn't you hear us calling your name?"

"No. There's so much noise tonight."

"It's okay now. Irene's under arrest. Let's get you into the house."

She gazed up at him. "Matt, you had me so frightened. How could you not tell me about the terrible risk?"

"I didn't want you to talk me out of it. You can be mighty persuasive, you know. Besides you were right. Character determines fate. You rescued an abused dog, and he repaid your kindness. Something wouldn't let me turn my back on Rochelle Ralston."

"Matt, are you strong enough to walk with me across the beach?"

"I'm okay, honest," he fibbed. He was exhausted, more from not having slept in days, he thought, than the surgery. "Irene is on the dock with the FBI and the local authorities."

"Perfect! I want her to know that she didn't get away with anything. She was responsible for everything Dexxter did. Now she has to pay the piper."

Matt heaved himself to his feet. "Let's go, babe."

Clinging to each other, they slowly waded through the dense mangroves. Jiggs dog-paddled along behind them. When they reached the beach, Matt saw the lights on the dock. Another boat had arrived.

"Matt! Amy!" cried his sister as they crossed the sandy crescent everyone called Half Moon Bay. "You're—you're okay. Thank God."

"Matt," called Clive. "I told you not to leave the hospital."

"Shelly—I mean, Amy, are you all right?" asked Trevor.

"I'm fine, just fine." She gave Matt a one-armed hug. "Matt's okay and that's all I care about, believe me."

"What happened with Irene?" Scott Phillips asked her.

In handcuffs Irene stood beside the policeman from Key West, her expression sullen, belligerent.

"Irene tried to kill me. She had a stun gun and a revolver. She must have thrown them in the water."

Scott's smile could have lit up a ballroom. "Book Irene Hanson for attempted murder. We'll add the other charges later."

Amy whispered in Matt's ear, "Let's get you to bed."

"Now, you're talking." He waved to the group as they started toward the house. "We're outta here."

Emily rushed up beside them. "Shelly, I mean Amy, please forgive me for the way I behaved."

Amy's expression softened, and he could see the woman he loved had already forgiven his sister. "You love Matt. I love him too. I understand how you felt. You were only trying to protect him."

"Em, I'll see you in the morning. It's time you got to know Amy. She's going to be family, you know."

His sister grinned. "Why am I not surprised?"

Arms around each other, they walked into the house, leaving the others to talk to the authorities. Matt suddenly felt even weaker than before. This time he realized it wasn't the surgery or exhaustion.

It was Amy.

He'd come frighteningly close to losing her. Now, he was weak with sheer relief. "I don't know what I would have done, if Irene had killed you."

"I wasn't going to let that happen." She explained how Irene had tried to trick her into believing he'd died during the operation. "Even when I thought you were dead, I wasn't going to let you give up your life just so that woman could kill me. I intended to die fighting."

"In your own way, you've always been a fighter," he said as she opened the door to her room. "Haven't you?"

"I suppose." She kissed his cheek and nudged him toward the bed. "You need to rest. I don't care how revolutionary microsurgery is, you've been through a terrible ordeal. Get some sleep."

He was too tired to argue as he watched her turn back the covers. He plopped onto the bed and let Amy pull off his shoes.

"Character determines fate," Amy whispered as she stretched out beside him. "Fate took care of you. Now we'll have a lifetime together."

"Believe me, you were worth the risk. I loved you too much not to take a chance."

EPILOGUE

Three Months Later

Matt leaned back in his chair and watched the group on the sand not far away from Half Moon Bay's terrace. His sister, Emily, and her husband were huddled under a huge umbrella. Beneath the shade of the blue and white stripped canvas cooed the baby they had struggled to conceive, Samantha Lynn.

Nearby, Amy was sunning herself, talking nonstop to Emily about babies. Despite a rocky beginning, the two had become the best of friends.

"Matt, here's the latest issue of *Exposé*," Trevor said as he came out of the house. "Your article is the feature."

Matt took his eyes off his wife as Trevor gave him the magazine.

"I've already read it," Trevor told him. "You'll certainly open the world's eyes to the latest techniques in brain microsurgery."

"I hope so," Matt replied.

Since his own brush with death and the hell of searching for Amy, his view of life had changed. He'd settled in a home on Sunset Key, not far from Half Moon Bay. His career in journalism had taken a different turn. Now, he was content to freelance, writing articles that interested him, so he could spend as much time as possible with Amy.

His latest article featured Dr. Dietz's revolutionary procedure, which was quickly gaining acceptance in the medical community. The German doctor had saved his life and could help hundreds of other patients with inoperable brain tumors—if the medical establishment would recognize the new procedure.

Trevor pointed to the picture of Matt helping Amy along the shore. "No one would believe you'd had a tumor removed just hours earlier."

"True, once the doctors would have made me stay flat on my back for days." Matt leaned forward in his chair, watching Amy take his sister's baby and cradle the infant to her breast. She was going to make a fantastic mother. "People need to know techniques are changing. Now, they're performing heart surgery without stopping the heart from beating. The medical world is being transformed every day."

Trevor sat in the chair next to him and nodded his head toward the group on the beach. "Why don't you do an article on reconstructive surgery, contrasting it to cosmetic surgery?"

"Good idea." Matt knew Trevor was proud of the new turn in Clive's career. After Matt's revolutionary surgery, Clive had devoted more of his time to helping patients disfigured by accidents or birth defects and performed fewer cosmetic surgeries.

"Shelly, I mean Amy changed us all, didn't she?" Trevor asked.

"Yes, I—" Matt began but the telephone rang and Trevor rose to answer it.

A few minutes later, he came back. "It's for you."

Matt didn't like Trevor's strange tone.

Amy cuddled the sleeping infant. "Is there anything more beautiful than a baby?" she asked Emily.

"No, and Samantha is the most beautiful baby on earth, right?"

Amy giggled softly, not wanting to awaken her niece. Niece. Once she wouldn't have thought it possible, but she had a family to call her own.

"Oh, Mama, you should see me now," she whispered under her breath as she gazed up at the flawless blue sky, doming over Half Moon Bay.

She knew her mother was in heaven, watching her. Her mother would be thrilled that she was married and expecting a child. Thrilled. "You would have made the perfect grandmother," Amy said to herself. "That's my only regret. You haven't met Matt in person, and you won't be here when I have the baby."

She put her hand on her stomach. A slight swell was the only visible sign of her pregnancy, but soon that would change. They'd only been married three months; she'd conceived shortly after the small wedding at Half Moon Bay.

Matt's voice interrupted her thoughts. "Amy, let's go for a swim."

She hadn't heard him coming, but she was glad to see him. She handed the still sleeping infant to Emily, then stood up. Matt was looking at her the way he often did—as if he couldn't get enough of her.

Once The Beast would have gazed down at her toes, but that person no longer existed. Amy smiled at her husband and took his hand. They walked along the shore together, heading for the shallow part of the cove where the swimming was best.

"Aw, man, look at that." Matt pointed to Bingo chasing Jiggs through the mangroves at the far end of the beach.

She laughed. "The odd couple, for sure. Now that Bingo is out of his cast, he's hell on wheels."

Matt stopped and turned toward her, his expression serious. "I just had a call. Irene has decided to plead guilty. You won't have to testify at her trial."

"That's good news, I guess. It'll save the taxpayers money, but I wanted to stand up in court and tell the jury how she tried to kill me."

He slipped both arms around her waist and pulled her close. "A long trial like that wouldn't have been good for you . . . or the babies."

"Babies? What are you talking about?"

"After I found out about Irene, I called Dr. Robinson for the Ultrasound results." He paused to give her a pleased grin. "We're having a boy and a girl."

"Twins?"

"Yes. You're happy, aren't you? I've always wanted a big family. I thought you did, too."

Tears seeped from her eyes. She seemed to be on the verge of tears all the time now. Hormones, Emily assured her, but it made Amy upset with herself.

"Of course, I'm happy. I'm just worried that I won't be a good mother."

Matt kissed her forehead. "That's natural, darling. I'm worried about being a father. I never had a role model, you know. But we love each other. That's what counts. We'll figure it out together."

"I'm the luckiest woman on earth."

"No, I'm the luckiest guy. I've got my life in balance now. I know what counts. You . . . my family, my friends." He kissed her on the lips this time, a light, tender kiss. "I owe it all to you. I can't tell you how very much I love you."

Please turn the page for an exciting sneak peek of

Meryl Sawyer's newest novel of romantic suspense

EVERY WAKING MOMENT

now on sale at bookstores everywhere!

PROLOGUE
FINAL DESTINATION

A gem of inspiration could appear anywhere. Out of the blue or from the Psalms. Today it had come over the radio.

"From the moment of conception, the journey begins. The final destination never alters. It is always death."

Perfect.

"Why hadn't you thought of putting death in such simple terms?" he asked his reflection in the bathroom mirror.

It was so true. Man was conceived and ultimately died. Some died sooner, and more violently, than others.

But eventually, everyone died.

Death fascinated people—especially brutal deaths. No doubt about it. Just tune into the evening news. Plane crashes. Car accidents. Drive-by shootings.

Brutal murder.

Well, he had to admit, murder could be interesting.

It beat death by natural causes, which was a major snoozer. Unless you were someone important, it was a nonevent for television. Your demise was confined to a few lines in the obituaries.

Not all murders were worthy of attention, he noted not for the first time. Most killings were pathetic, botched jobs.

Crimes of passion, not crimes of expertise.

The police had absolutely no trouble catching those idiots. But a cunning killer was a different story. Murder could be handled with finesse, and not be an impulsive, stupid act that left a trail of clues a blind squirrel could follow.

No. If he remained clever—and patient—murder could be elevated to an art.

"Wait!" he said, studying his reflection for a flaw and finding none. "Art is the wrong word. A game. Now, that's a better description."

Not just an ordinary game, but an intellectual challenge requiring strategy, like chess. He had to plan his moves, one . . . two . . . three and even four steps ahead of his unsuspecting opponent.

Revenge took time and a well-crafted scheme.

"Have no doubt. I can plan the perfect crime," he said, flicking out the light and leaving the bathroom.

It required the proper subtlety to carefully plot murder. He refused to rush it and have his name added to the list of bunglers who killed and were so easily caught.

When it all came together, the way it was now—nothing, but nothing was sweeter. Or more fun than orchestrating the final moments of the adventure called life.

A dead gasp of a laugh ricocheted through the room, music to his ears.

"Death *is* the final destination."

1

It was nearly ten o'clock, but South Beach was just beginning to wake up, Taylor Maxwell noticed as she strolled along Ocean Drive toward Brew Ha-Ha. SoBe thrived on the club life, which meant dancing until dawn to frenetic music. Not that she was part of the club scene. Taylor lived in SoBe to enjoy the diverse culture.

Or so she told her family and friends.

Taylor secretly admitted she'd stayed in the apartment she'd shared with Paul Ashton to feel closer to him. He'd adored South Beach, and before he had disappeared, Taylor had spent her free time here with him. SoBe wasn't far from Coral Gables, where she'd grown up, but it was another world entirely.

A teenage boy sauntered toward her, his bopping walk swaying to a beat only he could hear. Attitude blazed from his dark eyes, half hidden by a Dolphins ball cap.

"Yo, mama. Lookin' good."

Taylor knew better than to respond. If she did, he'd follow her down the street, refusing to take no for an answer. She'd dressed conservatively—for SoBe—white shorts, strappy high-heeled red sandals, and a sky blue blouse tied at the midriff, baring only a few inches of skin. No exposed navel pierced with rings or studs for her.

The kid strutted into a newsstand specializing in magazines featuring nude women. She walked along the nearly deserted sidewalk, gazing beyond the stately royal palms at the beach. Sparkling blue waves swelled, crested, then tumbled onto the sand, leaving a trail of froth as they lazily retreated.

In the distance, a pale mist hung over the ocean, blurring the horizon where the blue sea met the even bluer sky. A cat's paw of wind ruffled the umbrellas and towels early beachgoers had set up to stake out their places on the white sand.

It was February and pleasantly warm, the weather that made Florida a mecca for snowbirds. Taylor had lived here for almost thirty-two years, her entire life, but she never took the climate or the scenery for granted.

One of the bitterest lessons she'd learned was *nothing* could be taken for granted.

The ability to survive and thrive—despite being so heartsick over Paul—was one of her strongest points. Through sheer determination, she'd concentrated on her job and had become very successful.

Nights were the hardest time

Hours of hope would crash into mind-numbing fear that she would never see Paul again. The only escape was to work until it was almost dawn on her computer trivia game.

Driving herself hard and forcing herself to tamp down her grief, her fear, kept her mind off Paul.

Most of the time.

But on sunny mornings like this, she couldn't help thinking he should be at her side, enjoying the beautiful day.

Taylor strolled into Brew Ha-Ha, and the fragrant scent of coffee greeted her. Salsa music pulsed from speakers that hung from the rafters. The coffee house was little more than a bamboo shack with palm fronds for a roof, but its Cuban-style coffee drinks made it a popular hangout.

She looked around for her friend, but Lisa hadn't arrived yet. A glance at her Ebell confirmed that she was a few minutes early. She decided to order and relax with coffee while she waited.

"*Café cubano*," she told the girl behind the counter. "A double."

It would be like mainlining high octane caffeine—a legal high. Taylor could almost feel the adrenaline rush just watching the girl pour the thick, sugar-laced Cuban coffee into a pink cup not much bigger than a shot glass. The scent of the *pan cubano* slathered with butter and toasting on the grill reminded Taylor she'd neglected to have dinner last night.

"I'll have a slice of *pan cubano tostado,* too."

She paid for the coffee and toasted Cuban bread, then found a small table under the shade of the ancient banyan tree that arched over the area like an umbrella. She added a touch of cream to the coffee even though this was a no-no to most who drank the Cuban coffee for its pure, intense flavor. As she was stirring the mixture and munching on the crusty Cuban bread, Taylor spotted Lisa, coming up the street with her usual jaunty stride.

Even though they were the same age and height, Lisa Abbott was like the flip side of a coin. While Taylor was fair with blond hair and blue eyes, Lisa had raven-black hair and melt-your-heart chocolate brown eyes. The hot-pink bustier and matching shorts she was wearing captured the attention of every male in the vicinity.

Taylor sprang to her feet, waving. "Lisa! Over here!"

Lisa rushed up and flung herself into Taylor's open arms. "Oh, God, I've missed you!"

Tears welled up in Taylor's eyes as she bear-hugged her closest friend. Nine months had passed since they had seen each other, but to Taylor, it seemed like years. With her brother, Trent, immersed in a new relationship, and with Paul gone for two years, Taylor had missed Lisa more than she ever could have imagined.

"Sit, sit," Taylor said. "Tell me everything."

Lisa rolled her dark eyes. "Do I have time to get coffee first?"

"Sure, but hurry. I want to hear all about your trip."

She sat down, taking a careful sip of her very hot coffee, and watched Lisa put in her order. Brew Ha-Ha was beginning to fill, and Taylor recognized several of the regulars. Most mornings she stopped in here for coffee to-go before climbing into her small Beamer to head to the Coral Gables offices of To The Maxx where she worked in the family business with her uncle and brother.

Lisa returned with a cup of flavored coffee and a double thick slice of *pan cubano tostado*. The scent of vanilla wafted across the table as her friend gently blew on the coffee to cool it.

"What's new?" Lisa asked.

"You don't want to know."

Taylor realized Lisa didn't inquire about Trent because she wanted Taylor to volunteer the news about her younger brother. Trent and Lisa had been happily married for six years—or so everyone assumed—until Trent asked for a divorce.

Lisa had been devastated. As soon as the papers had been signed, she'd gone on an around the world trip to find herself. Since she'd left, no one had spoken to her, but she'd e-mailed Taylor and her parents to say she was okay.

Still, Taylor had been worried. After the way Paul had vanished while abroad, she'd wondered if someone had stolen Lisa's laptop and she'd met a similar fate. Taylor had answered the telephone last night and discovered Lisa had returned.

"Tell me about your trip. Which country did you like best?" Taylor asked, calculatedly avoiding the subjects it would be painful to discuss—Trent's new love, Paul Ashton, her mother.

"I've been dying for this bread." Lisa took a bite of the *pan cubano.* "India is my favorite country—hands down."

Interesting, Taylor thought. She wouldn't have pictured Lisa in India.

"I spent six months there studying the *Kama Sutra.*"

"Really?"

Taylor sipped her coffee to hide her shock, thankful she was wearing shades. It was difficult to imagine one of Miami's up-and-coming financial advisors spending months studying the art of making love.

Lisa flipped her long hair back over one shoulder with her hand, a gesture Taylor had noticed the day they first met at Yale. "I'm changing careers. I'm opening a shop here in South Beach as soon as I can find space."

Changing careers? This was not like the steady, goal-oriented Lisa who had married her brother.

Tragedy changes you, Taylor decided.

She'd like to make a career change as well. She wanted to start her own company and develop computer games. She was a trivia buff and had a game already half finished, but now, with her mother so ill, was not the time to leave the family's cosmetics business.

"What kind of shop do you plan to open?"

Lisa smiled at Taylor over the rim of her cup. "I'm not sure what I'm going to call it yet, but it'll be a boutique that sells everything from sexy lingerie to love potions. There'll be classes for women in the evening to teach them the arts of the *Kama Sutra.*"

It was such an outrageous career change that Taylor might have laughed, if she hadn't known Lisa for fourteen years. What was Lisa thinking? This was a ridiculous idea—even in SoBe.

Then the light dawned. Trent. Lisa hadn't seen the divorce coming, hadn't suspected a thing.

Lisa blamed herself.

Taylor recognized the pain in Lisa's eyes because it mirrored her own loss. At times she wanted to break something, hit something. Scream.

The only solution was to maintain inner strength and deal with grim reality any way you could. For Lisa it might just be a *Kama Sutra* shop.

Only the strong survive, Taylor reminded herself.

"You think I've lost it, don't you?" Lisa asked, her voice pitched low.

Taylor couldn't lie, not to Lisa. She'd pick up on it in a heartbeat.

"No. I don't think you're crazy. I think you're blaming yourself for something that was beyond your control."

Lisa downed the last of her coffee, got up from the table, and went back for a refill. By the time she returned, Taylor had marshaled her thoughts.

"If you want to help people, why don't you go back to school and become a therapist?" Taylor suggested. "Better yet, become a personal coach. That's what many therapists are calling themselves. Men don't like to admit they need a therapist, but a coach—."

"You don't understand. That's the Western way. I'm into Eastern methods. It's a sensual, hands-on technique."

Taylor didn't know what to say. This was her best friend, but after her trip Lisa seemed like a stranger. Her mind wandered and she couldn't help wondering what Paul would be like, if he should suddenly reappear after an absence of two long years.

Time had changed her, too. She'd never been afraid to make business decisions, but she was much more confident now. Some of her innovations had received attention from the major cosmetics firms. Now they were fielding offers for their small company.

"Your turn," Lisa said. "What's been happening?"

Taylor took another sip of coffee, stalling, trying to decide if she should mention Trent's new love or not. She caught sight of a tall, dark-haired man and a dog in the line that had formed at the counter. She pushed her shades to the top of her head, leaned closer to Lisa, keeping her voice low.

"There's the mole."

Lisa's dark eyes widened. "Mole?"

"The creep who moved into my building. He lives right across the courtyard. This is the first time I've seen him out in the light of day. He slinks off to work at nine or so and comes back at dawn like a mole."

Lisa wrinkled her nose. "The guy in the wife beater?"

Taylor shook her head, realizing Lisa meant the man in the tank top cut extra wide at the arms to reveal bulging pecs and biceps. "No, the guy with the dog."

"The hunk with the Labrador retriever?" Lisa flipped her hair over her shoulder. "A mole? Nah. He probably works in one of the nightclubs."

"I doubt it. He takes his dog to work with him."

Lisa studied her for a moment. "Okay, what gives? Why don't you like him?"

"I've never met the man. There's something strange about him, that's all."

"Like what?"

"I'm not sure exactly. Twice now I've caught him looking at my apartment in an odd way."

"He wouldn't be the first guy to be curious about a knockout blonde, especially if she's right across the courtyard."

"He's never seen me. Both times, I was upstairs in my office, hidden by that humungous fern. I looked down and he was staring at the first floor of my apartment."

"Maybe he's new to the area. You know how people are about South Beach architecture. He was probably studying the cool etched-glass mermaid panels beside your front door or the rounded art deco corners of the building."

Taylor glanced at the man, who was now placing his order. "True, but it . . ."

"Gave you the creeps? Well, I think the guy could benefit from some *Kama Sutra* enlightenment. Introduce me."

"I told you. We haven't met." She stole another peek at the guy. He was ordering, his back to them, but the dog was watching her. "His dog is positively scary. See the way he's glaring at me?"

Lisa looked, but the Labrador had turned away. "You love dogs, especially Labs and retrievers. If it weren't for Paul, you'd have a golden retriever, right?"

Taylor nodded; Paul had been allergic to dogs. It had kept her from adopting one from Retriever Rescue. She adored dogs, always had, so much so her family and friends teased her about it. This was the longest she'd been without a pet. Only the hope of Paul's return kept her from getting one.

"This dog is different," she told Lisa. "He never barks. He just stares."

"I don't get it. If you've never met the man, how do you know so much about his dog?"

"I was in the laundry room one night. I could feel someone

watching me. I turned around, and that dog was in the doorway. It was staring at me, one leg up, pointing like he'd spotted fresh kill."

A shadow of alarm touched Lisa's dark eyes. "Did he growl or bare his teeth?"

"No. He just kept his eyes trained on me, and his nostrils were flaring. Then someone whistled, and the dog ran off."

"That is a little weird. Did you report it to the building manager?"

"No. You know old Mrs. Bryant. She's nosy as all get-out, and she upsets so-o-o easily. I didn't want to make trouble for the dog. What if he's harmless?"

"If he does anything, even growls at you, take action. Remember that woman in San Francisco." Lisa brought the last of her *pan cubano* up to her mouth. "Oh, my God. The stud with the dog is coming this way. Be still, my heart!"

Taylor turned her head toward the busy street but kept her neighbor in sight. He *was* coming over to them.

He stopped directly in front of their small table and spoke to Taylor. "Hi, there. I'm Shane Donovan, your new neighbor."

"Wow! You live in Taylor's building," Lisa said, managing to sound as if this were news to her. "Sit down."

"I'm Taylor Maxwell," she replied, kicking Lisa under the table. Why would she ask him to join them?

"I know." Shane swung a chair around backward and sat down, straddling it. He placed his coffee mug on the table. He pulled off aviator style shades and shoved them into the pocket of his black T-shirt. His dark blue eyes seemed unusually intense under brows a shade lighter than his black hair.

She supposed most women would be attracted to Shane Donovan, if you went for tall jocks with linebacker shoulders. Personally, Taylor preferred lean runner types with sandy hair and green eyes.

Men like Paul Ashford.

"How do you know who I am?" she asked.

He smiled, his mouth canting slightly to one side and giving him a mischievous, boyish expression. "I'd seen you around, and Mrs. Bryant told me who you were."

Mrs. Bryant. It figured. The old biddy probably was trying her hand at matchmaking. She knew Taylor didn't date and had commented on it several times.

When had Shane Donovan seen her? Taylor wondered. She was certain he hadn't, but obviously she was mistaken. He must have been peeking through the curtains when she wasn't looking.

Creepy.

"Where are you from?" Lisa asked Shane.

"Germany originally, but I've been around a lot."

The way he said "a lot" implied something, Taylor decided. Danger or a situation he'd rather not discuss. His expression kept his secret—whatever it was—but the intensity in his gaze as he looked at Taylor revealed deep, powerful emotions.

She wasn't easily frightened, and she wasn't afraid now, but she had to admit this man made her uneasy. It was a subliminal message that Lisa wasn't picking up. Just from Lisa's smile, Taylor could see how taken her friend was with this stranger.

"I just returned from nine months abroad," Lisa told Shane.

"Lucky you."

He had an attitude, she decided. A grown-up, more sophisticated version of the teenager she'd passed on the street earlier. He was the kind of man who went after what he wanted, and he probably got it.

His dog had sat down next to Shane, but its eyes were locked on Taylor. This close, the dog appeared less threatening. His eyes were soulful as if he were sad or profoundly troubled about something.

Shane stroked the dog's back while continuing to listen to Lisa, who was asking if Shane had ever been in India. He hadn't.

"What's your dog's name?" Taylor asked.

"Auggie. That's short for Augustus." He jostled the dog's ears. "Right, boy?"

The dog's tail flitted, but it wasn't what Taylor would have called a real wag. "Your dog seems . . . different. He sniffs a lot, but I've never heard him bark."

Shane studied her for a moment in a way that unsettled her more than it should have. "Auggie's a Braveheart military dog. I'm de-training him, getting him used to civilian life."

"Really? Was he an attack dog?"

Shane chuckled. "No way. Auggie has an A-rated sense of smell. He's trained to detect explosives."

Taylor gazed down at the dog, intrigued. "Why isn't he still in the military?"

"Bad hips. He flunked the last field test. He had to be able to jump over a four-foot wall, but he couldn't make it." There was something almost wistful in Shane's voice, as if he'd personally failed the test.

"Were you his handler?" Lisa asked.

Shane shook his head, then drank a little of what appeared to be *café con leche*—Cuban espresso with steamed milk.

"No. I had connections and was able to bring Auggie here. Ex-military dogs need a lot of retraining. They've never been taught to play or enjoy people the way other dogs have. All they've done is work."

Interesting, Taylor thought. That would account for the dog's watchfulness. As if sensing her thoughts, Auggie inched a bit closer, and Taylor stroked the gloss-black fur on his head. The dog's tail thumped once.

Something inside Taylor ignited, a small spark of happiness. For a second she didn't recognize the feeling. It had been so long since she'd experienced a flicker of joy.

Her life had been reduced to hard work, business deals. And loneliness. And worries about her mother's failing health.

She reached down and rubbed the dog's chest, a touch she knew all dogs liked. Auggie leaned forward to get closer to her hand and flicked his tongue across the back of her fingers.

Maybe it was time to give up on Paul and rescue a dog. The minute the traitorous thought hit her brain, she yanked back her hand. Paul was still alive. If he'd been killed, she'd know it, feel it.

Wouldn't she?

"What business are you in?" Lisa asked.

"Security. Computer security."

No way, Taylor thought. There was an air of ruthlessness about this man that didn't jibe with the computer types she knew.

"Oh, gosh! Look at the time," Taylor cried, standing up. "We're late." She grabbed Lisa by the arm. "Nice to meet you," she said to Shane.

"Well, that was *so* not like you," Lisa said once they were outside Brew Ha-Ha. "You're never rude."

"That man is not a computer expert."

Lisa stopped, put her hands on her hips, and studied Taylor for a moment. "How can you tell? Did you turn into a mind reader while I was away?"

"No, of course not. I—I just feel something's wrong with him."

"Yeah, right. What's wrong with Shane Donovan is that he's interested in you."

Lisa put her arm around Taylor and gave her a heartfelt hug. "You're young and pretty . . . and alive. You have to face reality."

"Reality?" Taylor repeated, the word a hollow echo in her head.

"It's been two years since Paul disappeared." Lisa gazed directly into Taylor's eyes, hesitated a moment before saying, "He must be dead. It's all right to be attracted to another man."

Taylor squinted against the bright sunlight through a sheen of tears that appeared without warning. Trust Lisa, her dearest friend, to say what her mother and brother must have wanted to tell her for months.

Like a crack in the universe, hope drained from the pool of inner strength that had supported her all this time. A silent scream tore through her, as much a cry for what had been lost as a cry for help.

A dark and terrifying moment of truth nearly knocked Taylor to her knees. Every waking moment, she'd kept this thought at bay, but Lisa had forced her to face the truth.

She was never going to see Paul Ashton again.